Cartel Viper

The Cartel Brotherhood

Sabine Barclay

OLIVERHEBERBOOKS

Second chances aren't about repeating the past but forging a future together with a fresh start.

Find me writing Historical Romance as Celeste Barclay.

Happy reading,
Sabine

Subscribe to Sabine's Newsletter

Subscribe to Sabine's bimonthly newsletter to receive exclusive insider perks.

Have you read *The Syndicate Wars?* This FREE origin story novella is available to all new subscribers to Sabine's monthly newsletter. Subscribe on her website. www.sabinebarclay.com

Sabine also writes Historical Romance as Celeste Barclay. Discover her Highlander, Regency, Viking, and Pirate Romances. Browse Now

The Cartel Brotherhood

Chapter One

Javier

"Are you sure this is the right one?"

I look over my right shoulder at my brother who shrugs and nods. We've had meetings with—shall we say "clients"—in some odd places before.

Some shithole places, some strip clubs we own, and some of the nicest resorts in the world. I don't recall ever meeting at a three-star, run-of-the-mill hotel. It's not quite nice enough to write home about, but it's far too nice to be called seedy.

It's the type of place a family from middle America would stay if they wanted a cost-efficient visit to New York City. I glance at the room number again and match my brother's shrug. I tap the key card we got from the receptionist and push the door open with my left hand, my right holding my gun.

I raise it as I enter the room, not trusting anybody or anything because something feels off. The sound of glass hitting the floor, then shattering makes me spin to my left

1

where a woman stands cowering behind the kitchen counter in this extended-stay hotel. She stares at me; her gaze darts between my gun, pointing at her, and my squinting gaze.

This isn't who should be in this room.

What the fuck went wrong?

I won't assume anything until I get the all-clear from the men who came with my brother and me. I don't take my eyes off her as the men fan out, checking the bedroom and the bathroom. Two remain in the hallway, prepared for anyone who unexpectedly joins us.

"Get out."

The two words are spoken with authority that doesn't match the woman's shaken expression or how she continues to tremble.

"Where's Luigi?"

Her brow furrows. "I don't know, probably off with Mario."

It's my turn for my brow to furrow. Did she just make a video game reference? She cocks an eyebrow, and I see some of her initial shock wear off. Now, anger replaces it. She points toward the door.

"Get the fuck out of my room before I call the cops."

Joaquin and I chuckle, but it's hardly a mirthful sound. There's no way she's getting to a phone, let alone dialing any numbers before any of us stop her. Everyone here knows it's an empty threat, but it's not unexpected.

"Get out before I scream."

That could be more problematic. She opens her mouth, and I lower my gun. Since none of my men warned me of anything, I'm comfortable holstering it in my shoulder harness. I put my hands out to the side, and I sense Joaquin doing the same thing. The three men who entered with us make themselves unobtrusive near the windows and the bedroom door.

"Whatever you're here for, I don't have it. Leave, and we can pretend this never happened."

There's something about her voice, and the longer I stare, her face looks so familiar, but I can't place it. If we've met before, it was years ago. I'd certainly remember her if it had been recently.

"I'm serious. Get out."

She's faster than any of us expect when she pulls a butcher's knife from a block holding various sizes. The way she handles it and how her stance changes—this is a woman who's trained to use a knife, but in the process of grabbing a weapon, her shirt sleeve moves, and I see what are clearly bruised handprints around her wrist.

They're easy to recognize when you've inflicted them thousands of times. Joaquin shifts, not stepping closer, but to get a better view. I'm certain he sees the same thing I do and knows someone hurt her. The bruises are faded but still noticeable.

When neither Joaquin nor I order our men out or make any sign we're leaving, she grabs a second knife and draws it back. So, she's prepared to hurl it at one of us. I'm not inclined to get stabbed today.

I also don't want to take a woman hostage. And I won't kill one who isn't a mercenary. That puts me squarely between a rock and a hard place.

"Look, I'm not calling the police. And I haven't screamed. I don't need any attention from anyone right now and neither do you. If you kill me or take me, that's what'll happen. I know there're security cameras in the building. If anything happens to me, you'll be a suspect. Leave, and we can pretend we never met."

She's said the same thing twice. I narrow my eyes at her, and the feeling I know her grows even stronger, but I still can't place it. It'll surely come to me later.

We can't wait around much longer if we're going to get out of here unnoticed. This meeting's gone to shit. I'll have men posted here to watch her. They'll intervene if she calls the police or tries to go to them.

I take a step backward, and Joaquin follows my cue. With both of their leaders moving toward the door, our men know it's time to beat a hasty retreat. Neither she nor I take our eyes off of each other as I'm the last one to back out of the door.

I pull it closed but don't step away immediately. Instead, I'm pressing my ear to it. I hear nothing through the door, but I suspect she'll peek through the spy hole at any moment. My men and brother have the same thought I do, as they press themselves against the wall, so she won't see any of us. I continue to listen for any sounds inside the room, but it's as though no one's there. I look over at Joaquin, and he tilts his head toward the elevator.

We need to find out if the receptionist gave us the wrong room number on purpose. We head to the opening elevator doors as I pull my phone out and find the contact for the guy we were supposed to meet.

ME

What room number?

I shoot off the text as we head downstairs, and a second later, a reply comes through.

SENDER

We're at 552.

I turn the phone toward Joaquin as I follow him into the elevator. His hand shoots out to hold the door open. The room is in the opposite direction from where we just were, which was five-twenty-five. This is my mission, but I ask for Joaquin's opinion.

4

"Do we leave, or go to him, or go back to the vehicles to regroup?"

"I say we check it out but be prepared to run."

I don't want anyone to see us because that would bring attention to us. There'd be seven Latino men in tailored suits running through a Holiday Inn. It sounds like the shittiest spy movie ever, but we're all in excellent shape because these things happen. We have to be prepared in case we need to bolt.

We step away from the elevator. Joaquin looks at Paco, and he knows to stay here. We all have earpieces in, so we can communicate without making calls. If anyone questionable approaches, he'll let us know. He'll also notice if the woman tries to leave.

The rest of us hurry down the hallway. I draw my gun for a second time before knocking on the door. I hate not having the element of surprise, since the key card is to the wrong room.

I don't like people boxing me in, which is basically what waiting in a hallway is. It also means I'm not in charge of the meeting from the get-go. That's not a problem so much as an inconvenience. It doesn't set the tone the way I want it to.

The door opens a couple inches, and I raise my gun just like I did the last time. Except since I'm not opening the door, I put my shoulder against it and shove the man on the other side. He didn't expect that, so the door swings open. Joaquin, my men, and I flood the room. No sounds of shattering glass meet us, but my men do the same thing as before, sweeping the area.

This time around, they find two armed men waiting in the bedroom. These Chicago Mafiosos are no more thrilled to have guns pointed at them than the woman was. My men strip them of their weapons and force them onto their knees.

"This isn't a good start to the meeting, Luigi. Having men hiding, ready to jump us."

"They were watching the soccer game and staying out of the way."

Fat fucking chance, but I let that excuse go. I gesture with my gun to the sofa and coffee table. Luigi nods and leads the way. I already saw the suitcase just inside the bedroom door. Joaquin fetches it and brings it over.

"What took you so long to get up here?"

Presumptuous fuck. I don't answer to Luigi, so I ignore the question. I definitely don't want to admit we went to the wrong room.

"Let's see what you have." I control this situation, not him.

Luigi glances around before hoisting the small suitcase onto the coffee table and sitting on the sofa. He leans forward to do the combination lock. He looks at Joaquin, then me, before unzipping the luggage.

"It's all here, just like my boss promised."

His boss. That fucker. I'm certain Salvatore Mancinelli doesn't know Edoardo Rizzo is doing a deal with us. He'd shit a brick. Not only are we doing a deal with a *Cosa Nostra* family, we're doing it here in NYC. Right under his fucking nose.

But little does Edoardo know what's coming next. If we fuck him over, then we fuck over his in-laws, the Vizzinis in Boston. Why leapfrog to them? They fucked over my *tía*. *Tío* Enrique isn't done with Tommaso Vizzini for the shit position he put my soon-to-be *Tía* Elodie in just after my uncle and new aunt met. It'll be a long time before my family is good with his.

"Then let's see. The longer you take, the less I trust you." If negative trust is possible, that's where we're already at.

"Here you go."

They don't look like much, but the small Persian prayer rugs have micro-nano-chips woven into them and cumulatively are worth just shy of one-point-two billion. I pick up a rug and unroll it, running my fingers over the fabric, knowing what I'm looking for. It doesn't take long before Joaquin and I verify the shipment is as it should be.

"Good." I'm not known to be effusive.

I close up the suitcase but pull off the lock. I saw the combination, but I don't trust Luigi's, so I snap my lock onto it. I lift the suitcase off the table as Joaquin takes a messenger bag from Alvaro.

"It's all here. Just like my uncle promised." Oh, it's all there all right.

Alvaro is Paco's younger brother, and something like a second cousin twice removed. He's one of the few men we trust to carry a bag full of money. Joaquin opens and tilts it toward Luigi for him to see. My brother pulls out a stack and flips through them, picking three bills from the center and handing them to Luigi. They're the only three bills in there that're legit. Joaquin marked them before we left my place, so he'd be sure to grab the right ones.

Luigi holds them up to the light before nodding. "Thank you."

Joaquin zips the bag and hands it over. I'm passing the suitcase to Alvaro while another one of our guys opens the hotel room door and checks the hallway.

"*Todo bien.*" All good.

We get the signal it's clear for us to leave. None of us waste a moment. Joaquin heads out before me, but he and I stand just outside the door with our weapons pointed at Luigi and his goons to make sure all our men can get out. Once we're in the hallway, we don't wait around. We're not exactly running, but neither are we taking our time to walk down the hall to the elevator.

We don't linger for the parting gift we left Luigi to detonate. It's not a bomb per se, but we're certainly not exploding die packs on the bills. Instead, when he opens the bag and

7

rummages around inside of it, he'll knock the cap off the bottle inside.

"Did you have any trouble with it?"

Joaquin will have loosened it a bit more as he pulled out the stack of counterfeit hundred-dollar bills.

"No. I prepped it this morning. It was easy to unscrew it the last bit when I reached inside."

They may or may not realize what's happening, but they'll soon be dead. The bottle contained highly concentrated hydrogen sulfide. At an amount enough to make someone nauseated or give them a headache, it would smell like rotten eggs. However, at a thousand parts per million, it'll be scentless and immediately cause cardiopulmonary arrest.

Next, our team of men—our cleaners—will slip in and clean the room of bodies and anything else they left behind. There won't be even a scintilla of trace evidence that any of us were ever there.

It'll look like the Chicago Mafiosos left without paying their bill.

"Done." Joaquin turns his phone toward me, much like I did mine earlier.

He and I and our other brother, Jorge, aren't triplets, but we may as well be. Joaquin is eleven months older than me, and I'm ten and a half months older than Jorge. You never find one without another, if not both. We're known as *Tres J's*. We've been inseparable our entire lives. Out of necessity when we still lived in Bogotá and by choice now because my brothers and our cousins are the coolest men I know. If I'm forced to spend time with anybody, I prefer it to be my family.

Joaquin and I are quiet in the car on the way to our *tío's* house. I gaze out the window as we cross into New Jersey from Brooklyn. I can't get the woman out of my mind. That niggling feeling that she's familiar won't go away. I say nothing as

Joaquin and I head into *Tío* Enrique's house. We kiss our aunt-to-be on the cheek when we pass her at the front door. I really like Elodie a lot. My brother and I head into *Tío* Enrique's office where he and our cousins Pablo and Alejandro, plus our other brother Jorge, are. It's when *Tío* Enrique reaches for a paper on his desk that I suddenly know who the woman is.

Chapter Two

Maddy

Javier Diaz had no idea who I was.

Neither did Joaquin, and that's just as well. I'm at least fifteen pounds lighter than I was the last time we saw each other, and I don't look better for it. It makes me about fifteen pounds underweight.

He and his two brothers are men I've known since they moved to America twenty-odd years ago. That's because I grew up next door to their *Tío* Luis. I've known that man my entire life, just like I have their other uncle, *Tío* Enrique.

Our families were once super close. Luis and Margherita had two sons who were both older than me. The younger one, Juan, was the same age as my older sister, Laura. They were just a couple weeks apart.

I grew up with those two guys being more like my brothers than just next-door neighbor friends. But Juan fucked around and found out when he went after Laura because not only did she dare not love him back when he decided he was ready to pay attention to her, she also made the cardinal mistake of marrying the bratva's *pakhan*. I adore my brother-in-law, Maksim, and the rest of his family. I think of them—refer to them—as my brothers rather than in-laws.

Because of that, I'm not saying a fucking word to anybody about Javier bursting into my hotel room. Not only do I avoid shit between the bratva and the Cartel, I'm also not ready for anyone in my family to know I'm back in NYC. I've lived in Albany since I left for college ten years ago.

I've been a nurse up there ever since I graduated. I became a nurse practitioner midwife a few years ago. Right around the same time I met that motherfucking, shitty, son-of-a-bitch, cunt-eating bastard, otherwise known as my ex-boyfriend, Drew O'Sheehan. He can fuck all the way off with bells on.

I'm not bitter or anything.

He's the reason I'm fifteen pounds underweight and hiding out at a hotel, rather than being with my family. I'm not ready for my family to see me like this, and I don't want Drew to find me.

To say our relationship was turbulent is putting it mildly. Why I stayed for so fucking long *isn't* beyond me. I like to think I'm pretty intelligent, that I have common sense, and I'm not one of those women who thought I could change him. I knew exactly who and what he was, and that's the reason I stayed.

Of course, I didn't know who and what he was when I met him. I didn't even know who or what he was for the first two years we were together. He hid that so damn well he should've won an Oscar every year. However, I've known for the last two years, and I finally broke his hold on me. But I'm not just on the run from him. It's his entire family because you don't get one without the other.

That's what happens when you date somebody in the mob.

If I'd known who he was when I met him, I wouldn't have

even given him a second look. There are already enough ties to organized crime in my family. We sure as hell didn't need one more, but that's exactly what happened. I've been a virtual prisoner for the past two years.

The few times I tried to hint to Laura that something was wrong, Drew found the texts. I even switched to a burner phone and tried to hide those. I realized a while ago that he had cameras all over our apartment. He'd watch me when I was at home. He had people reporting to him while I was at work. I tried to leave twice, and he always found me.

There's a reason, even in summer, I wore long-sleeved shirts under my scrubs, and almost never took off my lab coat. I'd make the excuse I always run cold, but it was to hide the bruises. He didn't care that he left them places people could see.

It was his control. It forced me into wearing clothes that kept me covered up. His jealousy that anyone might look at me was only a minimal part of that. I couldn't really wear what I wanted to wear. I couldn't do the things I wanted to do because I was often too sore.

I'm free of him now.

At least, sort of.

I'm certain he's looking for me. What he doesn't realize is I learned a lot about hiding from him. Some of it was necessity, so people wouldn't know what our relationship was really like. A lot of it was from thinking about all the things he did to hide his real ties from me for two years, and all the things he did to hide who he was from the rest of the world.

He was a master class in subterfuge. And I was an A-plus student. Now, I'm employing all those skills.

But having two Diaz men burst into my hotel room, likely expecting to meet one of their associates, and instead finding me, puts a damper on my hopes that I can be anonymous for a while. I planned my escape for months. I made sure I had everything I needed.

Drew insisted we have a joint checking account, so he had control over my salary. What he doesn't know is that I'm an artist. The one place he couldn't have cameras was in my car. He had tracking devices on it, but he never put any cameras in there. He assumed between tracking me and having men follow me, there was nothing I could do he wouldn't know about. Except he had my windows tinted to where I'm surprised I never got pulled over or ticketed.

Some of that was for my protection, since rival syndicates knew who I was. Some of it was that possessiveness that nobody else dared look at his girlfriend. But it allowed me to draw in my car when I would pretend to nap there if there was no space in the on-call room.

Instead of napping, I would push my seat all the way back or climb into the back of my SUV and sketch. I even had my watercolors hidden in the well where the spare tire's kept. It certainly wasn't easy without an easel, just using my bent legs to hold my sketch pad or lying on my stomach with my canvas.

The sketch pad pictures were easy to deliver to the sketchy-ass art dealer. They were small, and I could pass them to him when I went to the grocery store. The canvases took some spy-level secrecy since men watched my car while I was parked. I'd pick this one spot in the employee lot that made it impossible for them to see the trunk. I had to trust the fucker enough to give him a spare key fob—which cost me nearly four hundred dollars that I saved from lunches I skipped buying at work—so he could open the trunk while I was inside the hospital and slide them out without Drew's men seeing him.

But selling my art made me extra money I kept squirreled away. I was motivated, so I found a way. Two years of doing that has built me a nest egg. I didn't think it would take that long for me to gain the chance to escape. The first time he hit me was the first time I tried to leave. I learned quickly to be as deceptive as him. And I also realized it would be no small feat getting away from him, especially as his net closed tighter around me by the day.

I look around the extended-stay hotel room I've been in for a week. I've been packing as I mull this situation over.

I only brought what I absolutely need. I knew a guy in college who used to make fake IDs. It was serendipity when his wife came in to deliver her baby. They were in town from Schenectady, and she went into early labor. I helped deliver their son. Then he delivered fake driver's licenses and fake passports to me. He even stole a couple social security numbers for me and made cards for those.

With my new identity, I went in and opened a bank account where I kept my art money. It was a branch of the same bank I already use but closer to the hospital than the one near my home where I use my real name. Since I already banked with them, it never raised any red flags to Drew when his men reported me going there. After that, I used online banking for the art sales.

Now I have what I need—money and a new identity—but another complication exists. I'm certain either Javier or Joaquin posted one or two of their men nearby to make sure I don't bolt or call the police.

I hear my phone buzz from the bedroom and hurry to grab it, worried anyone posted in the hallway could somehow hear it. I don't want any of the Diaz men returning because they fear I'm going to squeal.

"Hi, Mom."

This isn't who I want to talk to right now. She's going to ask questions I don't want to answer because it means I have to lie.

"Hi, sweetie. How're you?"

"I'm well. How about you?"

That was lie number one.

"Same. I haven't talked to you in nearly a week, so I thought I'd give you a ring. Do you have time to chat?"

Not really.

"Sure."

I pull my baseball cap low over my eyes and tuck my blonde hair underneath it, securing it out of my way. I grab the tube of disinfectant wipes I took from the hospital on my third to last shift.

"I have some news to share."

"Oh?"

"Enrique's getting married."

"What? No way."

That's not what I expected to hear.

"Yeah. He met a woman a few months ago, and he's head over heels. According to Laura, the few people who've met her think they're a lot alike."

Boss bitch.

No one gets anything past my sister. She was a corporate attorney, and that's how she met my brother-in-law. She's a shark and tiger combined. She's even more tenacious now that she's a mom. She has twin preschoolers. If this woman is anything like Laura, then Enrique's met his match.

"Is she Colombian?"

I assume he's marrying another Cartel woman like he did about fifteen or sixteen years ago. As far as I know, he's been technically single. I don't need more details than that since he was like an uncle for so long.

"No. She's from Boston."

"Huh? Is she younger than him?"

"A little. About ten years."

He has his other nephew Pablo to be his heir, so he doesn't

need to try for any sons. Makes sense he'd find someone closer to his age.

"When you see Luis or Margherita, pass along my *felicidades*." Congratulations.

My parents and their neighbors are civil but not friends anymore.

"Enrique's invited all of us to the reception."

My gaze darts toward the door.

Motherfucker.

"Really?"

Once I'm finished wiping down any surface I touched, I put the tube of wipes in my go bag. I do a sweep of the bedroom, pulling the sheets of the still-made bed a little tighter. I didn't sleep directly on the sheets, instead using my sleeping bag. I did my best to make sure I didn't leave any hair as a sign I was there. It's not like I thought somebody would send a forensics team in here, but in case Drew found me, I didn't want to leave any obvious evidence that this was my room.

"Yes. Do you think you can come down for it?"

Since I'm already here.

"I can try. I can't believe we're invited."

"You know Laura and Maks are, and so are the rest of the family. Laura's made as much peace with Enrique as they can, so they're on good terms right now. It's not like Luis and Margherita are Dad's and my enemies. We just aren't close anymore. As strained as it is, we've all been like family far longer than we've been estranged. Should I reply it'll be you and Drew?"

Fuck my life.

"Text me the date, and I'll let you know whether he and I can make it. It might just be me."

Or not.

"It's next week."

Shit. Shit. Fuck.

"Let me check my schedule, and I'll get back to you. I gotta run, Mom."

"Okay, sweetie. Love you."

"Love you too."

I hang up and look at my phone. I have to come up with an excuse besides work for why I can't go. It would be legit to say it's too late to get the time off, and my mom would understand since she's a doctor. But I've used that excuse so many times over the past two years, I know my family doubts me. I don't need to raise their suspicions right now.

With everything packed up, I ease the hotel room door open and use my cell phone camera to look down the hallway, angling it so I can see there's a man by the elevators. I yank my phone back as he looks in my direction. I wait for him to sound the alarm or come investigate, but nothing happens.

I slip out while looking toward the elevator. I silently close the door. I'm taking a chance since Joaquin or Javier might have posted somebody at the stairwell. I head casually down the hall toward the stairs, trying not to look suspicious.

If anybody asks why I'm using the stairs instead of the elevator, I'll say there was a large man standing at the elevator, and he made me uncomfortable. It's not a lie. I head down two flights before stepping into the hallway. I'm not in as good a shape as I once was, and I'm winded from those two flights of stairs. I hop in the elevator to ride the rest of the way down, chancing he has men outside of the elevator in the lobby.

The doors ping open, and I've never been so glad it's raining outside as I am now. I pull my hood up over my ball cap and zip my coat all the way up. I cover my nose and mouth with the collar, and my cap shades my eyes.

The hood keeps anyone from seeing the bits of my blonde hair that poke out from beneath the hat. The Diazes have a man in the lobby. He's pretty unobtrusive, but after growing up next door to the second most senior member of the Cartel, I know what to look for. My time with Drew confirmed it.

While I miss the tank of an SUV I had, which was perfect for winter in Albany, I'm glad I have something much more inconspicuous. I left my SUV behind when I ran. Instead, I have Maine plates on a small gas-hybrid hatchback. Part of the money I saved paid for it. I used my fake identification to register it. I considered putting on fake plates. I couldn't risk getting pulled over and having the cops run them. I toss my bags in the trunk and snap closed my umbrella as I climb in.

I need to get away from here, then I can plan further what I'm going to do next. I can't wait around in the parking lot to make up my mind. I'm in a part of Brooklyn I don't know very well, but I have a pretty good idea of where I am. I didn't want to go somewhere near my family in Queens. But I wanted to be somewhere where I could get to them fast if I absolutely had to.

Once I'm back on the road, the image of Javier entering with his gun drawn fixes in my mind. I always thought he was the hottest of the *Tres J's*. Javier, Jorge, and Joaquin. There's not an ugly one in that family. Enrique's a silver fox. Luis is too much like a second father for me to find him attractive. Same thing with Pablo; he's too much like a brother. But I can acknowledge they're good looking.

Their other cousin, Alejandro, is the pretty one in the family. The one that's almost too hot to be true. There's one in each of the four families. In the bratva, it's Pasha. In the Mafia, it's Lorenzo. In the mob, it's Finn.

But there's always been something about Javier that could drop my panties in a heartbeat. I haven't seen him in years, but nothing's changed about that. Yeah, Joaquin was there, but it wasn't because he was behind Javier for most of it that I barely noticed him. It wasn't because Javier did most of the talking.

It's his overall aura. There's something about the man that's drawn me to him since we were in high school.

If he realizes who I am, there's no way he'll ignore me. It's only a matter of time before he finds me if he deduces my real identity.

Chapter Three

Javier

I've been sitting outside the hotel for the last six hours staring at a whole lot of nothing. Once I figured out the woman was Madeline Doyle, I knew I couldn't ignore what I saw. It tempted me all over again to call Maks to find out whether he knew his sister-in-law was back in town. The bruises on her wrist bothered me before I remembered her, but they alarm me now. But I keep my suspicions to myself because she obviously doesn't want her family to know she's here. If she did, she would be with them, not in a hotel in Brooklyn. I keep telling myself that to assuage my guilt for not saying anything to anyone.

I went up to her room when I arrived and knocked, but she didn't answer. I considered using the key card to just walk in without invitation. But I've already done that once, and I doubt I'd get as warm a reception as I did the first time. Instead, I'm sitting in the parking lot like the stalker I am.

At least I'm multi-tasking. I look down at my laptop and

study the brief I'm drafting. I have a RICO case—Racketeer Influenced and Corrupt Organizations Act—to litigate. One of our men got picked up for extortion. He was running a hush money scheme with his employer that he screwed the pooch on. He fucked it up every which way from Sunday.

"Joaquin, I need the phone records. Without those, I can't prove his boss was in on it."

Therein lies the rub. The fucker got his boss involved, thinking it would lessen the share he owes us. They stole from the company together rather than our guy putting his employer to the screws. I'd let them both rot in white-collar prison, but to do that, I'd have to lose the case. That shit ain't happening.

I don't need the lawyers in the other families thinking I'm slipping. Reputation is everything in this world, and I can't afford to have mine tarnished. At least, not my courtroom one. Thanks to shit that's gone down over the past few years, my family's entire reputation got flushed down the shitter by my cousin Juan. Thank God that *cabrón* is dead. He was about to be our undoing. I feel bad for my aunt, uncle, and cousin Pablo. But not that bad.

"I told you I'm working on it. What's up with you? You've been in la la land since the meeting yesterday. Now you're snapping at me."

"Sorry. I'm still annoyed the receptionist gave us the wrong room number. I want to know if that was intentional. Did Luigi set us up?"

"I don't think it's Luigi or the employee. I think it was the woman."

I brace for my brother saying Madeline's name and pointing out that we know her. When he says nothing more, I wonder if he's waiting for me to admit recognizing her.

"That was messy. You know I don't like messes."

I'm not a neat freak, but I am—particular.

"Are you worried she'll figure out who we are and go to the police?"

No. I'm worried she'll go to Maks.

If Joaquin's asking that, then maybe he doesn't realize we've known that woman since we were kids. She's a lot thinner—too thin—than she was when we were in school, and the bruises were distracting. We didn't spend a lot of time around her since she and Laura went to school near their house in New Jersey. My brothers and I went to school with the other syndicate guys. But we know her from going over to Pablo and Juan's house. She and I ran into each other a few times outside of school.

That's one way of putting it.

In a fucked-up twist of fate, all the parents in the Four Families—except *Tío* Luis and *Tía* Margherita—have homes in the same two neighborhoods. The kids in the Four Families didn't grow up going to elementary and middle school together, but we wound up in the same classes in high school. They grew up playing peewee and little league sports together, though. Their moms always brought the good juice boxes. My brothers and I, along with our mom, were still in Bogotá. We stayed, even after rivals killed my dad.

"She might call them." *That's the least of my concerns.* "Or she might go to the news. She might tell a friend who calls the police. I don't know. I just don't like that an outsider got involved."

"She didn't look like she wanted to be found. I doubt anyone in her life knows where she is. I know you saw the bruises on her wrist."

"I did." And that's part of why I'm waiting for her.

"She's too old for it to have been a parent. Probably a significant other."

"That's my guess." And I'll kill the man when I find out who he is.

I'm unprepared for the wave of protectiveness that washes over me. I don't like the idea of any woman being mistreated. I'd defend anyone who deserves my protection, and that's usually anyone unaffiliated who's weaker or smaller than me. But knowing someone hurt Madeline bothers me more than I understand.

"Hopefully, she's safe where she's at, and she's out of whatever situation she was in. I'll have the records to you by tomorrow morning. I still have a few more strings to pull to get all of them."

I nearly forgot what we were originally talking about until Joaquin mentioned the phone records.

"Thanks. Just let me know when you're sending them over."

"Okay. *Te amo.*"

"*Te amo.*"

We will never get too big or too old to say I love you to each other or to hug our mom. It's a family law we say I love you to each other at least once a day, and we end most calls that way regardless of who's around us. You never know when you won't get another chance to say it.

I return my attention to my computer and reread what I wrote before I spoke to Joaquin. I do my best to concentrate and continue to outline the relevant case law, but I can't focus. I'm glancing at the hotel as much as I'm looking at my screen.

Maybe she has plenty of food and doesn't need to go out to eat. She has the kitchen, after all. I should leave it alone and go home, so I can get this work done. I should call Maks and let him know. She should be his problem. But I can't. I can't bring myself to turn my car back on. I can't get myself to leave the parking lot. Just a couple more hours.

It's been two days. I couldn't stay here the entire time. I had to go home, but I'm in the parking lot again. I wound up putting a camera on both ends of the building, so I could record the entire parking lot. I waited until it was dark and stuck them on the walls. They're up higher than most people can reach since I'm nearly six-three and stretched. The height makes them inconspicuous and gave me a wider view. I could've had Joaquin hack the hotel security, but I don't want to explain myself yet.

I've barely slept in case I missed her leaving. I napped here and there the last two nights and reviewed the footage. Madeline hasn't come out once. I'm really suspicious now. It's odd. This isn't the type of hotel where you'd want to spend all day. There's no spa or pool. There's nothing interesting within walking distance.

It's going to be dark soon, so I don't want another night to pass before I approach Madeline. I slip out of my car and head to the front entrance. I scan my surroundings for anyone watching me. I often have bodyguards with me, but not always. Today, I'm working solo. I prefer it that way. Joaquin is the shyest of all of us. He doesn't mind being around people, but he hates being the center of attention. He'd rather blend in. I'm the most introverted. I don't enjoy being around most people unless they're family.

I walk into the lobby with an air of confidence I cultivated on the streets of Bogotá when I was a tween. It was a means of survival. Without a dad, my brothers and I were an easy target for the street gangs. They would've loved nothing more than to beat the ever-loving shit out of the *jefe de jefes'* nephews. Everyone knows *Tío* Enrique even if he lives in New Jersey. He's the most powerful man in the Western Hemisphere, despite what Salvatore Mancinelli, Maksim Kutsenko, and Dillan O'Rourke might say. He's undoubtedly the most powerful man in Latin America. That made Jorge, Joaquin, and me high value for a ransom too.

My confidence wasn't always real, but the swagger looked it. Now I use that as I pull a counterfeit FBI badge from my pocket. Among all my crimes, pretending to be a federal agent is pretty benign. It's how Joaquin and I got the key card the last time we were here. We said we had a person of interest here.

It's a different man at the reception desk today, which is perfect. I don't want to explain why I'm back and asking about a different guest.

"Good evening. How can I help you?"

"Hello. I'm Agent Mendez, and I'm looking for one of your guests. They were in room five-twenty-five. Have they checked out?"

I show the man the badge before he can object. I don't give Madeline's name, instead wanting to see if he offers it. I watch him tap his keyboard before he looks up at me. I notice his name tag says he's a manager, so I won't have to wait for him to play any games, saying he needs to ask a supervisor before giving me the information. He doesn't ask for a warrant, so that's one less lie to spin. I shift my right arm, and he sees a hint of my handgun. That wasn't accidental.

"Ms. Henderson is still checked in."

Good. That means the key card should still work. But who the fuck is Ms. Henderson? As far as I know, Madeline didn't get married, so that is *not* her last name. How was she able to check in under an assumed name? She'd need a photo ID and a credit or debit card with that name.

Ding. Ding. Ding.

Red flags and sirens are going off.

"Do you need me to escort you up?"

Nosey fucker.

He isn't offering to let me in. He wants to know what the fuck is going on. So do I.

"No. I can knock. Thank you."

I could knock, but I won't. I make my way to the elevator, growing more impatient as each floor ticks by. When the elevator pings at the fifth floor, I put my hand on my gun. I peek out of the elevator, always cautious before stepping into a confined space. I see no one, and I continue to keep my head down like I did in the elevator. I don't need cameras recording my face. I turn toward the room I want, my ears peeled for anyone approaching from behind. I'm not paranoid, but I'm situationally aware even in my sleep.

I pull the key card from my pocket, not bothering to knock. I let myself in again, and immediately, I know the room is vacant. Just like in the parking lot, I sweep my gaze around the room. It's spotless. I walk to the kitchen, and everything looks like maid service came through. Not just the half ass tidying plenty of housekeepers do while a guest occupies the room. This is ready for the next guest kind of clean. I head into the bedroom, and the bed is crisply made.

Madeline didn't sleep in it. This isn't just she pulled the sheets up. This is there aren't any wrinkles. How she managed that, without fresh sheets, means she didn't untuck them. I walk into the bathroom, and there's a lingering scent of disinfectant. I have a sensitive nose. Spring and fall allergies are a bitch. If I don't take an antihistamine twice a day, I'm fucking Rudolph.

I move back into the main room and look around. She wiped down everything. She probably tucked herself into a sleeping bag to keep from messing up the bed. I know she's a nurse, so she knows how to sanitize things. She obviously did that here.

Touching nothing, I move through the rooms a second time —this time with a far more critical eye. I'm looking for any smudge or hair. A single thing that leaves a hint about her. Part of it is to gather evidence of I don't know what for my use. The other part is to make sure she left nothing behind someone else could use. If she went to this much trouble, she's definitely hiding.

I take nearly half an hour, but I leave knowing as little as I did when I arrived. I get back to my car and consider what I learned. She didn't check out, but I doubt she plans to come back. I wonder if she recognized me or remembered me, and that's why she left. Or did she leave merely because she was scared after having a bunch of narco-traffickers busting into her room? Will she come back to check out? Or will she do it online? Probably the latter.

Where did she go?

I don't know what she drives these days, so I definitely don't know her license plate. I can't run them myself, so it's forcing me to ask Joaquin for help. I pull out my phone and inhale.

Fuck my life.

"*Hola, hermano.*" Hello, brother.

"*Hola.* Can you get into the hotel's security footage?"

"Which hotel? The one we were at? Do you suspect someone went to see Luigi? Or—are you wondering about that woman?"

That pause was intentional.

"Find out what car she got into."

"Why?"

"Please."

"Javier, why?"

"Because I'm asking nicely."

He scoffs. I was a bit demanding.

"Give me a moment. I just sat down to my computer. Where are you?"

"The hotel."

He remains quiet. I can guess what he's thinking. I've already examined my feelings in the time it took me to get back to my car. Something's not right, and I can't turn away from this. If Madeline's hiding under a fake name, she's desperate to get away from someone or something. With the protection she could get from her in-laws, something is seriously wrong for her to be on her own. My brother isn't asking questions because he knows he won't get answers until I'm ready to give them.

"She got into a subcompact with Maine plates."

He reads them off to me as I put them in a note in my phone.

"Maine?"

"Yeah. It's a deep-blue four-door."

"Can you run it to see if it's a rental?"

"Give me a moment."

I hear him tapping on his keyboard again. I keep myself from tapping my fingers on the center console.

"It's registered to a Caitlyn Henderson. Who's that?"

"I don't know." *Why's Madeline using that name?*

"Do you want me to track it?"

"Yeah. Please."

I remember my manners a little faster this time. I'm usually way more polite, but this shit has my mind spinning. I know it'll take him a few minutes to get her whereabouts if he has to run through the city's camera records to follow the car from here to wherever she is.

"She's in Jersey. She left before we did."

Did she go to her parents? How the fuck didn't any of our guys see her?

"She took a weird route to near Montclair, considering she

didn't stop. She took the Verrazano Bridge to the Staten Island Expressway, then across the Goethals Bridge."

She went to her parents if she's near Montclair. "Did she take Ninety-Five up to the Turnpike then Essex Freeway?"

"No. That's part of what's weird. She took surface streets through Elizabeth, went up the Garden State Parkway, then got on the Essex Freeway."

She went south to go north. She could've just taken the Brooklyn Bridge into Manhattan, then taken the Holland Tunnel over to Jersey. From there, the Turnpike to Essex Freeway would take her close to Montclair. She really didn't want to be followed.

"Can you tell where she stopped?"

"Somewhere in Montclair. She got on surface streets that don't have cameras."

"Okay."

"Why do you think she took such a circuitous route? Was she worried we'd follow her? I have no footage of her leaving Montclair."

"Maybe."

I turn my Porsche on and look at the screen as I reverse out of my parking spot. It's not until I'm in drive that I speak again.

"Joaquin, she's Laura's little sister."

My announcement is met with a moment of silence before my brother responds with surprise.

"Madeline?"

"Yeah."

"No. She was way skinnier than Madeline ever was. She was way paler too. Madeline was always outside with Laura. While Laura used to fade in winter, Madeline had a perma-tan. We used to tease that she fake-baked to look like she belonged to Pablo's family instead of hers. That she wanted to be Pablo's little sister rather than Laura's."

None of us mention Juan if we can avoid it. Laura wasn't a bossy big sister, but she certainly had opinions. Pablo would stand up for Madeline because he would've swapped either sister for Juan. His younger brother was a real pissant. Pablo would let Juan pick on him because he knew if he unleashed his temper, he'd be the one in trouble for picking on his baby brother. He'd get back at Juan in other ways.

"Why on earth would Madeline stay somewhere like that when she was so close to home?"

"She's hiding something or from someone. You saw the bruises on her wrist."

"I did. What are you going to do about it?"

Even if I can't see him, I'm certain my brother cocks his eyebrow at me, already knowing the answer. Even if he can't see me, my answer is a raised eyebrow in return. I usually don't subscribe to "what my family doesn't know won't hurt them." At least, most of the time, I don't. In this case, I don't know what I'm going to do, so it's better if I don't speak out of turn. My brother trusts me not to fly off the handle, but I won't settle for less than the full story.

She owes me that.

Chapter Four

Maddy

"Mom, I'm ready?"

"You look lovely, sweetie."

"Thanks. Is Dad in the car?"

"Yes. Just let me grab my purse."

I step onto the front porch and look to the right. I've barely seen Luis or Margherita in the two days I've been with my parents. I wound up getting another hotel room under a different alias about two miles from the house I grew up in. I wasn't ready for them to see me, and I didn't want to explain why I came down early and unannounced. I needed more time for the most visible bruises to heal.

I glance down at the evening gown I'm wearing since it's a black-tie affair. It's modest but elegant. It has a single strap that crosses my chest and back. It doesn't plunge too low across my chest, so it hides where Drew would pinch me while we had sex—the only good part of our relationship—but he did that to remind me I was his. He was a shitbag everywhere but in bed.

He was decent there. The gown also covers most of my shoulder blades, the seam wrapping around just beneath my armpits. It hides the fading bruise over my right kidney.

As I walk out to the waiting SUV from the car service my parents reserved, I watch the Diazes' house. I spent so many hours playing there as a child. We had so many Sunday dinners there. We alternated weeks for more than two decades. It's odd to know that's over, even though it has been for nearly five years. It's not like I expect Luis, Margherita, or Pablo to step out of the house. Pablo doesn't live there anymore, and besides that, they're at the wedding ceremony. They only invited anyone outside the immediate family to the reception.

I glance in the side-view mirror before climbing into the third row. I would normally care about my appearance anyway, but I put extra effort into today. Some of it is feeling self-conscious about being at such an enormous event and having so many people look at me. I feel like somehow, someone will know what I'm hiding beneath my gown.

I want to look the part of the *pakhan's* sister-in-law, not that Maks or anyone in his family expects anything of me but being myself. Still, that family and the women who married into it are insanely attractive. My parents and I will sit at the same table as Maks and Laura.

And there's a part of me I don't want to acknowledge that wants to look good in front of Javier. I wasn't expecting guests, so I hardly looked my best when he burst into my hotel room. I'm certain he and Joaquin spotted the bruises on my wrists. If he asks, I'll say I'm into martial arts, and my opponent got me into a hold I couldn't break. I've refined that lie so well, I practically believe it myself.

I've tried not to think about him every waking moment of every day since I saw him, and I've succeeded. It's only every other moment. His family is another insanely attractive one. In fact, all the members of the Four Families are wildly gorgeous. There isn't a dud in the bunch. Not the men or the women. But there's always been something about Javier.

I watch the houses go by, then the buildings alongside the highway until we're in the city and at one of the most luxurious hotels in Manhattan. The Peninsula is where my sister had her reception. I sweep my gaze around the ballroom as my parents and I enter the receiving line with my sister, the Kutsenkos, and the Andreyevs—Maks's mom's side of the family.

"Madeline, you look stunning. Thank you for coming all the way down here."

Javier didn't tell him.

"Thank you, *t*—Enrique."

I barely caught myself before calling him *Tío*. That would have been uncomfortable. Laura glances back at me, hearing my near *faux pas*.

"I'd like you to meet my wife, Elodie."

"Hello. Thank you for including us on your special day."

"Enrique and I are both so happy all of you could make it."

I hear sincerity in her voice, and she didn't force it. But I know any happiness she has about us being here is for Enrique's sake. She doesn't know us, but I'm certain she's heard the stories. She's not quite an ice queen, but she's definitely regal enough to be *la patrona*—Boss Lady. She already looks the part of the *jefe's* wife.

My family makes our way to our tables. The four Kutsenko brothers, their wives, their mother, their four cousins plus the wives of two of them, their two aunts and two uncles make nineteen. Add my parents and me, and that's twenty-two. We take up three eight-top tables. I sit beside Laura.

"Can you believe he remarried?" Laura leans toward me as Maks pushes in her chair and mine.

I continue to look around the ballroom as I answer. "No. I

never imagined he would. He's been the perpetual silver fox since we were in college."

"I know. But he seems to really love her."

"I'd say as much as Maks loves you."

"I don't know how I'm happy for him while still not liking him."

"Are you ever going to make peace with everything that happened? Juan's dead—" I whisper that. "—and their family's left our sisters and cousins alone for years."

The bad blood with Enrique and his family stems from shit that happened with a couple of Laura's sisters- and cousins-in-law. They've always encouraged me to think of them without any qualifiers, just like Laura does.

"I'm not angry anymore. I just don't trust or like them."

"Could've fooled me. I'm surprised Enrique didn't have your butter knife removed."

There are place settings, so we all knew where to sit. Enrique has a large cross tattooed on his forearm with a P at the top, a J at the bottom—Pablo and Juan—and an L and M —Laura and Madeline—on the sides. Laura's threatened to carve her initial and mine out of Enrique's arm if their family does anything else to ours. I wouldn't put it past my sister to do that. And frankly, I'd hold his arm down. I miss my friendships with the Diazes, and I especially miss considering Enrique an uncle because he was always the fun one when we were little. But it'll always be my family over theirs.

The others join us, and the conversation moves on. Sumiko, Maks's cousin Pasha's wife, is expecting their first baby. They announced it since they can no longer hide it. I'm certain everyone else in the family already knew, but it surprises my parents and me.

"If you ever need anything or have any questions, you know

I'm just a phone call away. Nothing is too silly or insignificant to ask."

"Thank you, Madeline. It's reassuring to have a midwife in the family. I'll take you up on that if anything comes up."

I've made the same offer to all the women in the family as it's expanded. It reminds me how much I already miss my job. It's the only thing from Albany I miss. I love my work, but I don't know if I'll ever go back to it. No one here knows I'm hiding from Drew, and I'm praying it doesn't get back to him before I can disappear again. But once I'm living under another assumed name, I won't be able to practice.

I'm unprepared for Laura to elbow me as I chat with Christina, the fourth Kutsenko brother's wife. I look over to where Laura points.

"Go on. Maybe you'll get lucky."

I want to sink under the table. In no way do I want to join the other single women as Elodie tosses her bouquet. I don't want to marry, and I don't want to hear anyone in my family ask when Drew and I plan to marry. I've avoided telling more lies than absolutely necessary tonight.

"Go on. The middle of the pack looks like the best place since I bet she'll give it a good toss." Christina waggles her brow at me, and I want to hurl.

With a table full of expectant faces, there's not much I can do. I push back my chair and move onto the dance floor. I inhale a deep breath and steel myself for the jokes and giggles. I don't want to do this.

I glance over to where Javier sits at the head table. Our gazes meet as the bouquet sails through the air. I have no choice but to put my hands up to keep the bundle of flowers from nailing me in the face.

Fuck. My. Life.

I spot some annoyed expressions, and I'm uncertain

35

whether they're specifically directed at me or just overall annoyance because they need something to hound a boyfriend who hasn't popped the question. From these bitches' faces, I can't say I'm surprised if that's the case. But most congratulate me, asking me if there's anyone special in my life.

I shake my head as I extricate myself. I feel Javier's eyes boring laser beams into my back. Paranoid much?

"Congrats." Laura's gaze sweeps over me. "Let's go to the restroom."

My sister reads me too well. She's been suspicious all evening, but she's said nothing. She sees something in me now, and she'll wheedle it out of me. I'm not ready to tell her, and she's the only person who *always* knows when I'm lying.

"They're about to cut the cake. We can't step out. That would be rude."

It's her gaze that practically sets me ablaze, but she nods and settles back in her chair. I take my seat, setting the bouquet on the table. I'd offer to give it back to Elodie, saying I'm certain she wants to preserve it; however, this is a tossing bouquet. It's meant to go to someone else. I'm stuck with the damn thing. It's beautiful and smells wonderful, but it's a fucking beacon for attention.

We clap as Enrique's hands cover Elodie's, and they press the knife through the cake. I have a pang of envy. I definitely don't want Enrique, but I think about the life I once thought I'd begin with Drew. I thought that would be us one day. Now, who knows whether I'll have that chance?

I'd need to live in a state that doesn't require a blood test to marry and do a shit ton of other things to cover my tracks so well that I could marry under an alias. Not that doing all that shit would matter because to do that means my family wouldn't be at my wedding.

Maks invites Laura to dance. They make a stunning couple,

and they move together like a couple who know everything about each other down to their souls. They do. I shift my gaze to the other bratva couples as they join Maks and Laura. They've all met their soulmates too. My attention moves to the Mancinelli and O'Rourke families. All the couples in those families are as in love as the ones in mine. The Diazes have been the final holdout, and now Enrique's broken the seal.

A lump rises in my throat. My eyes burn with threatening tears. My chest tightens.

None of this is fair. I'm not always a good person, but neither am I a horrible one. But none of this seems attainable anymore.

My parents are the last to join them since my dad went to the restroom. They look at me, knowing I'm the only one left behind. Sergei and Anton, the two unmarried bratva men, are ostensibly here as guests, but they're the family's bodyguards. The men all guard their wives, but it doesn't hurt to have two extras. I know they probably assigned one of them to me. I'll know in a moment as I stand. I'm escaping to the restroom.

"Madeline, I'll go with you."

Anton.

"How're you?"

"Well. How about you?"

He has the same sexy accent as the other men in the family, and he's technically single, but I know we'll never be interested in each other.

"Same. It's nice to be back around family for a few days."

He glances down at me before going back to surveilling the area. Does he know something? Does the family?

I don't know all the ins and outs of the bratva, but I know my sister married into the ruling family. She's Elodie's equivalent. Anton is super senior but not quite the same as Maks and his brothers. He's like a big toe's length below them. Same with

Sergei. I know both Sergei and Anton are talented hackers, so it makes me think at least one of them gathers the family's intel. Have they been watching me? Digging into my life?

Paranoid much?

We reach the women's restroom, and Anton knocks. We hear no one, so he pushes the door open. All the stall doors are ajar, and there are no visible feet within. Anton nods and backs up, letting the door close behind him. The moment it shuts, the first stall door opens wider.

I glance over my shoulder at where Anton must be on the other side of the door.

"Javier." My voice comes out a hiss.

"Madeline—sorry, Caitlyn—it's good to see you again."

I refuse to flinch. My gaze locks with his, and I'm as defiant as ever. I'm unprepared for him to step forward and grab my forearm. His hold is surprisingly gentle, but he tows me behind him into the disabled stall.

"I'll scream."

"No, you won't. You would have already. You didn't want the attention at the hotel, and you hate having it here. What the hell, Maddy?"

"Madeline."

"Caity."

I practically snarl at him. He knows I hate having my name shortened. Nobody does it.

"I don't care what name you go by. You will tell me what the hell is going on."

He snags my other arm and lifts them both between us. He turns them over as he looks at my wrists. He spins me around—and frisks me! Except I know he's not patting me down for weapons. He keeps the pressure light, and he's respectful in how he touches me. But I shy away from his hand when it glides over my kidney.

He takes a step closer to me, and I feel the heat from his body across my back. He doesn't exactly cage me. I could slip out from between the wall and him—if he let me.

"Who hurt you, Maddy?" His tone's softer—gentler.

If I lie, he'll know, so I remain silent.

"I'm not a cop."

I snort.

"So, I won't Miranda you. You *don't* have the right to remain silent. You will answer me."

I twist to see him. Our gazes meet yet again, and I see the arrogance I've always known. But there's genuine concern there. He's worried about me. There's certainly an ulterior motive, but some of it really is about me. When I shift to face him, he leans back enough to let me. We're still standing so close, we're practically touching. Nothing about him scares me like it would with any other man his size or Drew's.

"Tell me who. Let me help you."

"Why?"

His eyes narrow.

"I am *not* my cousin. I've done things worse than you can imagine, but I've never laid hands on a woman out of anger or violence. I have *never* hurt you. Just the opposite, and you know it."

"And you promised never, ever to bring that up."

"You promised to come to me if you were ever in danger again. We both lie."

"That was a long time ago."

"So? These bruises were fresh."

"I release you from that promise."

"Fantastic. I don't release you from yours. If you don't tell me what the hell is going on, I will dig until I find out. I will be your shadow like I was for nearly a year, but you won't appreciate it. I will find out. I will hold it against you for keeping it from me. And I will retaliate against whoever this was tenfold for whatever I find out they did to you."

"You're threatening me into confessing, so I won't feel guilty about someone else's blood on my hands. That worked when we were in high school, but it doesn't work now."

"Am I too late?"

Simmering anger on the cusp of rage darkens his already perpetually tan cheeks. He and his high school girlfriend went to make out in the same park I did with a guy I'd just started dating. The guy wanted more than I was willing to give. Javier heard me banging against the window as I tried to get the guy off me. Javier left his girlfriend and ran over to the car. He didn't know it was me at the time. He just knew it was a woman screaming.

The guy locked the doors with his key fob once we climbed into the backseat. I thought we were going to make out a little, but the guy wanted full-on sex. I was a virgin and planned to stay that way. When Javier tried to open the door, he discovered it was locked. He ran back to his car, got the tire iron, and shattered the driver's window.

He got the doors open, then dragged the douchebag out of the car. I thought he was going to kill the guy. Instead, he broke a couple ribs with the tire iron. He wanted to call the cops—risk having them see him since he insisted on being my witness.

I refused. I didn't want anyone to know. I didn't want my parents involved. Stupid teenager that I was. The compromise was Javier appointed himself as my bodyguard. We didn't go to high school together since I lived in New Jersey, and he lived in Queens. But every day, he'd make sure I got to school safely before booking it to his school. I think he was tardy almost every morning for a semester. As soon as he finished practice for whatever sport he was playing, he'd go to my house to make sure I got home safely.

On weekends, he'd be my shadow when I went out with friends. He kept an eye on me when I went out with other guys. He was a ghost, but I always knew he was there. I wished countless times when Drew first started abusing me that Javier was around, that I could count on him. Then that fantasy fizzled.

"Maddy, answer me. Am I too late?"

I shake my head.

"Say it. I told you, you don't have the right to remain silent."

"I have to go. Anton's going to wonder what's keeping me."

"Let him. Tell him your stomach rebelled. I don't give a shit what lie you tell that asshat. You will answer me."

"No. You aren't too late. Nothing like that happened."

"But someone hurt you."

"I take a martial arts bootca—"

"Lie to me, and I'll spin you around and spank you just like I did that night."

He sent his girlfriend home in a rideshare and hid me in the bathroom while Joaquin and Jorge came to get rid of the guy. He told them the girl he was with took off. Once his brothers left, he stalked into the bathroom and demanded answers like he is tonight. He warned me if I didn't answer and insisted upon acting like a guilty child trying to stay out of trouble, he'd treat me like one. I crossed my arms and tried to look down my nose at him.

He pulled me out of the restroom like he pulled me into this bathroom stall. Took me to the closest bench, sat down, yanked me over his lap, and spanked me.

Hard.

I confessed everything, and he comforted me. When I stopped crying, I apologized for being awkward when he went to so much trouble to help me. I thanked him, and he helped

41

me to my feet. That was when we exchanged our promises. We got in his car, and he took me home. We never discussed it again, but I knew what he did to keep me feeling safe. I never got to thank him for that.

"Javi, please don't make me."

I thought I could sound strong, but my voice is a tremulous whisper. I feel weak, which makes me feel defensive. He pulls me into his arms, and I remain rigid.

"Maddy, it's me. Let me help you."

"There's nothing to do. You know I have a fake identity. What was happening is over now. Let it go, just like I did."

"If you want the spanking, then tell me."

It tempts me. I've heard he's into kink, and the idea appeals to me, even if it would hurt. It's not just that he's hotter than any man I've ever met—seen. It's that someone else would be in control of the shitshow for even a minute. All I'd be able to concentrate on is him. Not even. It would be the pain in my ass —the kind I'd enjoy rather than how he's being by not letting up on this.

His left hand eases down to my lower back, his pinky at the top of my ass. He does nothing more; just lets it rest there.

"Is that what you want, *chiquita?*"

Little girl.

It's not patronizing or condescending like it is when Drew would sometimes call me that in English. It's endearing. I feel safe again like I did that night fifteen years ago. I can't help how my body melts against him now. I tell it not to, but it does.

"Javi, I have to go. Anton will come in soon. He'll get worried. Or worse, he'll call for Laura."

"But you don't want to go, do you?"

I shake my head.

What the fuck is wrong with me?

I'm that fucking damaged.

Chapter Five

Javier

The woman in my arms should be nowhere near me. She's right that Anton could walk in at any time. It would be way worse if Laura did. Anton might ask what I'm doing. Laura would put a blade through my eye before dragging her sister out. But I'm not letting go.

Not until Maddy makes me.

I've always thought of her like that, but I've never called her it. Not before today, at least. No one around me ever shortened her name except for Laura, and that was only sometimes, so I didn't either. I never felt obligated to watch over her, but I always felt protective once I saw her fighting to keep that guy—who died for his sins three years later—from assaulting her. Back then, she was more like a little sister or even a cousin since she was like Pablo's little sister.

But she doesn't feel like any sister should. She feels good.

She feels right.

I feel out of my fucking mind. This is an invitation to my

death, but I haven't pushed her away. I haven't stepped away. I know what I should do, and I'm saying fuck off to my common sense.

"Javi, thank you for caring. I don't want to go, but we have to. This is a horrible idea."

"Yet neither of us is letting go."

She wrapped her arms around my waist when my hand shifted to right above her ass. I'm fighting so many urges right now, and one of them is to cup her ass and discover if it feels as good as it looks. I'm certain it's even better. I've wanted to gouge out every man's eye who even glimpses at her tonight. I know that's nuts, but I'd hoist her over my shoulder and carry her away if I could.

Fucking barbaric.

It would just confirm what the other families say about me.

I don't want to care, but I do. I do for Maddy's sake.

"*Chiquita*, I'll let you go, but you have to promise me two things."

"No."

"You haven't heard either thing."

"That I'll tell you what's going on soon and that I'll tell you if I need help. I won't do either of those, Javi. Don't ask and don't tell me to."

"Then you and I will walk out of here together, and I'll take you straight to Maks. Anton can keep up if his knuckles dragging on the ground don't slow his ass down."

The guy went to UPENN on a full academic scholarship. He's not stupid. He's just not as smart as me, who went to Yale on a full academic scholarship too. Mine was entirely meritorious and had nothing to do with my family's financial situation, which was far better than his at the time.

"No. Javier, don't do this. Please don't push me. I can't."

"You won't."

44

"I can't. I'm not ready to talk about any of this. I can't get anyone else involved."

"Too late for that."

"Joaquin isn't in here making a fuss."

"But he noticed the bruises too."

"I don't doubt that he did, but he's minding his own business."

I keep my left arm around her waist as my right hand tips her chin up. Our gazes search each other, and I've never wanted to kiss a woman so much in my life. I even think she might accept one if I offered. But she's a woman with bruises and secrets. That usually means one thing. Having a man take advantage of her when she's clearly vulnerable would be a move too despicable for even me.

"Madeline, I gave you a choice. You tell me the truth, or you get a shadow. You just made your decision, now you must live with that."

"No."

She tries to shake her head, but I'm still holding her chin. I pinch enough to keep her from moving, but not enough to hurt her.

"You can tell me no about any and everything. I'll listen to you every time. But I'll ignore it every time for your protection. You cannot convince me otherwise."

"I'm safe, Javi. I'm not in that situation anymore. Let it go."

"Is he dead?"

She goes rigid once more.

"Did you kill him, Madeline?"

She swallows before she shakes her head, and I let her.

"Did someone else kill him?"

She shakes her head again.

"Then whatever it was still is. You might not be in the same room as whoever this man is, but any man who'd harm you, like

I believe this shitbag did, is a man who had complete control of you. That's the only way it could've happened. He's not a man who will just let you go. He will hunt you, won't he?"

Her expression doesn't change except for something in her eyes. I see it. She wants to appear defiant by not answering, but she's crumbling inside.

"You are going to leave this restroom and go back to your family. You're going to say a friend called, and you're going to head back to your parents' place to change. I'm certain *Tío* Enrique and *Tía* Elodie already left for their honeymoon, so you don't have to stay. One of the Kutsenkos' men will drive you home. You will let me in the house when I knock on the back door."

"No!"

"Yes, Maddy. You will tell me absolutely everything."

"No. I'll turn the alarm back on, and I won't let you in. And I'm not going home unless I'm with my parents. You can't make me do any of this, Javi. Don't force me."

That's a bucket of ice over me.

"Then tell Maks and his family what's going on. If you don't, I will. You need protection, Maddy. I'll never force you. That's the last thing I want. But I will *not* back down. I kept your secret the first time, and it was against my better judgment back then. There were hours every day when I feared for you because I couldn't be close to you. I couldn't get to you if you'd needed me. I can be there now if you'll let me. If you won't, then it'll be a bratva man who is."

"What? Are you going to order Maks to give me guards? That would go over so damn well."

"The moment I tell him someone hurt you and is likely hunting you, Laura won't let you out of her sight. Do you want to be under house arrest with Laura and Maks as your wardens

—never mind your mom and dad—or do you want freedom to come and go with me as just your shadow?"

"You're manipulating me, Javier. I don't appreciate it."

"I'm not. I'm talking to you like a woman who knows more about the life I live and your sister lives than you should. It means you know what she can arrange and what I can do. Do you want one man as your guard or an eight-man rotation? It's me or Maks, his brothers, and his cousins. Choose now, *chiquita*."

"You."

She doesn't hesitate, but she resents it. I don't care.

"I can't protect you if I don't know the truth."

"You'll have to figure out how to. I won't reject your offer anymore, but I'm not telling you anything else."

"Then I will see the boogeyman in anyone who goes near you. Do you want me to confront every man in sight?"

"No. I'll tell you some of it, but not tonight. I want to stay with my family. It's been ages since I've had fun with them. I want to enjoy it."

I stare down at her before I nod. Relief settles over her, and a surge of guilt washes over me for pushing way too hard. I dialed it down about a million from how I'd be if I were interrogating a man, but obviously, I was still too much. I don't want to remind her of whoever I want to learn about.

I suspect it's the guy she was with, and I just want her to give in and tell me. But at the same time, if that's who did this, I'm not surprised she doesn't want to tell me. She fears him, and she doesn't want to admit she stayed with a man who mistreated her.

"Tomorrow, Maddy. That's as long as I'm willing to wait."

A knock on the door signals we've run out of time. I can't believe Anton waited this long, but I'm glad he did.

"Coming! Meet me at the park?" She says the second part to only me.

"Nine?"

"Okay."

She steps out of the stall, and I go back to standing on the toilet seat. I listen to her when she speaks to Anton.

"Sorry about that. I had to take a call about a patient. I needed privacy to discuss the case."

"No worries."

Anton's voice fades as he responds, and the door closes a moment later. I count to a hundred before I step down. I ease open the restroom door and count to forty before I step out. No one appears, but I know we have men hidden in the shadows as added security. There was nearly a scene between Olivia Mancinelli, the Mafia underboss's wife, and Cormac O'Rourke's date. We have history with the woman's family, so I stuck close by since the woman's brother was there too. Sack of shit he is.

Besides that, it's been the perfect event. The wedding was moving, and I don't remember a time I've been prouder to be part of my family than when I stood in the row of groomsmen as my *tío* married his soulmate. I glance in Maddy's direction as I return to the ballroom.

I wonder what she'd look like in a wedding dress rather than the gown she's in now.

My eyes feel like I rubbed them with sandpaper. I'm exhausted, and I wish I could blame it on a hangover or fucking a bridesmaid all night. Considering the three women who stood beside *Tía* Elodie are all married and connected to a different syndicate, I definitely didn't go after any of them.

Instead, I spent all night two houses down from Maddy's parents' house. I had to park farther down the street until *Tío* Luis and *Tía* Margherita got home. I couldn't risk them recognizing my car. Once I was in position, I remained camped out there until Maddy got in her car twenty minutes ago. I've followed her most of the way to the park, but I took a shortcut to get here first.

I've already swept the area, and it's clear. It's a state park, not one with a playground. There's no one nearby on the trails, but there could be at any minute. I park at the far end of the lot, nearly out of sight. It's where Maddy and I ended up with our dates that night. I hope she figures out this is the spot.

I only have to wait another two minutes before her car appears. She backs into the spot like I did and looks over at me. I climb out of my car, and she opens her door.

"No."

She hears me and looks over again as I walk around the hood of my car and approach her. Her door is ajar, so I open it. However, I block her from getting out.

"From now on, you don't get out unless I open the door or give you a signal that it's safe."

"A signal or open it for me? You're supposed to be a ghost. You can't come near me without someone noticing, and if you're hidden, I won't see any signal."

"Do not get out of the car again until I let you know it's safe, Maddy."

I step aside, and she climbs out. She opens her mouth to disagree, but when I shake my head, she snaps it shut. She pushes the car door hard enough to slam it, but I catch it, closing it with barely a sound. She turns toward some tables, but I open my passenger door.

"Until I know what's going on, I consider this is a safe place, but it's still exposed. We can talk in my car."

She narrows her eyes.

"For Pete's sake, Maddy. I know you have horrible memories of being in a car alone with a guy here, but do you really think I'm here to harm you? That's insulting."

She looks duly chagrined. "I'm sorry."

She gets in, and I close the door. I hurry back to my side and climb in. I watch her from the corner of my eye. I've pushed—shoved—as hard as I dare. Now, I have to let her open up to me. If I do more, I'll be nothing short of a bully. She won't trust me, and she'll either lie or omit a shit ton. I don't want her to feel like I'm interrogating her just with my eyes. I've been told my stare can be intense.

"Javi, I won't give you any specifics. Know that now. You won't convince me to, so don't try. I was dating a guy who got rough with me a few times. I was dumb enough to forgive him the first time it happened because he was drunk. I believed him when he said he thought I was someone else and shouldn't have walked up behind him."

She didn't believe him, and I can tell. The bastard knew who she was and hurt her, anyway. But I remain quiet.

"It happened a couple more times, and I felt trapped. He has money and connections, so I got scared he would track me down. I decided an alias would be better."

"An alias that must have a driver's license, a credit card, and car registration. That's not just breaking up and moving home."

Those were observations, not questions. But from the mulish set of her jaw, I can tell she took them as accusations.

"I wanted to disappear for a bit."

"So, you went to your parents?"

"Not my fault your uncle decided to get married this week *and* invited my entire family to the reception."

Once upon a time, they would have been at the wedding too. Maybe not Laura and Maks, but she and her parents would've been. Maks might've waited outside the church for Laura. Now that wasn't even a remote possibility.

"When did you tell your parents you're headed back up to Albany?"

"After lunch."

"Today?"

"Yeah. They think I need to get back to work."

"But you quit."

She remains silent.

"Last I heard, you were with the same guy for a few years. Drew something or other."

"I'm not with him anymore."

"Because of this?"

"Our relationship ended when there just wasn't anything left between us."

"Maddy, being evasive doesn't mean I can't read between the lines. Don't treat me like I'm too dumb to get the subtext."

"I don't think you're dumb."

"But you are being evasive."

"I told you I would be from the start. I won't give you details."

I twist in my seat, so I can look at her more easily. She's reluctant, but she turns toward me. Her hands are knotted in her lap, and her left thumb rubs the back of her right. It's an obvious tell, but it's been hers since we were teens. I reach out and cover her hands with mine.

"I can learn everything about the guy in five minutes if I want to. You can force me to dig, or you can just tell me. Either way, I'll know."

"Please, just leave it alone. If anyone you doubt comes near me, then do something. Otherwise, just fade into the background like you did when we were kids."

"I worried about you back then. Now I fear for you, *chiq-*

uita. The guy back then was a teen like us. He was a brute, but he didn't have the experience an adult man has. He didn't have the resources an adult man has. It's not the same. The danger was significant back then. Be reasonable about how much worse it is now. I'll protect you no matter what, but it would make my job exponentially easier if you told me everything."

"If it's that hard, then quit this *job.*"

The venom in her voice tells me something about that word cuts deeper than I can guess.

"You know what I meant, Maddy. I don't see you as an obligation or burden, so don't make me out to be the villain here."

"I don't have to."

That cuts deep.

She's throwing who I am and who I have to be in my face. She's pushing me away because I've gotten too close. I get her.

"You're being awkward for the sake of being awkward. Madeline, you're one wrong word away from that spanking. I told you I won't bend to your will when it comes to your protection."

"Don't scold me, *Javier.*"

"I'm sorry, *chiquita.*"

"How is that any better? I'm not a little girl, *Javier.*"

"Stop that." My hand tightens around hers. "I wasn't scolding you when I used your full name. I didn't mean for it to sound that way. You've always preferred it, and I wanted you to know how serious I am. You're not a little girl. You're *my* little girl."

That one word—*my*—reveals more of my feelings than I want, but I can't ignore the surge of possessiveness and protectiveness that consumes me. I don't want to ignore it. I want to devour her. I want to be inside her. I'm unprepared for how strong this wave of emotion is. I feel like I'm the vulnerable one now.

I lean in, but I won't kiss her until she lifts her chin. I won't take advantage of her when we've been discussing someone who's done nothing but take advantage of her, albeit in a different way. She speaks before I can bring my lips to hers.

"I'm not a Little, Javi."

That makes me pause. I draw back enough to look her in the eyes.

"I'm not a Daddy Dom. Were you someone's sub, and it got too rough? They didn't respect your boundaries? Is that what happened?"

"No. You are a Dom, though."

It's not a question, but I answer anyway.

"I am."

She swallows before her gaze drops to my lips. Hers part.

"You're not a sub, but you want to try, don't you?"

She remains quiet, so I continue to do the talking. I watch her to gauge whether I'm headed in the right direction.

"You want someone else in control right now. You want someone who'll take care of you. Make you feel special, protected, desirable, and deserving of their attention. You want to obey because you want your only focus to be on your Dom. You want the freedom to try new things. You want to know that ultimately you decide whether to stop or keep going. You need that power, even if you don't want to control the scene. It's why each time I threaten to spank you, you get wet."

Her nostrils flare. I suspected—hoped—but that confirmed it. When her cheeks flush a deep red, it's not desire like I feel. It's mortification. She thinks I know how she reacts to me from some embarrassing indicator. I lean forward and bring my lips to just behind her ear. I let them brush her skin as I speak.

"My dominance might make you wet, but you've been

keeping me hard since the moment I laid eyes on you in that hotel."

"Do I have to submit?"

"You already did, *chiquita*. But I won't force you to do it completely. Keep your wall around you—for now—but it's already crumbled in parts. You didn't leave the restroom the moment you found me. The moment I put my hand on you. The moment I insisted you let me help. The moment I told you to get in my car. The moment my hand touched yours. You've stayed, so you've already submitted."

"Javi."

It's a breathless whisper as I pull back. She turns her head, and our lips brush. Immediately, it explodes into more than any first kiss I've ever had. This is all my attraction to her from a decade and a half ago that's laid dormant along with everything I've felt since seeing her. Recognizing her only opened the vault. From the way she's kissing me, I think it's the same for her. My free hand tunnels into her hair, and she moans. I fist it, and her tongue thrusts into my mouth.

I let go of her hands to cup her neck, and she fists my shirt. The fucking center console is in the way, or I think she'd try to pull me over it. It's certainly the only thing that's keeping me from lifting her to straddle my lap. God, how I want her pussy pressed to my cock. I want to run my hands over her, but I don't dare.

As much as I want this—as much as I'm ready for this—she's not. Maybe the kiss, yes. But more? No. She's hiding from some man who abused her. I don't want to frighten her. I don't want her to think I'm some predator. I don't want to remind her of him.

"Javi, I know you're not him."

She pulled away to say that, and she kisses my cheek when she finishes. She brings our lips together again, and she's even more insistent. I test the waters by tightening my hold on her hair and resting my other hand on her throat. She moans again and leans into my palm. I press more weight against her throat, but nothing more. I kiss along her jaw until my lips are back to where they were when I whispered to her before.

"You're not a Little. I'm not a Daddy Dom. But you are my *chiquita*. You're smaller than me, and you're vulnerable right now. You deserve and need protection. You deserve and need someone who appreciates you, respects you, wants the best for you. You deserve someone who'll take care of you."

"You just described a father."

"Or a significant other. You deserve a partner."

"What are you saying, Javi?"

"I'm saying you deserve better than whatever you had."

She pulls back from me, searching my gaze for something. She doesn't know if I'm offering or just saying this in passing. She must have missed the *"my"* both times I said it. I've had a week to think about this. To imagine what this would be like. Not just the physical part, though Lord knows I've jacked off every day thinking about that.

I've thought about what it would be like to offer her those things, and what it might be like if she were my partner. She's vulnerable in more ways than one, but she's not weak. If she escaped whatever hellscape she was in, assumed a false identity, and still insists she can protect herself, then that steel backbone I remember from when we were teenagers is still there.

I infuse more command into my voice than I've used so far, but I'm careful not to make her think I want to intimidate her.

"I know you heard every word I've said, so you must be ignoring me calling you *my chiquita*."

"What am I supposed to call you in return? *Papi?* Daddy?"

We stare at each other, and something shifts in the air

between us. The words hang there, but neither of us shies away from them.

"Do you know how badly I wanted to kiss you like this when we were in high school, *chiquita*? How big a crush I had on you?"

"You never showed it. I didn't think you enjoyed being around Laura or me since you hated attending the Sunday dinners you got stuck going to at Luis and Margherita's."

"I spoke no English when my mom, brothers, and I arrived. I didn't understand most of it for the first two years. When I did, I hated the small talk. I hate small talk now. I already saw Pablo and Juan all the time, so there was nothing new to hear from them. Juan and Laura were practically twins and always together. You gravitated to Pablo. Joaquin, Jorge, and I could've just stayed home for all we talked to anyone else. But that doesn't mean I didn't have a crush on you."

I rest my hand on her waist as my other forearm rests on the center console. I've twisted toward her as much as I can. What I really want—want even more than a minute ago—is for her to straddle me. Now, it's so we can talk more easily not just because I want her cunt as close to my cock as I can get it with clothes in the way.

"I had one on you. I thought you didn't care about me. You had that one girlfriend, but otherwise, you didn't seem to date. That or you were so discreet, it never came up. You only paid attention to me once you rescued me, but even then, it's not like we hung out."

Her gaze doesn't waver, but her shoulders round a little when she admits she thought our feelings weren't the same. My fingers tighten on her waist. I want her to know how serious I am about what I'm confessing.

"Maddy, I had that one girlfriend because I couldn't be with you, so I used to imagine she was you. It didn't last because I hated pretending since she was never a good substitute. I had some decency to know how wrong that was, so I ended it. I didn't want anyone else but you. Then you went to Albany for college and stayed up there. I rarely saw you while we were in college, and it'd been years since we've been in the same room. I was so into you."

"I was into you, but you never gave me even a hint you were interested."

As she speaks, her gaze drops to where my arm rests on the console. I shift and draw one of her hands up, so I can still balance my weight while entwining our fingers. My thumb rubs over the back of hers.

"You were outgoing and into everything. You love being around people. I hate it. I've always been a homebody. I liked you, but I didn't think we had enough in common. Besides, there's no way your parents or you would want you with a guy in the Cartel."

"That's present tense. Not back when we were in school. Now."

"At any time."

"You know Laura and Juan had a past that went beyond merely being best friends. My parents didn't stop that."

"They never liked each other romantically at the same time. They might have been fuck buddies, but they were never a couple."

"So, fuck buddies wasn't what you wanted."

"And it's not what I want now."

"What're you saying, Javi? Do you want me as your sub?"

That makes me pull back and sigh. "No."

"You already have one."

"Technically, but I haven't seen her in two and a half months. It's over. I just haven't told her."

She lets go of my hand and leans as far away from me as she can. Any trust she had just evaporated.

"Maddy, she's not my girlfriend. It's never been romantic. It's a relationship, but it's not a friendship or a partnership. It serves—served—a purpose for her and for me. It's run its course. I just haven't had the heart to tell her because I wanted to avoid an argument."

"You've just been stringing her along. Making her wonder why you're not into her anymore. Making her sit around, waiting for you to pity her with your attention."

"No. She's free to see whomever she wants, and she does whatever she pleases. I've avoided it because she needed a place to stay a few months ago, so I let her move into one of my rental units on Staten Island. I don't want to kick her out, but part of the reason my interest fizzled is because I know she's taking advantage of living rent free."

"Taking advantage? She probably thinks she has a shitty boyfriend."

"Hardly." My laugh's hollow. "She's not some kept woman. Some mistress I keep tucked away in a fuck pad. I tried helping her out when her landlord upped her rent by five percent with barely the legally required advance notice. She knew it was a favor and changed nothing about our agreement. She knew it was supposed to be temporary, but she's stretched it out. I don't want an argument, and I don't want to dump her on the street. I've avoided it and just let her stay there."

Maddy stares at me, and I feel like shit on the bottom of her shoe.

"You've always avoided conflict when you can. I know your roles in your family mean you stir up shit, but it's never been your instinct to do it."

She watches me for another moment before looking down at where my hand now rests on her thigh.

"Why don't you give her the option to move out or pay rent?"

"I was going to do that once I ended our arrangement, but it's not like I'm going to do that over text or the phone. She deserves me seeing her in person to end it."

"But you suspect she'll argue with you about it, so you've been ignoring the situation. It won't just go away."

"I know. But I have a more important reason than ever to break it off."

Maddy cocks an eyebrow. She looks like she did in the hotel room and in the restroom stall. She looks beautiful.

"Maddy, I've thought about you nonstop since the hotel. I figured out who you were when I saw *Tío* Enrique's tat right after we left the hotel. I waited outside the hotel for you, but I discovered you'd already left. I knew you went to another hotel, then to your parents."

"You've stalked me?"

"Yeah."

She blinks three times before she laughs. Not the response I expected.

"If it were anyone else, that would be fucked-up and freak me out. But you're so honest about it, and I know it's because you're worried about me. I guess I can accept that."

"It's given me time to imagine a lot of shit between us, and not all of it was sexual."

"But some of it was?"

It's my turn to sit here blinking before I cock an eyebrow. She smiles and shrugs.

"Maddy, the list of whatever you aren't telling me is probably a mile long, but it all stems from you just ending a relationship. I have one to end. This is a shitty time for either of us to want someone new. Not to mention your in-laws will execute me when they find out

I've even breathed in your direction. But I know what I want."

"Oh?"

"Do you know what you want?"

I'm too chicken shit to admit it without a better idea of whether she might want anything similar.

"Yeah, I do. And I'm not afraid to admit it includes you. I've been thinking about you nonstop too. I had a massive crush on you for years, so some of that has come back up. You're not a boy anymore, and I'm definitely not that girl by a long shot. You're right that I want a partner. There are a lot of days when it's hard to remember I deserve anything good. I'm pretty fucking damaged right now, Javi. I'm a hot mess without a home or a job. You don't need a second woman in your life without a place of her own."

"Those are entirely separate situations that aren't alike. I don't want to be your rebound."

"A rebound only happens when there's enough air in the ball to bounce. I feel utterly deflated. At least, I do when I'm not around you. Last night... Now... It's different. I feel like my old self when I'm around you. But I don't know that I can handle much more than just breathing."

"Then I'll wait until you know."

Chapter Six

Maddy

Oh. My. God.

First, it was that kiss. My stomach's still in knots, and my pussy aches like crazy. It's taking all my resolve not to look at his dick while I wonder what it would feel like to have it inside me. I spent hours wondering that in high school and the first couple years of college. I've been wondering it for the past week. Now, I don't think I'll ever stop wondering it.

Second, it's knowing he was and is interested in me too. Shut the fucking front door. I thought he looked at me like a kid sister, and that's why he insisted upon watching out for me. Like a silent favor to Pablo and his family.

Third, I want what he's talking about. What he could offer. But what if I'm so fucking broken I don't know how to be a proper girlfriend anymore? What if I'm too weak now to be a partner to a man like Javi?

Fourth, Drew.

But, God, how I want what he's offering. I just want to say yes.

"Maddy, I'm sorry. All I've done is push too hard since last night."

"What? No! I'm thinking not retreating. Your family might be all right with me, but you weren't wrong about Maks's. Being anywhere near me puts you in even more danger with all of them than I can guess you already live with."

Not to mention what Drew would do if he ever found out. He's in the syndicate pee wee league compared to Javier. But that wouldn't stop him. The man is not right in the head.

I should tell Javi the truth. All of it. Come clean and even let him help me. Some of it is pride. I don't want to admit how weak I've been. There's so much shit I did that I'm not proud of just to keep the peace with Drew. Some of it is fear one of them will explode. Javi and Drew are both powder kegs, and there are way too many fuses around them. I don't want any harm to come to Javi. It's part of the reason I didn't want him to know anything about what's going on. I don't want to be the reason for something bad happening.

"*Chiquita*, give me two days to end things with her. Let me be truly available to you. Then think about what you do or don't want. I'll wait."

"I've thought about it nonstop. I told you that. But there's so much standing in our way. Our families won't approve."

"Your family won't."

What more can I do but nod? It's true.

"You also don't want to tell me the truth. If you agreed to be with me, you know you'd have to. You know I wouldn't settle for any less, and your conscience wouldn't let you keep it from me. Whatever happened, you don't trust me enough to tell me. You don't know me well enough as I am now."

"Javi, I think I trust you pretty fucking implicitly to be sitting in a car in a nearly deserted park with you."

"That's not what I mean, and you know it. You know I won't physically harm you. You know I won't kidnap you. You can imagine a sliver of what I would do to protect you from either of those things."

A sliver?

I know he's in the Cartel. I know what that means. I did before I met Drew, and I have a better fucking clue now. But I also know Javi and his brothers saw shit while growing up in Bogotá that they never should have. Not as adults and certainly not as young children. I probably can only imagine a sliver of what he's capable of.

Thinking about Drew doing those sorts of things used to make me want to retch. It disgusted me and tormented me. With Javi, it reassures me. What kind of sick fuck does that make me?

One who can rationalize why it's fine for Javi to be a torturing criminal and still want to curl into his arms while I wanted to slash Drew's throat once I found out.

He cups my face, and I meet his gaze. His eyes might be the shade of milk chocolate, but I'm the one who wants to melt into a puddle when he looks at me like he is now.

"I'm gun shy, and I admit it, Javi. But there's no one else who can tempt me to try again. End things with your sub, and I'll give us a chance. I can't promise what'll come of that."

"That's all I'm asking for. Keep your secrets, Maddy. I won't demand again. Lord knows I have secrets I can never tell you. I'll lie to you, little one. I'll omit the truth. I'll do whatever and say whatever I have to, to protect you and the people we love. It's hypocritical to hold you to a different standard than I hold myself."

I'm keeping my secrets to protect you and the people we love too.

"I understand why there's a different standard. I've known what your family is since I was a kid. I know the family my sister married into. I don't know all the ins and outs, but I know enough."

"Promise me something, though. Promise you'll call me the moment you feel unsafe. Don't brush it off. Tell me. If we're going to be anything to each other, then I won't be your shadow. I won't hound you. But I'll only agree to that if you swear to tell me if you get scared."

"I promise, Javi."

I cup his cheek and stretch over the center console to kiss him. His right hand rests at the side of my neck, but his left hand is reaching around for something. His seat slides back, breaking our kiss. Then his hands are on my waist, and he's lifting me onto his lap. The steering wheel digs into my lower back, but I'm straddling him like I ached to do. We're kissing again, and his hands guide my hips to move. I grind my pussy against his cock, and holy fuck. There's nothing little about this man.

When I'm moving in a rhythm he likes and is driving me crazy, his hands slide down to my ass. He grips it, and it reminds me how bony it is now. I used to like my ass back when I had one. But from the way he intensifies the kiss and how hard he's squeezing, I think he likes what I have. He reclines the seat, and I fall forward. It gives his hand room to draw back and spank me.

Over and over.

"Ow! Javi, ow! That fucking hurts."

"I know. It should."

"I thought we agreed I could keep my secrets. Are you punishing me for that?"

"No. I'm setting a precedence for you to understand what'll happen if you keep anything from me that could pose a threat to your safety."

He's not gentle about this. My ass burns. But he stops as abruptly as he started. When he wraps his hand around my throat this time, he squeezes. Not enough to scare me or make it hard to breathe. But it's possessive as fuck.

I love it.

I hated it when Drew would do it. It wasn't kinky breath play. It was to make me think he would kill me until I realized he wouldn't. He couldn't afford to do more than knock me around.

I feel safe while Javi does this.

"I'm going to say this a third time, and I'm going to keep saying it whenever I want. You are *my chiquita.*"

I wait for him to say more, but he doesn't. He's laid his claim, and I don't object. I have no idea what this will be like between us, but I love this dominant side. It makes me feel all the things he said I deserved to feel. Safe. Protected. Appreciated. Desired.

"I will take care of things with her today. One way or another, she won't be my sub by dinner. She might be my tenant, but that's it. I haven't touched her in nearly three months, Maddy, and I won't ever again. You are mine, and I am yours for as long as you want this."

"Me?"

"I told you I'll wait. That means I'm not walking away unless you tell me to. Even then, it won't be without a fight."

"After today, does that mean you're mine?"

"Absolutely."

"What does this mean, though? Like what will this look like?"

"I don't know. It depends on what you're ready for. I don't want to be just your fuck buddy, but if sex is all you want—"

"It's not. I just don't know how much of that I can offer, and I don't know how much nonsexual stuff I can offer, either. I just don't know."

"We move slowly. When we reach your boundary, we talk about it. I will never force my way past it unless it's—"

"About my safety. I know." I grin. "You sound like an old man the way you whittle. Maybe I should call you—"

Something in his gaze changes, and my heart races. Daddy and *Papi* are what we're both thinking. He rescued me earlier by changing the subject, but he just keeps looking at me. His left hand slides down the back of my jeans until we're skin to skin since I'm wearing a thong. I press into his right hand, increasing the resistance against my throat as I lean farther forward.

"Daddy."

If he practically devoured me before, I don't know how to describe this. His hand slides down from my throat to my tits. He's careful, uncertain where else I might be bruised. I don't mean to, but I can't help it when I shy away ever so slightly. Immediately, his hands grab the hem of my shirt and lift.

"You will let me see, Maddy. All bets are off. I'll take it all back if you fight me on this."

I close my eyes and lift my arms as he pulls my shirt over my head. He tosses my top on the passenger seats. His fingertips graze over my back, just enough pressure to make me wince when he gets to my kidney. He sits up and twists to see around me. I know the bruises are yellow. They're in their final stage of healing. I suck in a breath as his hand trails up my right ribs. He lifts my hands over my head, placing them on the head rest behind him.

I keep my eyes closed through all of this. I don't want to see

66

his expression while he examines me. Because I'm not watching, and he's so gentle, I'm unprepared to feel his lips wrap around my nipple or for his tongue to toy with it. I didn't even notice him move my bra cups.

"Javi."

"Mmm."

He just sucks harder after I moan his name. When he tires of that side, he moves to the other. His hands return to my hips to guide me again. He abandons my nipples to kiss over the remaining bruises my bra hid until he pulled the cups down. He smatters them with kisses before he sucks beside an existing bruise. I open my eyes and look down. He's watching my face, reading me. He knows these came from someone pinching me. He already knows I wasn't a sub, though I could've just been in a relationship with some BDSM.

He's marking me. Covering what Drew left with his own brand. He's replacing my terrible memories with good ones. He leaves fresh love bites in places that weren't marred. He's doing it because he can. When I look down in the days to come, all I'll see are signs I belong to him now.

I love it.

He draws me down, so we press chest to chest. My head rests on his shoulder. I feel his heart racing. Everything else about him seems so calm and unhurried. But I realize how much discovering what he suspected is real bothers him.

"*Chiquita*, let me hold you."

I let my body go limp against him, and his heart rate slows. He relaxes too. One of his hands slips down my jeans again to cup my ass. His other hand sweeps up and down my back. I kiss his neck, and I feel affection for the first time in years. I feel it as I give it and receive it.

"Don't let me go for a while."

His arms tighten around me. "I told you this ends when you

tell me to walk away. Until then, I will hold you and not let go. You're mine, Maddy. This is where you belong."

I've heard those words before, and I hated them every single time. But they were never said with reverence. With softness. With respect. Sure, they're possessive as fuck. But Javi's kind of possessiveness comes from his protectiveness. It's not him wanting to keep me from the world. It's not him wanting to limit me to only what he allows. His possessiveness comes from wanting to ensure I can have everything I need. He won't let anything get in the way of me having that.

"When can we see each other again?"

"Tomorrow, little one. I'll figure something out with work. If your family thinks you're going back up to Albany tonight, you won't be staying with your parents. Where will you go?"

"Back to the hotel in Brooklyn. I didn't end the reservation. I extended it. I figured it's been long enough that you wouldn't expect me to go back. It puts enough distance from my parents that I can't run into them. It's in a different borough from Laura and the others. You could come there."

"All right. What time?"

"Whenever. I'm not going anywhere once I'm there."

I don't know how long passes while we simply sit with me still straddling his lap and his arms wrapped around me. I nearly doze off a few times, but I know Javi's wide awake. I doubt he'd ever fall asleep somewhere so potentially exposed. This is the most relaxed I've been in—I don't know how long. I could stay like this forever.

"I love you too, Dad."

My dad gives me a massive bear hug like he has since I was a kid. Until this morning, it was the hug that made me feel safe no matter what. The moments when he engulfed me in his arms and pressed me against his broad chest were moments I felt untouchable from Drew, even when he was in the room with my dad and me.

Now, it's Javi who makes me feel that way. That sense of being shielded by the world is at least ten times stronger with Javi.

I step back, and my mom takes my dad's place.

"I love you, sweetie."

"I love you, Mom."

She's soft in all the right place, and I relax against her. If my dad is my shield, then my mom is the solution to the world's problems. There's nothing she can't help me sort out. At least, that's what I tell her. There's shit I'll never tell her. It's the same shit Javi tempted me to disclose, but I held back. I've never wanted to share any of my secrets with anyone, but I was close to relenting with Javi. I'm delusional to think I won't, eventually. I know I will. I'm just not ready yet.

It's almost noon when my parents walk me out to my car, and I have to remind myself it's mine. I still expect to see my SUV. I told them I borrowed this from Drew's cousin since it's more fuel efficient to drive down here from Upstate New York.

I know Javi has a Porsche, but he was in one of his family's Suburbans yesterday. I'm certain it was because he wanted a bulletproof shield around us. The Four Families have these behemoth SUVs that are souped up with a shit ton of after-market parts that make them practically tanks. Among other features, they're entirely bulletproof from top to bottom and all the way around.

As I consider it, I realize he's been showing me he's determined to protect me since the first moment we looked at each other last night. He's not a man to make false promises. At least not to the people who matter, and I must be among the ones who do. That makes my toes curl in my shoes as I load my bag into my trunk. I have to go back to the hotel here in Jersey that I was in before I arrived at my parents' place the day before yesterday. It's where the rest of my stuff is. I'll check out there and head back into Brooklyn.

It'll be another night alone, but I'll see Javi again tomorrow. I haven't felt lonely since I left Albany. I've felt free, even if I've been scared Drew or Javi would find me. As I drive away from Mom and Dad, loneliness settles over me. I refuse to be fucking needy and mopey when Javi isn't around. I won't give up my hard-earned independence. But I wish I were going to see him rather than one empty hotel room then another. Rather depressing after how things were in his SUV a few hours ago.

As I drive, I check all my mirrors in a rotation, along with looking through the windshield. I'm searching for any car I recognize or might be following me. As I merge into traffic in Brooklyn, I'm certain there's the same sedan I saw when I stopped at the Jersey hotel. I don't want to go to the next hotel and lead someone to me. Though, the first hotel would have been an easy place to corner me.

Did Javi send someone? Is Maks and his family suspicious, and one of them sent a guy? Did Drew track me down?

I'm tired of my paranoia. I wonder if I'll get over it. I want to tell myself it's situational awareness, but since nothing's happened—knock on wood—it must be an overactive imagination.

I circle the block a few times until I no longer see the car behind me. I breathe a little easier, but I still don't go straight to the hotel. Instead, I swing through a drive-thru. I'm not hungry yet, but I will be later. I would've gone to the store since I have a full kitchen at this hotel, but now that I think I'm being—or was being—followed, that doesn't seem like such a good idea.

I eat my fries to keep from winding up with soggy ones

later. I pull into the hotel parking lot as I finish the last one. I look for a parking spot, and I could swear the car I thought was following me is now in the lot. But it was never close enough for me to see the license plate, so I can't be sure. There's no one in it, and I don't want to get close enough to peek inside. I debate whether to go through the lobby or slip through the keycard-controlled side door like I did the few times I had to come and go before.

I decide to make an appearance through the lobby since I haven't been around for a couple days. I made a massive detour on the way to my parents' house, which was only a couple miles from my second hotel. I slipped back in here, messed up the bed, left a couple plates in the sink, and left a couple hairs in the bathroom sink.

That made me super anxious, but I hooked the hang tag on the door asking for housekeeping to come in. I knew their schedule for my floor, so I waited around the block until I figured they were done. I hurried back up to my room and put the hang tag back on the door but with the side saying Do Not Disturb showing.

Now I smile at the receptionist as I go by. Once I'm out of her sight, I hurry to the elevator. There's no one in the lobby, so I don't fear someone noticing me. I know there are cameras, but I keep my head down for most of my walk. I only wanted the receptionist to see me to confirm I'm still staying here. I don't dally once I get off the elevator. I put my ear to my room's door and listen. I hear nothing. I know I can't avoid the sound of the door unlocking, so I press down on the handle to keep it from relocking, but I don't open it.

Nothing happens.

I have my phone camera up as I lean against the door to make enough room for me to angle my phone without exposing myself. I use the camera to look around the limited area I can see. When I've done all I can to ensure no one's in there, I walk in. I bolt the door and flip the metal latch.

I'd just gotten back from the store when Javi and Joaquin burst in. It's why I was in the kitchen. I'd had my hands full, so I hadn't set the bolt or put the bar across the door.

I check every corner until I'm satisfied there're no cameras or listening devices I can find. I kick off my shoes near the sofa and turn on the TV. I'm still not hungry, but I force down my sandwich. By the time I'm done, my eyes are drooping. It's not even that late, but I'm totally drained. I toss the wrappers and bags in the trash and am ready to drag myself to bed when I hear someone try to unlock the hotel door.

Chapter Seven

Javier

I brace myself for impact as I unlock the door.

"Javier?"

"*Sí, Anna Maria, soy yo.*" Yes, Anna Maria. It's me.

For nearly six months, the promise of kinky sex excited me whenever I arrived, and my sub was already here. I've always let myself in, and that was part of the novelty. She didn't know exactly when I'd show up, and I didn't know exactly how I'd find her. But dread makes my gut churn now.

Anna Maria's an attractive redhead, and I enjoyed every minute of being with her—at least when it involved tying her up and fucking her until we were both breathless. But everything outside the bedroom, especially dealing with the apartment, became a chore. That's why I've been avoiding her. Believe it or not, my instinct is conflict avoidance.

Rather than just show up like I used to, I called ahead this time. She knows we're going to talk, but it doesn't surprise me when she steps out of the bedroom in transparent lingerie. It does nothing for me. It's like looking at any of the dancers at the strip clubs my family owns in New Jersey. The novelty of being around naked women wore off before I was even legally old enough to drink.

The only woman I want to see in lingerie—preferably naked—is Maddy.

"*Vestirse.*" Get dressed.

It's a command for sure, but it's not in the tone I used to use. I want her to know I'm serious about talking. I don't want her to think it's a prelude to what we used to share.

"*Pero, Jav—*" But, Jav—

We continue in Spanish since she's a Colombian girl from the block back in Jackson Heights. We're in Staten Island because once upon a time, it kept the other syndicate eyes off me. Fucking Cormac O'Rourke. So much for privacy once he found out.

"No buts. Get dressed, Anna. Please. We need to talk, and it won't be me giving you another order."

She studies my expression before she drops her gaze and nods. We'll see how submissive she feels by the end of this conversation. The red hair might not be natural, but her temper matches it. I've known her since high school, so I've seen what she's like when she unleashes. I'm not in the mood for that and won't tolerate it.

It only takes her a minute to toss on a pair of yoga pants and a sweatshirt before joining me in the living room. Before she can get too close, I point to an armchair. I take the spot in the middle of the sofa.

"Have you found a permanent place yet?"

"This is so convenient for you. I figured—"

"You've known since I offered this place that it's temporary. If you haven't found one you prefer, then you can stay here. However, it'll be as a tenant."

She stares at me, and I know she's fighting to master her shock then her anger.

"Paying you rent for you to come here and fuck me is fucked-up. Or are you a *puto* now?"

"Do you think calling me a prostitute is endearing? We both know you've been using me for the apartment to stay rent free. You've made no effort to find a new one, which tells me you think you can use me. I haven't come to see you because I didn't want to just toss you out. But knowing I'm being used doesn't exactly give me a hard-on."

"So, you want me out or to pay rent, so you can get it up again?"

"No. That part of our arrangement has been over for months, and you know that as well as I do. It's why you haven't texted me to ask where I am. You've been happy to come and go as you please without having to put out."

I'm being a tremendous ass, and I know it. I didn't mean to launch into the conversation and be a *cabrón*—asshole—but something in me just doesn't have any patience for her anymore. It's the way she looked at me. Sized me up as though she was guessing how much more she could get out of me.

"Just like that, you're going to kick me out and end our relationship?"

"Contract, and no, I'm not kicking you out. I gave you a choice. You can pay rent like any tenant would, or you can find somewhere else."

"You think I'd want you as a landlord after this?"

"Not particularly, but this is a rent-controlled building, so you won't find a better deal."

"It's fucking Staten Island!"

"That hasn't bothered you yet."

It hasn't bothered her because free on Staten Island is better than any amount in another borough. *La conchuda*—a moocher. That's what she is. She'll take what she can for free. What's worse is she believes the world owes it to her because she's beautiful.

"Why're you doing this, Javier? Why did you wait so long if you have a problem with me staying here?"

"I told you, I didn't want to kick you out, but I also told you this was a temporary solution."

"Do you want to move someone else in?"

I would never make that kind of arrangement with Maddy, even though I know she needs a place. I wouldn't bring her to a place I used to fuck my former sub. I wouldn't give her a temporary place without helping her find something more permanent. And I wouldn't want to set her up as a mistress. I definitely don't want her to be my sub.

"Yes. There's a couple that's been looking for an apartment in this neighborhood. An agent approached me, and I'm ready to rent it to them."

That's true. I just hadn't said yes yet. I will on my way home since I know Anna Maria won't agree to pay rent. I can already tell.

"You're unbelievable, Javier. You're going to screw me, and not the way we agreed."

"Then sign the lease I have with me and put down the first and last month's rent." I reach into my suit coat pocket and retrieve papers I folded lengthwise to fit.

"You really intend to charge me rent."

She's flabbergasted I'm following through with what I said. Why wouldn't I? I gave her orgasms when I promised them, and I punished her when I promised to. It sorely tempts me now to spank her and leave without pleasuring her. But the temptation doesn't outweigh my aversion to touching her. I won't touch any woman but Maddy.

"Yes."

"If I sign and agree to pay rent, will we go back to how things were? Will we be good again?"

"Anna, that's run its course. We haven't been together in nearly three months. We both know either of us could have suggested we see each other. Neither of us has."

"Is there someone else?"

"I don't have another sub waiting around." Which is true.

I have a woman I hope will be my *novia*—girlfriend—and maybe something more. I don't want to rush into anything, even though I've decided what I want. I need to be sure Maddy can adjust to life in my family because you can't have us without the Cartel. I have to be sure she can reconcile joining a family who generally loathes her in-laws. I need to give her time to decide what she wants in life and in a partner. I think she knows what she doesn't want, but I don't know if she's convinced of what she deserves in one.

"Fine. At least I know you haven't gone and fallen in love."

I keep my expression neutral. Anna Maria doesn't need to know just how easily that could happen now that Maddy's back in my life. I don't need Anna Maria's jealousy. I've seen it when we'd go to my club and do scenes there. We did a couple threesomes early on, but she was a pain in the ass afterward, interrogating me about how much I enjoyed the other woman. She was just as much a nuisance when we went and just scened together. She wanted to know why I looked at another woman or what I'd do with another woman if she weren't around. I stopped taking her, and we just came here.

"Does that 'fine' mean you want to stay here and will sign the lease?"

Please say no. Please say no. Please say no.

"Fine means whatever. I'm over it. I'll find a place not on Staten Island. Somewhere people actually want to live. I'll be out by the end of the week."

I look around the place. She's definitely made herself comfortable, but the furniture is all mine. She doesn't have that much to take.

"Three days. Go to your sister's."

"Fuck no!"

"Go to your dad's."

"Javier—"

"Go to Luz's." Her best friend.

"I can't. Come on, Javier."

"There are plenty of people you can stay with. You just don't want to leave a place you have to yourself for free."

"That's not why I stayed. You know I care about you, and you care about me."

I sit back and cross my arms, my sleeves straining across my biceps. I see her lust flare, and I regret my new position. She thinks she can seduce me back into letting her stay. I rise and step around her and the armchair.

"*Adios, Anna. Tú poder gorrear apagado alguien más.*" Goodbye, Anna. You can mooch off someone else.

I walk to the door and open it before looking back.

"I'll make sure Pablo knows you're moving out."

Her look of shock, then dismay isn't surprising. It's not as though my cousin has ice in his veins, but it's definitely colder than tap water. He won't hurt her, but neither will he put up with any bullshit because he doesn't have any personal investment in this.

It won't thrill him I'm passing the buck to him, but he'll understand. I slip out the door and let it click closed behind me. She has those three days, then I'll change the locks.

I'm at my condo in Manhattan with the live camera feed pulled up for the Brooklyn hotel. Nothing's been going on since I arrived home. It's not that I'm spying on Maddy so much as I don't trust whoever she left behind not to find her.

She already confessed he'll hunt for her. It terrifies me that this unknown man will find her when I'm not there. My conscience says I should stop stalking her and trust her judgment. But it also tells me if I were a good potential boyfriend, I would've assigned men to the hotel to watch her when I can't. I don't know which part I should listen to. It thoroughly tempts me to do both. Assign the men and I stop watching her, but I can't bring myself to do that. I'm not ready to make my interest public, and I'm not ready to relinquish control of the surveillance.

I haven't admitted I placed a tracker on her car when I staked out her parents' home. I didn't admit I spent the night watching the house. I left the reception before she did, and I worried she might think I left in a pissy huff. But as I moved toward the ballroom door, our gazes met again, and she offered me a half smile. I think she understood it'd been a long day for me.

What she didn't know was I wanted to arrive at her parents' home in New Jersey well before they did. Since she parked in her parents' driveway, it was easy to attach the tracker. I made sure it worked while she drove home from the park. I've already checked her vehicle's location, and it's at the hotel.

I'm starving, so I give in and head to my kitchen, bringing my laptop with me. I keep glancing at the screen as I make myself lunch. I am about to put the leftover *patacones con hoago*—fried plantains with a tomato and onion sauce—in a pan to reheat when I notice movement on the screen.

Who the fuck is that? I have no reason to suspect the two

men I see approaching the front of the hotel. But my brothers and I didn't survive growing up in Bogotá without a father, without having some Spidey senses. I don't know who these men are, but something feels remarkably off about them.

The way they move screams syndicate. It's an air of self-assuredness, along with their muscular build. It's not just "I'm hot shit because I'm bigger than you." It's "Nothing can stop me. 'No' doesn't mean no."

I wish I had a way to tap into the hotel's security feed, but I didn't put any cameras in there. I'm stuck with just the parking lot. I leave the food on the counter and grab my computer as I hurry to my bedroom. I continue to watch what's happening as I yank off my tie and button down, dropping them on a pile with my trousers.

I never leave my custom-tailored suits on the floor when I change, but I don't bother wasting a moment to pick them up. I watch over my shoulder as I yank black cargo pants and a black long sleeve shirt from my closet. I'm hopping from one foot to the other as I put pants on.

I know there's no possibility I can get to that hotel before something happens, if anything does. Maybe I'm being paranoid, but my intuition screams I need to get to Maddy. I'll call, but that won't be enough.

Once my clothes are on, I head back to my living room. Some instinct long ago told me not to delete Maddy's number from my phone, but I have no idea if it's still the same one it was when we were in high school.

I tap the button on my phone and give the command.

"Call Madeline."

I'm grabbing my keys as I speak, still carrying my laptop. I try not to lose my shit as I wait for the elevator to carry me down to the basement parking garage. When my computer loses the Wi-Fi signal from my condo, it links over to my phone's hotspot. I continue to watch the live feed of the hotel parking lot. Maddy hasn't answered even though I've called three times. It goes to voicemail, so I know I have the right number.

Maybe it's because she doesn't recognize mine.

"Text Madeline."

My phone follows my command, and I dictate my message.

ME

> Maddy, it's me, Javier. Answer when I call, otherwise I'm going to think something's wrong.

I give the message a chance to go through before I dial again. My car picks up the Bluetooth once I turn it on. It's still ringing as it switches over to hands-free. It rings through to voicemail again.

"Text Madeline."

ME

> Answer the damn phone, Maddy. I'm about to panic.

I call yet again.

Maybe she's in the shower and doesn't hear it ringing. Maybe she left her phone in her purse and can't tell it's vibrating. I'm certain there's a solid explanation that doesn't involve those men attacking her, but none reassure me. I keep one eye on the road and one eye on my computer screen.

Fortunately, it's Sunday, so I'm not facing too much traffic. But it still takes me a half an hour to cross over to Brooklyn. It'll take me at least another twenty minutes to get to her hotel.

Nothing's changed outside the building. Those men haven't come out yet. I haven't seen them before. They carried

81

no luggage as they walked in. That's part of what raised my suspicions.

Who're they there to visit? Is it a situation like what brought Joaquin and me there in the first place?

Unfortunately, the cameras can't zoom in enough for me to make out the license plate on the car I saw them walk away from. I can tell its make and model, but nothing more specific than that. I don't know if the tags are New York or out of state. And by that, I mean not New Jersey or Connecticut either.

Every light I stop at tempts me to blow through it, but there are still other cars on the road. I don't need to cause an accident or have anybody call the police and report my license plate. I drum my fingers on the steering wheel, impatience battling to take control of my usually reasoned mind.

I'm three exits away when I watch Madeline burst out of a fire escape and barrel down the stairs, nearly falling twice. She jumps down the last few steps on each flight before she bolts to her car. The men are right behind her and threaten to overtake her as she weaves through the parking lot. She waits until the last minute to unlock her car. She barely slams it shut before one man tugs on the handle. I can't see more specific details within the car, but he hammers on the window. The second guy stands in front of the hood. Not smart.

Maddy can pull through to the next spot, so she inches forward, letting her bumper push the man. He doesn't back up, instead pressing onto the hood. She continues forward, and the man scrambles onto her car. The moment she's free of the cars beside her, she makes a sharp turn while accelerating. She whips into another tight turn at the end of the row of cars.

The man goes sailing off the hood and smashes against another car. That'll hurt in the morning. I can practically hear her tires squeal from here as she peels out of the parking lot and onto the street. The guy on the ground staggers to his feet, shaking off what probably feels like a bulldozer hit him. The first guy's already pulling their car around to get the second one.

With one hand on the wheel and glancing at my computer, I pull up Maddy's tracker. I expect her to head to Queens where Maks and Laura live, but she doesn't go in that direction. It makes me think she might head into New Jersey to go to her parents, but she's pointed toward Manhattan. Does she think she can lose them in traffic there?

Chapter Eight

Maddy

The Do Not Disturb sign is still hanging on the door, so I don't know who's there. Did Javier come and is trying to use his keycard? I'm not prepared for him to walk brazenly in and out of wherever I'm staying whenever he wants. We're not there yet.

I won't call out to him, since there's a chance it's not him on the other side of the door. I creep toward it, and the hair on my arms stands straight up. I haven't even put my eye to the spyhole before I know it's not him. When I see who it is, my chest feels like a Mack truck just parked on it. It's hard to breathe.

How the fuck did those goons find me?

They're two of Drew's henchmen. Mikey and Pauly. About as generic mob names as you could get. Each of them shares names with at least six other men in their family. Sure, good Catholic names all the syndicates use but hardly original, especially since none of them are the kind of Catholic I was raised.

I rack my brain for whether any paparazzi snapped photos of me at the reception last night. They were outside the hotel since a syndicate wedding reception that has the who's who of the corporate world and criminal underworld gathers attention. I've learned the families do it on purpose to not only flaunt their wealth and thumb their nose at law enforcement, but they also do it to flatter the millionaires and billionaires desperate to do legitimate—and sometimes illegitimate—business with them. Apparently, there's a lot of wheeling and dealing that happens at the receptions. If only Maks had explained that to Laura before theirs.

I purposely kept my head down and turn my face away from the cameras. Did someone leak photos from inside the event? Did I wind up online? Drew knows my family's connections to the Diazes, so maybe he guessed I'd be there and had someone follow me.

"Madeline, open the door."

I shy away from the peephole, scared they can see in rather than only me seeing out. I press my back against the adjacent wall and tell myself to breathe. The door handle jiggles again, and I'm thankful I flipped the bolt and put the bar across the top of the door.

"We'll bring the hotel staff up here to let us in."

And how do they get around the bar even if they can open the deadbolt?

That's my only saving grace right now. I dash to where I put my purse on the sofa and snag my phone. I pray Javier's number is still the same from high school. I scroll my contacts for Xavi. Javier is Spanish for Xavier, but there was no way I could have either of those names in my phone since Drew checked it regularly. Like not just looked at the call log or text history since anyone could delete them. Of course, he has a cousin who works for the cell company he insisted we both use.

He forced me onto his plan. It meant I had to make it look like a girl's name. Since I never called the number, he never questioned it.

I tap the contact and tap the call button, but it never connects. I look at the phone screen and see I have no service. I glance toward the door.

Motherfuckers.

I check the Wi-Fi and try to make the call that way, but I have no signal for that either. They jammed it. They don't want me calling for help. There's no hotel landline either, which I thought was odd. Now I'm ready to panic. I can't call the front desk. I can't call the police. I can't call Javi. I can't call Laura. I'm truly fucked because I'm trapped.

Think, Maddy.

I've started calling myself that. I'm not sure when, but within the past two days. It clicked, and now it's stuck. But I don't want to hear my own inner monologue. I want to hear Javi reassuring me I'll survive this. I want to hear him promise to make all of this go away and know he can.

I slip my phone into my back pocket and look around the hotel room. I run through a list of things I most need and whether I can fit them into my purse. I go to the room safe and get my legit driver's license and passport out along with my fake ones. I shove them into my bag and look around again. The windows are sealed, so it's not like I could risk breaking my neck by slipping out one of them.

I have no choice but to wait them out.

They don't hammer on my door constantly, not wanting to draw attention from any of the other guests. But neither do they remain silent; they call out my name. After fifteen minutes, they move on to threats.

"This will piss Drew off even more. Let us in, Madeline."

Not by the hair on my chinny-chin-chin.

"Don't be awkward. He's waiting for you outside."

I stay out of sight of the window, but I make my way over there. I peer down to the parking lot, scanning the vehicles. I notice the one I saw earlier and thought was following me.

Why didn't they nab me in the parking lot? Why let me get up here?

I don't see Drew waiting outside a car, and he'd never ride in the mid-sized sedan. He'd insist on an SUV for something like this. Inconspicuous isn't his style. He thinks making his presence known intimidates people. Subtly isn't his specialty.

I don't believe he's here, but he could be nearby just as easily as he could still be in Albany. I just don't know.

I consider the knife I pulled on Javier and Joaquin. Could I stab and run? Maybe I'd hurt Mikey, but then there'd still be Pauly behind him. Do I take my chances because they're the only ones I have? I have a gun, but it doesn't have a silencer. If I shoot them, someone will hear it. Can I lure them in but get out before they can grab me? Definitely not.

I pull my phone out again, but I still have no reception. Not even a half bar. It's the little x over the wedge. I'd send up smoke signals right now if I could. It tempts me to set the fire detectors off. If they're in the hallway, then other people will urge them to leave. Once they're gone, then I could slip out in the crowd.

No. They'd find you in the parking lot. You could scream, but you don't want to draw attention to yourself. You need to leave with no one noticing. That's been the entire point all along. No one can know.

Bit late for that, don't you think?

Now isn't the time to dwell in negativity. There has to be something.

"Madeline, come home with us. We'll tell Drew you just wanted to go to Enrique's wedding. You can tell him you believed he wouldn't let you go. Accept the consequences, but refusing is only making it worse."

That's Mikey, but they both know what he'll do to me if I go back. There's not a chance in hell I will. I'll end it before I do that.

"You have a job to finish, Madeline. You don't get to just walk away."

Fuck you, Pauly.

That's a large part of what this is about. It's not just that Drew expects me at home with him. It's the job I ran out on. It sure as fuck wasn't delivering babies. I won't get sucked back in, and I'm not ready to think about that shit.

"Gentlemen, I believe no one is there. Please wait in the lobby or return later."

Oh, thank God.

I return to the door and put my eye to the peephole again. I haven't seen this person behind the front desk before, but he's a burly dude who's even bigger than either Pauly or Mikey. He's not chiseled like either of them, but there's no doubting he's a muscular man. I've seen Mikey and Pauly in fights, and my money would still be on the hotel staffer.

"The woman staying here is in the room. We think she might be in distress and can't get to the door."

Bullshit, Mikey.

"That's not what multiple guests reported to us. You can leave, or we can call the police."

Fuck.

Don't kill him, please!

I watch the man push back his blazer and put his fingers on a walkie-talkie call button. A red light goes on, so he's pressing it. Anything else that's said will get transmitted.

"Fine." Pauly begrudgingly concedes for now, but the look

he casts me through the door would make most mobsters wither.

Too bad I've gotten way worse from Drew, so it has no effect on me.

"We'll be back, Madeline."

I pray the receptionist doesn't correct Mikey and tells him the room's reserved under the name Caitlyn. The man's brow furrows for a moment before he twists to point toward the elevator. I shift to watch the men for as long as I can, but they disappear before they pass the next door.

I gather my purse and grab one of the larger knifes. I count to one hundred before I ease the door open. I hear nothing, but I still don't move. I wait for one of them to react to the sound of the door opening. I hear the elevator ping, and that's my cue. I bolt for the stairwell and push open the door. I don't let it slam, but someone must have heard me because Mikey bellows my name.

I get down half a flight to the quarter landing and notice a door that says an alarm will sound. I don't give a shit. It must lead to the exterior fire exit ladders I've seen. I burst through it, but no alarm goes off. I nearly break my neck a few times as I practically slip rather than run down the stairs. I jump down the last three on each flight. I hear men's heavy tread on the metal above me, but I don't dare look back or look up. Neither Pauly nor Mikey call to me, but I know it's them.

When I get to the parking lot, I zig-zag among the cars. If they followed me, they know what I drive and where I'm parked, but I work on the principle that it's harder to hit a moving target. I wait until I'm a car away before I unlock mine. It takes two hands to pull it shut as Mikey grabs the handle. I barely get it closed, but my finger is over the lock button when I do. I press on it and hear the mechanism.

I barely breathe before Mikey's pounding on the window. I

turn on the car as I watch him reach back and under his leather jacket. I know he carries a retractable billy club. If he gets that out, he'll smash my window. At the same time, Pauly's positioned himself in front of my car.

Dumb move.

I put the car in drive and give him a nudge. Fair warning. Rather than take the gentle hints, he climbs onto my hood. It's about to be Mr. Toad's Wild Ride.

I don't exactly gun it, but I press hard on the gas pedal. I need to get away from Mikey's baton and get Pauly off my car. Anyone watching would call my driving erratic. I call it strategic. I take a sharp turn in the parking lot at speed, and it flings Pauly off. He goes sailing into another car. I'm certain he'll survive, and they'll both soon be chasing me down. But it buys me time to get on the road.

I know where I'm going. I don't even have to think twice about it. I need to get into Manhattan. From there, I'm not entirely certain.

I pull my belt on, and my car stops yelling at me. I wriggle and pull my phone from my back pocket. I glance at the screen and see a dozen missed calls from Xavi.

Javier.

I see I have several texts too. I don't have time to read them, but he must know something's wrong. I unlock the screen with my thumb as I half watch the road and half look at my phone. I hit the missed call notification and tap the dial button.

"Maddy!"

"Javi, how do I get to your place? I need help."

"I know, *chiquita*. I'm watching it all. Did they hurt you?"

He knows? He's watching me?

I don't have time to be freaked out that he's stalking me.

No. That's not right.

I can take a second to appreciate he's following through on

his promise to protect me. That's what it means in this world. Tracking your loved ones. I know Maks tracks Laura. He doesn't monitor her every coming and going, but he can find her if something goes wrong. I'd call what's happening right now something going wrong.

"No. They didn't touch me. I got out of the room and down the fire exit without them getting close to me."

"But they nearly did when you got in your car. I'm almost to you, *chiquita*. I see your car. I'm in my Porsche. I'm going to hang a u-ie when I pass you and get behind you. Stay on the line with me, and I'll give you directions. We aren't going to Manhattan, even if it is a little faster. We're going to the Heights."

Jackson Heights. It's the Colombian Cartel-controlled neighborhood in Queens. Wherever he takes me, it'll have more protection than his condo in Manhattan, which is what I originally wanted to find.

Instead of jumping on NJ3—still an interstate with six to eight lanes—we head to the Garden State Parkway. I pray Javi knows what he's doing, and there's no traffic or construction on here. There's no avoiding tolls crossing over from New Jersey into New York, so my license plate will get recorded. Whenever I go through one, I keep my head tucked. I reach for the ball cap I keep on the backseat to help shield me from street and toll cameras.

I check my rearview mirror as a silver 918 Spyder zooms toward me. Of course the man owns the fastest Porsche ever made. At least it's a gas hybrid. I speed to give as much room between me and my—our—pursuers. He whips around, making the tightest turn I've ever seen a car do.

"Go, Maddy. Floor it. You have an open stretch until we get to the Parkway."

He must remember I have a lead foot. I push my car to go as

fast as I dare on a surface street. It doesn't take long for the Parkway ramp to come into sight. Since I know Javi's following me and knows where I'm going, I don't use my turn signal. He's practically riding my bumper to ensure no one can slip between us. The highway is empty along this stretch, so I put my pedal to the floor.

My car leaps forward, and I watch the speedometer jump up to ninety, then one-ten. It's been a long time since I've tested how fast a car could go on an open highway. I have no fear—not a moment's trepidation—about going this fast.

I know my car can't do what Javi's can, but it's holding its own for right now. But I have to slow when I turn off the Parkway and merge onto I-80. I have no choice as traffic slows for bridge construction over the Hackensack River.

"It's okay, Maddy. The lanes narrow, so they can't come alongside us. I'll keep them from catching up to you. Just keep going, little one."

"Okay, Daddy."

I keep looking at my dash clock. What should be like twenty minutes on this road creeps up to thirty as we inch along.

"Maddy, you're doing just fine. I know you're anxious, but they're three cars behind me and not catching up. They don't know where we're going, so we'll lose them when we hit Astoria."

"I'm trying not to panic, Da—"

Oh, fuck.

I catch myself before I say Daddy, but it's only then that I realize I already said it once. I cringe and want to sink into the floor of my car. It's way different—us both thinking the word and me saying it aloud. I'm utterly humiliated.

"*Chiquita*, I will protect you just like I promised. Once we're safe, I'll take care of you and everything else. You know that. It's why you called and were headed to me. We both know why I call you *chiquita*, and we both understand why you called me that. It works for us."

Us.

I want an "us" so badly I nearly burst into tears.

"Thank you, Daddy." I can barely respond above a whisper, but I want to be sure he hears me.

We both fall quiet as we crawl through the traffic until we can merge onto Ninety-Five and cross over the lower level of the GW Bridge and into the Bronx. I spot Yankee Stadium as we travel south along the Harlem River. I keep my head down as we pass through the toll and onto Randall Island. So many fucking rivers and islands in New York City. I breathe a little easier as the East River flows beneath me, and we finally hit Astoria Park in Queens.

"Maddy, we're going to get off on South Astoria Blvd. When we do, let me get ahead of you. I'll lead you the rest of the way. Be prepared for me to take sharp turns there might not be time to warn you about."

I hate knowing Javi won't be behind me to shield me, but neither do I love knowing he was their first target before they could get to me. I'd rather he not get caught in the middle.

We jump off the Grand Central Parkway, and I follow him along surface streets. I stick close to him, and I barely follow him around some corners since he takes them at the very last moment. If I weren't so attentive, I'd sail past them.

"Javi, they're still there!"

I watch Pauly and Mikey inch up to two cars behind me.

"I know, little one. I see them in my mirror. This last turn should do it. It'll be the third street on the left."

"Okay."

We've crossed through Woodside and Sunnyside Gardens. He's taking us into Elmhurst. These are parts of Queens I've only heard of. I've never been here. I've had no reason to. He's bringing us around the backside of Jackson Heights. I don't know if Mikey and Pauly figured out who was following me and now I'm following, but the moment we enter the Heights, they'll know it's someone from the Cartel. If they haven't already called Drew to tell him what's going on, they will now.

Chapter Nine

Javier

My gaze darts between my windshield to watch the road ahead of me, and my rearview mirror to ensure Maddy's still behind me and those two fuck nuts aren't any closer than two cars behind her. My fingers ache from how tightly I grip the steering wheel. My heart's racing. The knot in my stomach threatens to form a lump in my throat. I haven't been this scared in years.

I have a healthy fear of death. Having a sense of immortality is the fastest way to prove you're mortal. I'm not so ballsy as to believe nothing could kill me. I know how close to death I live every day. I know how close the men in my family live to death. It gives me a respect for life. I often fear for the other members of my family, but it's been a long time since I've felt this level of terror.

Not since I was new to killing. I'm used to my uncles, brothers, and cousins being with me. Men who are trained for high-speed chases and shootouts. Not being with a woman who's never been in a situation like this before. It took most of the ride to Queens to convince myself that it's safe for me to lead the way, rather than being a buffer between Maddy and whoever's chasing us.

But she doesn't know her way around Queens. I'm certain of that. It's not like my family knows every single person who comes in and out of this borough. However, we have a pretty damn good idea of many, since we track plenty of people and often tap into the city's street cameras, so we can monitor—shall we say—people of interest. I've never seen the car she's driving before or anybody who resembles Maddy.

I need to be certain we can get to the place I have in mind together without missing turns because she doesn't know how soon they're coming up. I glance in my rearview mirror again, and she's right on my bumper. I take the turn I told her about.

"Maddy, there's a building coming up on the next block on the left. I'm going to open the gate. You're going to follow me through. There'll be a ramp to an underground parking garage. I'm going to pull off to the right, just inside the gate. You're going to go down that ramp and park as far into the garage as you can get."

"All right, Javi."

Her voice is stronger than it was when she called me, but there's no disguising the tremor that remains. She's completely out of her element.

I click the remote on my visor and the gate crawls open. Never have I wanted a piece of metal to move faster. I pull through when it's only halfway open and swerve to the right. I'm already pushing the gear stick into park as she follows me through. My car's barely stopped moving as I fling the door open. I've already unfastened my seatbelt and am climbing out with my gun in my right hand. I crouch beside my car, letting three other vehicles pass before I stand.

I recognize the vehicle that was following us. It tempts

me to shoot the driver, then ask the passenger questions. Instead, I inhale a steadying breath and shoot out the two driver's side tires. The car careens to the right before it plows into a streetlight. Men are already running out of the building that's above the parking garage I told Maddy to pull into.

These are my family's men. With guns drawn, they charge across the street. We're in a neighborhood my family controls, so no one's going to ask questions about an unexpected car crash that followed two gunshots. They won't ask about any more noises they hear. People will just stay inside and watch from their windows.

I glance toward the ramp and see no movement. As much as I want to check on Maddy, I need to deal with these men first.

"They're dead, *el patrón*."

"What?"

How are they dead? They didn't hit the pole that hard. My men didn't shoot them.

I hurry across the street to where the driver's side door is open. It's obvious neither man was wearing his seatbelt. Maybe they thought about jumping out as quickly as I did. Maybe they never had them on to start with. But the passenger is practically through the windshield. The driver's head is between the steering wheel and dashboard, turned at an unnatural angle. He's half out of his seat too.

"Find out who they are. Deal with them. Deal with the car."

I spin on my heel and run toward the garage. Now, I not only need to check on Maddy but ensure she doesn't come up and see this. I know she's a nurse, but I also know she delivers babies. I'm certain she's seen a dead body or two, but I don't know that she's seen anything this grisly. There's blood splattered all over the car's interior, and both of the bodies are gruesome.

My eyes adapt to the dim light after the bright sunshine. As I look around, I notice she followed my instructions and parked all the way on the other side of the structure. I almost wonder if she's gotten out of the car when I can't see her. She must see me because her head pops up. She was leaning across the passenger seat. She doesn't open her door, instead winding the window down a couple inches.

"It's all right, *chiquita.* You can come out. I'm going to take you inside the building. I have somewhere safe for you."

"All right." She sounds much more confident now than she did before.

As I look back up the ramp, I realize she has an obscured view of the car that chased us. She can't see the front half or the light post, but she can tell the car isn't sitting on the street properly. I look down at her, and she's watching me with an expectant expression. I merely shake my head. She glances back toward the street before meeting my gaze and nodding.

"I suppose a nurse won't help."

I shake my head again. She winds up her window and turns off her car as I open the door for her. Once she's standing, our arms wrap around each other, and I hold her as tightly as I can. Her head burrows against my chest as she releases a shuddering sigh. It takes me a moment to realize my exhale matches hers. I finally have a sense of relief even though I know it's temporary since there's shit to sort out. I have obvious questions for her, but they can wait.

She kicks the door closed behind her since I didn't open it all the way just in case she needed to slip back in quickly and take off or barricade herself in there. I'm still situationally aware even though I'm focused on her.

"Javi, I'm sure you have to deal with whatever happened

out there, but when we get inside, will you stay with me for a minute?"

"*Chiquita*, I'm not letting you out of my sight or my reach until I'm satisfied you're okay."

She can tell me whatever she wants because I know she'll try to reassure me once she believes we're out of imminent danger. But until I'm convinced she's safe and assured I can protect her, I'm not going anywhere. My men will clean up for me. They'll dispose of the bodies; they'll sweep the car, then strip it. There's a good chance they'll take it to one of our salvage yards and instead of crush it, set it ablaze. We have space for controlled burns. Sometimes we need to ensure there's no evidence left behind, and merely smashing a car isn't always enough.

I keep my arm wrapped around her shoulders as I guide her into the building. I don't expect my cousin to be there, and I barely hide my grimace when Pablo recognizes Maddy. His eyes widen as his gaze darts between her and me. I feel Maddy lean against me more, which I didn't think was possible since I'm practically holding her up.

She's known Pablo longer than me and was far closer to him for years, but she doesn't rush to him. She barely acknowledges him with more than a weak smile. I'm the one she still depends on.

Guilt prickles at me for how satisfying that realization is.

"Hi, Pablo, what're you doing here?"

"I heard the crash, but I was on a call."

"I'll explain later."

I jump in before Maddy can say anything, since I'm uncertain how much I want Pablo to know yet. I'm unaccustomed to keeping secrets from anyone in my family, but this involves Maddy's safety. It's not like I think Pablo would jeopardize her, but there are still too many unknowns.

Until I can talk to Maddy about who those men are, I don't need any extra hands in this cookie jar.

"Is anyone in the office right now?"

Pablo's watching Maddy as he shakes his head. I steer us past him, and now he watches me. I shoot him a look of warning, which surprises him even more, but he says nothing. He doesn't follow us as Maddy and I make our way to the elevator. He understands I want to speak to her alone. He'll take it up after we reach the office, and he'll find something else to do.

We ride up in silence, and when we step into the hallway, I tilt my head away as I spot some of our men outside the back entrance to the storefront that's supposedly just a liquor store. Maddy and the general public don't need to know we run an illegal gambling ring in the basement, which is a floor above the underground parking garage.

We keep men in this interior hallway because our operations here aren't a well-kept secret from our chief rivals: the mob, bratva, and Mafia. They'll stay away until I tell them to return. No one in the store's front will know I have Maddy in the office.

I unlock the door and hold it open for her, and she steps inside. The moment I have the door closed, she's back in my arms. I want to devour her, taste every bit of her, touch every part of her to convince myself she's really okay. But the last thing I'm going to do is take advantage of a traumatized woman. I didn't do that when we were in high school, and I won't do that now.

"Javi, just hold me, please. Don't let me go."

Her voice is little more than a whisper, but I hear every word as though she's yelling. Our mutual need for me to protect her sharpens all of my senses.

Her arms wrap around me, and I don't bother trying to keep them away from the gun holstered at the small of my back.

When I've been involved with other women, whether it's casual dating or subs, I've always made sure I leave my gun and holster somewhere they're unlikely to find it, or I've ensured they never discover it by wrapping their arms around me. But Maddy's always known who and what I am.

It's a relief I don't have to hide that from her. She'll never know the extent of what I've done and what I can do, and what I inevitably will do. I will always lead a double life, but at least there are a few secrets I don't have to keep from her that I would if it were any other woman, since I have no interest in being with a Cartel daughter.

None of our men have daughters I'm interested in, and I'm wary to let a subordinate's daughter have that much access to my family. I never want to question whether the woman's into me or into my position. Since I'm the worst possible choice for Maddy, I definitely don't fear she's in it for a bad boy or to ingratiate herself into my family. She's already known us her entire life. I don't fear she's somehow a spy for Maks, since I burst into her life, not the other way around.

When she tilts her head back, I gaze into her fathomless green eyes. They're that translucent shade that's almost gray, not the deep emerald all those fuckers in the O'Rourke family share. The way she's looking at me only increases the temptation to kiss her. Apparently, that sentiment is just as strong, if not stronger, in her. She rises onto her toes and brings her lips within inches of mine. Our gazes haven't wavered.

Her offer is clear, but she's not taking control. She's letting me decide whether I accept her offer. I lower my lips to hers, and the rest of the world disappears. It's as good as it was in the car, except now we don't have a steering wheel in the way.

I reach back to double-check I locked the office door. Pablo won't interrupt—at least not without knocking. I guide her toward the sofa in the office. It's the most uncomfortable one

Tío Enrique could find. It's barely more than a plank. The desk chair is high-end, cushiony, and ergonomic. That's for my family. The bench sofa is for anyone unfortunate enough to be called before us for an interview. But it's the only place short of clearing off the desk where we fit.

I scoop her into my arms and sit. I'll deal with the planks of wood under my ass rather than let her be uncomfortable. The kiss continues as she clings to my shirt with one hand and cups my jaw with the other. I stroke her back with one hand while the other holds onto her ass. It's both comforting and possessive. It seems to be exactly what she needs.

It's definitely what I need.

When we come up for air, I kiss her forehead. "*Chica*, you know I need to know what happened. I won't push you to explain everything now, but it has to all come out."

She nods, and her body remains relaxed against me, but my sixth sense tells me she's in no hurry to reveal everything she should. For whatever reason, she doesn't trust me enough or isn't ready to rely on me completely. I know I could interrogate her, demanding answers with rapid-fire questions to trip her up, but I won't do that, even if it means I'm giving her time to come up with excuses or lies.

I'll sort that out because I don't want her to feel like I'm backing her into a corner to get what I want. That's not how I want any type of relationship to begin. I'll always hold more power than she will, so anytime I can make her feel like we're equals, I will because I want her to know she can truly depend upon me. I never want her to doubt that.

"Javi, can your men take care of all of that before anybody finds out who they are?"

"Yes, it'll already be done by now."

"Really?"

"I know it's only been a few minutes, Maddy, but you can guess this isn't the first time."

"Nor will it be the last."

She finishes what should have been an unspoken thought, but there's no point in denying it when I've just told myself to be open with her.

"Thank you for everything. Coming to my rescue. For dealing with all of this. For sheltering me right now. I didn't know what would happen once I got to you, but I just knew I had to."

"You can always come to me for anything, Maddy. I'll always be here for you."

I go quiet, silently encouraging her to share what happened before I found her near her hotel. My silence is met with hers. I don't think she's being awkward. I think she's not ready to speak. Maybe she's still gathering her thoughts.

However, as the moment drags into a couple of minutes, I realize some of this is stubbornness. Despite not wanting to interrogate her, it looks like I'm going to have to prod a little if I want to learn what's really going on.

Chapter Ten

Maddy

I owe him an explanation. I owe him more than just a kiss in gratitude. But if I reveal anything, I'm likely to reveal it all. I'm not prepared to do that yet. There's still shit I need to sort out in my head after that unexpected O.J. Simpson-style car chase. I didn't expect Mikey or Pauly to show up at my door.

I need to figure out how they found me. I need to figure out whether they had time to tell Drew not only where I was, but where I'm certain they guessed I headed and to whom.

I knew better than to let anybody know I was here. As glad as I was to see my family and to even be at Enrique's wedding reception, I knew I should've remained hidden. The risk of exposure was too great, and now I'm paying the price for it.

Mikey and Pauly certainly did. They weren't entirely bad guys in the grand scheme of things. They were following Drew's orders just like they always did. But of all of Drew's men, they were among the nicest to me. It's probably why my ex-boyfriend sent them after me. He figured if anyone could convince me to give myself up and go back to Albany, it would be them. Not a fine fucking chance in hell, but he wasn't too far off.

Once I know how much Drew knows, then I can adjust my plans. As much as I'm enjoying a moment's respite here on Javi's lap, tucked away in a locked office in a building his family not only owns but guards, this is temporary. I won't intentionally bring more danger to him and to his family than they already have on their own.

I also don't need a syndicate war on my hands. As much as the O'Rourkes hate Drew's family, they're still honor-bound to support Drew as fellow mobsters and the head family on the East Coast.

And there's no way Javi will let this go. He'll not only go after Drew, once he finds out my full involvement, he'll wipe out his entire family. It'll be a war on two fronts. First in Albany, then down here.

Because my sister's married to the bratva *pakhan*, they'll get involved too. They'll fight the O'Rourkes because they're guilty by association. Then they'll fight Javi's family because there's no way Javi will let them defend me alone.

Both sides will have their feelings hurt. The bratva won't appreciate that I went to their rival for protection. The Cartel won't appreciate the bratva getting involved because they'll think it looks like they can't take care of me on their own.

I need to defuse the situation, at least for now. At least I can tell myself that. Fat fucking chance that's going to happen.

"Maddy, who were those men?"

I take a moment too long to answer.

"Don't lie to me. I know I've given you time to come up with excuses, but don't lie. Refuse to tell me, but don't say something you can't take back."

"If you give me that out, then don't ask me questions you don't want to hear my answers to."

"Oh, I want to hear your answers. I just want truthful ones. If you won't tell me who they are, then at least tell me why you won't admit that."

"If I won't tell you the former, how can you possibly think I would tell you the latter?"

"So, you admit you won't tell me who they are?"

"I'm certain you'll find out on your own within the next five minutes."

If either of the men were carrying their legitimate IDs, it'll be easy for Pablo to look that up. If they weren't, but they each used one of their known aliases, it'll only take two minutes longer than it should. If they were smart and didn't carry any ID, then I might get lucky. I don't know if the Diazes have access to dental records.

I'm certain they won't recognize the men as being ones from the city or even New Jersey, so that leaves Albany. It won't take much of a guess to know these guys are from a syndicate. It won't be difficult to narrow down which one. So, all this shit's going to come to a head in the next few minutes.

My mind's rapidly working through this devolving situation, and I'm realizing it's getting worse by the moment.

"Maddy, I'm certain you know I'll figure out who these men are. Do you really want me to learn the truth from Pablo, or would you rather I hear your side of the story first?"

I'd much rather he hears my side of the story, but he'll ask more questions I can't answer. Then I'll just look awkward. That'll make it worse.

No, worse is you being resistant. Be forthcoming, and perhaps there's a chance to salvage whatever might have been between us.

I can't fight the temptation to rub my forehead anymore.

My head's pounding, and the closer I come to sharing any details, the more I want to vomit. The bile's burning the back of my throat, and tears sting the inside of my eyelids. I feel my heart rate racing, and Javi must feel my increasing sense of foreboding or hear the death knell over my head.

"All right, Madeline—"

"Don't call me that."

I try to get off his lap as he rejects me, but his hold only tightens.

"You're not going anywhere until I'm certain you're safe, and the safest place is in my arms."

"You still believe that? You still want that?" My voice trembles with each of those questions.

"Of course I do. You're the one who doesn't seem to agree."

"Is that why you used my full name?"

"Yes, you're the one putting distance between us, but I'm not the one who wants to."

"Using my full name says you want distance."

"And you refusing to tell me any of the truth—give me even a clue what's going on—screams far louder than what I said. It's obvious since the moment I walked into your hotel room, you're hiding from someone. I already figured out someone mistreated you. I didn't grill you on who, and I haven't dug around even though I could. I've wanted you to share this on your terms, but you're not giving me much of a choice but to either demand you share what's going on, or I pry into your life with or without your permission."

"Prying implies you're not looking for permission, Javi."

"True. So, decide now, Maddy, what's it going to be? Do you tell me the truth about what's going on, or do you leave it to my cousin to tell me, or for me to assume the worst before I dig?"

It would be so much better if I just told him the bits I can.

I've spent years keeping these secrets, cultivating stories to deflect. I could tell him ones I've used before, but he'll see through those lies. He's already told me not to tell him any. He'd rather I refuse to answer, but that option's no longer available. I'll start out slowly. Hopefully, feeding him a couple of bites will tide him over for now. I'm kidding myself to think that, but it makes it a little easier for me to start.

"The guy I was seeing back home got into some shit he shouldn't have."

That makes it sound like it was a choice.

"It complicated things between us, and I discovered he has a temper. When things went wrong, he needed a scapegoat, or an outlet. That became me. I don't know all the inner workings of what he was doing, but he was also very possessive. He didn't want to let me go."

That's such a bland version of the truth, that if it were chicken, it'd be unseasoned and boiled.

Javi remains quiet, waiting for me to divulge more, but that's what I'm ready to share.

"Little one, I won't push you any further for now, but those men weren't just petty criminals. It's obvious they're in a syndicate, and considering you lived in Albany, it makes it pretty damn easy for me to guess which one."

Fuck my life.

"I'll keep my word, and I won't ask for more. Just know I'm already figuring things out. I'm waiting for you to confirm them."

Hopefully, he thinks one of them was my ex-boyfriend, and that the guy I dated was pretty low-level.

"Maddy, we can stay here for as long as you like. Once you're less scared, I can take you to Laura's."

"What? No. I don't want to go to my sister's." It's the last thing I want.

"Are you worried about bringing danger to the twins?"

"Of course, I'm worried about my niece and nephew. No, Javi, Laura will grill me until I'm burnt to ashes. I know she'll defend me tooth and nail, and I know Maks and his family have all the resources needed to protect me, but that's not who I want to be with."

I glance toward the door when I hear a sound on the other side. He must be able to see more of my face than I thought.

"Do you want to go with Pablo?"

I jerk away and twist to look at him. "No. Why would I want to go with him?"

"You grew up practically as his little sister."

"Practically. I'm not and never have been. You know our families aren't close anymore. It's been years since I've hung out with him. Whatever's happened in that time has made him a man I don't think I know anymore."

Javi's gaze shutters, and I know I'm right.

I've suspected for a long time Pablo deals with the worst of the worst his family faces here in the U.S. I don't want to imagine the crazy, twisted, fucked-up shit Alejandro must deal with since I've heard he's always going back and forth to Colombia.

I know Javi and his brothers' reputation, but I also know they cultivated it to protect themselves as three teenagers who moved here not speaking the language and without a dad. They feared it would be as dangerous for them here as it was in Bogotá. I figured out why they did the things they did early on. I tried dropping hints of that explanation to Maks a few years ago, but he didn't believe me. He said he knows them better than I ever could.

That's because no one besides Javi knew our secret. I'm positive he never told his brothers.

"Then what do you want, Maddy?"

109

"Do you have something else you need to do? Is there some-where else you need to be?"

"No. Did you think I was trying to pass you off?"

"Maybe."

"That wasn't it. I just want you wherever you're most comfortable and will feel the safest."

I feel vulnerable as fuck admitting it, but if I don't, then I won't get what I want and need.

"I want to stay with you."

There. I said it.

I avert my gaze, but he lifts my chin until I can't keep from looking at him unless I close my eyes. It's tempting.

"Look at me, little one."

"Yes, Daddy."

The words slip past my lips, and I'm embarrassed once again, even though it feels right to say them.

"You know why you call me that, and it has nothing to do with daddy issues or wanting me to replace Killian."

It's funny to hear him use my father's name since he's always been Mr. Doyle to the Diaz guys in person.

"If you want to stay with me, then that's exactly where you'll be."

"Thank you, Daddy. That's exactly what I want. I know I'm safe with you. You're the only one I feel safe with."

"You need to understand something. You know more about me than most, even if we haven't been around each other in years. If you don't know for a fact, then I'm certain you've guessed things about my family too. I will never, ever force you to do anything you don't want to. I won't intentionally put you in danger. But you have to accept I'm a man with no limits. You've known my reputation since we were kids. It was a complete exaggeration back then."

He pauses while he looks at me, the rest of that thought heavy in the air.

"That reputation is earned now. It means there's nothing I won't do to protect you. I'm certain there's plenty you aren't telling me. I'm certain all of it puts you in more danger than I know already. I want you to promise me something."

His gaze bores into me. I know he doesn't expect me to swear my promise without hearing it first. I've refused every time in the past. He just wants me to know there's not an inch of wiggle room in this.

"If you even remotely think something would worry me, then you will tell me immediately. It doesn't matter whether you think it's a big deal or not. It's whether I would think it matters."

"I can't—"

"No, not yet. I'm not done."

My chin jerks back.

"I'm not looking for domestic discipline with you or anyone else. I know you're not a Little either. But if you don't come to me, if you put yourself in danger by my standards, then I will punish you. It'll be more than just a spanking. You'll give up certain freedoms until I decide to give them back. Regardless, you're going to have a security detail. But I will put you under lock and key if that's what it takes for *me* to feel you're safe. Can you live with that?"

That's a shit ton to take in, but it's not unappealing to me. As I consider what he's telling me, it should freak me the fuck out. It's so close to the threats Drew made, but they were never about keeping me safe. They were about controlling me so I couldn't leave. Drew never asked for my agreement. He just dictated to me. He punished me when I didn't obey, but those punishments were abuse. They were never consensual.

So even though what Javi says sounds so much like the

threats Drew made, they couldn't be more different. And as I continue to think about what he said, the idea of domestic discipline isn't wholly unappealing, which makes me think my head's not screwed on right. It's not what Javi's into anyway, but it makes me curious.

"Maddy?"

"Yes, I promise I'm good with all of that."

"Is there something else you want to say? Something else you want?"

"I don't know."

That's honest, because I'm not sure what I want at this point. Things are moving so fucking fast right now. I barely know up from down, left from right. The only certainty I have is I'll do just about anything Javi tells me at this point.

"What I just said, Maddy, about it not being domestic discipline. Is that what you were used to?"

"No, I definitely wouldn't call it that."

He stares at me, and it's so intense, it tempts me to look away. But I'm pulling on my big girl panties again, and I sit here unflinching.

"He abused you frequently, didn't he?"

I dip my chin.

I've just signed Drew's death warrant, as though it isn't already a foregone conclusion once Javi figures everything out. But now that I've admitted he abused me, there's no way Javier Diaz is going to let Drew live. It's not in his nature to be that forgiving of something like that.

I know it, and I've accepted it.

"Then do you want domestic discipline between us?"

"I don't know exactly what that would look like, so I don't know, Javi. I want to share my thoughts and disagree with you. I don't feel like I need you to correct me if I do something you don't like or don't agree with. But knowing you'd be in charge—

112

in control even—is reassuring. It takes a weight off my shoulders. It's not that I can't deal with my own problems, but it certainly would be nice to have the burden shared and to know you take my well-being seriously enough you won't accept anybody, including me, putting it at risk."

"So, if I consider whatever you do a danger to you, then you give me permission to punish you or correct you however I think you need it?"

"Maybe. I don't know. This is a lot."

Am I really considering giving a man who's even deadlier than my ex-boyfriend carte blanche to punish me?

Yeah, because he's not the one who'll beat you to death if he catches you.

Chapter Eleven

Javier

This is *not* the direction I envisioned this conversation going.

I'm already hard from her being on my lap and the kisses we've shared. That she'll cede that much control to me is arousing as fuck. I've never had a domestic discipline relationship because I haven't been in a romantic one since high school. By the time I got to college, I knew I couldn't bring anyone home to my family. Not because they wouldn't accept the girl, but because she'd run straight to the cops. It seemed pointless to start something that would invariably end. That's why Dom/sub arrangements were perfect.

Now Maddy's offering me not only a BDSM relationship, but also a romantic one where we both feed my need to protect and have control. I never imagined she—or any other woman I'd meet—would be into that. I hadn't entertained the idea, so it's never been something I've thought through. Yet, here we are.

"*Chiquita*, we'll figure out what's right for us."

She gazes into my eyes, and I wonder what she's thinking. It's like she's searching for something. Is she trying to determine whether I'll ever mistreat her like her *pinche gonorrea carechimba* boyfriend? Fucking shitty face of a vagina doesn't really lose much in translation.

"Javi, I had reservations when I started dating my ex-boyfriend, but I pushed them aside because he seemed like such a nice guy."

The idea of me seeming like a nice guy is completely foreign to most people. I can be charming when I want to be, and it's not like women run from me. But anyone who spends more than the time it takes to appreciate my looks soon learns my name and "nice" usually aren't in the same sentence. Not even the same fucking paragraph. Not the same fucking conversation.

"You've been right that I know more about your family and you than I probably should. I know the man you are most of the time. But I have no reservations with you. Just the opposite, and that's terrifying when I stop to think about it. How easily I trust you when we haven't been around each other in years—most people would think I'm not right in the head. You are who you are, and I know that from the beginning. You aren't going to turn into a monster I never knew lurked around the corner. You're turning out to be nicer than most people will ever know."

I suppose that's a compliment.

"Javi, my point is, I trust you, and I want that 'us' you just mentioned. I didn't give you my promise because I don't intend to break it. I gave it knowing I will, but I'll accept the consequences. That's what I promised. There are secrets that aren't mine to tell, and there are secrets that aren't safe for anyone if I do. If that means you keep me under lock and key, then I'm probably safer that way, anyhow."

115

I feel my temper flare, and I look toward the door. There's only so much we can do with men in the hallway and my cousin around here somewhere. I glance toward the window, wondering if it's safe to take Maddy to my place.

"You need to tell me right now whether those men would know who I am and if they would've told someone you were with me."

"They might not have known which Diaz you are, but they knew you were one once we crossed into the Heights. I don't know if they had time to tell anyone."

"Will whoever sent them kill you?"

"Possibly."

I expected that answer, but it isn't the one I want.

"We're going back to your hotel to get all of your belongings. You are checking out. Then you're coming with me."

"Where to?"

I put her on her feet and stand in front of her. My left arm wraps around her, and my right hand rests on her throat.

"You want to keep your secrets. Fine. But I'm keeping mine too."

I press against her throat as I claim a savage kiss. She melts against me when I thought she might put up a fight. My tongue slips past her teeth, and a moment later, she bites. Not hard enough to hurt, but more than a nip. My hand tightens around her throat, not as retaliation but to let her know I understand what she's doing. She can be defiant, but it'll come with consequences.

I kiss along the underside of her jaw until I get to her ear. My teeth tug her earlobe with more force than she used on my tongue. She shivers, pressing her hips forward against my dick.

"I'm going to do dirty, dirty things to you tonight, Madeline. You are going to submit to each thing unless you clearly say no. You will take whatever punishments I dole out. You will wear

116

my cum inside and out. That's what happens to my *chiquita* when she keeps things from me, and I've given her plenty of chances to confess. When we get where we're going, you will strip naked and remain that way until I give you back your clothes."

I know I'm being outrageous.

I know I sound like a twisted fuck.

But she's panting beside my ear, and she crossed her wrists behind her back on her own and is keeping them that way. She didn't object to me using her full name this time. Just the opposite. She moaned when I did.

"Daddy."

She whispers the single word in surrender. I tighten my hand around her throat as I kiss her. I count to ten in my head before pulling away and letting go. I step back, and she nearly falls forward. She barely catches herself. We stare at one another, and an understanding passes between us. That might have been dirty talk, but at the heart of it, it was all real. It's what we both want. What we need from each other.

"I'll go wherever you take me, but after you punish me, are you going to leave me there?"

"You make it sound like you fear I'll leave you in some prison cell. I know you know where I live, and you've probably heard of some of my other properties. Between what's mine and what the rest of my family owns, nowhere we go will be a hardship. I'm not dumping you in Bogotá with *Tío* Luis."

Pablo's dad is our mutual *Tío* Enrique's younger brother, and my mom's older brother. *Tío* Luis's in Colombia—again—dealing with another *cabrón* who thinks he doesn't have to pay his taxes on time. Alejandro does a lot of business down there for us, but *Tío* Luis is the one who slips in and out of prisons down there like he's best friends with the wardens. They pretty much are for how much each of them has made in hush money.

"I don't care if you put me in a two-by-two hole in the wall of a twelve thousand square foot mansion. Just stay with me, please."

There's genuine nervousness in Maddy's tone, and I don't like it.

"Maddy, I will *never* abandon you. I will never dump you somewhere and not explain as much as I can. I'll be evasive, and sometimes that's me being a Dom, and sometimes it's me protecting everyone in my life. But I won't wage psychological warfare on you. I'm not interested in you being with me because I gave you Stockholm Syndrome."

"I know all that. I didn't think you planned to fuck with my head. I told you when we got here, I only feel safe with you. It's being clingy and needy, but I'm scared, and the only person I'm comfortable with is you. I don't want to be left somewhere with just your men to guard me. I don't know them even if I trust them as an extension of you. I'm fine with everything we've talked about, with what you just said, because it's all based upon you being with me."

My left arm wraps around her again as my right hand cups her jaw. I lift her so she can sit on the desk before I step between her legs. She tilts her head back to look up at me.

"*Chica*, I'm going nowhere unless you tell me this is over. I'll fight for you and for us. I won't walk away the first time you tell me to go. We knew the moment we saw each other, neither of us was done with the other. The moment you got in my car, we both knew an 'us' is our fate. You belong to me now, Maddy. I protect what's mine. I cherish it." I sweep my thumb over her cheekbone. "Let me be yours."

"Daddy, I've wanted that since high school. If you're offering, then I'm accepting. I've always believed we belonged together. I just didn't think it would ever happen."

Before I can respond, there's a knock.

"Javier?"

"*Sí.*"

All our men here are native bilingual speakers, but I don't know what the guard on the other side of the door's going to say. He'll know to speak Spanish.

"*Pablo necesita hablar contigo. Dijo que está de camino.*" Pablo needs to speak to you. He said he's on his way up.

"Pablo's coming."

I lift Maddy off the desk as I speak. She looks toward the door and nods. She's less than thrilled. I'm uncertain whether it's the interruption or whether it's Pablo. Maybe both. I walk to the door and unlock it. I open it as Pablo raises his fist to knock. I step aside and let my cousin in before shutting and locking the door again.

"*La llevaré al castillo.*" I'm taking her to the castle.

It's an estate our family owns on the Long Island Sound in Connecticut. She wasn't wrong about the twelve thousand square foot mansion, even though I'm certain she knows nothing about this place. It's one of the best-kept secrets in our family. My father bought it for my mother as a wedding present. If ever we needed to flee Bogotá, it was where we were to go.

It's on a private island with woods that meet the water. There are plenty of places to hide in the house, and no one approaches without the occupants knowing. It's where we all go now when we want people to believe we're vacationing together in the Med or South Pacific. Sometimes we really go to those places, but if most of the family is traveling together, it's not abroad. That's too predictable. Too easy a target.

My announcement shocks Pablo. He says nothing as his gaze darts to Maddy. He looks back at me, and his expression hasn't changed. At least, not in a way Maddy could tell. I can, though. He'll have plenty to say about me taking anyone—

119

especially a woman—extra especially Maddy—to our family haven.

I don't give a shit.

"*¿Lo sabe?*" Does he know?

Pablo doesn't want to say uncle or Enrique because Maddy will know who we're talking about. I don't know if her Spanish is better than it was in high school, which was mediocre on a good day. She studied French instead because she wanted to do a semester abroad once she got to college. Damn. I haven't thought about that in over a decade. It surprises me I remember.

"*Todavía no. ¿Vas a chismear o me vas a dar tiempo para explicar?*" Not yet. Are you going to tattle or give me time to explain?

That was an asshole thing to say.

"*No actúes como un culo. Yo iba a encargarme de ello por ti, para que puedas concentrarte en ella.*" Don't act like an ass. I was going to handle it for you, so you can focus on her.

"*Gracias. Ya te imaginarás por qué estoy un poco tenso ahora mismo. Quiero llevarla al lugar más seguro que tenamos, aparte de la bodega.*" Thank you. You can imagine why I'm a little tense right now. I want to get her to the safest place we have short of the bodega.

The bodega is the place our family uses to handle our most unsavory business, so I'm definitely not taking Maddy there. We may sterilize the place after every time we use it, but I swear the place is fucking haunted. Lord knows there've been enough dead bodies in there to fill a cemetery. I refuse to go on *Dia de los Muertos*. Day of the Dead. We all avoid the place on November first and second.

Pablo nods, and we continue our conversation in Spanish. But I want us to hurry because we're being rude to Maddy, and I want to get her out of here before it gets dark.

"Don't worry. I'll explain what's going on and where you're taking her. He'll agree since it's her."

Tio Enrique's still extremely protective of Maddy and Laura, even if Laura doesn't believe it. There's a shit ton that's happened behind the scenes to thwart crap aimed at the bratva simply so Laura doesn't have to worry about Maks's safety. We don't need to brag, but we're prepared to call in a favor if we need to. Nothing in life is free.

"I'm taking her to her hotel to grab her stuff, then we'll head out. She doesn't know where we're going."

"Will you blindfold her?"

I stare at Pablo, incredulous that he asked that.

"What? It's safer if she doesn't know how to get there. No one can force her to take them there, and we keep our privacy."

"Who's being an ass now? She's my girlfriend, not my prisoner."

There. I said it. As far as I'm concerned, Maddy's my girl-friend even if we haven't defined our relationship down to that term. It's what we mean. At least, I assume that's what she means because that's how I see it.

I glance at her, and our gazes meet. We spoke quickly, so she may not have understood everything, but I'm sure she knows *"novia"* means girlfriend. She confirms it when she dips her chin in agreement. Pablo's expression hardens when I focus on him again.

"And she was like my little sister from the day she was born. Whatever you have going on between you isn't my busi-ness but making sure she's safe sure as fuck still is."

"Then explain everything to anyone who needs to know and keep your phone on. I'll let you know once we're there."

I offer Maddy my hand, and she slips hers into mine. She offers Pablo a smile that's far warmer than when we arrived. Maybe she followed our entire conversation after all.

"Pablo, I don't know what's going on, but I know your distinct tones. I trust Javi just like I always trusted you. Whatever he thinks we should do, I'm going to listen to him before anyone else. I'm sorry for the trouble I already caused, and thank you for cleaning up the mess."

Pablo watches her as she speaks, and I know he's trying to read between the lines both about what's going on between Maddy and me and why those men chased her. Before I stormed into her hotel room, I would've said Pablo understands her better than I do because of their lifelong friendship. But I don't think that's the case anymore because when he looks at me, I know he has more questions than answers.

"Always, Madeline."

"If you're allowed to let anyone besides Enrique know where Javi's taking me, tell your mom and dad hi for me, please."

Pablo merely nods.

"We're taking a car from the fleet."

I don't want anyone who's figured out what Maddy's driving to follow us, and the car I have with me today is far too flashy. If I'd known what I was getting myself into when I raced out of my place, I would've driven my mid-size BMW. It's far less conspicuous than the Porsche.

"I'll have a guy pull an SUV around."

It won't be a large one we use on missions. Those damn things are veritable tanks. Pablo knows I want something reinforced and sturdy, but nothing that'll stand out. He hesitates a moment before stepping forward and kissing Maddy on the cheek. She wraps her arms around him, and I know she relaxes. But I also know it's not the same as when I hug her.

"Is your number still the same, Pablo?"

"Yeah. Call it if you need anything at all. Listen to Javier.

He'll do whatever he needs to, to keep you safe from whatever's going on."

"I will. Thank you."

"We'll be down in a couple minutes." I want Pablo to leave us alone before Maddy and I head down to the garage.

He says nothing before he leaves, just a last look at me and a nod. I turn to Maddy, and she accepts my offered hand. She'd held it when she got off the desk but had to let go to hug Pablo. Now we lace our fingers.

"How much of that did you understand?"

"Bits and pieces. You usually don't speak that fast."

"True, but Pablo and I weren't just chatting. I'm taking you somewhere only my family knows. No one outside the family and our most trusted guards go there, so it's the safest place in the U.S. I can take you."

"That's why he suggested you blindfold me."

I guess she understood plenty.

"Yes. We can stay there as long as we like. We have everything we need to last there a couple months, not that I think it'll come to that."

"A luxury fallout shelter?"

My expression turns grim, and she merely nods. I turn toward the door, but she puts her free hand on my forearm.

"Javi, is this going to make life harder on everyone else? Will they have to do your work for you?"

"There's nothing coming up that'll be a burden to anyone else."

"But you're your family's lawyer. Do you have court?"

"No. My calendar is clear for the next three weeks. I can still work from there since we have secure internet. And if anything comes up, *Tío* Enrique and *Tío* Luis are both attorneys too. They may not openly practice, but they're still licensed in New York and New Jersey. I'm replaceable."

Nails on both of her hands dig into my hand and arm. "Never, ever say that. No, you are not."

"Shh, *chica*. I'm not going anywhere. Bets on how fast I annoy you because I'm up your ass."

"If you're offering, then how about three hours? Is that long enough for us to get wherever we're going?"

I stare for a moment before I grin. My free arm wraps around her hips, and I squeeze her ass. I lean in to whisper to her, even though there's no one to overhear me.

"I'm going to fuck your pretty little mouth, your tight little cunt, and your perfect little ass tonight. Then I'll do it again in the morning, then the afternoon, then tomorrow night. I'll do any and all of that whenever I want. Do you know why?"

"Because I belong to you?"

"You are mine to pleasure, Maddy. I want to watch you come while you forget about everything besides us. I want to make you happy."

"Thank you, Daddy."

"Let's get on the road. We need to get your stuff from the hotel, and I want to set off well before it gets dark. I told you I wouldn't push you for more information, and I won't. But you have the time we take to get to the estate to come up with more of the truth because you won't enjoy the consequences if you don't."

Chapter Twelve

Maddy

Just like Javi told me, we stopped at the hotel. I've still been using my sleeping bag rather than mess up the sheets. I have my own towels too, so I've left as little trace of me as I can. He helped me wipe down all the surfaces before we headed out to the midsize SUV we're in now. We aren't going as far as I assumed, only into Greenwich.

This part of Connecticut lies along the Long Island Sound and about an hour's drive from Queens with some traffic. It's like an entirely different world, though. The properties around here are estates, not just houses. They have mansions and are on "grounds," not front and backyards. As we approach the gate to a particularly secluded one—it's on a fucking island by itself—I realize my comment about a twelve-thousand square foot mansion wasn't far off.

We turned off the main road and onto little more than a dirt path that would be easy to miss if you didn't know what to look for. It turns into a paved driveway as we emerge from a forest and approach a gate. I can see it's the first of two, the second standing across a causeway. Javi pulls up to what looks like a regular tree, but I realize it has a keypad on it. He punches in the code, and the gate slides open. I watch guards step out of a hut tucked away against the tall brick wall. The two men nod at us.

They're dressed like the ones who patrol Enrique's property. They have Kevlar vests and helmets with black fatigues. They're both armed with high-powered rifles and handguns in thigh holsters. I'm certain they carry knives just like Javi and his family always do. When I see more men like the first two as we approach the second gate, I breathe much easier.

"There are a dozen men who live here full-time. Four are always posted at the gates, and four patrol the grounds while the last four are off-duty. It might seem like a boring assignment, relegated to the middle of nowhere, but very few people in our organization know this place exists. The men stationed here know they're among our most trusted because we can't afford anyone to follow them here when they leave. With only a dozen men here, they have to be among our best."

I swallow because the implications are grave. This place may be the pinnacle of luxury, but it could also feel like a prison. I hope it's more like a romantic getaway than a secret lair. I don't know yet. I scan my surroundings as we continue along the driveway until we circle around the side to the six-car garage. I've never seen one so large. It's more like a barn attached to the main house. A guard materializes out of I don't know where and holds out a remote, pointed toward the garage. One door rises, and Javi pulls in. The moment he's in park, the door closes.

"Wait."

I look over at him when he issues the command. I haven't even unfastened my seatbelt or reached for the door.

"You don't get out until the door closes. I'll turn off the engine immediately, and once I do, you'll know it's safe."

I look over my shoulder as the door stops moving. Holy shit. The rule's in place in case Javi needs to reverse out of here or in case someone or something rolls beneath the door before it closes all the way.

Fucking intense.

Not quite as much as the high-speed chase, but it's another overwhelming thing to take in today.

I unfasten my seatbelt and reach for the door. He covers my left hand as I pull the handle.

"Maddy, when we're outside somewhere, you either wait for a guard or me to open the door for you. We will have scanned our surroundings and are confident it's safe for you. Only exit your car in a closed garage if the house is secure or someone you trust is inside.

"Are these the normal protocols, or is this because I was followed?"

"Unfortunately, these are standard. But they're doubly important now."

"Yes, Daddy."

"*Chiquita.*"

He must hear the fear in my voice because his other hand cups my jaw, and he brushes a soft kiss against my lips. I lean into it and savor it, even though it's brief. I climb out of the car and walk around to the trunk. Javi already popped it open, and we both reach for my luggage. He's gentle, but he brushes my hand away before gathering all my things. He has keys in his hand that he passes to me as we turn toward the door leading into the house. I unlock it but then step back, knowing he won't want me to go in first despite his hands being full.

He elbows the door open and immediately sets my stuff inside to the right. He blocks my way in as he looks around.

When he's convinced it's safe, he moves aside and holds out his hand. The door leads into a mud room, but I can see through the far door to a living room. Peeking down the hall, I see the kitchen door open. We don't exactly creep through to the main entrance area, but we move with caution. Even with the security, Javi's natural tendency toward caution is there.

I didn't realize how large the foyer was from where we entered through the garage. The living room is even more expansive than I thought. It has to be to fit Javier, Joaquin, Jorge, Alejandro, Pablo, Luis, Margherita, Luciana, Catalina, Matáis, Enrique, and now Elodie. There are a dozen people in his family, and none of the men are small. Alejandro has the broadest frame, and most people consider him the hottest in the family, but I disagree. I think Javier is hands down more attractive. Alejandro's almost too good to be true.

He's a near replica of Enrique, but he sounds like and has Matáis's mannerisms. He has Catalina's personality. He's a perfect blend of his parents. I never met Javier, Joaquin, and Jorge's dad since he died before they moved to America, but their mom, Luciana, is a firecracker. None of *Tres J's* are as extroverted as her. Margherita's genes got little say in Pablo since he's a mirror of Luis from looks to attitude.

As I watch Javi continue to assess our surroundings, I have a brief thought about what kids with him would be like. I used to wonder the same thing about Drew when we first got serious. Then I made sure I did everything I could to never get pregnant. I'm certain he would have liked me to just so he could trap me. He thought he had when he threw out my birth control four months after I moved in with him.

I'd already seen a hint of who he really was, so I'd had one of the OBGYNs I worked with insert an IUD for me. He was irate when he found out, but he couldn't get it out, and he knew he couldn't march me into a doctor's office and demand they remove it. He punished me for it, but I refused to give in. I consider whether I'd remove it for Javi if we got serious enough to marry. The idea of kids with a Cartel member is unappealing. The idea of a family with Javi makes me imagine dark-haired little kids with perpetual suntans running around.

He catches me smiling to myself and pulls me into his embrace. Our gazes lock, and I could drown in his whiskey-brown eyes. The sunlight from the window above the front door is lightening them from the milk chocolate they usually are.

"You're so damn beautiful, Maddy."

That came out of nowhere.

"Thank you."

"The sunlight on your hair looks like a halo, and your eyes match the water in summer. I know I should give you a tour of the house, but all I can think about is stripping you, so I can finally see all of you."

"The rooms aren't going anywhere, Daddy."

"I know, but are you tired after everything that's happened today? Are you hungry?"

"Your mother's etiquette rules are great, but I don't want polite Javi right now. I want the man who promised to do dirty things to me."

I squeal as he pounces, backing me against a wall. His kiss steals my breath as he presses me into the hard surface. Aggressive is the only way to describe him, and I'm here for it. His possessiveness makes me feel protected. His certainty that he can do whatever he wants promises me pleasure, but it also reminds me there's nothing he won't do to keep me safe. I feel cherished.

When he leans back and our gazes meet again, I recall the crush I had on him in high school. It started before he rescued me from the fucking sack of shit who locked me in the car. It got stronger after that, but I never imagined in my wildest dreams everything I daydreamed about would come true.

"Maddy, I've wanted this since I met you. I was angry at the world that someone murdered my father, that we had to move to a country where I didn't speak the language. I just wanted to be left alone most of the time. I was a dick to everyone until I met you. Even when I scowled, you smiled at me. You did your best with your Spanish to make me feel welcome whenever I was at *Tío* Luis and *Tía* Margherita's the same nights your family was there for Sunday dinner. I wasn't appreciative enough, but I had a massive crush on you. I'd never spanked a girl before I did you, but I'd never feared for one the way I did for you that night. That spanking made me realize things about myself I never believed I could have with you. Just the opposite. I believed there would never be a chance to do it again."

He's opening up to me. I'm certain part of it is he hopes I'll do the same and tell him all my secrets. So fucking tempting, but I can't. Never mind the danger it would put him in, he'd never respect me again. I'd rather take them to the grave.

"I had the same crush on you. No other man has spanked me, Javi, and you're the only one I've ever wanted to."

He keeps watching, but I see regret in his gaze now.

"*Chiquita*, I wish I could profess I haven't shared that with anyone else, but I've spanked other women. The one thing I can swear to you is that it never meant what it did with you. I didn't spank them out of fear for their safety or because I wanted to protect them."

"I guessed as much, but thank you for telling me."

He waits, and there's no doubt he expects me to share more. Temptation nips at me, but pure stubbornness—and likely indisputable stupidity—make me keep quiet. I didn't think about what parts of the truth I would share while we drove up here. I struggled to stay awake while driving through New York City, then our destination intrigued me too much once we left the state.

When I'm not forthcoming, I feel him retreat. I rise on my toes and kiss him, partly to reassure him and partly to distract him. But he doesn't take the lead like he has in the past. It's not even about me leading. He's passive despite returning the kiss. I've dropped a wedge between us.

You knew that's exactly what would happen. You need to figure your fucking shit out.

"Daddy, is there a soaking tub here?"

"Yes. More than one. Do you want to take a bath?"

"Only if you'll let me wash your back."

He considers my offer, and he takes so long, I wonder if he's punishing me or really thinking about saying no. Instead, he steps around me and gathers my belongings again. I guess he trusts the entire house is secure if we're headed upstairs without him checking everywhere else. The tour will come later if there is one. He still seems reserved compared to a few minutes ago. This is the Javi who doesn't like to be around people and would prefer to be left alone. The untrusting one.

I follow him up to the second floor and along a hallway to the last room on the right. It must overlook the backyard with a view out on the water. As we walk in, I realize the angle of the house means bedrooms on both sides must have views. It's a masculine room, painted in a deep gray with cobalt curtains. I can see into the bathroom to where the walls are cobalt too. The bedding is a more muted gray and blue. The furniture is surely mahogany—not mahogany-colored, but the actual wood. On every surface, there's some type of assembled Lego set.

I look up at Javi, and I'm certain he's blushing. Did he forget they were here? Does he think I'll tease him? Mock him?

"You're still into them, aren't you? Do you and your

brothers still line up for the special edition releases? Didn't you used to camp out to be at the front of the line?"

He nods. He offers nothing else, and I fear I really fucked things up.

"That's really cool that you, Jorge, and Joaquin still do that together. Laura and I are still super close, but it was impossible to do anything like that with me in Albany and then once she had the twins."

"My brothers and I enjoy each other's company, and they know how much I still enjoy them, even though I'm in my thirties."

"Age has nothing to do with it. I always figured you'd become an engineer or something since you used to make the most complicated designs before you'd assemble them into the official design."

"You remember that?"

"Of course. I overheard you talking to Juan about it once, and then I heard Margherita tell my mom. I know once your English was good enough, you were on your school's Science Olympiad team. Why did you become a lawyer?"

"Because *Tío* Enrique and *Tío* Luis won't live forever."

I open my mouth, then snap it shut.

Duty.

Joaquin has the degree in computer science. Jorge's the accountant. Pablo's the scientist and Enrique's heir. Alejandro's got the MBA. They needed an attorney, so it fell to Javier. Does he not like what he does?

"Maddy, my J.D. is my second degree. My undergrad was in electrical and mechanical engineering. Now that I'm a lawyer, I don't use it as much as I could, but it's not like I forgot anything."

That makes my chest tighten. Pablo's concentration was chemistry and biology. I can guess what he uses that knowledge for. Now, I'm thinking about what Javi uses his for. Nothing that comes to mind is positive.

"I'll run the bath. Strip, *chica*." He waggles his eyebrows at me.

Maybe things are okay after all. Maybe he'll give me some more space, but I know he won't wait forever. Maybe—

I hear my phone ringing in my purse. It's one of my burners I stockpiled before I left Albany. Since it's the one in my purse, I know it's the one that has calls forwarded to it from my real number but has no kind of GPS or location services. It's the one I answered when my mom called to tell me about the wedding. I can ditch it and tell Laura or my parents I lost it. I know I have more than a hundred voicemails from Drew. I stopped listening after the first ten because they were just profanity riddled threats. Not even the first couple worried about my wellbeing.

I pull it out and check the screen. Wonderful.

"Hi, Laura."

"Where the fuck are you, you worthless cunt?"

My blood freezes in my veins.

"What did you do to my sister?"

"Wouldn't you like to know?"

"I'm calling Maks."

I hang up, but the phone rings again immediately. I have Maks's number memorized since I have none stored in this phone. I smashed my actual phone and disposed of it before I left. I feel badly polluting, but it's at the bottom of the Mohawk River, and the sim card went wherever the sewer goes. Even though the Hudson is closer to where I lived, I could just imagine, in some twist of fate, the phone floating into the city. Even though the Mohawk is a tributary to the Hudson, I threw it in ahead of the falls. The rocks and pressure should have obliterated the little pieces left after I took a hammer to it.

I ignore the call, but before I can dial my brother-in-law's number, mine rings yet again. I answer after all in case Drew's willing to give me information about my sister. I wish this phone had a three-way feature, but it doesn't. I look toward the bathroom, and I know I'm going to have to ask Javi for his phone to call Maks.

"I want to speak to Laura. Now, Drew."

"Meet me, and you can see for yourself that she's fine."

"Tell me what color fingernail polish she's wearing."

There's a pause. "Pale pink."

Good memory, but wrong. My sister *never* wears polish. Not even gloss, but she buffs them. He might have thought it was polish, but it wasn't. He doesn't have Laura.

"You spoofed her number."

"And you fell for it."

I remain silent as Javi steps out of the bathroom. His eyebrows shoot straight up, and he rushes across the room. I tried to keep my expression neutral, but I'm certain he senses the anxiety roiling within me.

Who is it? He mouths the words.

I'm a deer in the headlights.

"*Chica?*" He whispers this time, and I'm certain I'm the only one who heard him.

"You're not alone, are you? You're with that shithead Diaz."

I guess his men called him before they died. If they did, then he knows I was in the city. Has he guessed I left? He asked where I was earlier.

"What do you want?" I think my voice sounds stronger than I feel.

"You fucking know what I want! Bring back what's mine and bring your sorry scrawny ass with it!"

Javi wraps his hand around my wrist and tugs, but I resist. He must have heard some of what Drew yelled. He tries again, but I won't budge. His hardened expression is the only warning I get before he lands the hardest spank he's given me yet. It forces me a step forward. He grabs my pants' waistband and yanks me back. He swats me again. Tears prick the back of my eyelids. I still don't want to give in.

"You are two seconds away from me baring your ass and spanking you hard enough and long enough for whoever that is to hear it."

He whispers that in my ear, and even spoken that softly, I hear the warning I need to heed. With a shaking hand, I lower the phone from my ear and press the speaker button.

"Drew, I'm not going back up there."

"You are if you want to live."

Rage pulsates from Javi. My ex-boyfriend's name or voice gave him away; he knows who I'm talking to. He puts his hand out, but I still don't want to give him the phone. My resistance is too little too late, but I claw at the last thread. He leans over until our noses nearly touch. I want to flinch away, but his gaze captivates me. He plucks the phone from my hand before I know what's happening.

"O'Sheehan, you sack of piping hot shit."

"Which Diaz are you?"

"The one who's about to fuck your whole world up. You're about to find out what it's like to pick on someone your own size. Stay the fuck away from Madeline, or I will ruin everything you have and everything you've ever thought of having. I will take it, crush it, then burn it to the motherfucking ground. You know my family. You know I'm not lying."

"Tell the bitch to give me back what belongs to me."

"What did you just call *my* woman?"

"Yours? She fucking you too? Whore."

"Drew." I hiss his name in warning, but I don't know why I do.

135

"There's no 'too.' Only me, and I don't share. Stay the fuck away from her, Drew. I won't say it again."

"Tell *Madeline* to give me back what belongs to me."

"I don't have it anymore."

"Bull-fucking-shit. You've never been a good liar."

I laugh, and it sounds more like a snort.

"I lied well enough to get away from you a month ago. I lied well enough that you haven't found what you want. I lied well enough to make you a shit ton of money for the past two years. Here's the truth. Rot in fucking hell. Come near me, and I'll kill you."

There's a moment's pause because he knows I'm serious. When he laughs, it's hollow. Javi's brow furrows. He can tell it's bravado now, and Drew isn't as confident as he was a moment ago.

"Did you forget about that?"

I'm pissed. Since I'll have to explain everything to Javi now, I may as well get most of it out with this call.

"No." Was that a tremble in his voice?

"You know what I'll do when I'm backed into a corner. You watched it all. You're lucky I left. I could have done to you what I did to them."

Javi's staring at me as though he's never seen me before. As though I'm some aberration. If only he knew how much worse it's about to get. Drew digs my grave when he speaks again.

"You don't have the backbone to do shit to me. They were easy marks. That's all you could handle."

"I doubt Javier will agree with you when he finds out what you made me do."

"What the fuck is going on, O'Sheehan? What's Madeline talking about?"

"Maybe you should tell your boy toy, fuck buddy."

"O'Sheehan, I'm already going to kill you. How drawn out

I make it depends on how you speak to Madeline. Keep it up, and I will make it last for days."

"And leave her unprotected?"

"She's with my family now. I motherfucking dare you to come near any of us."

"Challenge accepted."

All I can do is stare at Javi when the call suddenly ends.

Chapter Thirteen

Javier

What the fuck did I just listen to?

I'm staring at the phone in my hand, unable to bring myself to look at Maddy until I'm certain I won't lose my ever-loving shit. I'm equally pissed at both Drew and Maddy. Drew for mistreating Maddy, and Maddy for hiding her boyfriend's—motherfucking ex-boyfriend's—mob connections. How on earth could she have kept this from me? It all makes sense, but what the fuck?

"Javi?"

Usually, I'd feel badly about how timid she sounds, but today isn't the day for me to dredge up any sympathy. At least not yet. This is too incredible, and not in a good way. I inhale three deep breaths before I lift my head and meet her gaze.

Now, I feel horrible because of how terrified she appears. I don't think she's faking it. Her hunched shoulders, wrapped arms, and trembling might be from Drew's threats and my obvious outrage, or perhaps it's simply my presence.

This isn't what I want, even if I'm angry at her.

I twist and toss the burner phone on the bed before I open my arms to her. She steps into my embrace but doesn't unwrap her arms to return my hug. Instead, she stands there, shaking like a leaf.

"Maddy, you know secrets aren't an option anymore. You must tell me what's going on."

She nods but says nothing.

"I can't protect you if I don't know everything from start to finish."

"I know, Javi."

Silence lingers between us for so long I wonder if I'm going to have to command her to tell me what's going on. Just as I'm ready to put my hands on her arms and press her back, she leans away from me, and our gazes meet.

"I'm sorry. I'm sorry I didn't tell you the truth. I'm sorry I got you into the middle of this. I'm sorry those two words aren't nearly enough to make up for what's already happened and what inevitably will happen. All I can say is this is why I tried to keep my distance from everyone. Getting involved with the O'Sheehans never ends well."

"You've been with Drew for a while."

"I *was* with Drew, not have been. I'm *not* with him anymore."

She snaps her mouth shut, and I know she's unsure whether to say she's with me. My gut screams, "of course she is," but this isn't just about me. It's my entire family she's brought into this mess. There's no way it won't roll downhill and wind up in my family's lap. There's no way I can deal with this alone. Inevitably, it'll draw them all in. It makes me want to scrub my hands over my face, but I withstand the temptation.

"I met Drew at the hospital where I was a midwife because his sister had her baby there. I helped deliver the little boy. It took me a while before I agreed to go on our first date. He was persistent but charming. It never felt like too much. He seemed interested, but my new job had crazy hours, so dating didn't feel possible. It wasn't exactly that he wore me down because I liked him, so I found ways to make it work. For the first two years we were together, I had no idea who and what he was. He kept it all from me."

She pauses, and I sense she's trying to gauge whether I believe her. I nod, and she flashes me a half-hearted smile.

"Two years ago, he fully embraced his role as boss. It was just before we moved in together. I'm still amazed he pulled off hiding everything from me. Rather than break up with me, and I suppose risk me telling people I'd been with a mob boss, he just tightened his hold on me literally and figuratively. He became insanely possessive and began to hurt me. He'd always had a nasty streak to him when we argued, but it wasn't enough to make it unbearable. He'd say things to be hurtful, but it got far worse once I found out who he was. The things he said and the things he did. It was about two months into me fully knowing what was going on that he pressured me to help him. It began with little things like patching up his guys when they got injured. Then it was having me come on some of his missions in case the guys got hurt."

"He what? He had you go on missions with him?"

Incredulous. That's the only way to describe how I feel hearing that.

"Yeah, I was always a couple blocks away, but I was there. I didn't argue with him because it just didn't feel worth it. The consequences were too many bruises or threats. He wound up controlling all of my life, or at least he thought so. He thought he controlled who I saw, who I called, where I went, and how I spent my money. He doesn't know I took on some extra jobs here and there and sold my art, but I also skimmed off the top."

When she says that last bit, I think I finally found what can make my jaw truly hit the floor.

"Skimmed off the top of what, Maddy?"

"Off the deals he made me do."

"You better explain exactly what you mean by that because right now my mind's going to the worst possible scenario."

"He didn't whore me out or anything like that, but I spent a lot of time going back and forth between Albany, Rochester, Buffalo, and Ontario."

I let that sink in, not because I don't understand, just the opposite.

"He made you a drug mule?"

She's pulling a "me" right now. Just like I'll go silent when she asks questions I can't or won't answer, she's doing the same thing to me. But her silence tells me everything I need to know.

"Maddy, why? Why did you stay with him for so long? You could've told Maks. You could've told *Tío* Enrique. You could've told your parents. You could've even told the O'Rourkes. You had so many options. Why?"

She grits her teeth and clenches her fists.

"I take it you've never been the victim of domestic violence, have you? Why does any woman stay in a situation like that? It sure as fuck wasn't because I thought I could change him."

"You really believed there was no way out?"

"If you'd seen what he did to me the couple of times I tried to leave, or he thought I was telling Laura something, you'd understand. I didn't believe I'd survive the time it took for Maks and his family to get to me if he found out. But it finally got too unbearable, so I risked dying. That would have been better than staying."

I cup her jaw and brush my thumb over her cheekbone. I do it often because it soothes me.

"*Chiquita*, if only I'd known."

"I know that, Javi. I'm certain everybody in my life will say that when they find out." She looks toward the window, her voice distant, her mind obviously far away. "But it just wasn't as simple as walking away."

I let the silence envelop us; this time in no rush for her to continue. I'm happy to give her time to process everything. I take her hand and lead her over to the bed. We both kick off our shoes before climbing on. I sit propped against the headboard and lift her onto my lap. She sits sideways at first, but then doesn't like it, moving to straddle me, making it easier for us to see each other.

"Javi, I have a lot of his money tucked away. Far more than I'm certain he suspects. But I also hid more than half of his last shipment that he wanted me to run across the border."

"Do you use it?" I don't want to ask that question, so the words are slow to come out.

"No, never. I'm a nurse. I know what that shit does to you. I kept it as security. It's hidden somewhere he'll never find."

"Maddy, you need to tell me exactly where it is."

She bites her bottom lip, and I know she wants to shake her head. I don't think it's because she doesn't trust me enough. I think she fears how I'll react.

"Little one, I can't help you if I don't know."

She takes a deep inhale, and I watch her chest cave as she exhales.

"I promise you it's the one place none of them would think to look. You're going to believe I'm the worst kind of person for this. But it was the only place I felt certain was safe."

I want to tell her to hurry up and spit it out, but I'm not interrogating some guy I'm getting bored with and just want to kill to be done with it. This is my terrified girlfriend.

"You're going to think I'm the worst kind of Catholic."

All I do is cock an eyebrow to that, considering I'm about as lapsed a Catholic as there can be. All the members of the Four Families have complicated relationships with God and their faiths. Three families are Roman Catholic, and one's East Orthodox. We all grew up being altar servers as kids. I sang in the children's choir at my church in Bogotá. But it's difficult to do the things we do and believe confession is enough for absolution when we know we're going to commit the same sins repeatedly. Willingly.

"He thought I wasn't back yet after my last run. So, one night, I visited the cemetery where they buried his grandparents. They cremated his maternal ones, so they're in a mausoleum, but his paternal ones have plots next to each other. It was almost too dark to see what I was doing, but I made it work."

From the way she watches me, I know she wants me to deduce what she means rather than having to confess it.

"You buried his drugs with his grandparents."

She bites her bottom lip again before she raises her gaze to meet mine. Her shoulders go back, and her chin comes up.

"I did." The note of defiance in her voice is a tremendous relief.

"Good. You're right. That's the last place they would think to look."

"You don't think I'll burn in hell for disrupting someone's eternal resting place?"

"No. His grandmother wasn't too bad, but his grandfather was a piece of shit. A complete douche. It's not surprising Drew turned out the way he did."

"Did you know his grandfather?"

"No. All four of his grandparents died before I moved to America, but I've certainly heard enough about them. I've seen video and heard recordings of his grandfathers along with stories that would've been better left untold. Where's the money you took from him?"

"Some of it's in the secret bank account I opened under an alias. Some of it is with me, but most of it is with the drugs. Javi, what I said to him—it—wasn't an empty threat."

"I didn't get the feeling it was. Have you killed before?"

"Yes."

Her gaze is unwavering as she answers. I don't know if she's really as brave as she looks, but she's certainly doing her best to convince me. I know she has to be pretty fucking brave to have endured what I'm figuring out she already has. She's only giving me a hint of what the entire story is. I sense it's all she'll give me for now.

She's kept her secrets for so long, it won't be overnight that she divulges all of them. I know it's not a matter of not trusting me. She's terrified and has been for years. She still thinks she needs to hide the truth to survive. It's on me to show her she isn't misplacing her trust after the disaster she discovered the last time she trusted a man.

"*Chica*, you're safe here with me. That hasn't changed just because you spoke to him. I know your burner doesn't have GPS, but I'll still dispose of it. You must have had your calls forwarded to that one. You can check your messages from my phone, and you can tell anyone you need to call back that you lost or broke it. The house has jammers, VPNs, and spoofers. No one is tracking you here."

"Thank you, Daddy."

She watches me for a long moment before shifting her gaze to her lap. She moves only enough to breathe. She's not any more relaxed now than she was while we stood beside the bed. I press her against me and kiss the crown of her head.

"Nothing changes between us, Maddy. Not unless you want it to."

"Are you going to punish me for keeping all those secrets?"

"I hadn't planned to. All of that happened before we reconnected."

She chokes a laugh at that last word. It's the mildest way to describe how I burst into her life and haven't left her alone since.

"I wish you'd been forthcoming, but your secrets aren't that different from some of mine. Ones I can never tell you. I know I'm a hypocrite for expecting you to confide in me. To make me your confessor when I won't do the same. But I think your heart will be lighter if you keep telling me, and I can better protect you. I've always had my family as my shield. You've been on your own and done an admirable job, but you aren't alone anymore."

"I know. It's like I can breathe again for the first time in years. It's been like breathing through a wet washcloth. I could do it, but it was hard. There was never enough air."

"Do you want to talk to Maks? He'll eventually tell Laura what he can, but I'm certain he'd keep this secret from her and your parents for as long as he can."

"No. I don't want to put him in that position. They'd understand, but I don't want to be the reason he keeps even more secrets from my sister. Laura would forgive him, but it would put a strain on them. It's better he doesn't know yet."

"Whenever you're ready. But, Maddy, we have to tell my uncle. We can stay here indefinitely like I've already said. He'll want us to. This just isn't something I can keep from him because Drew will strike. They need to be ready."

I'm unprepared for her to burst into tears. She's been dry-eyed this entire time, though I think tears have threatened a couple times. Now she's sobbing.

"Maddy?"

"Laura told me some of the stuff that's been going on

recently, and I know Margherita's still recovering from the last round of treatment. The last thing I want is to draw attention to your family, put any of you at risk when things have already been tough lately."

"Shh, little one. Things are always tough." I joke, but unsurprisingly, it falls flat.

Instead of giving her false platitudes, I simply hold her. I keep kissing her head and stroking her hair. I think the tears are cathartic, so I don't stop her. It's not long before the tears are a steady stream, but there are no more heaving sobs. She sniffles and swipes at them half-heartedly. It's ten minutes before she heaves a sigh and goes still. Her breathing evens, and I wonder if she's asleep.

"Javi, I'm still awake. You can move me if you want. Your arms must be tired, and you must be bored."

"I will never be bored holding you. I'll relish any opportunity I get. Let me do it for as long as I can."

"You said you hadn't *planned* to punish me. Past tense. Have you changed your mind?"

"You sound like you almost hope I will. Would it make you feel better if I did? Ease your conscience?"

She hesitates before she answers, and I barely hear her when she does.

"Yes. It's what we agreed to."

"I don't think that it is. We—"

"You made me promise to tell you anything that puts me in jeopardy. I did everything but that. You warned me, and I knew what I risked by not telling you. I risked a shit ton."

I consider what she's saying, and she's right. But I don't know that her nerves—or mine—can handle that right now. She's so tense, she feels brittle enough to snap.

Then again, maybe a spanking is what she needs to ease her anxiety.

"Maddy, if I spank you, then you need to know I'm doing it because it's what you need not what I think you deserve."

"You don't want to do it? I don't want to force you to do something you'll resent. I don't want to diminish—"

"Maddy, I'll always do anything you need. If this is it, then strip, little girl. I believe I told you that earlier."

She climbs off the bed, and I follow her. She watches me as she peels off her t-shirt. Next go her jeans. She pauses when she's standing in her bra and panties. I twirl my finger, silently telling her to turn around. My eyes gorge themselves on her. Her body's even better than I imagined. She needs to regain some weight, so her ribs don't show so much. She's still the most alluring woman I've ever seen. Her body does things to mine.

When she finishes her slow spin, she reaches back to unfasten her bra. She lets it fall to the floor, and I'm practically salivating. When she hooks her fingers into her thong, I'm ready to shred it. She isn't teasing me by lingering. She's nervous. I think it's a combination of trepidation about how I'll punish her and self-consciousness at showing her body to someone new.

"Take your time, little girl. It's the last time you're wearing panties."

"What?"

"No more panties."

"Why?"

"Because you belong to me. All of you, so that includes that pretty pink pussy. When I want it, I'll have it."

I waggle my eyebrows, and she giggles. It softens my words, and I'm certain I look as excited as I feel.

"Yes, Daddy."

The panties join the pile of clothes on the floor. She'll learn I'm serious even if I made her laugh.

"Come here."

I extend my hand, and she takes it. I tug her toward me. When she's standing nearly toe-to-toe with me, I put my index finger's knuckle beneath her chin and tip her head back. Now we're gazing at each other rather than her attention being on the floor.

"Maddy, we've never done this before. I've spanked you but not given you a genuine punishment before. I don't know what you can manage, and you don't know my strength yet."

Her eyes dart to my chest then my arms. When she focuses on my face again, I see the spark of lust.

"I'm plenty aware of your strength, Daddy."

"You know what I mean. Have you ever had a safe word before?"

As soon as the phrase leaves my mouth, I want to wince. Of course, she hasn't had one with a boyfriend who beat her. If she did, he never respected it.

"Drew wasn't my first boyfriend, and he didn't start abusing me until a couple years in. It was when I moved in with him. Before that, we were a little kinky."

I don't want to know what that means, but I know I should understand her experience with anything to do with BDSM.

"Bondage?"

"Yes. Handcuffs, his ties. Sometimes it was my wrists behind my back or tied to the bed. He'd give me a playful swat, but it was never a spanking. There were some toys too."

"Pick something I can't confuse for stop when you don't mean it or misunderstand when you mean enough."

"Fallopian."

"As in the tubes?"

"I am a midwife."

I stare at her for a moment before I shrug and smile. If Fallopian is her safe word, so be it. It's not mine to reason why. It's something I'm certain she's said a million times and can remember, but it's not something I imagine she'd ever want to say during sex.

"Is there anything that's a hard pass?" *Will anything trigger you?*

I can't ask that second part aloud. Maybe I should, but I can't bring myself to. From her expression, she knows I'm thinking it.

"I'm not into any R. Kelly stuff, but I don't think there's anything else I wouldn't at least try with you. We might find something I can't do, but I don't know yet."

"That's fair. If anything reminds you of the past, scares you, makes you even a smidge uneasy, you tell me immediately. Safe word or not, you tell me, Maddy."

"I know. I promise."

"How serious do you think your transgression was?"

She stares at me as though I'm an idiot. She takes a moment to respond because she can't believe I asked something she clearly believes is asinine.

"Which part? All the illegal shit I did? The keeping a monumental secret from you? Endangering you, your family, and my family? The selfishness that goes along with all of that? I'd say about as serious as it can get."

"Lean over the bed. Turn your feet inward. Hands tucked under you. Do not reach back because I risk spanking your hands and hurting you."

"Yes, Daddy."

She does as instructed, and I have the finest view I've ever seen except for looking at the front of her. I step to her right and place my hand in the center of her back, the pressure light. I use my left hand to land the first spank. It's firm, but not as hard as it'll get. I watch her expression since her face is turned toward me. She closed her eyes, and her hands are beneath her shoulders, gripping the sheets. The anticipation is worse than the swats right now. I'm slow to land the next five, building her nervousness rather than alleviating it.

The next five are swift, my large hand landing across both cheeks rather than alternating sides like I did to warm her ass up. Her skin's a rosy pink now. I'm watching carefully to ensure I won't leave any bruises. I study her face, observing every flinch. I listen to every wheezing inhale and how she struggles not to cry. It's clear she has a high tolerance for pain because I'm in no way gentle.

"Maddy, do you feel better yet?"

She tries to shake her head, but she can't do much with her cheek pressed against the mattress.

"Answer with words, so I'm certain I understand."

"Yes, Daddy. And no, I don't feel better yet."

"Do you think you deserve more than this?"

"Yes."

"What will it take to feel absolved, *chiquita*?"

"More than just your hand."

All the men in my family are kinky fuckers—literally. But it's not like we keep a communal stash of toys anywhere. Certainly not where our parents come to vacation with us. We bring no one with us, so no sexual partners have been here before Maddy. With no crops, whips, or paddles, my only choice is my belt. I'm wary of indulging her wish because I fear underestimating my strength. My gaze skims over her, looking for the aftermath of years of abuse. I noticed the bruising on her wrists have faded, and I see no scars. At least not on her skin, though I know there must be plenty on her soul.

I sweep my hand over her ass, feeling the heat emanating from it. It will burn by the time I'm done. I continue to observe her as I unfasten my belt and pull it loose from my cargo pants. I flatten and wrap the buckle end around my hand. I have far too much experience doing this. The single layer will be intense immediately. It'll sting like a motherfucker.

She shifts her weight nervously. She opened her eyes, so she knows what's about to happen.

"Are you certain, little one?"

"Yes, Javi."

We're not truly in a D/s relationship because I wouldn't allow her to use my name in a situation like this. She'd call me Daddy, sir, or master if we were. I don't think she's earned this, so I won't insist. We agreed to domestic discipline, so if this is what she needs to make recompense, then so be it.

"No matter how tempting it is, do not reach back, Maddy."

"I know."

Chapter Fourteen

Maddy

What the fuck did I agree to?

Domestic discipline.

Why the fuck did you ask for this?

That second question whirls around in my mind as I brace myself for the belt to land across my ass. I used to have a lot more meat on it, and I wish I did now. There's not nearly enough to absorb the imminent pain. I inhale as I watch Javi raise his arm. There's about six inches of the belt hanging from his hand. I clutch the sheets even tighter as I hear the swish as it moves through the air, then there's the hiss I make as I grit my teeth.

Motherfucker.

Not Javi. The pain. It's like a band of fire just ripped across my ass. But I asked for exactly this. I want to feel like I've paid my penance for all the wrong decisions I've made for the past four years. The decision to stay with Drew after the first time he insulted me. The decision to stay with him after the first time he slapped me. The first time he hit me. The first time he made me go on a mission. The first time he made me sell drugs. The first time he did any of the fucked-up shit he did.

I want the penance for not mustering the courage to tell my family the moment shit went sideways. I want the penance for not confessing everything to Javi the moment I had the chance. Hell, I could have asked for his help the moment he walked into my hotel room. He would have given it, even if he was there for his own illegal transaction.

I want to finally clear my conscience. I know this won't be enough, but it's a start. So, I focus on each time the belt lashes me, forcing myself not to arch my back or scream. If I start, his men will hear all the way at the gate and think he's skinning a fucking cat. I doubt any of them would even bat an eyelash. As a woman, they might check on me, but I doubt it. I'm here with Javi, so they won't rescue me from him. They'll follow his orders.

I breathe through the pain, forcing myself to focus on it and not let my mind wander. I wait for the next swat, but it doesn't come immediately. That was only five. I expected several more. I open my eyes yet again, and I see he's unwinding the belt. I open my mouth to disagree, but I watch him fold it in half.

He brings it down on my upper thighs, and I stomp my feet. He landed the first five in the same spot. Now he covers my ass, including my horizontal crack. The pain's different. It's not as breath-stealing, but it still hurts far more than I imagined. It's more of a diffused pain that radiates up my back and down to my knees. I swallow over and over, stomping my feet to keep from crying.

"Maddy, it's done."

He tosses the belt halfway across the room like it's a snake ready to strike him. He helps me up and pulls me against him. His heart's racing even though he appears calm. He didn't enjoy doing that. I wonder if this ever happens when he's—fuck it. Let's be real. I'm certain he tortures people. There's no delicate way to put it.

"Are you all right, *chiquita*? Talk to me. Was it too much?"

He sounds ready to panic. Fuck. This hurt him as much as it did me.

"I'm all right, Daddy. I needed it. I feel—"

I stop to think about that. How do I feel? I mean, beyond the obvious pain. Did this help?

"I feel lighter. All of it is still on my conscience. I haven't absolved myself completely. But some of the guilt from not telling you sooner's eased. You don't seem to feel better for it."

"I hate knowing you feel guilty enough to need that. I don't enjoy inflicting this kind of pain on you when I don't think you need the punishment. If I use a belt again, I'd rather it be part of bringing you pleasure."

"You've sworn to take care of me, and this is what I needed. It didn't fix everything, but I'm not carrying those secrets anymore, and I don't feel so ashamed of everything I've done or let happen. I know you know I repent, and that's really important to me."

"You won't sit comfortably for a few days. You'll remember exactly what you did wrong, and you'll remember you've taken your punishment. Maddy, I want to be sure you know my forgiveness is unconditional. When you admitted what happened and apologized, I forgave you. These problems aren't over, but anything that might have come between us is gone. We'll deal with all of this together."

"Thank God."

He squeezes me around the waist before scooping me into his arms. He carries me into the bathroom, where the full tub is waiting for us. I completely forgot he'd run the bath. He puts me on my feet and sticks his fingers in. I'm certain it's completely cold by now. My ass would love it, except he flips the plug and lets half the water out. He refills it with water warm enough I see some steam.

"Test it, *chica*."

I stick my hand in and nod. "Perfect."

He turns the water off and gestures for me to get in, but I shake my head.

"I told you I wanted to wash your back. Aren't you getting in?"

"If I strip, I'll fuck you. Let me take care of you a little more before that."

"Fucking me would definitely count as taking care of me, Daddy."

"You know what I mean, tease."

I shrug one shoulder as I take the hand he offers and step into the tub. He put in enough bubbles that they're practically overflowing from the tub as displacement pushes them up when I slide down to cover my shoulders. The water's cool enough to ease the sting in my ass without me getting cold easily. He perches on the edge and nudges me to lean forward. I wrap my arms around my shins, and he rubs my shoulders. My eyes drift closed. I'm in heav-en!

I feel my shoulders lower, and my head rests heavier against my knees. I inhale enough to fill my lungs and marvel at Javi's magic fingers. They find knots I didn't know I had. Knots upon knots upon knots, apparently.

"Please, join me."

"Lean back first."

He helps me lie back, and I slip under the water, soaking my hair. When I emerge and wipe water from my eyes, I find he already has his shirt off. He's fucking magnificent.

"Keep looking at me that way, and I shall embarrass myself."

"I doubt that. I think you're going to do just fine."

Am I drooling? I'm practically salivating as I watch his pecs and abs flex as he undoes the button and zipper on his pants. They fall to the floor. It doesn't surprise me when he picks them and his shirt up and loosely folds them before putting them on the counter. He's not the fussy type, but I know he likes things tidy. He slipped off his socks when we kicked off our shoes before getting on the bed. Even his feet are sexy. He has high arches and long toes. I'm not particularly into feet, but even that part of him is manly. He pushes his boxer briefs down, and they show the sexy AF V over his pelvis like an arrow to his dick. Then I see the grooves on the side of his hips that scream for me to put my hands there while he thrusts into me.

And oh, my word. That dick.

I've seen my share in porn, my medical profession before specializing in midwifery, and from my sexual partners.

His...

His is magnificent.

Like he could be a dildo model if there were such a thing. Like dildo makers would make casts of his cock and use them to make their artificial dicks.

I enjoy the power giving blowjobs makes me feel. But I'd gladly get on my knees and submit to him just to taste him. I want to feel the weight of it on my tongue. Feel his fingers in my hair as he presses my head to him. Feel him brush the back of my throat as I suck, and he fucks my mouth.

I have a dirty mind.

"Keep looking at me like that, Maddy, and I swear I'll come before you even touch me."

"Excited much?"

"Fucking hell. Yes, Maddy. Excited barely scratches the surface of what I feel."

He steps out of his boxer briefs, and I slide forward before turning around. I want to watch every moment of him getting in the tub with me. He eases in, making sure none of the water sloshes over the side.

"Come here, *chiquita*."

"Yes, Daddy."

I love calling him that. I love that it's something special between just the two of us. It's not like I have Daddy issues or make my voice sound childish. I just love the term of endearment.

"Will you teach me more Spanish?"

He freezes. Shit, that didn't come out right.

"Javi, it's not so I can understand your private conversations. I want to speak enough that it won't sound weird if I call you *Papi*. I think 'ay, Papi' can sound sexy as fuck."

He grins before snagging me, his hands on my ribs, and pulling me closer until I'm kneeling between his open thighs.

"You can call me *Papi* whenever you want, *chiquita*."

His accent is enough to make me wet even if looking at his body hasn't already done that. The spanking made me wet. Seeing him drenched me, and now I'll blame it on the bathwater for how sloppy wet I am.

"All right, *Papi*."

He moves my thighs, so I straddle him. I'm still kneeling with my pussy above the tip of his dick.

"Maddy, we can wait until we get out. I can run to the town and get condoms. I don't do random hookups, so I don't have any."

"I don't have any either. I have an IUD. I tested for a bunch of shit right before I left Drew. I didn't have sex with him again after I did. I pretended to be sick and slept on the sofa. I know I'm clean."

"I am too. I ended things with my sub, and I tested afterward. I was able to rush the results. I wanted to be certain it was safe to be with you, little one."

"Thank you. I don't want to wait unless you do."

"Not even another second."

I ease down onto his cock, and he fucking glides into me. It's erotic as fuck, and the best feeling I've ever had. If him entering me is this good, I can only imagine what orgasms are going to be like. Fucking out-of-body experiences.

"*Chica*...Fuck, Maddy."

There's reverence in his tone that makes me feel like a million bucks. His left arm wraps around my waist, and his right arm fits between my shoulder blades, his hand on my shoulder. He holds me tight against him as I settle my weight onto his lap, my thighs squeezing his hips. We simply marvel at the feeling of being joined and the emotions swirling between us.

I thought I loved Drew. I thought I would make a life with him. I thought I'd found my happily ever after. It was all a fucking nightmare. I want to close my heart off to any and everyone. Protect it from that pain.

As I watch Javi, I'm willing to risk it all over again. I think this time—this time I got it right. But I won't jump the gun. I can't be sure he feels the same way, but his expression makes me think he does.

The hand on my shoulder slips into my hair and cups my skull. He presses lightly, and I gladly lean in for a kiss. The rest of the world no longer exists. It's just Javi, me, and the erotic feel of the water around us. Only our mouths move as the kiss draws on. Our arms are around each other, our lips are melded together, and he's inside me. There's no getting closer than we are now. We are truly one.

When my body will no longer be ignored, I rise and fall on his cock. I've had plenty of sex in my life, but nothing like this. I exaggerate not. This is a spiritual awakening. The way his hands move over my skin. The way he kisses me. The way he holds me. I've never felt so desired. So precious. So grateful for someone who cares for me the way I care for him. Nothing about how we are now makes me think he's just trying to get himself off or that he'll make me come so that he can too.

I want to pleasure him the way he does me. I want him to feel as cherished as I do. I pour that into my kiss and every caress as we move together. My pussy feels full. A sensation I've been needy for but haven't had fulfilled—near pun intended—until now. I rise and fall on his cock, loving every groan I elicit. It's a fucking symphony to my ears as my own moans blend with his into a sexual melody.

"*Chica.*"

"Yes, *Papi.*"

"Fuck."

He really must enjoy hearing that because he grasps my hips and grinds my clit against his pubic bone. He moves me faster than I was on my own. He's demanding. Unrelenting.

"Come, Maddy."

"I'm close. Don't stop."

"My dick would kill me if I did. I'm close too."

I grip his shoulders as I hold on for dear life. I mix rising and falling with grinding.

"May I come?"

"*¡Sí!*"

He roars his response in Spanish, and it's sexy as fuck. It pushes me over the edge, and I don't hold back. I let myself enjoy every moment of my orgasm. It rips through me, starting low in my belly and spreading throughout. I want to scrunch my eyes closed, but I don't want to miss a moment of watching him as he makes me come. He's so fucking intense as he works to get me off again. He truly makes it seem like his pleasure comes from my pleasure. That knowing he got me off excites him. Makes him enjoy this even more.

"You are so fucking hot all the damn time, Maddy. But when you come—it's a fucking work of art."

"I want to do the same for you, Javi. Tell me what to do. How do I make you come?"

"Keep moving, little one. I'm fighting not to finish before you get off a second time."

"My heart might explode if that happens again so soon. I don't know that I can take it. But what a way to go."

We fall silent again, except for our grunts and moans. I lean in and nip at his earlobe, sucking it before licking the shell of his ear. He pinches my nipple, and I arch my back. He squeezes my tit, and I want nothing more than for him to suck on it. I lean back, lifting both breasts to him, my offer obvious. He covers my hands with his as I continue to move with him. He lowers his head, his tongue circling my nipple before he sucks on it. His teeth graze the sensitive skin before using his tongue to toy with it.

My head falls back as I focus on each sensation. Not able to see him anymore anyway, I close my eyes. I focus on how my body reacts to his. His fingers dig into my ass as he grips my hips once again. His lips kiss up the length of my neck. It's all so fucking erotic. My head falls forward to his shoulder as I hold on.

"I'm close again."

"Come in five...Four...Three...Two... One."

My body listens to his commands.

"Yes, Daddy!"

I scream, uncaring if anyone hears me. Let them all know he fucks like a God. I doubt it would surprise any of his men. Let them think whatever they like about me. I couldn't give a shit. I just know that I've finally been with a guy I've wanted since I was fourteen. I've spent more than half my life attracted to him.

"Maddy!"

His teeth sink into the flesh just above my collarbone. His lips soon wrap around it. He sucks but not long enough or hard enough to leave a mark. It's more like a drawn-out kiss. Then he's leaning back against the tub, and my chest is pressed to his. I rest my head on his shoulder, and this is utter perfection. He laps water over my back to ensure I don't get too cold.

"*Chica?*"

"That was perfect."

"It was. I never knew—never imagined—not even when I used to—"

He snaps his mouth shut. I practically hear his teeth click together. I'm too relaxed to move, so I can look up at him. I stroke my hand over his chest instead. I love the feel of the hair between my fingers. It's just enough to be hot. He's not a wooly mammoth.

"When you used to what?"

"When I used to jerk off to a photo of you I took at Laura's wedding reception. I snapped it while no one was looking. You were so fucking gorgeous. I was looking at perfection."

"You took a photo of me?"

He freezes, and I'm certain he thinks I'm pissed. I laugh and kiss his throat.

"I took one too."

"You did?"

"You looked more handsome than any man I'd ever seen. You could have stopped traffic in that tux."

"I thought the same thing about you in your evening gown. I know the attention is supposed to be on the bride, but I couldn't tell you a single thing about Laura's dress beyond it was nice. You had my entire attention."

"I never guessed. I kept stealing glances at you, but you were never looking at me."

"I was always looking at you. I'm just sly. I assumed you were looking at me because of something Laura told you about Juan."

Silence falls between us. His cousin caused a shit ton of trouble for my sister when she started dating Maks. I know there was more shit than she told me, and I know it kept happening until he disappeared. Supposedly, he moved to Chicago, but I never believed it was true. Laura confirmed it a few months later. He was a douche to everyone but Laura, and that's because my sister never put up with his shit. He was taller than Pablo for about a year, and he was a complete asshole to his older brother. Pablo put up with it, so he wouldn't get in trouble for picking on his baby brother. Juan believed that was the green light to be a complete asshole to Pablo for years.

While Laura and Juan were off playing, Pablo looked out for me like his little sister. He helped me with my math homework and would play soccer with me in their backyard. He'd come over and hit a tennis ball against the side of our house for hours while we shared our interest in science. He told me about some of the stuff Juan did to get him in trouble, but neither Margherita nor Luis ever bought Juan's lies. He wound up in trouble for what he did and for trying to blame his brother. It still didn't stop him from doing it. I know it hurt Laura when Juan was unkind about her and Maks, but I haven't missed him for a second.

"Laura hadn't told me much before the wedding. I knew they were fighting, but she was nervous about joining a bratva family. She was nervous about being the *pakhan's* wife. She and Lanie weren't getting along back then either. She took Juan's side and believed whatever bullshit he spewed about

Maks. I'm glad Michelle was there to stand with me at the altar since there were so many men there on Maks's side."

In a twist of fate that I now know was just starting, Laura's other best friend, Michelle, married Lorenzo Mancinelli. He's the Mafia's accountant. Her sister, Elizabeth, married Enzo's brother Marco. Now I'm with Javier. Four girls from a rich neighborhood in Jersey wound up with four syndicate men. Who would've thunk it? Sure as hell not me.

Javi tucks hair behind my ear before kissing my temple. My heart's so fucking full, it feels like it'll burst. His left hand holds my ass, and his right strokes up and down my back.

"You're going to put me to sleep. I haven't been this relaxed in years. I'm completely content."

If only his body cooperated, but his cock does its own thing. I still feel just as connected, even if he isn't inside me anymore. I'd happily stay like this for days, except we both hear his phone vibrating on the counter. I sit up, and he reaches for his pants. He slides it out and looks at the screen before looking at me.

"We need to get dressed, Maddy."

Chapter Fifteen

Javier

Why can't things just be simple?

> TÍO E
>
> Drew O'Sheehan? You need to explain now
> then get back to the city.

I can practically hear my uncle's voice in my head. I know he isn't pissed that I brought Maddy here even though it's our family retreat. He thinks I don't have her protected well enough. In case he truly orders me to bring her back, we need to get dressed.

But not until we finish our bath.

Maddy's ready to climb off me, but I reach for the shower poof and body wash. I didn't open the text, just read the preview. It's a family mandate that we have read receipts on, so I don't need my uncle to know I saw his command. I'll call him back, but not before I'm ready. He said nothing that makes me think there's imminent danger if I don't.

There's a lead glass window above the tub. It's difficult to see through, but I can still make out things on the ground. I've been able to see the men patrolling. If anyone breached the security, I'd see it, and we'd hear the alarm. Anyone who comes through the first gate without the code or anything heavier than a pigeon sitting on the top of the property wall sets off the alarm.

I rub the poof over Maddy's arms, back, and chest before she takes it and does the same to me. I pour shampoo onto my hand and rub it through her hair. She moans with satisfaction as I massage her scalp. After a few minutes, she returns the favor, her magical fingers massaging my scalp.

Fucking bliss.

All of this. Making love to her—there's no way in hell that was just fucking. Feeling her hands all over me. Talking to her. Spending time with her. This is far more than I deserve, considering the fucked-up things I do every day. I'm going to appreciate every second of it, since I fully expect fate to rip it away from me.

First it took my *abuelito*—grandpa—from me. I was super close to my dad's dad. My mom's father was murdered before I was born, but I remember my paternal grandfather. I was six when he died. He used to take me fishing and play card games with me.

Then it took my dad. He was murdered for marrying my mother and joining the Diaz Cartel. My *abuelito* never had a problem with *Papá* working for *Tío* Enrique even though he had to spend time working for my great-uncle—the one who killed his own brother—my grandfather.

"Javi?"

"Hmmm?"

"You suddenly seem a million miles away. Was it the text?"

"No. I was just thinking."

"Did something happen? Are you in trouble for bringing me out here?"

"No, but it was *Tío* Enrique. I have to check in with him. He knows we're out here. He wants us to come back to the city, but I don't think it's a good idea."

"Will it piss him off if you refuse?"

"Possibly. Probably. But I'm not taking you anywhere until I'm certain it's safe. He knows how I feel about this place."

She's sitting back and watching me now. I know she won't ask what I mean, but she wants to know.

"*Tío* knows I feel safest here. It's where my mom, brothers, and I fled to when we couldn't stay in Bogotá any longer. Men were pressuring my mom, trying to trap her into marriage to get to my uncle. They either wanted to kill him or make friends. Either way, it was dangerous for *Mamá*, and my brothers and I were leverage. When we came to America, we came straight here. *Papá* bought this place as a wedding gift for *Mamá*. It was a getaway for them that allowed them to enjoy everything New York offered without being in the city. They could just enjoy each other's company when they wanted solitude and take advantage of everything else when they wanted to go out. When it was no longer safe to stay in Colombia, *Mamá* brought us here. I come out here when I need time away from everything else."

Maddy listens, and I think she appreciates me opening up about my family. I'm certain she knew why we came to America, but there was no way she could know about this home. I observe her as I speak. I'm ready to share things with her I've shared with no one else. Things about my family's past that've always been top secret.

"Do you know much about my family and how we came to be who we are?"

"A bit. Only things Pablo and Juan said when we were

really young. Stuff they didn't know not to tell girls they thought of as little sisters."

"My dad's side of the family wasn't Cartel until my dad met my *Tío* Enrique in college. My *abuelito* did some business with my *tíos'* family, but they weren't Cartel. Beside *Tío* Luis, *Papá* was *Tío* Enrique's best friend. When *Tío* Humberto—my mom's uncle, so my great-uncle—started trouble, my *abuelito* couldn't ignore it. He recruited my dad when he was in his twenties. Back then, *Tío* Humberto lived in NYC, and he headed up the Colombians here. *Tío* Humberto believed *Papá* worked for him. My dad rose up the ranks fast because *Tío* Humberto favored him. *Tío* Enrique and *Tío* Luis had been out of college for a few years, and my mom and *Tía* Catalina were back in Bogotá after college. It didn't take long for everyone to realize the shit *Tío* Humberto wanted him to do was meant to screw my *abuelito* and to keep *Tío* Enrique from inheriting anything. Not here in New York or back home in Bogotá. *Papá* couldn't just walk away because he knew the shady shit *Tío* Humberto was doing endangered my mom's entire family. He met *Mamá* when he was gathering information to give to *Tío* Enrique. He couldn't tell *Mamá* that, so she thought he was a complete *cabrón*. Arrogant, apparently. I wonder where I got that from."

I try for some self-deprecating humor, and it works because Maddy flashes me a smile. I don't think I'm freaking her out too much, so I keep going.

"*Papá* never got over being unable to warn *abuelito* in time to save him. He told *Tío* Enrique about the first plot, and *Tío* thwarted it. But he didn't learn what *Tío* Humberto planned the second time until it was too late. *Papá's* the one who had to tell *Tío* Enrique, who had to tell *Tío* Luis. Together, they called *Mamá*, *Tía* Catalina, and *Abuelita*. I can't imagine how that must have felt for any of them. It wasn't *Papá's* place to tell

Mamá, but he was with her just after her brothers called. He made sure the three women were together. *Tía* Catalina was engaged to *Tío* Matáis at the time, so he was there too.

"No one ever doubted *Papá's* or *Tío* Matáis's loyalty because they were the first to get *Tío* Enrique's orders to strike back. They did what needed doing until my *tíos* could get to Bogotá. I'd like to say the stories I've heard are just urban legend, but I'm certain they only scratch the surface of what happened when *Tío* Enrique took over. He went from being a pretty recent college graduate to running New York City to running all of Latin America in the space of a couple phone calls and one gunshot."

That's an abridged version of history. From what I know, *Tío* Enrique and *Tío* Luis went full vigilante when they returned to Colombia for my *abuelito's* funeral. They sent *Mamá*, *Tía* Catalina, and *Abuelita* to the family's compound on the coast near Venezuela. It's where our ancestors' lived before migrating to Bogotá. We still speak the indigenous language when we don't want anyone around us to understand.

While the women were gone, *Tío* Enrique led five missions that practically decimated every rival they had in the country. He's only helped law enforcement once; he ensured *Tío* Humberto's extradition from the U.S. to Colombia. Once he had his uncle back in Bogotá, he made sure it benefited the government to hand the *hijo de puta*—son of a bitch—over to my uncle.

Tío Luis started infiltrating prisons to ensure we had men on the inside who'd keep the incarcerated men from *all* the cartels on our side. Whenever the government released any of them, they were ready to work for my uncles, not *Tío* Humberto. *Tío* Enrique personally captured his uncle and imprisoned him in a lavish estate that makes Pablo Escobar's look like a cabin in the woods in comparison. He gave *Tío*

Humberto the luxuries to taunt him because *Tío* Enrique hasn't allowed him to leave the place in over thirty years.

He oversees things when *Tío* Luis or Alejandro aren't there. *Tío* Enrique goes down to visit every few months to beat the shit out of him—to remind him he lives because my uncle lets him. He started doing that after *Tío* Humberto failed to look out for *Mamá*, my brothers, and me. He had the power to keep men from pursuing *Mamá* for her money and connections. He could've kept men from approaching my brothers and me to recruit us into rival cartels. He could've kept the street gangs from attacking my brothers and me. But he didn't.

Mamá did an excellent job protecting Jorge, Joaquin, and me until we became tweens. The street gangs got more aggressive, and my brothers and I were getting in fights regularly. By the time Joaquin was fourteen, I'd just turned thirteen, and Jorge was nearly twelve, I'd already killed three men. Joaquin had also killed, and Jorge had already stabbed guys. It was imperative we get out, so we fled to this house.

Everyone believes the Kutsenko brothers had it the hardest because their old leader was a fucking psychopath. Bogdan was eleven when they immigrated to the U.S., just like Jorge. I know they tortured Bogdan during their training, and I can say none of my brothers or I experienced that. But we saw and did shit that rivaled what the Kutsenkos experienced, yet they only call us the fucked-up ones. They should look at their pretty little faces in the mirror and stop being such hypocrites. We're no more psychopathic than they are. We do nothing worse than what they do to protect our respective families.

As I watch Maddy, I know that's shit I can't share with her. She can never know I killed for the first time when I was ten. The guy tried to kidnap me and held Jorge at knifepoint. The man assumed because I was so small compared to him, my rage wouldn't be as strong as any man's. No one touches my brothers.

"Javi?"

Maddy's voice pulls me back into the present again. My thumb rubs away lines where her brow furrows as she watches me.

"Just slipping back into memories again, *chiquita*. I wish I could tell you more, but I can't."

She observes me for a moment more before she nods.

"Javi, I'll never ask because I don't want to bring up painful memories. But I'll always listen. I know there are things from your childhood I'm certain you believe would scare me away or that I'd reject. There's not. You're the man you are today because of what you've experienced. I'm here with you because I want you, which means I accept everything that comes with you. Past, present, and future."

She appears nervous with the last word.

"Past, present, and future, little one."

"There's more for me to tell you about what I've done, but I can't manage that today. I'm scared you'll reject me for it."

"Have you hurt children or animals?"

"No!"

"Then I won't reject you, Maddy."

"I'm not who you thought I was, though."

"Yes, you are. You're intelligent, resourceful, funny, kind, giving, fearless, strong, sexy, and mine. That's who I thought you were, and that's what I still think."

"You thought I was yours?"

"Well, I imagined it enough times."

"If only we'd known back then what we know about each other's feelings now."

"True, but maybe God knew neither you nor I were ready

to be an 'us' back then. Maybe we needed to get to who we are now to be ready."

"You're right."

I doubt her relationship with God is as complicated as mine, but we grew up with the same faith. I think she gets what I mean.

We finish our bath and dry each other off. Running the fluffy towels over each other tempts us to do a lot more, but we both know I can't ignore *Tío* Enrique much longer. Since she has clothes with her—she told me she'd done laundry at the hotel—she has something fresh to put on. I remember I have a couple t-shirts and pairs of athletic shorts here, so I grab a set.

"Are you hungry, little one?"

"Is there anything here?"

"Yes. We keep the house supplied with nonperishables. I can send men into town to get anything fresh we want. But I can make us plenty of things with what we have."

"Okay. If you want, I can go to the kitchen and rummage around. I'll cook while you call Enrique."

She gets that she probably can't hear most of the conversation. Her Spanish isn't good enough to understand everything, but I don't know what she can, and I don't know how much of it will be things she can't hear.

I wrap my arm around her waist and pull her against me as she turns toward the door.

"Not so fast."

We share a kiss that tests my resolve to care about what my uncle has to say, but I can't risk not speaking to him if it would endanger Maddy. I've always followed *Tío* Enrique's rules, even if I bent them sometimes. I don't want to start ignoring his commands now, but I know without a doubt I will if I don't agree with what he says about Maddy. I'll put her safety first.

That's a shocking realization.

I watch her close the door and wait a minute before opening it to peek down the hall. I want to trust her, but I know what temptation it is to listen when you're scared and aren't in control. I wouldn't blame her if she didn't fully trust me or just wanted to know what I'm planning without her. But I don't see her. I leave the door slightly ajar, so I can watch as I hit my uncle's contact in my phone.

"Took you long enough, *sobrino*."

"Sorry. I didn't see your text come in."

I realize I still haven't read it. I put the call on speaker, so I can pull up the message.

TÍO E

Drew O'Sheehan? You need to explain now then get back to the city. We can protect you and plan. Hiding her won't fix this.

"Sure. What do you know about her relationship with O'Sheehan?"

He dismisses my excuse, and I can imagine what he assumes we were up to. He's right of course. I consider what I can share without breaking Maddy's confidences. I'm certain she shared things she doesn't want anyone else to know.

"He abused her and forced her to do some jobs for him. She didn't know what he was at first, and by the time she did, he had complete control over her."

"Why's he after her? Because he can't accept that she doesn't want him?"

"There's that. She knows things about his business he doesn't want her to share. He spoofed Laura's number when he called, so she answered. I didn't hear all of it, but I know he threatened her."

"Can you get her here?"

"I don't want to bring her back into the city. It's not just the drive back. I don't want her somewhere so obvious. We're better hiding here."

"I can send the helicopter."

"No. I really don't want her back where Drew can guess where we are. I don't want him to have any opportunity to attack. Even if we shield her and resist him, she could get hurt. I don't want her around the violence."

"Are you certain no one followed you?"

"Yeah."

"Should I send your brothers?"

Part of me thinks yes, the more men to protect Maddy, the better. Part of me thinks no, I want no distractions and all the privacy we already have. And a third part thinks no, I don't want to risk anyone following them up here. But my brothers could take the helicopter rather than drive, so that would keep anyone from following them. And coming here was about keeping Maddy safe not have a sex retreat.

I know what the selfish part of me wants, and I know what the responsible part of me feels duty-bound to do.

I barely contain my sigh. "Yes, send them, please."

I know they'll give Maddy and me privacy, so I shouldn't worry. But I don't want to embarrass her since she'll know they'll know why we slip away. Then again, as spectacular as our bath sex was, maybe she'll change her mind. Regret what we did and realize we shouldn't get more intimate. I don't think that's what'll happen, but it's a possibility.

"They can be there in an hour."

"Tell them to bring me some clothes. We left unexpectedly, so I only have what's already here."

My brothers and I are worse than teenage sisters. We can share clothes without a second thought. We share suits whenever we need to since we often have to change. Things can get messy when we're working, or we want to be certain we leave no DNA behind. It means burning our clothes. It's a good thing we're all billionaires because our wardrobe costs us a fortune. We have different tastes for our more casual clothes, so I may not love what they bring me. But I'm just glad I'll have clean ones.

"Pablo's here. He wants to speak to Madeline."

Why?

I want to demand a reason my cousin, who's known Maddy since she was a baby and had a super close relationship, wants to speak to my girlfriend. That means admitting stabbing insecurity and jealousy. Between the two of us, Pablo's always been the one women gravitate to. They're curious about his brooding nature and looks. I'm such a homebody that I have no patience for small talk. Women approach me, but they usually get bored quickly. I don't date, so having a woman who enjoys the kind of sex I like made having a sub so appealing. I don't want that anymore, so I want no competition. Reasonably, I know Pablo isn't. But he could be.

Chapter Sixteen

Maddy

I fought the temptation to stay in the hallway and put my ear to the door. I want to know what's happening because I'm scared Javi will decide we need to go back to the city. I won't feel as safe there as I do here. I know Javi will ultimately decide, and I'm fine with that. I'm just tired of feeling like life is happening to me. I've felt so out of control for the past month while also feeling like I've had more control than in the past two years. The conflicting emotions are exhausting.

I trust Javi, so I made myself put one foot in front of the other until I arrived in the kitchen. I'm making pasta since there are several boxes and jars of sauce. It's easy and fast, so we can have something quick if we're going to leave. I'm lost in thought as I mix the sauce in with the noodles. I nearly jump out of my skin when Javi slides his arms around my waist and nuzzles my neck.

"Did you find what you need?"

"Yes. There's plenty here. I made something simple in case we're pressed for time."

"We aren't. Jorge and Joaquin are coming out here. They'll take the helicopter, so no one can follow them. I trust the men here, but not like the men in my family. Pablo wants to talk to you."

I stiffen before I turn in Javi's arms. "Why?"

"I don't know. *Tío* said he did. You can call from my phone."

"What do I say if he asks questions about Drew? What do you want him to know?"

"That's up to you, Maddy. I won't dictate what you can say to the men in my family since it's best if they know as much of the truth as you can tell."

"And if he asks why I went to you instead of him or Enrique?"

"Tell him the truth."

"I can't tell him the entire truth. I won't say, 'I've never wanted to fuck you, but I can't wait to jump your cousin's bones again.'"

I grin, and he pins me against the counter as he kisses my neck down to my collar bone and squeezes my left breast. He trails his lips back up my throat until he gets to my jaw, kissing along it until he nips my earlobe.

Pablo who?

I want nothing more than another round of what we did in the bath. Shower sex, pool sex, ocean sex. The water made it more erotic than anything I've ever experienced before. Javi is hands down the sexiest man I've ever been with. I'm insatiable.

I have a loose shirt on with buttons that run halfway down. He unfastens them and tugs my bra out of the way. Then he alternates tits as he sucks and licks. I lean back to make it easier, my right hand bracing me as my left clutches his shoulder. I don't know if I'm hanging on for dear life or making sure he can't get away. I'm unprepared for him to wrap his hands around my waist and hoist me in the air, suspending me in place.

"Pull your shorts down."

I unfasten them and hurry to obey, though it tempts part of me to disobey or just move slowly to see how he punishes me. But I know my ass can't take much more. The bath helped soothe the skin, but it's definitely sore. I push them down and kick them off. He carefully places me on the counter, knowing I have no cushioning against the hard surface. He presses my knees apart before drawing me to the edge.

He squats as he kisses along my left inner thigh until he gets to my vag. His tongue does magical things as he licks the length of my pussy lips then swirls his tongue over my clit. He presses the tip into me before wrapping his lips around my clit. He sucks while licking back and forth, and I want to squirm. His hands pin me in place. I get what he offers, and he decides what that is. He's completely in control of pleasuring me. He'll deny me if he wants, just to intensify my need then the satisfaction when he lets me come.

When his tongue flicks my clit over and over, I use the cabinet behind me to hold me up. I'd melt into a gooey puddle of lust if it wasn't there. He keeps working me, and I feel the ache in my pussy growing into a burn. I want him so badly it's almost painful being empty.

"Javi, please. I need you."

He obliges—partly. He thrusts three fingers into me as I tilt my hips farther forward. It feels amazing, but what I need is his cock. I need to know he's inside me, but I also need the sensations only a dick can give. Fingers are great, but they're not enough.

"Javi, I need more. I need *you*."

He doesn't stop fingering me or sucking my clit, but he looks up at me. He must see my frustration because his brow furrows. His mouth lets go, and he withdraws his fingers, sucking them with a wicked gleam in his eyes. He lifts me off the counter and carries me to the kitchen table. He pushes down his shorts, and I love that he's going commando. I reach over my head to grab the far edge as his fingers press into my ass, and he thrusts into me.

"Javi!"

"Sí, chiquita."

"Fuck. You feel so good. Hard, Daddy."

He grunts as he plows into me. He loves hearing that word as much as I love saying it. It's proof I trust him. That I surrender to him and will let him take care of me and protect me. It doesn't mean I can't do things for myself. It doesn't make me a child. It doesn't make me subservient to him. It makes me free.

"Fuck, Maddy. I'm going to come too fast."

"I want to make you come."

I Kegel as hard as I can every time he bottoms out inside me. He leans over me, pressing his chest to mine as our gazes lock. I'm entirely entranced. I'd do anything he told me right now. Not out of fear. Not to keep the peace. The excitement is intoxicating, and I want him to feel it too.

"Keep doing what you're doing, and I will. Are you close?"

"Yeah. Keep going."

He supports his weight on his elbows as his hands wrap around mine. I splay my fingers so we can intertwine them. I pull my feet up to the edge of the table—I think for a moment how unhygienic that is, but then again, we're having sex where people eat—and use it for leverage. My hips rise and fall in rhythm with his as he grinds against my clit. My eyes droop closed for a moment, not because I don't want to watch every moment but from sensory overload. I need a moment to focus on just what I feel, not what I see and hear.

When I'm ready to handle it all again, I open my eyes. Javi's expression is so intense, but I can tell his focus is entirely on me. He's observing me, gauging what I need and want, doing his best to please me. My heart's pounding from exertion, but it expands with a depth of feeling I'm not ready for. I want him to be my future, but I'm not ready to fall in love again. This is a marathon, not a sprint. Yet my mind and body are on a mad dash to the finish so I can claim my happily ever after.

I push my thoughts away from that since the only finish line I want is where I win an orgasm. I'd love it to be a tie and come with Javi. He lets go of my right hand and pulls back enough to bring his tongue to my nipple. He wraps it around the puckered flesh, toying with it. He flicks it just as he did my clit before practically swallowing my breast. I used to be a solid C cup, but with the weight I've lost over the last couple years, I'm barely a B without padding.

I've wondered how no one's ever mentioned I'm on the thin side. It's made me think I must look better as I am now than I did at the weight I got to through college and when I became a nurse. I also wear scrubs most days and a lab coat, so those aren't exactly form fitting. I noticed my parents and Laura watching me eat at Enrique's reception, so I think they noticed I'm skinnier. I feared Javi would find me scrawny, but from the way he can't stop sucking my nipple and touching every part of me he can reach, I think he likes what he found.

"Maddy, are you close? I can't wait much longer."

I let go of his hand and move mine to grasp his hips. I press on the grooves, encouraging him to thrust and stay in me. I grind against him and feel the beginning of my orgasm.

"I'm coming, Daddy...I'm coming."

I arch on the table, and my fingers move to his back as I

press into his muscles. He thrusts four more times before I know he's there. He pulses inside me. I'm not certain whether I want to have kids, even if I've thought about them with Javi. But the idea that he could impregnate me as a way to claim me completely is maybe a bit fucked-up but totally hot to me.

"One day, if you want children, I'll fuck them into you, little girl. There'll be no way to deny you're mine when our child grows inside you. No one will doubt you belong to me, and I belong to you."

Fucking mind reader!

I observe him, trying to figure out if that was entirely dirty talk or whether he meant it. I think it's the latter. I think he'd never push me into having children if I didn't want them, but if I did, he'd keep me barefoot and pregnant if that's what I asked for. I also think he'd be deeply involved in his children's lives since he lost his father so young.

"Yes, Daddy."

We keep our gazes locked. I think he's trying to figure out whether I'm reacting to what I believe is dirty talk, or whether I'm responding with a truthful answer to a truthful statement. Neither of us wants to clarify, and both of us would rather keep the kinky dynamic for now. We share a kiss, though, that's far more tender than one would expect after such a declaration. We don't pull apart as he lifts me and kicks back a chair. When he sits, I wrap myself around him as our kiss carries on. He leans back as we both take a breath, and I rest my head against his chest. His hands cradle my ass, and I could stay like this forever.

Unfortunately, we both feel his phone vibrate in his pocket. It surprises neither of us to see Pablo's name on the screen. He offers me the phone, and I look at him as if to say *what do you want me to do with that?* I didn't mean to sigh as loudly as I do when I accept it and slide my finger across the screen.

"Hi, Pablo."

"Madeline, are you all right?"

"Yeah. We got here without any problems."

I put the call on speaker.

"Javier spoke to *Tío* a while ago, so I expected to hear from you sooner. I got worried."

I suck my lips in for a moment as I observe Javi. He seems less than thrilled to hear from his cousin.

"We were having lunch."

Javi might have while I was on the counter, but I look down at where my body meets Javi's and waggle my eyebrows. He relaxes, his shoulders dropping away from his ears.

He's nervous I'll pick Pablo.

"Madeline, whatever happens, listen to Javier. Do exactly as he says. It doesn't matter if you don't understand why or disagree. Just do it."

"I know that."

"Javier, I'm certain you're listening, so don't kill me for this. Madeline, my entire family still considers you my little sister. Everyone except Javier. He's been in love with you since he moved here. There's nothing he won't do to protect you. I trust him with you. Not just because he'll protect you. I'm trusting you not to endanger my cousin."

I've seen no one blush as deeply as Javi is right now. His cheeks are a deep burgundy, and even the tip of his nose is too. There's a tinge of pink on his forehead. He looks away from me, but I won't let him feel embarrassed. I press his chin to turn his head back toward me and lean in for a kiss. I rock my hips since I know he won't be inside me for much longer. He grabs them and moves me. I didn't mean for us to have sex again. I just wanted to feel us remain connected. He's going to make me come while I'm on the phone with his cousin.

Wasn't Pablo's comment enough to prove his cousin wants

nothing to do with me romantically? Does Javi have to prove I'm his by getting me off while I'm speaking to a nonexistent rival?

It disappoints me a moment later when he stops guiding me at the rhythm he wanted. I realize he did it to keep him hard, not to get me off. Wishful thinking, I guess.

"Pablo, I'll obey whatever Javi tells me to do. He knows that because I already promised." I mouth *Daddy* at the end.

No sound comes from Javi when he responds with *good girl*. I can't stop my smile. His approval means more to me than Drew's ever did. It means more than any past boyfriend's.

"I'm certain you told Javier things he didn't tell *Tío*. I'm also certain there's more you haven't shared. You weren't secretive as a kid, but you only shared what you wanted people to know. If you trust my cousin the way you say you do, you need to tell him absolutely everything. He'll know what he can keep between you and what he needs to tell us to keep you safe. The more you try to shield him or us, the harder you'll make it to protect you. Know that nothing will make him give up on you. Not after nearly twenty years."

I cup the end of Javi's jaw, my fingers at his nape, and my thumb brushing over his cheekbone.

"I will, Pablo. I'm where I belong because I'm with the person I trust most."

"Javier?"

"Yeah." He sounds less than enthused to speak to Pablo.

"I doubt I'll survive this conversation once you're both back. Madeline used to doodle Madeline Diaz in her Chem notebook in the back. She thought I never saw it. Knowing Drew, I'm certain there are a few reasons Madeline never married him. Some of it was because her heart belonged partly to you, not entirely to him. Watch out for my little sister, and do whatever you must because she'll hold on as tightly to you as you do to her."

It's my turn to have a bright-red face. I'm fairer than Javi, so I'm certain I practically glow magenta. I had no idea Pablo ever saw that. He tutored me in Chemistry, but I thought I kept those doodles hidden. I'd love nothing more than to sink into the floor.

"I will, Pablo. We gotta go. My brothers'll be here soon."

"You know I'm a call or text away."

"Thank you." Javi and I respond at the same time.

Javi hangs up and tucks his phone back into his pocket as I climb off his lap. When his brothers arrive, I don't want them walking in while I have no shorts on. He follows me over to where I left my clothes and the now congealed noodles. They hardly look appetizing.

"Maddy?"

I look over my shoulder as I consider whether there's any way to rescue our late lunch. Javi reaches past me and moves the bowl aside and eases me around to look at him. Heat radiates from my cheeks all over again. Having my back to him gave me a chance to gather my composure a little, but that evaporated.

"I didn't know you shared my feelings back then. I never imagined you could. I don't think you've been pining for me this entire time. I know it was puppy love back then, so I don't think I had anything to do with why you didn't marry Drew."

"It was puppy love, and I feel differently about you now. My feelings are ones of an adult. But those lingering questions of what it might have been like to be with you and the last shreds of hope that I could be with someone like you... They never went away. I don't know where we are with how we feel now, but I know where I want to get to."

"Same. I won't profess love right this minute, but I know

183

I'm already falling in love with you. We're both different from when we were kids, but not so much that we fundamentally changed. I want to be in a relationship with you that's unlike anything I've had in the past. I don't know how to be a boyfriend, but I hope you'll let me try."

"And I'm worried I don't know how to be in a healthy relationship anymore. You're the only one I want to try with. Please be patient if I get skittish. I know what Pablo said is true, and I will tell you everything. I just don't think I can do it all at once."

"I get that. But is there anything I don't know that is dangerous enough to not only get you hurt but also get my brothers killed?"

Where the fuck do I even begin?

Chapter Seventeen

Javier

Maddy's gaze doesn't waver, but I know she'd rather talk about anything besides her past with Drew. She's promised to tell me more, but she's not ready to do it now. However, procrastinating may not be a luxury she has for much longer. If what she knows can endanger my brothers, then I'll be unrelenting. I won't intentionally be cruel, but I won't let her past end my brothers' futures.

"Javi, I don't know what you know about the O'Sheehans' businesses. I assume it's far more than I can guess. They have dealings with the O'Rourkes when they must, but they're usually happy to avoid Dillan's attention. With all that's happened in Boston and Trenton over the past few years, Drew's family has flown under the radar most of the time. They answer when Dillan or any of the other O'Rourkes call, but they don't pick up the phone first. However, they do business with the Tremblays."

The Tremblays are Montreal's leading mob family. Talk

about a complicated cultural ancestry. A French-speaking Irish mob family. Tremblay is a fairly common last name in Quebec, but there's nothing common about the man who runs that family. He happens to be Sean O'Rourke's grandfather-in-law now. His daughter had a regrettable one-night liaison with the former head of the Boston mob nearly thirty years ago. His granddaughter is a highly intelligent and remarkable woman, but it's bound the Tremblays to the Boston O'Malleys ever since. It means the O'Rourkes now have indestructible ties to both cities that go beyond business.

That's been a royal pain in my family's derriere ever since.

"How much of that business does Sean know about?"

"Not as much as he probably should."

"Maddy, what does that mean? I need you to just tell me. I don't want to badger you, but you can't be evasive anymore. Not with my brothers' lives at risk."

"I know, Javi. But it's not as simple as just opening my mouth and letting all the secrets I've been punished for knowing come tumbling out."

That makes me pause. My gaze skims over her, and it would be easy to pretend I didn't see the bruises on her wrists days ago or how she shied away when I brushed my fingers over her kidneys at the reception. My life is like a theatrical performance every day since I reinvent myself depending on the situation. I can pretend anything does or doesn't exist depending on how it serves me. But there's no forgetting what Drew's done to Maddy, and I barely know any of it.

"He forced you to know his secrets, then punished you for it?"

"Yes. It's part of how he controlled me. He put me in situations where I couldn't help but learn his secrets, then he'd threaten me if I ever told them. He'd blame me for things that made no sense, but he'd try to gaslight me. I didn't buy into it being my fault, but it didn't change how I had to react to avoid him lashing out."

"How did you react?"

"I'd tell him—"

The windows rattle, and we look toward the helipad that's visible outside the kitchen. The door slides open as the helicopter touches down. The blades haven't slowed by the time Jorge and Joaquin jump out, bent low toward the ground.

"Shit!"

She scrambles to grab her clothes and rushes to put them back on as my brothers run toward the dining room glass doors.

"I'll let them in and keep them in there until you join us."

I hurry through the pocket door and slide it closed behind me. Just as I open the left French door, the security system beeps. Someone's at the first gate.

"*Hola, mano.*" Hello, brother.

Jorge gives me a loose hug, and I return it, but I'm looking toward the driveway. There's no way I can see it with half the house in the way.

"Hey. Did you see anyone pulling up to the gate?"

Joaquin glances in the gate's direction, but he can see no more than I can. "No. Did one of the guys run out to town?"

"They were all accounted for when I checked the video feeds when we got here."

I checked them while I turned on the bath. Every room has screens with the surveillance feeds, so you know where everyone is at all times. There aren't cameras in the main house's bedrooms, but there are ones right outside the doors. There are cameras in all the rooms in the guards' bunkhouse. They aren't afforded the same privacy my family gets.

The alarm beeps again, and we know that means whoever arrived just made it through the second gate. I don't like this.

"I need to get Maddy."

Jorge and Joaquin pull their guns from their lower backs as they spin around and step back onto the patio. Jorge fishes in his pocket and pulls out an earpiece he tosses over his shoulder to me. My brothers and I all put ours in, knowing they'll operate on a different frequency from the ones our men use. But we can easily flick them over to that one. We can hear everything the men say, but we can also communicate privately.

We won't speak Spanish either. We'll use *Macaguán*, one of sixty-five Amerindian languages spoken in Colombia. Only about five hundred people still speak it and almost exclusively in a remote region near the Venezuelan border. It's my family's ancestral language and great for keeping things private these days.

I watch my brothers move back-to-back as they creep toward the end of the patio before I slip back into the kitchen.

"Javi?"

"Something's going on, Maddy, but I'm not quite sure what. We need to get you in the safe room."

"Drew?"

"Possibly, but I don't know for sure. Come on."

I reach for her arm and wrap my hand around her right elbow, but before we can move toward the door that'll lead to the foyer, all hell breaks loose. The sound of automatic weapons firing blasts through the air. My grip tightens on Maddy as I tug her toward me, pulling a gun from the drawer closest to me. We have weapons scattered throughout this house, in places people are least likely to imagine.

"Javier?!"

"In the kitchen, Jorge."

My brother's voice bellows at me, even though the tone is neutral. His volume makes me realize those gunshots weren't fired by anyone on our side. Both of my brothers burst into the kitchen, not having made it far down the patio before turning back to find Maddy and me.

"We need to get Madeline up to the safe room."

"That's what I just told her. Come on, Maddy. Who is it? Did you recognize them?"

"No." It's Joaquin who answers this time.

His back is to us as he scans the scene outside the kitchen window. Maddy covers her mouth and smothers a scream as the window next to my brother's left shoulder shatters. We all dive for the floor, taking cover. I land on top of Maddy, trying not to squash her but shielding her with my entire body.

"Javi, I recognized that man."

I barely make out what Maddy says since her voice is muffled from me being on top of her. I push up onto my forearms and roll slightly to my right, giving her enough space to lift her head and look at me.

"That's one of Drew's men. How did he get here?"

I look over at my brothers. "Did someone follow you?"

Jorge shrugs one shoulder. "I don't know how they could have. Our flight pattern didn't follow any roads. It was as the crow flies. The only way anyone could know we were here is to already know where we would be headed."

More gunfire rips through the air, drawing closer to the house. Where the fuck are our men who're supposed to be loyal to us? Obviously, at least one of our men has sold us out. Otherwise, these people wouldn't have made it through the gate. No vehicle would survive ramming them. They'd come back as mangled metal. So, the only way strangers are on our land is if somebody let them on.

There's a moment of silence, so I push up onto my hands and knees, then crouch before reaching out my hand to Maddy. I only straighten long enough to look out the broken window to see if anyone's approaching our part of the house. It's still quiet for now. The four of us ease out of the kitchen and into the foyer. But we don't make it beyond there before we hear voices yelling out Maddy's name.

"Madeline Doyle, this is the United States Drug Enforcement Agency. We are here to serve a warrant for your arrest. Come out with your hands raised."

Maddy turns a panicked expression to me and shakes her head.

"We know it's not real." My whispered reassurance does little to ease her visible fear.

"Madeline Doyle, come out with your hands up."

"Javi, that's Jacob McIntyre. He's Drew's cousin. He is a DEA agent, but there's no way he'd serve an arrest warrant on me."

"If he thinks you're gullible enough to turn yourself over to him when you're on a Diaz property, then he's insane. I wouldn't let you go to anyone outside of my family, period. Let alone anyone connected to law enforcement or to another syndicate. He knows you're not leaving my side. He's banking on you fearing Drew more than you trust me and going along with what he says to avoid whatever Drew's told him to do to you if you don't cooperate."

I'm focused on Maddy, but I hear Joaquin speaking to somebody through our earpieces. The radio's suddenly gotten noisy with men loyal to us calling out orders to help barricade us in the house. I caught the name of the man who betrayed us. But there's nothing I can do about him right this minute.

Jorge barks a command to keep the guy alive but out of the way. Apparently, two SUVs rolled in with sixteen men against the eleven still loyal to my family, my brothers, and me. I don't know how many men we lost when our attackers breached the gates and opened fire. Not all the men have sounded off when the head of our guards told them to do a check-in. They could be injured or dead or must remain silent to hide, but the majority of our guys responded. Unfortunately, my brothers and I can't afford to trust any of them completely.

We don't have the luxury of making a mistake, so the three of us will err on the side of caution and only trust each other and Maddy.

"What are we going to do?" Maddy's voice is barely more than a whisper, and it pulls me out of my thoughts as I consider all the possibilities.

"We still need to get you to the safe room."

"No."

My brothers and I spare her a glance, all three of us shooting her a look warning her not to argue.

"No, Javi, you don't know which of your men have been compromised. I want to believe there's only one person who would violate your trust, but maybe there are more. Right now, it's three of you against an unknown number of men who could want you and me dead. Give me a gun."

"Maddy, no."

"Javi, give me a gun."

Something changes in her posture, her expression, and her tone. It hardens to a shard of ice. There's a warning in it that she's more prepared for a situation like this than I want to acknowledge.

"Have you killed before?" Jorge blurts the question I already know the answer to.

"Yes."

My chest tightens, hating that Maddy's ever been in a position to take a life for whatever reason. She chose a vocation that brings new life into the world, not one that takes it out, but she's been forced to do that. I wish there was a way I could shield her from more death and destruction, but that's not an option. At least not for today. And I don't see it being one tomorrow or the day after or the day after that if she stays with a man like me.

"Javi, come on."

She holds out her hand, our gazes locking. It's with reservation that I hand over the pistol I pulled from the drawer. She accepts it and immediately checks the barrel. She's handling the weapon with expertise I didn't expect. I know she learned how to shoot when she was a kid, but there's nothing rusty about her technique.

Joaquin elbows me and hands me his second handgun that he pulled from his ankle holster. It was naive of me not to keep mine on me, assuming that because we've never had a breach in the past we couldn't have one now. Obviously, I was wrong, and I'm left unprepared to properly defend my girlfriend.

"Come on, Maddy, I'll get you into a more secure part of the house."

Jorge and Joaquin glance over at me, and I meet their gazes as they nod. We all know Maddy is renowned for her stubbornness when she wants to be. There's no way I'll easily convince her to go to the safe room now, but hopefully, I can convince her to move into a part of the house that'll make her less of a target.

I see her hesitation, but when her gaze flicks toward my brothers and back to me, I know she understands my attention will be divided between them and her. My brothers understand she's now my priority in a way no one else ever has been besides our mom. She's always been a shared top priority. I can't expect the guys to understand what Maddy means to me, but I know they don't begrudge me wanting to keep her safe.

"Go."

Jorge barks the word as he leans forward and fires through the broken glass, taking out two men approaching the house. Their hair isn't bright red like the O'Rourkes', but their fair skin and freckles certainly don't scream Colombian. I lead the way up the stairs toward my bedroom, and Maddy follows on my heels. She's so close I'm surprised neither of us trips, but I'd rather know she's within my reach than not.

Instead of going into my room, there's a billiards room at the end of the hallway. What's not obvious is the exterior wall is thicker than it appears. I move aside a painting of my grandfather—the grandfather all the men in my family my age share—and reveal a biometric pad. It does a retinal scan as I place my four fingertips to it. A fake brick facade slides open, and I point into the dark.

"Maddy, there's an escape out to the beach. If you take these stairs down to the basement, you'll be able to follow a hallway to the beach. Just before you get to the sand and a sea gate, you'll find an inflatable zodiac boat. Everything will be ready to go if you need to flee. Come here and let me set your access in case you need to go, and my brothers and I aren't with you."

"I'm not going anywhere without at least you."

"If I tell you to go, that's exactly what you'll do, little girl."

I infuse steel into my command, and once more she looks at me like she did downstairs. I know her response will be just as determined as mine.

"I am not leaving you behind, Javier."

"Fine, either way, let me get you set up."

This isn't the time for an argument neither of us will be satisfied with. So instead, I program her retinal scan and fingerprint access.

"You're safe up here, Maddy. Just don't leave. I need to check on Jorge and Joaquin. No one will make it up to the second floor."

"Go do what you have to, Javi. I'll be here."

193

My hand rests at the base of her throat as I give her a quick, hard kiss before bolting to the door.

"This will lock behind me. Don't open it to anyone for any reason. Doesn't matter who it is, even if it's Jorge, Joaquin, or me. If it's one of us, and it's safe, we'll let ourselves in. If we come up here and say anything to you, pretend you're not here. I don't care how convincing we might sound. All right?"

"Yes, Javi, go help your brothers."

I give her one last long look before I rush through the door and pull it closed, hearing the lock automatically set. All of the rooms on the second and third floor have automatic locks that remain secured unless someone with access opens them. The rooms on the ground floor have doors that stay wide open unless somebody closes them. But once locked, no door in this house can be opened with anything other than a combination of biometrics or passcodes.

I hear voices yelling as I fly back down the stairs. I head toward the sound of more gunfire, but these are handguns, not rifles.

"Javier?"

"Where?" I respond in *Macaguán*, and Joaquin answers me in it.

"Sunroom."

It's our mother's favorite room in the entire house. If it gets destroyed, she'll be beside herself. There are things in here left over from my parents' honeymoon. They could have gone anywhere in the world. The most romantic places. The most exotic places. But all they wanted was time alone with just the two of them.

My mom is a photographer, and my father was a painter. There are several pieces of their art hanging on the walls or framed on various surfaces. When I enter the room, I find my brothers kneeling beside sets of French doors. Every room on the ground floor has sets of these doors. It's wonderful to open them in spring and summer for the cross breeze. The sound of the ocean wafts in and can be super relaxing. But right now, I see them as nothing but a liability.

"I thought *Papá* had all of the glass replaced everywhere and put in bulletproof windows."

I didn't want to bring that up in front of Maddy. Joaquin frowns, and his brow furrows before he answers me.

"So did we. I took a look, and someone's changed the glass recently. These aren't the windows that were here when we moved to America."

"Did somebody compromise the house's security? Or did *Mamá* order repairs and didn't mention it to us?"

Neither of my brothers have an answer to my questions. It's unlike our mother to do something like that. None of us think her doing some remodeling is the answer. But that means we must consider this betrayal goes far deeper than we initially believed. Somebody has been planning for this for ages, hoping for an opportunity where they can get to us.

I squat beside Jorge as we peer around a curtain and look toward the beach.

"How do things stand right now?"

I can't tell what's going on because none of our attackers are on this side of the building, but we can hear stuff happening around us.

"Miguel and Tómas just led four of our guys around the windward side to disable their vehicles." Joaquin points over his shoulder to where the surveillance screens are in this room.

I barely tear my attention away long enough to follow where he points. I see one SUV on fire, and the other clearly has all four tires punctured. The hood's raised with smoke coming out of the engine block.

"How many have we lost?"

"Three." Jorge names the men.

I know my brothers will inform the families when this is all done, so I can be with Maddy throughout whatever comes next. I don't envy them the job at all. It's one of the worst duties we have in this world. But we never pass it off to our men. Someone in the *jefe's* family always informs the survivors.

"So that leaves us with eight because somebody betrayed us."

"It was José."

Joaquin's answer sends fury through me unlike anything I've felt in years. Not since our father was killed. Hearing his name aloud from my brother was different from hearing it through the earpiece from someone else.

"Our José?"

"None other." Jorge's rage matches mine, even if no one outside my family could hear it.

That *hijo du puta* is our second cousin on our dad's side. *Tío* Enrique did José and his brother, Miguel, a favor by bringing them to America and giving them jobs when they each turned eighteen. He could've left them on the streets of Bogotá to fend for themselves against the street gangs our mother packed us up and brought to America to avoid.

Instead, *Tío* Enrique gave them jobs, the opportunity to get higher educations, and even work outside the family. They chose to remain in this life when they could've started fresh here. Both of them swore their loyalty. Clearly, only Miguel meant it. That betrayal runs so deep it makes me want to vomit.

José was one of the men just inside the first gate when we arrived. He looked straight at me and at Maddy. I don't know if someone put him up to this or how he made a connection with the Albany mob, but for whatever reason, he's put my *chiquita* in grave danger. José will pay, and it won't be with a quick death either.

My brothers and I remain quiet as we listen to what's happening around us.

"Jorge, where'd Jimmy go?" That's the pilot who flew them in.

"He's been guarding the helo along with Pete."

"Can we get out of here? Or do they have artillery to take out the helo?"

"Nothing we've heard or seen on the cameras makes us think they can take the helicopter down, but we can't be totally sure."

"Why haven't they attempted to breach the house yet?"

They seem to have stalled or something because they aren't picking off our guys, and they aren't storming the house. What are they waiting for?

"Your guess is as good as mine at this point." Jorge shrugs as he answers.

Joaquin has nothing to counter that, so he remains quiet. None of this feels right at all. We're missing something. One man ordered Maddy to come outside. A few shattered windows that were supposed to be bulletproof. Random bursts of gunfire that accomplish nothing more than a failed scare tactic. Three dead or unaccounted for guardsmen and one traitor.

Our men neutralized their vehicles, so they can't leave on their own. They aren't forcing their way into the house or scrambling to retreat. I ease my way over to the security screens. I tap on them, running through the live feed. Two of our men have five of the intruders at gunpoint. The Albany mobsters are bound and gagged, so some of our other men must have helped before moving on. Our pilot and a regular guard are near the helicopter. Jimmy's in his seat, and I can tell he's ready to flip the switches the moment we can get to him. Pete's got his rifle raised and is scanning his surroundings. No one's approaching without one of them noticing.

That's three out of eight guards.

Where're Miguel, Tómas, and the three other guys?

I keep swiping the screen to run through the security feed. I watch in horror as one of our attackers point-blank assassinates one of our men. He puts a bullet through Miguel's forehead as Miguel and Tómas try to approach a different invader. I'm even more blown away—for lack of a better cliché—when the man who shot Miguel staggers backward, blood geysering from his left eye socket.

All of this happened beneath the billiard room window, so I know it was Maddy who shot the O'Sheehan guy. It draws attention upward from the men Miguel and Tómas tried to approach. Before anybody lifts a weapon toward the upstairs window more men fall. This isn't a spray of bullets with Maddy praying she gets lucky. She's picking the men off methodically.

She's evened up the numbers for us, but she's left two men with their kneecaps blown out, rather than dead. She must recognize these as men of value, even though I have no idea who they are.

"NO!"

The wail fills the air, and I know José just discovered his brother's dead. It might have been an O'Sheehan who put the bullet through Miguel's forehead, but José pulled the damn trigger the moment he got in bed with the O'Sheehans.

I press the earpiece to put me on the right frequency with our men.

"Don't kill them. Hold on to them."

I wonder if my command will permeate the rage Tómas must be in right now. I know how infuriated I am that anyone's endangered Maddy. I can only imagine the state I would be in if I watched her die. Tómas just had to watch his husband die right in front of him. It's one of the most guarded secrets in our organization, since there are plenty of people who are still too old-fashioned for their own good.

Nothing about today is the way I thought it would be when I woke this morning.

Tómas storms up to José, who drops to his knees beside his brother's body. Tómas puts the muzzle of his rifle to José's temple.

"I have no choice but to let *el patrón* decide what happens to you, but you better believe I will find you in hell and make you pay for what you did to your brother all over again."

My men can hear Tómas. They won't think twice about it because some have likely figured it out, but others believe they're best friends and roommates. They're in their mid-twenties, so being unmarried hasn't raised too many eyebrows yet. My family would have figured out what lies to spin to protect them for the rest of time if we needed to.

"We have to go out there." I look over my shoulder at my brothers.

"Do you need to check on Madeline? We can do it."

"Thanks, Joaquin, but we all saw who did the shooting. She's safe."

Chapter Eighteen

Maddy

Javi's going to kill me for getting involved, but when I recognized the guy who's a real DEA agent and Drew's cousin, I knew I needed to step in. He's one of the guys whose kneecaps I blew out. I'm certain Javi will have questions for him.

I certainly do.

The guy I killed, Derek, was a complete and total dickwad to me since the day I met him. It happened to be the day I met Drew. He was at the hospital with Drew and his family because he was Drew's driver and is a close friend—was a close friend, I should say.

I found out later he played the asshole wingman, so Drew had a reason to step in and seem charming when he came to my rescue. It irritated me to discover how badly I'd been manipulated, but I didn't learn that for an entire year. It was one of many secrets revealed to me too late to keep from having any attachment to Drew.

I don't have a moment's doubt I made the right choice killing him, but I'm certain Javi won't agree. Not based on just that sliver of a story, but I don't want to go into full detail about the things Derek said to me over the years. It won't bring a dead man back for Javi to kill all over again. They were just crude comments, but they've humiliated me every single time.

I also suspect he was the reason one of my deals went south. I think he ruined it on purpose, hoping I'd get caught in the crossfire. He didn't approve of how much Drew came to rely on me. I would've been happy to follow Derek's insistence that I not be as involved as Drew made me, but Drew insisted upon doing things his way as always.

I scan the scene outside the window and watch as Javi and his brothers emerge from around the side of the house. I pull myself away and go to the security screens and swipe through them. I see no more attackers lurking anywhere, but that doesn't mean there aren't more hiding, waiting. It tempts me to leave the room, but I know Javi only has so much patience. I refuse to make today even worse by walking out of here without permission. I strain to hear the conversation below me, but it's far too quiet.

I head back to the window only to shift my weight from foot to foot because there's shit I know about Jacob that would be useful for Javi and his brothers. I don't have my phone with me though. It's in the bedroom. The only way to get that would be to leave here, which I just swore to myself I wouldn't do.

Do I lean out the window and call down to Javi?

Do I gesture to him, hoping to catch his attention and potentially distract him from what's going on around him?

I don't know what to do.

Thankfully, Javi solves that for me.

"Maddy, do you know him?" I watch Javi tilt his head back as he calls up to me.

"Yeah, I do. He's the DEA agent who tried to get me to come out earlier."

"So, he's the Fed?"

I know that question isn't really meant for me now that Javi's looking at Jacob. The guy's sitting on the ground with blood still gushing from his right leg. I can only imagine the agony he must be in. But it certainly doesn't match what I see in the two men kneeling beside one of Javi's guys. I hear one repeating *"mi hermano,"* over and over. My brother.

The other one could just be the dead guy's close friend, but I sense there's far more to it than that. There's something in the way the second guy is staring at the body. His entire bearing vibrates with devastated loss that's almost palpable all the way up here. They must have been partners or even husbands.

What a needless loss that's entirely my fault. The only reason any of Drew's men are here—the only reason why Javi and his brothers and their men were exposed—was to protect me. The crushing guilt envelops me and tightens its hold to the point where my chest burns, and I rub a fist over my heart because it's hard to breathe.

This wasn't the first time I've killed. I've admitted I've done it before. I've seen some of Drew's men die, but it never affected me the way seeing Javi's men does right now. My hatred toward Drew blinded me from any regret or remorse when his men died. But human decency makes me regret Javi's losses today. My connection to him makes it even deeper.

That's part of what spurred me to action. A deep sense of obligation to help protect the men who protect Javi and his family.

I lean forward a little farther, but I can't hear what's happening any better than I could a moment ago.

"Javi."

I risk calling down to him. He looks up at me and raises his eyebrows.

"I know things about him you should ask. I'd call you, but my phone isn't in here with me."

"Hang on. I'll come up and get you."

It feels like an eternity before I hear the door unlock. I don't raise the gun since you don't point a weapon anywhere you don't intend to shoot. But if it's not Javi, I'm prepared, and I'll shoot to kill, then ask questions later. The relief that washes over me makes my hand tremble. I click the safety back on and walk toward him, leaving the gun on the billiard table as I pass it. I don't breathe easy until I'm in his arms.

"We're both safe, *chiquita*. It's okay now."

"This is entirely my fault, Javi."

"No, it's not. Don't think that. If you've been part of this life now for years, you know these things happen far too frequently. They're usually not one single person's fault. It's the price we pay."

"Javi—"

"I brought you here. I didn't know anyone would betray us, but you were in danger because one of my men betrayed my family. You were supposed to be safe here. This was the one place in the world I was supposed to have faith that no one could touch us."

"Do you think this estate's completely compromised? Will they have told any of the O'Sheehans where they are and what they found?"

"Probably, but that's a problem for a different day. Right now, I'm just glad you're all right."

The kiss he gives me makes my toes curl, and I grip his shirt as though I might wither away if I don't hold on for dear life. I don't want it to end. I don't want to face the reality that I caused this. That I brought this to his family and have now

203

endangered them and ruined something special. He may tell me it's not my fault, but no one will convince me otherwise.

"*Chiquita*, tell me what you know now before we go out there. I can't afford any surprises."

Like my sniper level accuracy.

"Jacob's father paid a fortune to get his son's background check forged. He passed the academy legitimately, but he's dirty as a hog in slop. He feeds Drew internal information that's kept them from getting busted for years. What Drew suspects but hasn't proven is that Jacob also sells information to other families. So far, it hasn't compromised the O'Sheehans, but I believe Jacob's just biding his time. I think he'll fuck Drew over when the right deal comes along."

"But for now he's helping Drew by trying to kidnap you."

"That's my guess. That or he wants to ransom me to Drew. It wouldn't surprise me if Drew didn't order my execution today to get revenge for you helping me."

"You believe Drew would do that, knowing you came to my family for help?"

I glance at the floor as shame floods me. Not for what I did, but for what I didn't do.

"Drew got injured badly enough to need a hospital about eighteen months ago. A GSW to the chest. It was only a couple inches above and to the right of his heart. It was way more serious than I could deal with, but he wound up at my hospital. I was worried about a bunch of things, but I also wanted to know how serious it was to estimate how long they'd keep him admitted. Once I got into his records, I did some scrolling. I know I shouldn't have, but at that point, what was another law broken?" I shrug. "I found out a shit ton about his past, including some psychiatric records that included info from when he was a teenager. None of it truly shocked me. It confirmed what I suspected. He has borderline personality disorder and antisocial personality disorder. Basically, he's a psychopath—even if that isn't really the popular clinical term anymore. Discovering that made running away even more terrifying until I hit my limits and risked it. Now look at what I've done."

"You did *not* do this, Maddy."

I ignore him rather than argue.

"I put nothing past him, Javi. Jacob's not as maniacal as Drew, but they're cut from the same cloth. When you go down there to interrogate him, his mother and sister are sensitive topics. She walked out on his dad and left Jacob and his sister with a mobster to raise them. He's super protective of his sister, even though she's three years older than him. She hates him because he suffocates her. But his real trigger is his dog. Like *John Wick* triggered. He'll lose his shit if you threaten the dog, but he's not as resourceful as the movie character. He'll cave eventually if he thinks it'll protect the animal. Jacob would shoot his grandmother if he thought it would get him ahead in life, but he's a pile of mush with the dog. Only creature alive that loves him unconditionally."

"What's the dog's name?"

"Yeller."

"As in *Old Yeller*?"

"Yeah. He was a stray the Humane Society was trying to catch because he was rummaging through trash and stealing food. Jacob found him and was going to do Lord knows what— since it wouldn't surprise me if he didn't abuse animals as a kid. It was obvious the dog's been in fights before because it snarled at one on the other side of the street while Jacob tried to corner him. The other dog broke free from the woman walking him and charged. Yeller jumped in front of Jacob when the dog ran toward Jacob. He said it was like the dog in the book protecting the boy from the bear. The dog isn't much to look at, but he's loyal to Jacob."

Javi looks over my shoulder and out the window. I can't imagine what he's thinking after that story.

"Is there anything else?"

"He's been fucking his boss for the past six months, and she's pregnant. He didn't know I pick up extra hours at an OBGYNs' office, and he went with her for her first ultrasound. Neither seemed thrilled to be there. It wasn't a joyous occasion."

Javi watches me, and his eyes narrow.

"What aren't you telling me?"

I hesitate because I know he won't outwardly lose his shit, and I'm certain he'll still be rational when he does whatever he's going to do to Drew, but he'll be irate.

He spins me toward the billiard table and presses me to lean forward. He reaches around me to unfasten my pants and pushes them down faster than I can react. His hand lands across my ass, and it hurts more than I expected. After the earlier punishment, it burns like the fire of a thousand suns. I anticipate the next one and squeeze my eyes shut, but he does nothing.

"If I spank you again, I'll harm you. That's not the goal. You want domestic discipline, Maddy, so I'll punish you when you keep things from me that affect your safety. Whatever you don't want to say must be something you believe will push me around the bend. Tell me now, or your punishment will continue. I haven't decided how, but it won't be over yet."

He eases me to stand before him. I see fear in his gaze, and I know it's because he wants me to know he's more than just worried about me.

"I'm pretty sure he's the reason a deal blew up. I nearly got caught by the local police when a brawl broke out at a Buffalo nightclub. I was supposed to collect payment for product another guy delivered that night. The fight was massive, and I couldn't get out of the corner where I was talking to the owner. The guy sheltered me, then got me out the back. One of his bouncers led me to my car and made sure the police thought I was just passing by. I tried to tell Drew my suspicions, but he—"

I don't need to finish for Javi to guess. He wraps his arms around me, and I lean against him. That was one of the most terrifying nights of my life. Men got stabbed and shot right in front of me. I thought I would die when a guy charged the owner, who shot him through the forehead. I feared he'd turn his gun on me and blame me. Instead, he rescued me. He saw a bruise and guessed what Drew was like. He watched a man beat his mom to death when he was six. That was all the explanation he gave me.

"We have to go down there, Javi."

"Let me hold you for a moment longer. I know which fight you're talking about. I had no idea you were there collecting for Drew. I'm certain Dillan didn't because he never would've sent men to collect from the owner. I saw photos of what the place looked like after. Just let me hold you."

He repeats himself, and I hear his heart racing. I tried to downplay it, but if he saw the aftermath …

"I think Jacob is the one who told Dillan that Drew was creeping into the O'Rourkes' territory, knowing I would be there that night. Jacob distracted the DEA, supposedly to keep them away from Drew. I believe he did it because he wanted the O'Rourkes to attack. He prayed I'd either get caught in the crossfire or rot in jail until a trial with evidence he probably would've strategically placed at the scene."

I run my hands up and down Javi's back, and I feel the tension ease from his body as he exhales.

"That's it, Daddy. That's all I can think of right now."

"I'm going to bring you outside with me, but I want you in the circle my brothers and I will form. If you need to tell me something, tap my shoulder."

"I understand. I won't distract you."

He gazes into my eyes, and there's something there I can't describe. No man has ever looked at me this way. There's warmth that makes me feel precious.

"You are not a distraction, *chiquita*. No one could make me more focused than you. I will end this threat to you, and it starts now."

He lets his arms drop, and I pull up my pants. He slides his hand into mine. He's cautious as he leads me downstairs, scouting our path to ensure no one lies in wait. We head outside, and immediately, Jorge and Joaquin help Javi surround me. If they get any closer, they'll step on me. But it keeps me virtually invisible except for my legs.

"Doesn't Old Yeller get shot at the end?"

All right, then. Javi's diving straight in. Fucking hell.

"Leave my dog alone." Jacob tries to stand, but his leg is too weak to support him.

"Tell me what I want to know."

"Fuck off."

Javi laughs, but it's got no mirth. I wonder if he'd say something crude in response if I weren't here.

"Tell me what I want to know, and your dog lives. Give me only part of what I want, and I go after your sister. Give me nothing, and your dog is dead within the hour."

"Fuck my sister. Leave Yeller alone."

"That's an offer I wouldn't touch with a ten-foot pole."

"Nah. You're fucking the bony bitch hiding behind you."

I cringe. Not because he insulted me. Javi puts a bullet

through his other knee. It didn't take a genius to see that coming.

"You think you can piss me off enough to lose my shit and kill you. The more you piss me off, the longer it'll take me to kill you."

If I were any other woman, he'd never confess something like that. Then again, another woman wouldn't have shot a man through the eye.

"I can keep putting holes in you that'll make you bleed but won't kill you quickly. You're still talking with two bullets in you. We can test your pain tolerance by putting a few more holes in you before you pass out."

Javi points the gun at Jacob's hand that rests on the ground beside him. The latter looks at where Javi aims, so he's unprepared for the knife Javi flips open and flings at him. It imbeds in Jacob's chest just beneath his collar bone near his left shoulder.

"I didn't say how I'd make the holes."

Javi jerks his chin toward Jacob, and one of his guys jogs forward. I peer between Javi's and Jorge's arms to watch the man twist the blade before yanking it out. He wipes it on Jacob's shirt before bringing it to Javi.

"You going to have him play fetch?"

Jacob's an idiot to keep taunting Javi. I can almost guarantee Javi has far more experience interrogating a guy than Jacob does. I don't doubt Javi can draw this out.

"Did you cause the raid that nearly got Madeline killed?"

"Fucking inept local cops let her leave."

Not quite an admittance, but practically.

"Did Drew send you or do you have your own plans for Madeline?"

"That piece of shit can barely think straight. He's so pissed he doesn't know what the fuck to do. You don't want to be in the middle of this. Trade Madeline to me, and I'll make sure the DEA'll focus on the O'Rourkes instead."

"The DEA isn't going anywhere near them now that a former agent is part of that family. I should call Shane right now and let him know what's going on."

"You didn't deny you don't want to be in the middle of this. Give me Madeline, and I'll give you something better in return."

"Impossible."

"Come on. Everyone knows *Tres J's* don't give a shit about women. You'll do anything to keep your family ahead. She's only worth something to Drew because she knows shit."

I sort of know what he's talking about from what Laura's told me. She's hinted at some stuff to warn me away from *Tres J's*. I heard my big sister, but clearly, I didn't listen. Javi doesn't flinch at the taunt.

"That shit she knows seems worth something to you. Either you want her to tell you what she knows, or you want to manipulate Drew by holding onto her. What you want and what's going to happen aren't the same thing. Madeline goes nowhere. We're back to where we started. Answer my questions, or I make sure your dog is dead within the hour."

Javi reaches into his pocket and pulls out his phone. He unlocks it with a code, and I realize he probably doesn't have biometrics set up in case someone captures him. A retinal scan and a fingerprint won't do any good. He taps the screen a few times before he puts the call on speaker.

"Javier, what's going on?"

"Pablo, you're on speaker. I have a DEA agent in front of me with bullets in both kneecaps. I need you to find his address and send men over to it. It might be in Albany. Have them video call me before they shoot the dog. The *carechimba* doesn't want to talk. He's the one who led the raid to get Madeline."

Pussy face. Juan taught Laura and me that when I was twelve. His mother found out and threatened to take a *chancla* to his backside. She made him clean all the bathrooms and peel any and every vegetable they ate for a month. I'd seen Margherita angry at her sons before, but she was livid. I really thought she would go after him with the wood-sole sandal. She apologized profusely to my parents, who took it in stride. However, they didn't allow Juan to hang out with Laura that entire month his mom punished him.

"*¡Está bien!*" All right.

"Wait! No!"

There's no way Javi or Pablo would follow through on Javi's empty threat. Neither would hurt the animal, but Jacob's so attached to the dog he'll protect Yeller like a mother bear with its cubs.

"I'll talk. Just leave my dog alone." He glances down at his watch. "It's already too late. Killing my dog won't undo what's already done by now. You're going to kill me anyway, so I have nothing to hide now."

Chapter Nineteen

Javier

What the fuck is he talking about?

I won't show my confusion or how this rattles me. I cock my left eyebrow instead as I shift the barrel of my gun to aim at the center of his chest.

"You want to know so bad, but you refuse to ask. Tough shit because I refuse to tell."

"Javi, I thought of something."

I barely hear Maddy's whisper as her chest brushes against my back. The feel of any part of her touching me reassures me, but it reminds me at the same time she's in the middle of a volatile situation. Could Jacob mean more men will be here? Will there be an aerial strike?

I turn my head a fraction of an inch, but she leans closer.

"He has a sixteen-year-old son no one is supposed to know is his. I've seen them both barefoot. The guy inherited Jacob's webbed toes. It's a paternal hereditary trait. I don't know about cartels, but the mob's initiation is pretty loose, apparently.

They swear their oath after a needle pricks their right index finger. For the O'Sheehans, it requires killing someone. Timmy's supposed to join officially this month. It wouldn't surprise me if Drew tests him and marks a senior rival. If Drew already knows I'm with you, then he'll pick someone in your family. Timmy's more boy than man. If he can't get the right target, he might be desperate enough to go after someone he thinks is easy."

"My mom or aunts."

"Yeah."

"They're far less forgiving than the men in my family. That kid's fucked. Jorge?"

"Yeah, I'm calling *Tío* Enrique right now."

I remain focused on Jacob, but I hear my brother speaking to our uncle and filling him in on everything. In the near quiet, I hear a whirring sound from above. Jacob laughs as I spot the drone.

"Get Maddy inside!"

I put a bullet through Jacob's forehead as I step backward, forcing Maddy to do the same lest I step on her. I don't turn around, but I know my brothers and Maddy do. They'll shield her as I watch the drone. It could just be surveillance, but I doubt it. I suspect it carries explosives or bullets.

I watch Tómas have the wherewithal to grab José and drag him away from Miguel. He's only saving the *puta de madre*—motherfucker—because he knows I have questions. It's not because he cares about his former brother-in-law. A bullet strikes the ground where José knelt only seconds ago. While Jorge, Joaquin, and I guide Maddy through open French doors to a family room, Tómas and José lure the drone away.

"What the hell?" Jorge peeks through a window.

"Did it follow them?" I try to see past this shoulder.

"Yeah. But will there be more?"

213

We can only guess the answer to that, and we all assume it's yes.

"Your sanctuary's completely compromised."

Maddy sounds near tears as I turn toward her. Shame practically vibrates from her. I'd be furious because she's right, but she doesn't need to think I blame her.

"It's just a house."

The look she shoots me screams she doesn't believe me. I stay quiet since more platitudes won't solve this or make her feel better. Joaquin moves next to me before he speaks. I already know he's thinking the same thing Jorge and I are.

"We need to leave."

"How?" Maddy looks at all of us before staring out the window.

"Remember the Zodiac I told you about?"

"Won't that keep us exposed?"

I point out the window toward the left. She can't see much, but at least she knows which direction I'm talking about.

"See how the island curves toward that cliff? The cove will shelter us until we can get to the cave in that cliff. From there, we have a way out."

She watches me rather than looks out the window. She nods, and I know she trusts me implicitly. There's no time for that to warm my heart, but it would if we weren't on the verge of dying. Joaquin shuts the French doors as Jorge rushes to the security panel. He enters a code, and metal panels slide down the outside of the window and doors. They seal every entryway, making the mansion into a fortress.

This is why we have the fully stocked pantry. In case we go into lockdown. Our uncles and cousins will get the alert, so it surprises neither my brothers nor me when our phones all ring. *Tío* Luis calls Jorge while Pablo calls Joaquin, and *Tío* Enrique calls me. None of us notice we default to Spanish until Maddy wraps her arms around her waist and appears entirely lost. Without being fluent, there's no way she can keep up with our rapid conversations. We're speaking in code, anyway.

I slide my arm around her waist and hurry her toward the door leading to the foyer. Her fingers slip into the waistband of my shorts as though it tethers her to me. It's as reassuring to me as it is to her.

"Come on, *chiquita*. We need to get to the basement."

I hear my *tío*'s sharp inhale, and I realize he could still hear me even though I whispered.

"Should a priest meet you here?"

"Give me the chance to propose first."

I glance down at Maddy unsure if she understood that since it was only a sentence. She doesn't appear to since she's focused on keeping up as three men with far longer legs than hers run as we form a circle around her again.

"Fine. Call me when you get there."

He won't say the car we have hidden on the mainland just in case someone's gotten through our jammers and tapped the call or bugged the house. My brothers and I hang up our calls as we reach the basement door. Jorge leads with Maddy and me in the middle. Joaquin secures the door and follows us down.

"This way. Keep holding onto me."

I felt Maddy freeze when we took the last step because it's pitch black. While he was still alive, our father drilled it in Jorge, Joaquin, and me how to navigate the basement in the dark. We know how many steps it takes to get to the backup generator, the armory, and the tunnel leading out to the water. I hear the door to the armory open with a quiet whoosh. Joaquin'll grab an arsenal. Jorge hands Maddy and me life-jackets when we reach the hidden pocket door to the tunnel. They're stored outside the tunnel, so anyone donning them has time to do it while running toward the sea gate. Like the armory, this door requires a code and biometrics.

"You won't get separated from me this way or bump into the walls."

I scoop Maddy over my shoulder, and she once again grips my shorts' waistband. We make our way along the tunnel until we meet bright sunlight. Joaquin has better vision than anyone I've ever met. He peers through the metal gate that looks like it guards a prison cell.

"We need to wait. I see two of them. They likely have infrared, so they'll see us once it's dark, but it'll be easier to hide in the shadows."

"That's at least five hours. We can't wait that long." I look at Maddy, who I set on her feet, so we can both don our life-jackets.

"I'm all right."

It's cold and damp down here, and neither she nor I are wearing enough layers. But I worry about her since she's still under-weight. Maybe it's an old wives' tale, but I don't want her getting sick. Jorge must think the same thing because he passes her his suit coat. We all slide down to the floor, but I lift her onto my lap. Her eyes widen as she tries to look at my brothers. I wrap the jacket around her and ease her head against my shoulder. Her arms wrap around me as she huddles for warmth. She's already chilled.

"We can wait until the sun moves. It'll put the cove and cliffs in the shadow. We don't have to wait until dark. We just have to keep our movement to a minimum on the boat." Jorge offers the compromises, and the rest of us nod.

"Rest, *chica*. I don't think you've slept well in ages."

"I haven't."

I stroke up and down her back and over her ass until she relaxes. I tilt my head back to lean against the wall reinforced with concrete. It's smooth against my shoulders, so I force myself to take my own advice. I shut my eyes and listen to the ocean. We know from experience that Joaquin takes the first shift for lookout, then me, then Jorge. We never intended to go by age; we just always have.

"Maddy?"

"I'm awake."

"It's my watch. I need to move closer to the gate."

It's been an hour, so I need to take my turn.

"It's fine. Stay there." Jorge nudges his chin toward Maddy as he stands.

"Jorge—"

"Madeline, don't worry. He'll make it up to me."

"I'm not giving you my Porsche."

"You have two. *Mamá* says you need to learn to share."

"You can have last year's Lego set."

"You must really love me."

Maddy looks up at me and grins. She knows I've always liked fast cars, but giving up any of my Lego sets is the ultimate sign of devotion to my brother. I just have to remind him he's the little brother, so I'll only give him one I've already assembled.

Jorge exchanges places with Joaquin, and I keep my arms around Maddy. Having her in my lap calms me. I can physically shield her if need be, but having her close reassures me she's unharmed despite the attack. With the suit coat around her, no one can see her hand slip under my shirt. She grazes her nails up my abs before resting her palm on my heart. She kisses behind my ear before she whispers.

"Daddy, your mind might be a little relaxed, but your body's still tense. I feel completely safe here. I'm not scared anymore. If you won't let me blame myself for what's happening, then I won't let you do the same. Your legs are like steel plates under my sore ass."

I gaze down at her in the dim light, and I inhale as I make my body soften as much as it can.

"Mmm. Still rock hard."

Maddy's soft breath against my ear tempts me to shiver. She could be talking about my legs or the way my cock can't help but react to her being near me. If this weren't life or death and my brothers weren't a foot from us, I could fuck her while she straddles me.

"Later, Daddy."

She must have felt me twitch. She settles back against me, and I don't notice the time passing until Joaquin whispers to us.

"It's time."

That rouses the rest of us, and I lean to my right to see the sky more clearly. The sun is farther to the west than it was when we came down here. Jorge unlocks the gate while Joaquin, Maddy, and I push the Zodiac forward. The four of us drag it into the water. The inflatable boat is heavy. It would be a struggle for any of us brothers to move it alone and nearly impossible for Maddy. If she were alone, she'd have to wait for the tide to come in.

With four of us, it slides into the waves easily. I point to the hull, and Maddy crouches before curling into a tight ball. My brothers draw their guns and sit facing out while I go to the outboard engine. My gun rests on my right thigh while Jorge and Joaquin sweep their gazes over our surroundings. I steer the boat as close to the shore as I can without running aground.

We enter the cave on a wave that drives us into the depths without the motor's help. We're nearly to the back where we can step onto a ledge when that telltale whir echoes. I go full throttle while my brothers each take out a drone. I fully expect to hear an explosion when they hit the water, but there's not even a fizzle.

"Did you see any others while we waited?" I look at Joaquin and Jorge, but they both shake their head.

If there had been, they would have told me, but the question tumbles out as my fear ratchets up. Being in such an enclosed space with Maddy and machines sent to kill us has me speaking before thinking.

I maneuver us to where there's a natural ledge that's also reinforced with concrete. My brothers and I pull the boat out of the water and drag it to an enclosed area where the tide can't reach it and drag it out to sea. Past another secured gate with a code and biometrics, motion-sensor lights illuminate our path to a hidden location.

At the end of what feels like a long hallway, we come to a set of stairs. Once more, Jorge leads, and Joaquin follows. We enter what looks like a garden shed, but it's a garage. We have one of our armored SUVs that's a veritable tank parked here. I open the back passenger side door for Maddy, and she climbs in before I go to the trunk and grab additional rifles for all four of us. As I pass the open door, I look inside to Maddy, who nods before I hand her one stock first.

I give two to Joaquin before he climbs into the front passenger's seat. Jorge goes around to the driver's side. We're all fearless with just about everything, or at least we can appear that way. We all have a lead foot and love fast cars, but Jorge drives like a pro. It doesn't matter what kind of vehicle he's in; you'd think he's trying to win the Indy 500 or the Paris-Dakar Rally. He hits a button on his visor, and the garage door opens.

"Maddy, these windows are bulletproof, just like the Kutsenkos' SUVs, but stay low."

"Yes, Javi."

She doesn't hesitate to agree even though I know she's

prepared to shoot if she has to. I heard her checking the chamber while I gave Joaquin the other two rifles. I shut my door just before Jorge puts the vehicle in drive. All of us are on the lookout as we leave the safety of the small building.

The shed's tucked away on a property we also own but rarely visit. We have it as a backup but also to ensure we don't have neighbors. Many of the properties around here are vacation homes, so it's not unusual for them to sit empty much of the year. *Tío* Luis and *Tía* Margherita come here just enough to keep people from wondering if it's abandoned.

It's not long before we emerge onto the road, all of us with our eyes peeled for anyone lying in wait. Rather than going back the direction Maddy and I came from when we arrived, Jorge heads in the opposite one. Half a mile down the road, he turns off onto what's not even a dirt path, but *Papá* had trees cleared farther in to make it accessible for an SUV as large as ours.

The periodic gaps between trees are the only indicators of the path we take to get us away from *Mamá* and *Papá's* hideaway and back to a main road. Maddy keeps her voice down when she speaks, but it would be pointless to whisper since my brothers would probably hear. It just feels like a regular volume would be too loud for the situation.

"Are we headed back to the city?"

I meet Jorge's gaze in the rearview mirror before I shake my head. "No, we'll go to *Tío* Enrique's."

"Are you going to call Maks?" Nothing but dread fills those words.

"Do you want me to?"

It's an unnecessary question, but I want to be sure I understand her wishes. She vehemently shakes her head.

"No, not unless you absolutely have to. I don't want Laura

to know yet. She'll worry, and there's nothing she can do. The fewer people involved, probably the better right now."

She bites her bottom lip and looks toward the floorboards.

"Maddy, it's okay if you don't want to endanger your in-laws. I understand."

Her gaze flicks up to me, and there's guilt there. I cover her hand and draw it onto my lap.

"As much as I dislike them, they're your family, so I won't needlessly endanger them, either."

"Thank you." She more mouths the words than speaks.

I give her hand a squeeze, keeping it on my lap. We go back to looking out the window for any unusual movement or unexpected vehicles. It's disconcerting that no one and nothing greets us. Rather than put me at ease, it makes me wonder where Jacob's other men must be hiding. I don't want to assume the men who breached the property are the only ones he brought, but perhaps that's the case. We're still alert, nonetheless.

Chapter Twenty

Maddy

I heard the same sound as I did before the first drone attack. I was already curled into as tight a ball as I could make myself. Javi hovered over me as a human shield. While it made me feel loved, the last thing I ever want is for him to sacrifice himself for me. I heard the bullets strike the drones, then the splash. I fully expected some type of explosion, but there was barely anything to indicate we were about to be under attack.

Once we come ashore, it's a blur as we move through tunnels until we reach an SUV I never imagined could fit into what looks like such a small shed. There's just enough room for us to get the doors open and climb in. Then we're on our way. I watch our surroundings mostly in silence only responding when Javi speaks to me. It's a quiet ride back from Connecticut into New Jersey. I grew up in northern Jersey, so I recognized the area despite taking a roundabout route to avoid the city.

I've spent hours of my life here playing in Enrique's back-yard. It's like a third home to me after my parents' and Luis and

Margherita's. As I walk through the door, I see Enrique and his new wife, Elodie. It's strange to know a woman lives here with Enrique, but it still feels as familiar as it always has. It's comforting to know I'm with Javi's family. Enrique always seems so untouchable, even though as an adult, I understand there've probably been countless threats to his life over the years.

I watch as Enrique whispers something to his wife before she walks over to greet me.

"I didn't get to say more than just a passing hello at the reception, Madeline, but I'm happy we can be here to help. Whatever you need, let us know, or just go ahead and get it. I haven't changed much about the house, so things should be where you remember them."

"Thank you, Elodie. I really appreciate that."

I don't know how much more to say because I have no idea what Enrique already told her or will tell her about this situation. He's hesitant when it's his turn to approach. One smile is all it takes before I'm in his arms again just like I was as a kid when Laura, Pablo, and Juan would tease me about being the baby of the group. It was Enrique who always insisted they make time for me and allow me to play with the rest of them.

"*Tío*" slips past my lips before I realize what I'm saying.

"Madeline, you're safe here. You know I won't let anything happen to you. Neither will Javi nor anyone else in this family. You can stay here as long as you want."

I lean back to look up at him and nod. "Javi said he won't call Maks unless I want him to. Are you going to get them involved?"

He hesitates for a moment, but his gaze doesn't waver. "Not until we know exactly who's involved in this. This is a private family issue."

My eyebrows shoot straight up. "You don't think the Kutsenkos could be behind any of this, do you?"

"No. Not even remotely. They would never do that to you. That's not what I meant. Whether it's the O'Sheehans or someone else, they targeted you while you were with my family. I hate to say it, but whoever this is probably would have done the same thing if you were with your in-laws. However, you're with us. Until we know how widespread and far-reaching this is, I'd rather fewer people know."

"Do you really think it's more than just Drew?"

"I don't know that Drew O'Sheehan truly has the *huevos* to attack my family on our private estate without someone much more powerful backing him."

I want to blurt all the questions roiling through my mind, but I'm certain he can't and won't answer most of them. Besides, I doubt I'd like the answer to any of them, so I opt for quiet instead. When I step away from him, I look over my shoulder to find Javi.

I don't see him immediately, and a spike of fear shoots through me from the tips of my toes up to the top of my head. It only lasts a moment because I spot him on the other side of Alejandro, but it was nearly paralyzing. He's watching me, and I should've known he would be. I don't know what his cousin was in the middle of saying, but he abandons that conversation to join me. He slides his arm around my waist, and I sag against him. He keeps his voice low when he speaks to me, but Enrique hears him.

"*Chica*, are you tired? Do you want to lie down for a while or just have some peace and quiet? We didn't get to have a late lunch or early dinner. If you're hungry, I can make you something."

"No, I'm all right."

I look up at him and force myself to inhale deeply, letting the air fill my chest and calm me.

"I just didn't see you for a moment."

He observes me before he nods. "I won't let you out of my reach, little one, if that would make you feel better."

I force a tightlipped smile, not wanting to sound needy, but he understands me. I glance over at Enrique, embarrassed that he'll think I'm clingy after being the reason for all of this shit that's raining down on them.

He isn't watching me; instead, his gaze pierces Javi. I look up at the man I've wanted since I was a young teenager and who I'm rapidly falling head over heels for. I recognize the mulish set of his chin and the way he lifts it as he stares back at his uncle.

I've heard he's defiant to plenty of people, but never any of the adults in his family. I guess I should say the older generation since we're all adults now. Though in moments like this, when I feel so lost and unsure, it's good to have Enrique nearby.

I can't even imagine half the things he's witnessed or experienced. I know Javi, his brothers, and cousins have done plenty, but Enrique and Luis are still decades older and more experienced than them. I shift my focus back over to Enrique as he nods.

It's some type of acknowledgement to Javi, but I'm not exactly sure about what. Enrique steps away as the back of Javi's fingers brush against my cheekbone before his fingers wrap around my nape, and his thumb replaces the back of his hand.

"*Chiquita*, he gets how serious I am about you. That this is for keeps."

I swallow as I nod. Tears prick at my eyelids, but my smile is genuine.

"Maddy, I'm not walking away from you just because

things are hard. I don't want to sound flippant or callous, but if you're in this for keeps too, this is only one of a lifetime of storms we'll weather together. This may not even be the worst of what we face, but we'll do it together."

"Yes, Daddy." I whisper the words, and he offers me a soft smile.

"Maddy, there's nothing I won't do to protect you, and I think you've always known that. You've seen a sliver of what I'm willing to do. That will never change, but if this is too much for you—if this is a lifestyle you can't accept—I won't force you to remain. I might beg and plead and cry, but I won't hold you hostage. I never, ever want you to feel you're trapped with me."

"Javi, nothing about this feels like what I've experienced before. There's danger that surrounds you and your family every day, all day, but I don't fear you'd intentionally put me in the middle of it. That's where I find myself now, and unfortunately, I might find myself in this position again, but not by your doing. Just the opposite. If we ever face anything like this again, I only want to be with you. In the past, I wanted to be as far away from Drew as I could get. Instead, I don't want to let you go."

"Maddy, I will never ask you to do the kind of things he did."

My eyes could practically fall out of their sockets as I stare at him.

"Javi, never in this lifetime or the next would I ever imagine you'd ask, let alone force me to work for you. That thought never crossed my mind. I know and have known since we were kids what people say about you guys, but I also know how you helped Misha's wife and how you helped Maria Mancinelli. You aren't the things people say you are. It's the role you have to play. I think if I even considered the type of activities Drew

226

forced me into, you'd make sure I couldn't sit for a month of Sundays."

"That's right, *chiquita*. I want you as far away from these things as I can get you. I can't guarantee you'll be as far removed as I want, but I need to make sure we're on the same page about those things. It should probably go without saying, but I don't want there to be any misunderstanding."

"There's not, Javi."

"Madeline?"

I turn toward Elodie who's coming down the stairs with a stack of clothes. She joins Javi and me where we stand near the entrance to the living room.

"I don't know how well these will fit, but the pants all have drawstrings. I thought you might like to have some options."

She sounds confident, but I notice her cheeks tinge pink as she hands me the fresh clothes. I realize she's embarrassed that her clothes will be too big on me. It embarrasses me that I won't fill them out and will look like a child wearing her mother's clothes. Goes to show the grass is always greener on the other side.

"Thank you."

"The guys all have rooms here. I made sure there are fresh towels in Javi's bathroom. I found an extra toothbrush too. You can order any other toiletries you need, and we'll have them delivered within the hour."

"Thank you, Elodie."

"Elle. I know you know your way around, so truly, get whatever you need from the kitchen or hangout wherever you want."

"I spent most of my time here in the backyard, but I don't think I'll be allowed out there." I glance ruefully at Javi.

"No. You can go swimming another day."

He crosses his arms and cocks an eyebrow, but I see he

struggles to keep a straight face. He knows I love the pool here because it has a swim-in jacuzzi and wide steps I used to sunbathe on. I loved having the water lap over me while I baked myself. Laura loved it because it's an infinity pool where she could swim laps. I playfully huff.

"I'd love to take a shower, actually."

Elle smiles and turns away. Javi guides me up the stairs, his hand at my lower back until we get to the landing. Then it presses against my ass. His room is at the end of the hall. Not only do all the guys have rooms, but so do Luis and Margherita, Matáis and Catalina—Alejandro's parents—and Luciana—*Tres J's* mom. The house is shaped like a T, so Enrique and Elle have one end while everyone else has rooms across the landing, either to the left or right. Javi's room feels private since it's so far from the older generation's.

"*Chiquita,* I wish I could stay up here with you, but I don't want to embarrass you since everyone would know why. And despite saying I don't want you out of my reach, I need to meet with *Tío.*"

"I know. I won't take long."

"Don't rush. You can soak in the tub. If you aren't down yet, I'll come up when I finish the meeting."

"Thank you."

I lay the clothes on the bed and turn toward the bathroom. Javi steps in front of me and unfastens my shirt before peeling it off me. He unclasps my bra and leans forward to suck on just my left nipple. While he does that, he unfastens my shorts and pushes them down. He switches to my other nipple as he toys with my clit.

"Since you have no fresh bra or panties, I expect you not to wear any."

"Javi! I can go without panties, but I have to wear a bra. I can't go without. I know my tits aren't big en—"

"Do not finish that word, *chiquita*."

"I'm practically flat chested these days."

"If that were the case, what was I just feasting on?"

"Fine. Regardless of their size, I can't go around with my nipples showing. The guys in your family wouldn't stare, but they'll notice. I'm certain Enrique has men coming in and out of the house, so they'd notice."

"Only family comes in unless he invites them. Our men have no reason to since they can enter from the patio if he calls them into his office, which he almost never does."

"It's still not appropriate."

The thought mortifies me because even if they don't want to stare, nipples are like anything else you see then can't unsee. Since you don't expect them on display—at least not in America—you can't help but keep looking at them when it's obvious a woman's not wearing a bra, and they show through the shirt.

"No panties, *chiquita*."

"Yes, Daddy."

"Lean over the bed."

My brow furrows, but I do as he says. He steps behind me and spreads my ass cheeks.

"Tell me what toiletries you need. I'll order lube along with it. I'm fucking your ass tonight."

That wasn't the declaration I expected. "You said that to shock me into thinking about that while you're in your meeting and I'm alone."

"You didn't say no."

"Of course not."

"You like the idea enough to get wet just hearing it."

To prove it, he swipes two fingers between my pussy lips then trails them over my asshole.

"Don't get yourself off in the shower, little one. I'll know."

I don't believe that since I'll dry off with a towel, and I'll be horny and ready to fuck regardless of whether I get off before tonight.

He fists my hair and draws my head back as he leans over me, bringing his lips beside my ear. He grinds his cock against my ass.

"You don't believe me. You think I won't know. There's nothing about your body you can hide from me, Maddy. You know you'd confess if I asked because you won't enjoy how I edge you if you refuse to answer or lie to me."

"And if you come up here to shower alone later? I'll know if you get yourself off."

"Because you think I'll need time to recover between rounds? You know you keep me hard even after I come. I won't do it because I have no interest in having an orgasm without you to come on or in."

Come on.

He'd mark me, and I love that idea.

"Get in the shower or bath, little one. Your naked body and this conversation are too tempting."

I shake my ass against him before straightening. He squeezes it with both hands hard enough to make me gasp, but I don't shy away. When he lets go and turns, I step around him. I watch him leave the bedroom as I walk into the bathroom. I stand under the showerhead for far longer than I usually do. But the feel of the water running over me soothes me. There's masculine body wash and shampoo on the built-in shelf. There're also travel-size bottles of women's shampoo, conditioner, face cleanser, and a neutral-scented body wash. Two shower poofs hang on a hook. Elle was thoughtful and quick.

It feels good to scrub my hair, face, and body. It's a fresh start to a complicated and exhausting day. As I dry myself, knowing the bed is on the other side of the bathroom door tempts me. No one needs me, and Javi knows I'm safe up here. I hang up the towels and walk out to the bed. I'm about to pick a pair of yoga pants and an oversized shirt when I wonder about the time. I don't want to be up all night if I nap too late. I pull my phone from my shorts pocket where I shoved it at some point.

It's already nearly evening, so it's way too late for a nap. My shoulders sag. Sleep would be a better escape than just a shower. I'm about to put it away when it vibrates. This is the same burner that calls to my real phone get forwarded to. I scooped it up before I left the bedroom and headed to the kitchen at the estate. Javi never got a chance to dispose of it like he offered. That's the only reason I answer when I recognize the number.

Chapter Twenty-One

Maddy

"You can run, but you can't hide, Madeline."

I say nothing, instead, scrambling to get clothes on.

"Bad day? It's unfortunate Luciana's old love nest didn't survive the drones I sent."

Did he blow up the house once we left? We heard no explosions. He's probably just taunting me.

"I won't stop until you come home, Madeline. I'll punish you, then we'll move on. But if you stay with that piece of shit, I'll kill him in front of you. You're not the only one who's been busy today. Your niece and nephew are adorable."

My phone vibrates again as a text comes through. I dread opening it, but I have to know. There's a photo of Laura walking with her twins, each holding one of her hands. They're headed into the grocery store. I can see the guards with them, but it still rattles me.

Once I'm decent, I rush down the hallway. I mute the call as I dash past Elle, my finger to my lips as I shake my head because she greeted me. I know where Enrique's office is, so I knock once before opening the door. The men rise as I thrust out my hand, the phone held screen up on my palm. Drew's still talking as Javi comes to stand beside me.

"Konstantin begged for the cinnamon applesauce Auntie Christina lets him have. Laura's too much of a bitch and makes her kids have the unsweetened shit."

Christina only lets them have the unsweetened cinnamon, but neither of the twins is old enough to read and know that. Why that's the detail caught in my mind is beyond me. Maybe it distracts me from the terror that this psychopath knows something so specific.

I unmute the phone.

"You might have gotten a photo of them, but you won't get any closer than that. I know the men guarding Laura and the twins. One of them is Pasha."

He's Laura's cousin-in-law. He's as ruthless as Maks and just as protective. He won't let anyone get close to Laura, Mila, or Konstantin. His wife, Sumiko, is pregnant. As a soon-to-be father now, he's even more over the top than he was before. All the couples now have kids or are about to, and Laura and Christina both have two. The men will go berserk when they find out someone took pictures of Laura and the twins.

"You may as well put that black suit on now because your wake'll be tonight once I show Maks this photo."

"You won't tell Maks a damn thing because then he'll demand you go to him. You won't leave your hiding place to risk me getting you. You know it'll cause a fight between the Kutsenkos and Diazes, and you don't want your little fuck boy getting his pretty face fucked up."

I watch Javi, not knowing what to say. Joaquin walks over and lifts the phone from my hand. He plugs it into his computer but gestures for me to keep going.

"Or both families will go after you. They've worked together in the past."

"Ha. The Diazes might have helped the Kutsenkos when Misha needed them, but it doesn't go both ways. They'll destroy the Diazes, and you know it."

Enrique rolls his eyes and shakes his head. I didn't see Pablo earlier, but he's here now too. He makes an obscene hand gesture—like he's jerking off—until he realizes Enrique saw him do that in front of me. He drops his hand and grimaces. Alejandro shifts, catching my attention. He looks the most like Enrique, so when he rolls his eyes and shakes his head too, it's like a delayed replay of his uncle.

"Drew, you might have been a pain in the ass today, but I'm still with the Diazes, and you're still shit out of luck. I'm not going near you ever again."

"Is that a challenge, Madeline? I tracked you down twice. I—"

"And it took you more than a month to do that. I bet the only reason you figured out where I was is because you saw a photo of me or something while I attended Enrique's wedding reception."

It's Enrique's turn to grimace. I shrug. It was ultimately my choice to go, and I knew what I risked. I shift my focus when Joaquin spins his laptop around, and I see a digital map. There's a pulsing circle with a red dot in the center. I dart my gaze to Javi, whose expression tells me I can end the call. They know what they need.

"Madeline, do you want all the Diazes' deaths on your conscience? You couldn't survive that guilt."

"Neither your dick nor your balls are big enough to do shit personally. That's why you sent Jacob, and he died for it. It's why you had to send machines to do what your men can't. I left you, and I'm never going back. Come near me, and I'll kill you myself. You know I can and will kill. You wouldn't be the first today."

I hang up as I stare at the device that's back in my hand again. I can't believe I spoke so crudely in front of Enrique, but I think the circumstances can excuse my lack of manners. Anger pulses through me now that the initial shock and fear have eased. The urge to hurl my phone across the office tempts me, but I restrain my temper. It won't get me anywhere, and I refuse to have a meltdown in front of men who've had stoicism drilled into them since the cradle.

"Maddy?"

I look up at Javi who appears uncertain what to do. I can tell he senses my changing moods, and he wants to help but doesn't know how.

"We have to call Maks, don't we?"

"Absolutely."

A resolute answer, but he hardly sounds eager. We shift our gazes to Enrique who hardly looks thrilled, considering he told me this was private family business. I'll have to admit more than I want.

"Should we call from my phone or yours?"

"Javier's." Enrique's not deferring to his nephew, but it'll signal to Maks that Javi decides how best to protect me.

"Do you want me to step out for this?"

"No. You can stay. Maks and his family are all fluent Spanish speakers. If we need to discuss something, we'll switch to that."

Javi's attention moves to his brothers, and he jerks his head. They vacate the loveseat they shared—one that looked ready to collapse under their massive frames but is still standing—so Javi and I can sit. When our gazes meet, I know we both wish I could sit on his lap. That would be way too much in front of everyone else. We settle for his arm around my shoulders as he pulls out his phone. He dials and puts the call on speaker.

"What the fuck do you want?"

"Maks?"

"Madeline?!"

"I'm okay, but I need to talk to you. I'm at Enrique's with Javi and his family."

"What are you doing there? You shouldn't be near them."

"Maks, is Laura around too?"

There's a pause. "Yeah. Hold on."

We hear Maks moving, then my sister's on the line.

"Madeline, why are you with *them*?"

"Laura, there's—I—" I inhale a fortifying breath. "I left Drew a month ago because things have been—I wasn't safe there. I am now. I'm with Javi, and I don't want to be anywhere else. Drew found me, and he's threatening me again. He sent me a photo of you and the twins going into the grocery store today."

"Madeline—" My sister's speechless.

"Laura, I'm okay."

"Take me off speaker right this minute and go somewhere private. I'm speaking to you alone. Now, Madeline."

I glance up at Javi and nod. I stand and look around the room. None of the men appear surprised. They all know Laura. They know she has an iron will no one can bend. But they also know she wants to ask me things only I'd share with her or Javi. Shit that's private.

I step out of the office and look around. I see Elle and her dog in the living room. He's just like Laura's Mastiff but a different color. I can't take this call in front of her. I head up the stairs.

"Madeline?"

"Just a moment. I was in Enrique's office with the guys. I'm headed to Javi's room."

"Why do you keep calling him Javi? And Enrique has enough guest rooms in that mansion that you don't need to go anywhere but to the one we used to share."

We spent several Christmases here when we were kids. When we were really little, we'd fall asleep before the evening was done. She and I would climb into a bed together and whisper about the gifts we got or the ones we thought we'd get the next day. I didn't think about that room until just now. I still go to Javi's.

"You're going to lose all your shit, but you have to let me tell you everything while I have the courage to say it."

"You better hurry because a comment like that doesn't calm me down."

"I know. I don't know which end of the story to start with, and it might jump around as I think of things."

"I can follow. Get on with it."

She doesn't snap at me. I hear dread instead, but I know she's already formulating a plan to rescue me. She just needs to know enough details to figure out how. I need to stop her.

"When we were in high school, Javi and I wound up with our dates in the same park. The guy I was with didn't like it when I said no. Javi heard me scream and got me out of the car. He took care of the guy. After that, he insisted on being my shadow for nearly a year. I had a total crush on him throughout high school, so I accepted and felt safer for it."

"You did a shitty job keeping that secret, Mads. I knew about your crush."

"Did you know Javi was watching out for me?"

"No, but I suspected it. I thought you might have been hooking up."

"You never said anything."

237

"Back then, I trusted that he might have been an asshole to everyone but never to you."

"You need to trust that's still the case. He and I ran into each other a while ago. I trust him even more now than I did back then. He found out what's been going on with Drew. I ran away from Albany a month ago. Things haven't been good with Drew since I moved in with him. Do you know who he is? Has Maks told you?"

There's a protracted silence before my sister answers.

"Maks warned me that he's mob. I know you've figured out a lot of stuff about Maks and his family without me telling you. That was all Maks needed to tell me for me to figure shit out. Since you don't ask me about shit I can't tell you, I figured I'd do the same."

"I appreciate that. But Maks and Drew couldn't be more different. Laura, Drew's been—he's—fucking hell."

"Madeline, did he hurt you?"

I don't answer fast enough.

"Maks! Maks!"

"Laura?"

"Drew hurt Madeline. I want him now."

"Laura, wait." I knew she'd blow up.

"No. I know you won't tell me everything. I'll make that piece of shit tell me every secret he's ever had. If he touched you with anything but love and adoration, he will die for it."

My sister doesn't exaggerate. She's always been protective of me, but since becoming a mom and marrying into the bratva —there's nothing I wouldn't put past her when it comes to defending her family.

"Laura, I will tell you everything. You can tell Maks what you want after, but I can't do this with him to hear it. I'm sorry, Maks, but I can't. It's too—"

"I understand. *Malyshka*, find me when you're done talking to your sister."

I hear a door close, but Laura remains quiet.

"I looked that word up after the first time I heard Maks call you that. It sounds so sweet, and it is. Javi calls me *chiquita* for the same reason."

I let that bomb land, but it doesn't explode the way I fear.

"You're going to marry him, aren't you?"

It's not an accusation. It's not even resigned acceptance. There's a tinge of humor that lightens things for a moment.

"I don't know."

"Mads, if he's calling you that, then it's as good as a proposal. These men are affectionate with their family not outsiders. They don't date, and they don't have relationships with women they don't plan to marry. If he has a pet name for you, then you need to understand whatever promises he makes, he will keep them. Whether it's to love you till his last breath, to do his best to make you happy, or to protect you from anything—Mads, Javi plans to marry you. I also bet it's the best sex you've ever had. Kinky as fuck."

"Laura!"

"What lie did I tell?"

"None. I just can't believe you said that."

"Yeah, well, I've always been the blunt one. I don't like the idea that you're becoming a Diaz, but I'll deal. Tell me what the fuck is going on with Drew. No more detours."

"Things were fine for the first two years. Drew became the boss around the same time I moved in. He became possessive and controlling to an extreme. He could be a little nasty when we argued, but it blindsided me the first time he hit me. I tried to leave. I tried more than once, but he stopped me each time. I couldn't get away before he'd find me, and the consequences convinced me it was safer to just stay."

"He abused you for two years. Madeline, I've been married for nearly six. You must know the Kutsenkos not only would have helped you, but they would have ensured he couldn't retaliate."

"Laura, he heard every conversation I had with you. Read every text, every email. He had me followed *everywhere*—even at work—and kept cameras in our house. I was never truly alone. I discovered he bugged our place when I bought a burner and tried to call you. He sent men in. They broke the phone and locked me in the bedroom until he got there."

My voice trembles as I remember that day. I thought I would die, but it didn't stop me from trying to use a burner two more times.

"I couldn't communicate with you without him finding out. I couldn't warn you he sent men to watch you periodically. Just enough to scare me into staying quiet. I spent months painting in secret and selling my art covertly to hide enough money to finally get away. I was in Brooklyn for nearly a month before my path crossed Javi's. I tried to hide from him, but he's— persistent. I confessed to him like I am you."

I don't want to explain the sketchy ass man who picked up my art from the darkest depths of the employee parking lot while I was inside the hospital. I can tell her about that later when she realizes I couldn't have worked entirely alone. I also don't want to tell her about the money and drugs I hid because that's now the Diazes' business.

"I made a huge mistake going to Enrique's reception. I should have stayed hidden and lied about having work like I've done in the past. Drew found out. Probably saw a photo of me online or something. He sent men to get me. I went to Javi."

"You could have come to me. To any of us."

"I know, but Javi is who I needed."

Laura sighs, and this time I hear resignation. "I know I

could go to anyone in Maks's family, and I know deep down I could still go to the Diazes. But I will always want Maks before anyone else. I will only ever feel safest when I'm with him. I get it."

"I know you do. But when you add the twins to this, I refuse to go near you. I will not have Drew or any of his men get near you, Mila, or Konstantin, or any of the other Kutsenko kids because I'm his target."

"We can hide you without you being at one of our homes. Though you'd be safer on one of our properties than anywhere else."

Each Kutsenko couples' home—plus their Andreyev cousin's—is in a gated community with a private wall and gate around their property. They have armed security patrolling around the clock. They aren't out of shape rent-a-guards. These are bratva men. It's the same as here at Enrique's.

I never understood why Luis and Margherita didn't have the same security as Enrique. I figured it was because he wasn't the *jefe*, just the *jefe's* younger brother. Then I've watched Maks's relatives marry and move into properties like his and Enrique's. I think it's Luis's reputation. I overhead Maks's brother call Luis *el Espíritu Santo* once. The Holy Spirit. I asked Laura about it. She frowned but told me if Luis visits someone, they know their soul is about to depart their body.

"Laura, you know why I'm safest with Javi. You already said it."

"Madeline, Javi can finish him, but I will see Drew before he dies."

"I don't want you in the middle of this."

"Too fucking bad. You're my sister."

"Laura, there's still more to this story."

Chapter Twenty-Two

Javier

I'm about to knock on my bedroom door when I hear Maddy's voice. I lower my fist, though I know I shouldn't listen to her call with her sister.

"Laura, I am *not* going to your house. You already admitted you understand why I came to Javi and why I'm staying here."

I can't hear what Laura says, but I can guess.

"No. Absolutely not. I didn't tell you what Drew made me do because I'm asking for help. I'm admitting the fucked-up shit I've done for the past two years. The weight of these secrets has been strangling me, and you need to know because he threatened your family. What I did for the O'Sheehans has no bearing on whether the Diazes can protect me properly."

Yet again, I don't know what Laura's saying. However, I've known her for more than twenty years. I might not guess the exact words, but I know the sentiment.

"I'm not going the fuck over there, Laura. I—"

Fucking hell.

I knock, and Madeline goes silent for a moment.

"Who is it?"

"Maddy, it's me. May I come in?"

"Yes."

I step in and shut the door behind me. Splotchy red patches darken her cheeks. She's pissed. A year before I rescued her, she found out about a huge fight—a melee—the guys in my family got into with guys from the other rival families. She was pissed and disappointed in me the next time we wound up at my aunt and uncle's for Sunday dinner.

My brothers and I were complete douche's to Maria Mancinelli because we were all too immature to handle finding out one of her friends had a crush on Joaquin. We all thought our balls had dropped. He thought, as a senior, he was too good for some freshman girl. Maria stood up to him, and I made a comment she misunderstood. I didn't say it loud enough for her to hear clearly.

Before I could correct her, she was yelling for her cousin Carmine. With him came his goon of a friend Gabriele. That got all the Mancinellis' attention along with the Kutsenkos and their Andreyev cousins. They stuck up for Maria, and the O'Rourkes egged us on along with telling the Mancinellis they couldn't defend Maria without the bratva's help.

She swore I said *perra de pecho plano*. She told her family I called her a flat-chested bitch. Before I could correct her, fists were flying. Then there were knives and guns. It was an utter shitshow. All of us wound up in more trouble with our respective leaders than any of us could've ever imagined in our relatively brief lives. *Tío* Enrique was ready to cut out my tongue. I barely had a chance to tell him what I really said. I was fifteen and hiding behind *Mamá* to do it.

The only part Maria caught was *perro aplanado*—flattened dog—which is what I said my brother would be if any of our uncles found him sniffing around a fourteen-year-old girl. She was only proficient in Spanish back then, and there was too much noise with the music for her to hear me properly.

Maddy looks the same way now as she did that night at dinner when she had to sit next to me.

"Is everything all right?"

"No."

Laura must have heard me because they answered at the same time, and I could hear Maddy's sister.

"Can you call Laura back in a few minutes? I need to talk to you."

I see her hesitation, but she understands that if I don't want Laura to overhear, it's something private about our family—my family is Maddy's family now.

"I gotta go. I'll call you back ... I'll call you back. Bye."

Laura must have argued, but Maddy taps her screen, then tosses the phone on the bed. She scrubs her hands over her face. I scoop her into my arms and carry her to the bed, where I perch on the end.

"I'm sorry you fought with your sister."

"It wasn't a fight. She's scared, which just makes her feel out of control. Neither of us do well when we're like that. It's why you and Maks—"

Her cheeks darken, but this time she's blushing.

"If we weren't enemies, the Four Families would probably all be best friends. *Chiquita*, it's no secret how similar the men are in each family. Not just within one but across all of them. We're all into similar things, and the couples all have similar dynamics. It stands to reason Maks and I would have similar personalities, and you and your sister would have similar preferences."

"She did call me out on us being kinky, and it was pretty much an admission too."

She whispers that, and I know she's only confiding that in me as her partner. She would never tell anyone else something so private.

"Little one, we got some information while you were up here. I need to go out, and the others are coming with me. You need to go to Maks and Laura's after all. You're safe here with *Tía* Elle, but we think you'll be more comfortable being around people you know better. I don't know how long this will take."

"You have a 'place,' don't you?"

A wall drops between us. How the fuck does she know that? Did Laura tell her when they discussed Maks's family? Or did she accuse us of something and mention it?

"Daddy, I went to the O'Sheehans' multiple times."

"What?!"

Rage. Pure, unadulterated rage. It burns hotter than anything I felt earlier today.

This...

This...

This I cannot forgive. Not that I could forgive Drew anything, but this is whole other level shit.

She sighs and closes her eyes as she leans against me. I gaze down at her as my right hand strokes her left hip.

"The first time he took me there, he did it to shock me. To make me realize what he's capable of. To frighten me into thinking he'd do some fucked-up shit like that to me if I narced or ran. After that, there were a few times I led or took people there as though we'd do the deal somewhere private. I know he never let me see the worst of it. Just enough to terrify me and control me. I saw shit that confirmed my worst fears about him. When we got home after the first time he took me there, he explained all syndicates have a place they go where they control all of it. A place off the records and maps. A place cops know not to go if someone reports screams. A place that doesn't officially exist, so the feds can't get a warrant. They go to a barn in the western part of Albany, the hill towns. When he'd go there, he couldn't talk to me. His phone was off, so law enforcement and rivals couldn't track him. They were the best days because I didn't have to see or hear him. Fucked-up, I know. It meant someone else was dying, but I didn't care. It meant I was safe. If you're going to be away for a few days, my guess is you'll be at your family's place."

My heart races, knowing she witnessed any type of torture. She's killed before and obviously seen other people get shot. But the things that happen at these places—it's far worse than any mobster movie or the news could guess. The Mexican cartels leave heads in the streets and bodies dangling from bridges and overpasses. They use that to intimidate people into obeying. That's messy and leaves a trail.

New York Colombians prefer to make people disappear without a trace. We erase a person's entire existence. That absolute control is far more powerful. I don't want her to know these things about my family—about me. It's one thing for her to wonder. It's another for her to have confirmation.

"Javi?" She cups my neck and presses a kiss to my cheek.

"Hmm." I'm still lost in thought.

"Daddy, I know you hate that I know this. Knowing isn't a bad thing. It means I won't fear for you because I'll know you're in control. I won't question where you really are."

"You mean who I'm really with?"

She shrugs her right shoulder. "That too."

"I'm certain you know some places I do business are nothing short of seedy. My family owns strip clubs because men like to measure their dicks in places like that when they do

246

business with families they think they're superior to. If they didn't need us, they wouldn't do business there. Strippers and dancers have never been my thing. There's only one set of tits and ass I'll spend my life looking at. It's not possible for me to always admit when I have to go to one of the clubs, but it'll never be recreational. Have I led women on before to get information? Yes. Have I been with women because they've been as useful to me as they hoped I'd be to them? Yes. Will either of those things ever happen again? Absolutely not. I swear, Maddy. If I couldn't be faithful to you, I never would have touched you."

She nods, but she takes a moment to appear confident in her agreement.

"I believe you, Javi, even if I feel insecure. If nothing else, any member of your family would castrate you if you cheated on a woman you're committed to. I think your mother's disappointment would be enough to keep you from doing that regardless of the woman you're with."

"That's all true. I can understand why you'd feel insecure knowing I spend time in a place that operates on beauty and sex appeal. But the way I want you—fuck. I can't get enough of you. There will never be enough time with you even if we spend the next seventy years together."

"You expect us to live into our hundreds?"

"I might not get my dick up by then, but I'll still have my fingers and tongue."

She giggles and shakes her head. "You're ridiculous, but I get your point."

She sighs as she burrows against my chest. Would that we could stay just like this, but we both know we can't. She pulls away as I loosen my hold. We share a soft but far-too-quick kiss, then she's climbing off my lap.

"Do you need me to do anything to help you get ready?" She glances around the room as she speaks.

"No. I have everything I need. *Tío* Enrique wants to speak to you, then we'll head out. *Tía* Elle will take you to Maks and Laura's."

"Is it safe for her to go out?"

"Nothing will happen to her there."

Her eyes widen. "I never thought it would. I meant on the way there and back. Is it safe for her to leave the house?"

"Yes. You'll take an SUV and have guards too."

"Then why does she have to come? Javi, I don't want her to take any unnecessary risks for my sake."

"She said she had some errands to run, so she's going out, anyway."

That's sort of the truth. One of countless half-truths I'll tell Maddy in the seventy years to come.

"I'll text Laura. I don't want to hear her or Maks gloat."

"I called Maks already. He knows."

She stares at me, then nods. When she turns toward the door, I catch her forearm.

"Maddy, his family and mine had things to discuss, including my over-the-top demands for your protection. For your safety and his family's, he has to know some of what's planned. But he doesn't know all of it. No one outside my family—not even our men—know for sure. After what happened at the estate, we trust no one who doesn't share our DNA within one degree."

"Daddy, I believe you, and I trust you."

She rests her hands on my waist as both of mine cup her neck. I lean forward to kiss her as she rises onto her toes. This is more than lust. It's more than infatuation. It's not quite love—at least I don't think so, but how the fuck would I know since I've never been in love—but we're getting there. When we pull apart, her expression tells me she knows this is something real. Something deep. Neither of us is caught up in the moment. It isn't danger propelling us toward each other. It's longer lasting than that.

I hope I survive to enjoy it.

"How the fuck did they know where we were?"

I swing the crowbar at José's left ribs, making sure the hook catches on the bone. Tómas brought him to our place. It's a bodega the other families assume is in Queens. We have one there where we run our underground—literally and figuratively —gambling rings and where *Tío* Enrique can hold court with people who survive the meeting but need to understand it's only by his good graces that they do.

This bodega is on Long Island. The bratva and Mafia have their places in Queens. We suspect the mob is in the Bronx, and we're out here. The O'Rourkes and my family prefer some subterfuge. The Kutsenkos and Mancinellis couldn't give two fucks from Sunday and are willing to risk being discovered for the sake of convenience.

José is on death's doorstep. He looks like shit. Tómas knew we'd expect to see his former brother-in-law. That meant he got in a beating before it was our turn. He knew he risked our wrath by taking it upon himself, but he counted on us under-standing why he wanted his pound of flesh. The damage Tómas did meant José couldn't put up a fight, but he wasn't so incapacitated as to be useless.

"They found out."

"No shit. You told them where we were."

"No. They found out about Miguel and Tómas."

"Why the fuck would the mob in Albany give a fuck about a couple of our guys tucked away in Connecticut?"

"Not the Irish in Upstate. The bratva here."

That gives me pause. There's not a damn thing homophobic about the Kutsenkos or Andreyevs. They're modern Russians. They have reason to be *very* accepting of any lifestyle. Why would a gay couple in our organization matter to them?

"Were they blackmailing you because of it?"

"Yeah. They don't care, but they know other families would. They weren't going to use it against you directly. It was information to sell to anyone who wanted to fuck you over from the inside out. They knew not everyone would accept my brothers. It was tell them where you disappear to, or they'd sell the information to a Mexican or Colombian rival."

"You believed them? *¡Qué pelota eres!*" What an idiot you are.

"I'd do anything to protect my brother!"

"Shitload of good it did you. He's dead because of you."

José wails with grief. For the few hours left of his miserably pathetic life, he'll regret that to his last breath.

"*¡Lo sé!*" I know!

"So, they told the O'Sheehans where our family's most sacred place is because you told them."

I rear back with the pipe ready to crack more ribs on his left side. There are at least two I haven't gotten to yet.

He shakes his head. "No. I knew they were bluffing about telling any New York family about the estate. That was an empty threat. The Kutsenkos went after the O'Rourkes' ancestral home to punish them, and it's cost them millions ever since. We know Pasha, Misha, and Aleks nearly died last year in the Czech Republic because the O'Rourkes' reach is that far. I believed them when they said they'd tell someone in Mexico or

Colombia about my brothers. I figured they'd sell the info to your rivals in exchange for someone in Latin America going after the O'Rourkes for them. I didn't guess they'd tell someone in Upstate."

"Why were they even in contact with the O'Sheehans?"

"I don't know. Probably something to do with your woman since she's Maks's sister-in-law. When Drew sent men to find Tómas and Miguel, I tried to lie. I said they were just best friends since they were kids. I said I was as close to Tómas as Miguel was. They had photos of them on vacation in Jamaica."

I told them not to go there. I told them too many syndicates do business there for them to ensure their privacy. They didn't fucking listen. A horseback ride into the mountains to a coffee plantation likely cost them Miguel's life.

"Why'd you tell anyone about the estate if you knew your brother was there?"

"I was supposed to get a text before the attack. I was supposed to get enough heads up to get my brother and me away from there."

"And the text never came in."

José shakes his head again. He's strung up, naked with his arms over his head. He can't even hold it up anymore, so it lolls to the side, resting against his left bicep.

"I got the text, but it wasn't an alert to get out. It said dead men don't tell tales."

"No shit. There was no way they'd let you live once they attacked. They didn't want anyone to survive that. You were their first target outside my family. If they hadn't killed you, how did you think you'd survive my brothers and me? If we'd died, how would you have survived my *tíos*? If you hadn't confessed, they would've killed every survivor to ensure the guilty were punished. They'd never have trusted you again."

251

"¡Lo sé! But I had to take the chance if it could save Miguel."

"You should've come to us the moment anyone approached you with that information. You know we supported them. *We* would have protected them. Instead, you got your brother killed. *No one* is to blame but you. *You* did this. It's all *your* fault."

"¡Lo sé! ¡Lo sé! ¡Lo sé!"

He keeps repeating himself, the emotional anguish worse than the physical pain he's endured. I know Tómas made José confess all of this to his parents, made him be the one to tell them he got their other son killed. They're an old Cartel family, so our relationships with the other families is no secret.

"Let's go back a moment. I want to be completely clear. Drew approaches you with the knowledge that Tómas and Miguel are a couple. He threatens your brother. How do you get from there to telling them about the estate? They would have been safe there."

His hands fist and unfist, and he trembles. It makes the rope he's hanging from vibrate, which makes him swing and twist since only the tips of his toes touch the ground.

"It was the *señorita* or my brother. I told you we were supposed to have time to get away. It was tell him where you took her, or he'd hunt down Tómas and Miguel."

"Which Kutsenko told Drew to approach you?" I'll kill whichever one it was.

"I don't know. Drew never said." I believe him because Drew knows if he survives my family, he wouldn't survive selling out the Kutsenkos.

"Why'd he think you'd know in the first place?"

"He didn't for sure. I was his only contact who might know anything useful. He called me right after his guys told him she was with someone in your family and demanded to know where you might take her. It was before you even arrived. I only confirmed it when you pulled through the gate."

"So, you called him? You could've kept quiet."

"*Sí, patron.*" Yes, boss.

"Were you involved with the windows?"

His head drops all the way forward before it bobs. It lolls back against his arm as he answers.

"I faked a purchase order and lied about your mother ordering new windows. I had them replaced the day after I spoke to Drew for the first time."

I stand back and assess him. I consider how much more torture he can withstand. Plenty. I consider how much more information he has left to give. Probably not much. What Tómas did was to punish him. What I've done so far was to coerce him. I haven't even begun punishing him for putting Maddy and my brothers in danger or for violating the sanctity of *Papá's* gift to *Mamá.*

I turn toward Jorge and Joaquin, who took turns with a set of pliers. He's minus a few teeth, and he's had his balls in a vise for a while. They shrug in unison. I put the crowbar down on a table near the door to the office we built. It has a couple of cots and three showers along with a desk and some chairs. We often spend days at a time here depending on who we're working over. We've already been here for five hours. To José's credit, it took longer than I wanted for him to crack.

My brothers and I leave him hanging as we enter the office. We'll let his fear of the unknown keep him company for a while. I look at *Tío* Enrique, Pablo, and Alejandro. They've stayed tucked away in here. *Tío* will speak to José before I kill him. A final goodbye.

"Are you ready for me to see him?"

"You don't think there's anything left, do you?"

"Probably not. He might come up with something more

when he believes I'm the one who's going to kill him. But I doubt it."

"I want to know which one told Drew. It seems so unlikely for Maks or any of the others. There's plenty of shit they'd gladly tell a rival if they knew, but not about Tómas and Miguel. And Maks admitted he knew who Maddy was dating, but he didn't know Drew was hurting her. He wouldn't have put up with it if he had, and he certainly wouldn't help Drew, even if it was to strike us."

"Could one of their men have overheard the Elite Group discussing our guys?" Jorge poses the question that's already run through my mind.

The Elite Group is the bratva's senior leadership. Technically, it's the four Kutsenko brothers. But their cousins, Sergei and Anton, are in the positions just below them. Their other cousins, Pasha and Misha, are their most senior generals. When we use the term, we mean the entire eight tentacle octopus. Eight bodies and one communal brain.

Alejandro disagrees. "I can't imagine why they'd bother talking about Miguel and Tómas. Even if they had, they'd never do it where any of their men could hear them. I can't believe someone in their inner circle who would. Considering the lengths they've gone to protect their cousins, I just don't think it was them selling that information."

No one knows for sure, but the other three families that matter in NYC suspect there's a reason Anton and Sergei are the final holdouts not to marry. The Kutsenkos and their Andreyev cousins know no one in the O'Rourkes, Mancinellis, or us would say shit about any relationship those men might have. It's not our business, and frankly, none of the families care. If we wanted either of those men dead, we'd just shoot them. That's why this makes no sense.

"Who in the bratva approached José? He said he doesn't

know who told the O'Sheehans, but who blackmailed him to start with?" Pablo's looking out the two-way mirror, knowing we can see José, but he can't see us.

I follow his gaze for a moment before turning back to the rest of my family. I'll let someone else finish José. There are more important things now.

"Good question. We already explained enough to Maks. Now it's time for him to answer my questions."

Chapter Twenty-Three

Javier

"Why?"

"*Por qué qué?* If you can't speak in complete sentences in English, Javier, maybe Spanish will help."

"Don't play moderately dumber than you already are, Misha. You know what I'm asking."

"No, I don't. Get on with it, Javier. I have other things to do right now."

"I don't need to know what you and your wife are up to."

"Fuck you."

"No, I figured that's what you were going to do to your wife."

"Fuck off."

It's no secret all the syndicate couples can't keep their hands off their partner. Maddy and I are no better—no worse— than anyone else.

We're breaking a cardinal rule and using the sat phone at the bodega to call Misha Andreyev. Normally, this phone is only for emergencies, but we need to plan what we do next before we go anywhere else.

"Once you tell me why you targeted Madeline."

My temper is already on its last thread. He needs to fucking answer me.

"Targeted her for what? What the fuck are you talking about?"

"Drew O'Sheehan. Why'd you target Madeline to get to him?"

"I didn't target Madeline."

Misha sounds pretty adamant, but he could lie to God and get away with it.

"I never would. What does she have to do with this?"

"You knew who she was dating."

"So?"

I inhale, trying to regain the patience I lost the moment I heard his voice. Going around in circles won't help us, and me continuing to be belligerent will only shoot me in the foot. I exhale slowly before I try again.

"You know Madeline's been involved with Drew. You know who and what Drew is. How could you not believe going after him wouldn't affect Madeline?"

"Because, unlike your family, he keeps women and children out of our business."

I grit my teeth, reminding myself I can't explode at him over something he couldn't possibly know. Obviously, he hasn't spoken to Maks, or Laura hasn't told Maks everything yet.

"Misha, O'Sheehan's the worst of all of us. Not only did he get Madeline involved, he made her one of his mules."

I don't want to confess much more than that. But I may have to, and it won't remain a secret among their family for long, even if I'm not the one to say anything.

"What are you talking about?"

The edge to Misha's voice isn't directed toward me. I've known him since I arrived in the States, which wasn't too long after he and his family arrived from Russia. I know when he's being pissy or threatening me, and when it's for someone else.

"Ask Laura for more of the details. She'll know what Madeline would want shared. I won't divulge anything else."

"How the hell would you know more than Laura?"

I cock an eyebrow, even though I know he can't see me. My silence says just as much.

"Motherfucker, you cannot be serious. There is no way in hell Madeline Doyle picked you."

"Well, I sure am a far sight better than the piece of shit she's been with."

"So, you think she's trading up?"

The snideness in Misha's voice makes me want to throat punch him. But again, belligerence won't win the day here.

"Misha, when you went after Drew, you gave him information that allowed him to track Madeline. She ran away from him over a month ago."

"Ran away? Not broke up, but ran away?"

"Yeah, so what does that tell you about their relationship? She's been hiding ever since."

"She wasn't hiding when she went to your uncle's reception."

"Exactly, and she realizes what a misjudgment that was because it meant Drew discovered she was near the city. But you meddling in my family's business meant he tracked her to her specific location."

"We don't meddle in your business."

I snort a laugh. "*Cabrón*, we meddle in each other's business. None of us have the secrets we want to think we do. Just like you know things about some of our men, we know that about your family."

He knows exactly who I'm referring to.

"Is that a threat, Javier?"

"No, it's merely an observation. Why did you sell any of our secrets to the O'Sheehans? Tell me the truth, Misha, because this is about Madeline's safety. You don't have to give a shit about me or anyone in my family. But she's Laura's sister, and the one thing we can agree upon is keeping her safe. The only way for me to do that is to know what the fuck is going on, so I'm going to ask you one more time. Why'd you sell secrets to Drew?"

I hear voices in the background, and I'm certain it's Maks. He's either asking Misha what he's talking about or he's filling his cousin in on more details. When Misha speaks again, the volume is different, so I know he's put it on speakerphone. I remain quiet now that he's decided to fess up.

"Unsurprising to anyone, we've done surveillance on some of your men. We observed something interesting by entire coincidence while Niko and I were in Jamaica for a meeting. We are having complications with some of our deals in Eastern Europe, thanks to the O'Rourkes. We figured that nugget could be valuable."

"Complications, my ass. They're encroaching upon your territory in Eastern Europe. You want a way to push them out. Let me guess. You sold information to the O'Sheehans in order to get them to help you fuck over the O'Rourkes. They're pissed at the O'Rourkes for having a stranglehold on all their imports and exports along the St. Lawrence."

"Very good. Then again, Javier, you never ask a question you don't already know the answer to."

"I figured out that part. But you must have sold this information to the O'Sheehans before anything went on between Madeline and me. What did the O'Sheehans plan to do with this against us?"

"You know the O'Rourkes run their guns down the St. Lawrence. But your family has control over the other major product up there."

Products of the semi-organic type.

I need to keep listening to keep from losing track of his explanation.

"The O'Sheehans are getting pissy that you're expanding your reach upstate. They already hate that the O'Rourkes are stronger in Rochester than they are in Albany. They don't want you pushing out any of their rivals in Buffalo to take over there. They think they can handle their rivals, but they know they don't stand a chance against you once you dig in. They were going to blackmail you with that information or sell it to rivals in Latin America."

"And you—what—thought we wouldn't find out that all of this originated with you? You think you're in any position to sell those kinds of secrets? Motherfucker, don't come after my family. You can piss all the way off, Misha. You pretend your family is so fucking angelic, like your shit don't stink and nothing sticks to you. But you're just like everyone else. You'll fucking sacrifice anyone—man, woman, or child—to get ahead. We're not like you, *carechimba*. We've never used what we figured out about a couple certain someones in your family against you, and we never would. But you're fucking hypocrites to the nth degree to tell anybody what you figured out about Tómas and Miguel. We could very easily do the same thing to your family, but we never would. You want to call us psychopaths as though we have no bound-aries. But when push comes to shove and women in your family and the Mancinellis and the O'Rourkes have needed help, who the fuck has always been there? Us. Who the fuck caused problems in the first place? Not always us. You can't pin everything that goes wrong on us because you can't fucking protect the women in your family. Grow some balls, Misha."

He lets me unleash as I allude to what my family knows about Anton and Sergei. I know he's letting me vent my spleen because he's figured out Madeline is mine. He'd do the same thing if we were talking about his wife, Katerina.

"Look, right now that's neither here nor there, Javier. I didn't know the extent of Madeline's involvement in any of this. If I had, I would never have spoken within earshot of Drew O'Sheehan. Regardless of whether she's a woman, she's Laura's family. You know I wouldn't do anything to compromise Laura's family's safety."

"Bull-fucking-shit, *cabrón*. You knew full well Madeline could've been caught in the crossfire of this, and you still did it anyway. You know Drew's temper. You didn't think he'd take this shit out on somebody if it went wrong?"

"Yeah, take it out on his men, not on his girlfriend."

"What about Drew O'Sheehan has ever made you think he can control his temper once it gets fired up?"

Misha's silent for a moment as he considers what I said. He knows I'm not exaggerating. I can't fault him for his wishful thinking or believing Drew wouldn't hurt Maddy since they've been together so long. For assuming that if Drew ever hurt Maddy, she would've left.

"Look, Misha, what's done is done, and we'll deal with that later. But for right now, I need to know what the fuck else Drew knows about my family and what he could do, what he could leverage against us to get to Maddy."

I've tried not to use her nickname, hoping being more formal would keep him from manipulating me if he didn't know how deep my feelings ran. But I don't have the bandwidth to worry about that, and now that I've made it clear she's mine for keeps, there's no point in downplaying it. A man like

Misha is like any other in this world. He didn't draw his wife into his life without being certain he would marry her from the get-go. He knows it's the same for me with Maddy.

"There's nothing else I can think of."

"Fine."

"What's she doing right now?"

"I don't know. Are you not at Maks's?"

"I am."

I glanced at the clock on the desk. "Misha, she should've been at Maks's house ages ago. Is he not wondering where she is?"

"I don't know. Wait a minute. Maks!"

"Jav—"

"Maks, what do you know?" Do I sound as panicked as I feel?

"The last you told me, she was coming over, but you didn't say when she would be here. I figured she was still at Enrique's."

"Fucking hell, Maks. I don't have a tracker for her yet, so I don't know where she is."

I look over at my uncle, and his expression shows he's as alarmed as I feel. We're using our satellite phone for this call, not any of our cells. They're all off, so he can't easily ping *Tía* Elle's phone or the necklace she wears with a tracker in it.

"I have to go, Misha. I need to get back to my uncle's house and see what's going on with Madeline."

"We can head over there."

"No. You've done more than enough. Stay the fuck away from my girlfriend."

"Girlfriend?"

"Like you hadn't already fucking figured it out. Don't be a douche on top of all of this, Misha. I have to go."

I hang up the call while I'm unfastening my cuffs, then

unbuttoning my shirt. I changed into my regular clothes—a suit —before I left *Tío* Enrique's. It's cliché as fuck, but José knew all six of us showing up in suits meant we were there to do business. I took off the jacket, so I had full range to swing the crowbar.

I strip as fast as I can, hopping from one foot to the other as I prepare to jump in the shower. It's not just a way to freshen up after a night here on a cot. We scrub away any evidence we might have picked up in order to preserve our anonymity here and to protect us against bringing any evidence with us.

It also means we go through clothes faster than a group of sorority sisters. We burn everything when we leave. Pablo's already collecting my cast-off clothing to put in the burn bin. Alejandro's pulling something out of the community closet we have since we can all share clothes just like sorority sisters.

My heart races with a sense of urgency I'm all too familiar with. But as I shower, it grows to an intensity that alarms me. It wasn't that long ago we needed to rescue my *Tía* Catalina. She's always been like a second mom to me since she and *Mamá* are best friends and have been since they were little. There've been times when my brothers, cousins, and uncles have been in danger too.

This is different. It's never been the woman I want to spend my life with. It's never been the woman I can't imagine taking another breath without. She's become my everything in what seems like a matter of moments. But in truth, I've always had feelings for her, and she's had the same for me. It just took us two decades to admit it. Considering how long it took, I refuse to give up now that I finally have her.

I'm barely dry enough to get my clothes on without them sticking to me.

"Do you want me to drive?" Jorge holds out his hand for my keys.

We could've all come here together in town cars or our SUVs, but I knew I might want to leave before we finished in case Maddy needed something. Did I tempt fate by wondering that?

I nod to my brother, knowing his lead foot will allow me to concentrate on trying to track Maddy. Even though no one knows our place is here on Long Island, we still turn off our phones at least five miles away to give us a perimeter to protect our secrecy.

I know the others will finish up with José, and I know they'll begin a plan to retaliate against Misha. The bratva'll lose a few men or a few thousand dollars' worth of goods over this just to remind them they fucked up.

However, we can't hit them as hard as we'd like. Otherwise, we could wind up doing something that endangers Laura, Maddy, or some other woman in their family. We refuse to be like them. My phone pings within seconds of me turning it back on. There's a voicemail from my aunt Elle's number. My heart may have just stopped as I listened to Maddy's desperate plea for help.

Chapter Twenty-Four

Maddy

"Madeline, we can head over there whenever you're ready. Enrique said Maks knows to expect you. We just didn't say what time, so if you want to have something to eat before we go, you can, or we can set off right now."

I wound up staying upstairs for a couple hours after Javi left. He was concerned that I looked exhausted and got worried. He said it was safe for me to stay at Enrique and Elle's for a while if I wanted to nap. Once my niece and nephew see me, they won't leave me alone until their bedtime. I admitted I felt ready to drop. I was going to rest on the bed, but of course I passed out. Hard. I came downstairs after my siesta.

"I'm sure Laura's kitchen is fully stocked just like yours is with that many large men coming and going. There's always food in the house. Plus, one of their moms is usually dropping off something."

Galina, Svetlana, and Alina are all superb cooks who still

spoil their sons and daughters-in-law. It gives them excuses to go over and see their grandkids as well.

"Thank you for the offer, but Laura's only going to freak out more if I don't get over there soon. She's likely to come banging on your door. I didn't realize how long I slept."

Elle grins. "Enrique tells me all the time she's a younger version of me."

I tilt my head as I study her, then nod. "I can definitely see that. I got that feeling a little at the reception, but we really didn't have a chance to talk."

"I know, and I hope we can remedy that soon. I know how things stand between your family and mine, but I think it'll soon be your family and our family."

Her knowing look makes me blush. She's nearly old enough to be my mom and has adult children of her own, but a moment ago she felt more like an older sister. Now she feels like a knowing parent, like Javi and I were getting into trouble together upstairs, not like a couple of people in their early thirties.

"Madeline, I know what it is to keep the gravest of secrets, not only to protect yourself, but those around you. I'll never ask you to divulge anything you know about the Kutsenkos or the O'Sheehans. Just know that if you need an ear or a shoulder and you wish you could go to Laura, but you can't, you can always come to me."

She offers me a friendly smile before she turns toward the shoe rack by the front door. She won't belabor the point, but she wants me to know I'm not alone in this right now. Even though she recently married Enrique, she understands. I get the distinct impression she's not exaggerating. A lifetime of secrets is what it sounds like.

I put my shoes back on as well, glad that I had her fresh clothes to change into. Laura is a little closer in size to me than

Elle, but these are definitely comfortable. We head out to the garage after we both say goodbye to Constantine, her massive softie of a dog. He absolutely reminds me of Laura's dog Sebastian. I may not be ready for kids right this moment, but I think I might be ready for a Mastiff. It surprises me when we get into her SUV instead of one of the Diazes' vehicles.

"Madeline, I don't know if the O'Sheehans know how to distinguish the vehicles that belong to the Four Families. A massive black SUV or spit-polished town car headed toward Queens—particularly Forest Hills—will give away that you're in the vehicle. Drew may already be watching any of the Diazes' properties. Even though my windows aren't tinted as dark as any of the vehicles in Enrique's fleet, it still has darker windows than most. We have guards who'll be in unmarked vehicles who'll surround us as we go. We want to be as inconspicuous as possible."

"Do you know your way there?"

She shoots me a glance from the corner of her eye as she fastens her seatbelt. "I'm familiar with the area."

That's just about as vague as she could get. It makes me uncomfortable, yet I'm not scared.

We pull out of the driveway and head out of the neighborhood. We've barely made it a block before a car comes barreling toward us on this residential street. It's wide enough for two cars to pass easily, so there's no reason for this one to be on our side of the road. The vehicle in front of us speeds away from us, and I realize they're trying to intercept whoever this is. I watch in horror as a game of chicken plays out in front of us. Neither Enrique's guy nor whoever's driving this vehicle gives way.

Elle and I watch the head-on collision. I gasp and cover my nose and mouth with my hands.

"Elle, we have—"

"You stay in the vehicle. I don't care if you're a nurse. You're not getting out."

I look over at her and realize there's no way I'll convince her otherwise, even though I feel compelled to check on at least Enrique's men. I shift my gaze back to the street in front of us, and it amazes me to see the car with Enrique's guards is still intact enough to push the other vehicle. Both men in the Diaz vehicle lean out the window to shoot.

I glance in the passenger side-view mirror to see a car speeding behind us.

"Elle!"

I call out her name just as our guards behind us get rear-ended. Whoever's attacking us is trying to box us in and disable our protection detail, except the car behind ours is doing the same thing as the one in front. It shifts into reverse and pushes the other car. It's clear that, even though these are unmarked vehicles that look like they could be someone's everyday car, they're reinforced to be virtual battering rams. The cars that probably intended to drive us off the road are no match for them.

I don't know what to make of any of this since I've never been in a situation like this. However, when I look over at Elle, she's cool as a cucumber. Nothing seems to faze her about this. She maneuvers around the vehicles in front of us, turning and moving us into a wide U-turn.

"Madeline, get down. Cover your head like you're in an emergency-landing position on a plane."

"What about y—"

I don't even finish my sentence before I hear the first ping-ping against the metal of her car.

Is someone shooting at us?

As I look around, she does a complete mom arm, except

rather than holding me back, she grabs the back of my shirt just below my neck and pushes, forcing me to bend in half.

"Stay down, Madeline."

I'm inclined to follow directions as someone fires more shots toward us. I squeeze my eyes shut until I sense, then hear, Elle opening the center console. I peek with one eye and watch her pull out a handgun. The way she now drives with her knee as she checks that it's loaded and ready to go tells me this isn't her first rodeo.

She hasn't even been married to Enrique that long, so how does she know to do all of this? Who the hell was she in a previous life?

I heard she was an accountant and now writes psychological thrillers.

Is she trying to live out some fight or chase scene she came up with?

After winding down the window, she switches hands, and it's clear she's as comfortable holding the gun in her left hand as she was her right. She doesn't hesitate to shoot out the tires of a new car approaching us.

"How do—"

I don't get to finish that question either before she swerves and turns onto a side road a moment too late. We go up and over the curb as she fires the gun again.

"Madeline, climb into the back seat and get down on the floor."

"But—"

"No 'buts,' Madeline."

"No, I can shoot too."

"This isn't some range."

"I know."

"Madeline—"

It's my turn to cut her off. "I don't have time to explain

everything I've done, but I can help defend us. You're not the only one who shoots to kill."

She glances over at me before she nods. "Get into the back seat. Pull down the narrower side. There are rifles back there. Have you shot one of those before?"

"Yeah. I've only shot those at the range, but I'm comfortable with various calibers of pistols. Should I call Javi?"

She nods as I unfasten my belt. I clamber into the back before I pull out my burner. It rings until it goes to voicemail. Fuck. I debate whether to leave a message. We need help now, but he needs to know where I am while I can still tell him. I know Elle can hear me, but I keep my voice down.

"Javi, we're on our way to Maks and Laura's, but there are cars all over the place trying to drive us off the road. Your men blocked two of them, and Elle shot the tires of a third."

I glance over my shoulder.

"But there are more behind us. We're on Vandergrift, so we didn't make it very far. I don't know where we're going. Call me as soon as you get this."

Our gazes meet as she hits a button on her steering wheel.

"Call 'Place.'"

Place?

She must have the number to a sat phone the men have wherever they go to do whatever it is they do that I can never find out about. Before it can connect, her phone rings. The moment she answers, a voice comes through the car's speakers.

"*Tia* Elle, where are you? Maks says Maddy never showed up at his house. I expected you to leave hours ago."

"Javi?"

"Maddy?"

"I'm all right. I fell asleep, and Elle didn't wake me. But as soon as I got up, we left to go to Maks and Laura's."

"Is that gunfire I hear?"

"Yes, Javier." Elle cuts into our conversation. "I'm taking her back to my old house."

"That isn't yours anymore."

"That won't stop me from getting inside."

"But I thought you got rid of the panic room."

What the fuck did Elle need a panic room for in her old house?

I want to ask, but that seems neither here nor there at the moment.

"It's still reinforced, even if the new owners just think I was some kind of doomsday prepper. They'll be at work right now. It's the safest place to take Madeline—the one place whoever this is, is least likely to know about."

"Maddy, I'm coming. I'm already on the road."

"I know, Javi. Just hurry."

"I will, little one."

I'd give anything to hear him call me *chiquita* right now.

"Elle, behind us!"

I watch as a car comes around the bend we just took. They're driving as fast as we are, so I know these aren't people who live along this road. They're definitely pursuing us.

"Javier, tell your uncle where we're going."

"I will, but he doesn't have his phone on. It'll be from the sat. Expect it to be a foreign number."

I suppose Javier means Enrique will call back from the satellite phone. I'm getting a crash course in shit that was only whispered around me when I was with Drew. I always suspected they had some type of satellite phone for when they were at the barn, since I knew they turned off their own phones.

"They're getting closer, Elle."

"There's a 9mm back there. If you pull up the spare tire

271

cover, you'll find other weapons. If you're not comfortable with the rifle, then grab one."

One? Just how many other weapons does she have? I lower the back seat like she told me and scramble into the trunk, so I can lift the lid to the compartment where the spare tire is kept. It's there, but I also see a bag that fits into the center of the well. I pull at it, not expecting it to be as heavy as it is.

Metal clanks against itself before I unzip it and find a veritable arsenal in here. There's a disassembled shotgun, a disassembled rifle, at least three handguns I can see, and I suspect several knives. The bag is larger than I expected.

I look over my shoulder at Elle, who meets my gaze in the rearview mirror. The look she gives me is a hardened one. This isn't the easygoing woman who offered me something to eat twenty minutes ago. This is a woman who could be a cartel leader. I don't even know what the female version of *jefe* is. Maybe that's gender neutral.

I force myself to concentrate again as I consider my options among the handguns. I choose a 9mm similar to what she has up front, but I check the other ones as well. I'm comfortable with all of them and can easily switch among them before I need to reload.

"Elle, they're close enough I can see the outline of their bodies."

"Maddy, get down!"

Javi's shouting commands at me, but I ignore him when Elle shakes her head. I hadn't realized neither of them hung up. The glass in front of me lowers. This is one of the few SUVs that has a back window that winds down. It makes me wonder if the reason Elle has this particular make and model is for something like this.

I steady my hand by cupping it with my other. I aim for the front tires and take each out. The vehicle careens off to the side and nails a tree but not before the passengers open their doors. However, they're unable to get out when the airbags inflate. It gives us more time.

"Maddy, what was that? What's going on?"

Before I can answer, I hear the beeps from another call.

"Javier, that's your uncle. I have to go."

"Madeline, do you still have your phone?"

The urgency in Javier's voice conveys his near panic as much as him using my full name.

"Yes, I'll call you when I get to Elle's house. I don't want to talk over her when she tries to speak to Enrique."

"All right. Maddy, I love you."

"I love you too, Javi."

This isn't how I wanted to admit my feelings, and I doubt it's how he wanted to, either. But if this could be the last time we talk, then neither of us wants to go without the other knowing. These aren't emotions that have come out of nowhere. They're just ones that came back to life after lying dormant for so long. They're ones that have matured into something more than they originally were.

This isn't puppy love by any stretch. And this isn't just heat of the moment, deathbed confessions either. I can tell it's more than that. It's so much more.

We have a reprieve from anyone following us for the moment. I hear Elle speaking to Enrique, but I miss some of it, as I remain lost in thought. However, I snap back to the present as we pull up in front of a house.

"Grab the bag, Madeline."

We're here.

We don't drive toward the garage, but we're as close as we can get on the street in a gated community. I suppose someone could assume the car belongs to someone else who lives on this street. It doesn't directly tie us to Elle's old house.

I realize Elle didn't live far from the neighborhood she and Enrique live in now. She moved into his home. This neighborhood isn't as lavish as his. It's more like the one I grew up in, definitely more than just comfortable, but not mansions.

There are trees on one side of the house that provide a measure of privacy from her neighbor. I follow her to a side gate, uncertain what she holds up to the security box. She doesn't enter any code, but I hear it unlock. She pushes it open and shuffles me through. She closes it with barely a click. We move together. She with her gun raised facing forward, and me twisting to look behind us. She leads me over to the back door before she pulls out a lock-picking set from her purse.

She's fucking Mary Poppins of cat burglars.

Who knows what she'll pull out next? She opens the back door and freezes. I hear an alarm system beep.

"Stay here."

She keeps her voice down, but I realize hearing the alarm system reassures me no one else is home. She hurries to the keypad on the wall between the kitchen and living room. She enters something that must bypass the code the new owner's set. I can't imagine how she would have theirs. The beeps stop for a moment. Then I hear three more as she somehow resets it. She comes back over to me.

"If it stays off, it'll send an alert to the owners. I just needed it off long enough to set it to the perimeter rather than the internal sensors."

I nod. It makes complete sense, but I don't know what to say, having just broken into a house for the first time. She's had her phone cradled against her shoulder since we got out of the car, so she continues her call.

"Enrique, we're in. I'm taking her to the basement. You know I'll lose the call once I'm down there."

"Do you have jammers with you?"

"Yes, I'll set them up in the basement outside the panic room."

That shouldn't surprise me since Drew kept cell jammers in the house too. That's the least alarming thing I've heard so far. She hangs up with Enrique as we head down to the basement. I watch her pull a small device from the gun bag I'm carrying. She sets it up outside the door to what looks like a basement pantry or storage closet. We go in, and she flips a light on. The room is empty with nothing on the shelves.

"You said this was a panic room originally."

"Yes, my boys and I made it when I moved in. When I sold the house after Enrique and I got engaged, we remodeled it to make it look more like a storage room than anything else."

"Why did you even need that?"

"There's stuff in my past you'll learn about in time. But you should know I've been Mafia adjacent my entire life."

"Mafia adjacent?"

What the fuck does that mean?

Chapter Twenty-Five

Maddy

"I know that's vague, Madeline. But for right now, it's best if that's as much as I tell you."

My brow furrows at that. Elle doesn't trust me. I'm not family yet, so she won't tell me anything more. I get it. But it certainly leaves far more questions than answers. The best I can do is nod. There's nothing to sit on in this room now, so we both lower ourselves to the floor. I tilt my head back and close my eyes for a moment as I catch my breath and try to regroup.

"Madeline, I don't know Drew, but I know of the O'Sheehans. I know that family's reputation. Do you know what I mean by that?"

I shake my head, dreading whatever's coming next. There's been entirely too much revealed to me in the past few days. My head feels like it might explode if I learn anything else. Perhaps I can figure out more about Elle from whatever she shares now.

"I just told you I've been Mafia adjacent. You must know by now that means a specific type of family."

Italian, specifically Sicilian.

"Yeah."

"Did you know I lived in Boston before I moved to New Jersey?"

"No, I don't know that much about you, to be honest."

She offers me a soft smile. "Well, I grew up in D.C. while my dad was in med school, then doing his residency and specialty training. Then we moved up to Boston, where my parents are originally from. I went back after college when I got married. I didn't stop being Mafia adjacent until I moved down here. The ties that bind were finally severed when I married Enrique. But I know a guy or two."

Her gaze pins me in place. That sounded about as Guido as it gets. To fit the Jersey Italian stereotype, she just needs to be a short, overweight, balding, middle-aged man with gold chains.

"The O'Sheehans have a reputation about how they treat women. Drew's a chip off the old block. I don't know how your in-laws don't know that. I have to assume it's something they never learned. There's no way on God's green earth your brother-in-law would've allowed you to be with Drew if he fully knew what he's like."

"If Maks doesn't know that, how do you?"

She stares at me for a moment before she frowns. "Just like Maks must not know about Drew's family history, I didn't know you were the woman he was with. I knew he was involved with someone and had been for a few years. But your name never came up. Do you know how Drew came into his position?"

"Yeah, his dad died. I knew nothing about their family business until then. He kept it entirely hidden from me. I don't know how he did because I don't want to think I was entirely blind to everything. But I never suspected. It wasn't until he took on the role as boss that he stopped trying to hide things from me."

"Drew's father, Donald, was a shitty man who did shitty things to good people. He did one too many shitty deals in Boston, and it came home to roost. He didn't die of natural causes."

Her gaze still pins me in place, but now it bores into me like a jackhammer. Not only do I get the sense she knows how Donald died, but she had a part in it. Her expression tells me I shouldn't ask questions. That whatever I deduce is probably a fraction of the real backstory.

"Madeline, you can tell I'm familiar with Drew. I don't know him personally, but I know about his family. I know *a lot* about his family. What do you know about his mother?"

"That she's a retired librarian."

Elle snorts. "Librarian. Okay, I haven't heard that one before, but sure."

"I thought she worked at the public library."

"Madeline, that woman kept books, but they weren't the type you read."

My brow furrows.

"She kept the books that recorded everybody who did *business* with the O'Sheehans."

The way she stresses that word, it makes me think I've been stupidly naive the entire time I've known that family.

"Do you mean like a little black book of names and numbers and dates?"

She arches her left brow but remains quiet. That's exactly what she means.

"I thought women were supposed to stay out of things."

"Like how Drew kept you out of things?"

Touché.

Her expression softens, and it becomes motherly.

"Madeline, you only knew what Drew let you know. You probably pieced together other things without confirmation. But the absolute secrets his family wanted to keep are ones they'll take to the grave and would have even if you married him. The O'Sheehans don't get along with their Canadian neighbors in Quebec. They've tried expanding over the years into Rochester and into Buffalo and up along the St. Lawrence into Canada. They've stomped on the Montreal mob's toes too many times. Now that the O'Rourkes have a connection to the Tremblays, they're even more pissed and feeling even more shut out than ever."

She pauses and observes me. I suspect she's going to tell me far more than anyone else ever would.

"I know where they buried all the skeletons, Madeline. I also know who wants to dig up each one. There's more than one way the Diazes can make Drew suffer for how he treated you."

I stare at her for a moment before I lift my chin. "Javi can do whatever he wants to Drew, but only after I've had my turn. I want Drew to lose it all and see every bit slip away before he takes that last breath."

Until this conversation, I merely wanted to fade away and never see Drew again. I would've been happy to never hear his name again. But in no uncertain terms, Elle is giving me the opportunity for revenge. I can't think of anything I want more besides knowing Javi is safe next to me.

"Do you have a shovel or two?"

"Madeline, I've got every tool we could possibly need to unearth things that have been buried for generations."

"What do we go after first?"

"I need to get in touch with a couple of contacts. Do you know where Drew would be right now?"

I shake my head. "He could still be up in Albany and

sending men down here to deal with me. Or he could've come down here and is hiding somewhere."

"He believes Javier's family won't find him?"

"I don't know."

"Then that's the first thing I need to do. Once we know where he is, we can decide what to go after first. It all depends upon how easily he could get in the way. You can't overhear these conversations I need to have." She stands. "And it's safer if you stay down here. You saw me turn on the jammers, but that's no guarantee someone hasn't figured out where we are. I have to turn them off long enough to make the calls and wait for a response."

I bite my bottom lip but nod. There's nothing I can do, and it's not worth arguing over something that's none of my business. She might already know several of my secrets, but that doesn't mean I'm entitled to know hers.

I stay in the panic room while she heads into the main part of the basement. Once the door's closed, I can hear nothing. I'm left to my own thoughts, but I force myself to sit and count. I'm not trying to get to a specific number. I'm not even counting the seconds or minutes. It's something to focus on so my imagination doesn't run wild.

With the lack of reception down here, the burner I have doesn't register the time. I don't know how long it's been since Elle stepped out of the room, but she comes back in with a smile.

"I made some calls."

I don't ask for any specifics. Even if I wanted to know, she can't and won't tell me.

"You said your boys helped you make this into a panic room and then into a storage room. What are they like?"

Her smile broadens. We chat for the next hour and a half about her three adult sons. They sound like nice guys, but if she's Mafia adjacent, I wonder if that means they're full-blown Mafia. She tells me funny stories about them when they were younger, and she's clearly a proud mother as she describes them now. I tell her more about growing up knowing Enrique and what things were like with my sister.

The time passes faster than I expected, and it's given my nerves a chance to calm down after our fucking car chase. I can almost convince myself it didn't happen. That it was the product of my imagination. I know it wasn't, but I don't feel as panicked. I'll feel a hell of a lot better when Javi gets here. Fucking traffic. I refuse to consider any other reason's delaying him.

We pause mid-conversation when her phone pings.

"It didn't take my contact that long to figure out Drew's still in Albany."

She turns her phone toward me, and I see he's in his favorite bar. The TV on behind him has the stock market ticker across the bottom. I can see the time and date and know someone took it an hour ago.

She turns the phone back to face her and taps on the keyboard.

"I texted Enrique that I know where he is."

"Do you have any idea when that'll be?"

"Probably five or ten minutes after Javier arrives."

"How long do you think that might be?"

"Depends on traffic."

That could be five minutes or five hours since I don't know where in the tri-state area he's coming from. It's the same for Javi. I spoke to him before Elle made her calls, and he said he was on his way, but he's still not here. I swallow my frustrated sigh as she continues to talk.

"Madeline, with Drew still in Albany, there's plenty we can do to fuck him over without him knowing who's doing it. He might assume it's Enrique or Javier, but he won't be able to trace it back to them. He doesn't know enough about me to ever guess I could be involved. He won't think it's you because I doubt you have the skills or contacts to do what I can."

I open my mouth, but she shakes her head.

"Told you, it's a story for another day. We start with the Tremblays in Montreal. I have a favor or two to call in with them. What I can tell them about the O'Sheehans is information they'll gladly pass along to the O'Rourkes. Then Dillan can owe them a favor. It'll also keep me in the Tremblays' good books in case Enrique needs to have any dealings with them in the future."

My brow furrows. It's all so complicated when it exists in only half-truths and semi-secrets. The best I can do is remain quiet and nod.

"Do you know Drew's cousin, Jacob?"

"He's dead. He's the one who came for me up on the island. Javi killed him right before the second wave of the attack."

"Do you know about Jacob's son?"

"Yeah."

"They're supposed to initiate him soon, so it wouldn't surprise me if Drew doesn't push him to take out a big target."

That makes me consider the few initiations I heard about in the past. "You're right."

"Before all of this started, his mark could've been just about anyone. Madeline, I would guess dollars to donuts you're the mark. He's a good kid, eager to please, and eager to show up his father. However, once he learns his dad is dead, he'll feel honor-bound to avenge him. It'll only make him more determined to get to you. But he's a boy, not a man. He doesn't have nearly enough experience to go up against anyone in the Diaz family."

"Or you."

She offers me a half-smile, as though I've stated the obvious needlessly. I pretty much did.

"Drew's looking for a protégé, and he thinks this kid could be it."

"Madeline, you may be his mark, but he's mine. He's younger than any of my sons, but he's fair game. The moment he took up the O'Sheehans' banner, and especially once he agreed to the initiation, he made himself fair game. I know he's still young, so if you're not on board with that, then look away."

She doesn't say she won't put a hit on him. She's telling me to suck it up, buttercup.

"If Timmy is willing to come after me, then he's fair game for any of us to go after him." I'm resolute in my statement.

As we watch each other, I feel like I've found a kindred spirit. It truly is a shame she and Laura can never become friends because they were cast from the same mold.

"There's more we can do. Fucking the O'Sheehans over through the Tremblays and going after Drew's protégé are pretty big. Depending upon how long Javier will hold out will determine what else we do. I can make his life a living hell by getting every federal agency up his ass and out his mouth."

"I thought the rule was—"

I bite my bottom lip. I'm unsure how to phrase my question without sounding like I'm accusing her or lumping her in with an official membership into a syndicate.

"You thought the rule was to never help law enforcement. I'm not. It's not helping them so much as it is fucking over the O'Sheehans. It's not like I'm turning state's evidence. But I can drop some anonymous tips that'll push them in the right direction. I can have the FBI, ATF, DEA, and the IRS all pushing at each other to get to Drew's door first. Hell, I can even stagger it so there isn't a day until his death that he doesn't have a fed come knocking on his door. Even once Drew's gone, that'll still fuck over the O'Sheehans."

"None of them ever did anything to help protect me from Drew. None of them deflected his attention. None of them tried to shield me from his temper or the things he expected me to do. They were all willing to fuck me over, so they can all get fucked."

Enrique's known me since I was born. The idea of swearing in front of him makes me feel like a guilty child. I have no such hesitations in front of Elle.

"Then, regardless of what Javier does, we can set those things in motion today." She studies me for a moment, considering what she wants to say. "Just how far and deep does your hatred reach, Madeline? Because if you want the O'Sheehans gone, I can make them gone."

"You mean, like, *really* gone? Or just lose a lot of assets, so they're not a major player anymore?"

She chuckles, and it makes my blood run cold.

"Madeline, they've never been a major player in anything except the kiddie pool. I don't know what Drew told you or what he tried to make you think, but the O'Sheehans have been pretentious little fucks their entire existence in Albany. It wouldn't take much to have them replaced. And I'm certain Enrique has a preference for who would take over. It would certainly be useful for him if he chooses the O'Sheehans' successors rather than the O'Rourkes. I could tell him it's a belated wedding present."

I stare at her. Even with my sister's questionable ties to the underworld before she met Maks, I've never heard anyone speak like that. She's basically saying she'll kill off an entire family as a gift to her husband, who's the most powerful syndicate leader in the Western Hemisphere.

I don't even know what to do with that. The best I can do is shrug and nod at the same time. I don't have words for it.

"Madeline, this is one of those things where you have to answer me out loud. If you're not ready to do that, that's fine. Think on it. But a shrug and a nod aren't enough for me to commit to this."

My chin moves a few times as I prepare to answer, yet no sound comes out. I swallow and inhale enough to make my ribs expand.

"Let me think about it. Elle, you know what you're telling me now will go to my grave, right? I won't tell my brother-in-law. I sure as hell won't tell the cops or anything like that."

"I know you won't. You wouldn't do that to Javier because it would implicate him. And like it or not, anything that happens to this family would trickle down and hurt Laura because it would draw attention to her family too. Syndicate life is a four-party cold war. It's a war of attrition based entirely on mutually assured destruction. It's why the balance of power exists. These families may take turns being on top, but it's really a seesaw. What goes up must come down over and over. It's in everyone's best interest to keep that seesaw balanced lest both sides—or in this case, all four sides—fall off. The men talk big games about which family is the most powerful. It's no secret Enrique is the most powerful leader of them all. But even this family takes turns coming in first. Machismo and bravado might keep them from ever admitting that amongst the men. Trust me. It won't take you long to understand I'm right. Their posturing is as much about their ego as it is convincing the rest of the world they're too strong and too dangerous to come after. Drew thinks he can be a major player in this war, but he's not. He's just part of a proxy war."

"Sort of like how the Korean War and the Vietnam War

were really just battles in the bigger war between democracy and communism?"

"Yes, exactly. Fights involving the O'Sheehans are stand-ins for conflicts between the four major families."

I consider what Elle's explaining to me and realize I'm getting more insights than anyone else will probably ever give me. It's not that Laura will believe I couldn't understand this. It's not that she doesn't already know this. I'm sure she does. But if I stay with Javi, which I know I will, then Laura and I won't always be playing on the same team anymore. Even though we'll have even more in common than we did the last few years, this isn't the sort of stuff we'll discuss.

It'll lie between us. I don't think it'll get in the way or push us apart. It's something we'll silently acknowledge but can never really talk about. I don't want to think it comes down to picking sides, but Elle is already a Diaz, and she believes I'll become one too. As I look at her, I realize she's not actually old enough to be my mom. She's younger than Enrique by at least a decade, so she really is like an older sister. That's probably why she reminds me so much of Laura and not really of my mom.

"Thank you for explaining this to me. It's a lot to take in, but that makes sense."

I'm about to say more when a light flashes in the room's corner. We both turn toward it.

"Stay here. Somebody arrived."

Chapter Twenty-Six

Javier

"*Hermano*, it could be worse. We could be over on that side."

Jorge jerks his chin toward the oncoming traffic. It's the end of rush hour, and there are far more people coming on to Long Island than leaving it. So at least we're on the reverse side of traffic. But it still doesn't feel like we're moving nearly fast enough. Even though *Tía* Elle lived not far from where she and *Tío* Enrique now live, it's still over an hour's drive from Long Island to that neighborhood in northern New Jersey when there isn't traffic. We're nearly at two hours since we left the bodega.

I'm waiting for Joaquin to give me more information. He's had me on hold without any shitty elevator music to distract me.

"Joaquin, come on. Is there nothing else you can find?"

"I'm digging, but I can't make the internet move faster than the internet's going to move. I found banking records. I can see who's paying them. From the leapfrogging I did, it looks like the Tremblays have done some deals with them recently. My guess is the Canadians are only doing it as a favor for Shane, and some of that money will make its way to the O'Rourkes rather than staying with the O'Sheehans. I can see money going out. My guess would be for the shipment they just got last week from their brethren in Ireland."

They must be smuggling more whiskey than we realized. Booze or guns is what usually comes in through the Irish. Not exactly the most original.

"What about who just attacked them? Can you get into any of the CCTV's feeds?"

"There aren't any around them. It's a residential area."

It's not like I ever want us to be captured on a recording, but there are times when it would be great if the tri-state area was covered in cameras like half of Europe. Since we tap into all the city's surveillance cameras, having more would be useful.

"I need confirmation it's Drew who went after them and not somebody connected to *Tía* Elle and her old life."

Jorge snorts. "It's not like you have ever believed in coincidences."

I glare at my younger brother.

Even though I'm sitting next to him, I can see him frown and roll his eyes as he speaks. "What part of any of this makes you think it's a coincidence? Sure, somebody could come out of the woodwork after *Tía* Elle, but it seems pretty unlikely when you consider what's going on right now with Maddy."

None of us want to say wishful thinking since none of us would ever want something to befall our aunt. But lord knows we wouldn't be surprised if a ghost from her past life came back to haunt her—there's enough of those.

"Our guys gave me the plates already, but as you'd expect,

they're coming back fake, so it's taking me a moment. Javier, I know you need this yesterday, but I can only go as fast as I can go."

That's the second time he's basically reminded me this situation isn't entirely under our control. No shit, Sherlock. But I can't say that to my brother. It won't get us anywhere, and there's no need to be mean when he's already trying to help me. We can only do what we can do. But I feel like climbing out of my skin as I wait to see Maddy. There's a beep on the call, and I look over at the screen on my dash. Jorge and I exchange a quick glance.

"Joaquin, I gotta call you back. It's that fucking piece of shit."

"O'Sheehan?"

"Yeah."

"All right. Talk to you soon."

What the fuck could this piece of crap have to say that isn't just going to piss me off more? I hang up with my brother and click over to the new call. Before I can even say anything, he's laughing hysterically.

"Not a good day for you, is it, *amigo*? You've already lost one home. You're about to lose a second, and she'll be taking my cock up her ass before she falls asleep tonight sucking on it."

I look over at Jorge, but he's concentrating on the road as we merge onto a different highway.

If he's saying we're going to lose a second house, does he not know where Maddy actually is because *Tía* Elle doesn't own that home anymore? It's not ours to lose.

Does he think she's at *Tío* Enrique and *Tía* Elle's?

Does he think she's at my place?

Where's he targeting next?

"The shirt she was wearing earlier was much cuter than what she has now. Her bony ass barely fills out anything, but what she's wearing now looks like shit on her. I've seen scarecrows with better bodies than hers. Those drawstring pants couldn't be pulled tight enough since she has no ass."

He's goading me, but I refuse to take the bait. I won't respond at all, even though everything in me wants to scream she's the most beautiful woman alive. That if she was that unattractive, then he wouldn't want to touch her. But I know his comments are about control. If he were to get near her, anything he did would also be about control and not just lust.

It's disconcerting as fuck for him to know the type of pants Maddy's wearing. To see there are drawstring means someone got awfully close. It makes me wonder if he had more drones. It almost reminds me of the flying monkeys in *The Wizard of Oz*.

"You're wondering how I know so much. You're wondering how I got so close to her."

It's not like I think he reads my mind the same way Maddy does. These are obvious things anybody would wonder in this situation.

"She may have hidden from me for a while, but now that I've found her, I won't let her go. There's nowhere she can eat or sleep, even breathe without me seeing her. She's been mine, and she still is mine."

He's still prodding me, but I bite my tongue, hoping the more I let him speak, the better the chance is he reveals something we can use. Even though Jorge's focused on the road, I know he's listening just as keenly as I am. There has to be something he lets slip.

"You might have enjoyed her tight little cunt for a couple of days, but I've been fucking her for four years. And I'll be fucking her until I decide to squeeze the life out of her. You're a kinky fucker, so I bet you've already wrapped your hands around her throat. I'll do the same, except one of these times I won't let go. She betrayed me, and there's no going back. How you could want a bitch like her is beyond me. If she's willing to tell my secrets, then she'd tell yours too."

"You believe I already know things about you and your family. If that's the case, then antagonizing me isn't a good idea. I could just use what she's told me against you."

He practically cackles. "Who traded who? Was it sex for secrets or secrets for sex? My bet is she was ready to jump your bones the moment she saw you. She's always been a slut. Did you know she likes being watched?"

My right hand curls into a fist where it rests on the door's armrest. I don't know all of Maddy's sexual past, and I don't want to. I definitely don't want to discuss mine with her, but I couldn't care less how many guys she's been with. And the idea of being watched isn't something foreign to me. I'm not thrilled at the idea of anyone seeing her naked, but if that's something she's into, we can discuss it. Those thoughts aren't ones I would share with anyone—not even my brothers or cousins who are my best friends. I continue to wait out Drew to see if he tells me anything more useful.

"I can see Elodie. She knows we're here now. One of my guys must have tripped a sensor somewhere. I've heard she shoots better than anyone in your family."

"My aunt shoots better than anyone I've ever met. If she's looking out the window, then she already has her eye on her targets."

"That may be, but there are a lot more of my men than there are her. All it will take is one bullet through that window, then we'll be in the house."

I know there's no way my aunt has left herself exposed to be shot through the window. Maybe she wanted them to see motion in whatever room she's in, but she definitely hasn't allowed herself to become a target.

"It's a good thing her dog isn't here, otherwise, one of my guys would have already shot the beast. Fucking Cujo."

Constantine is the furthest thing from that rabid dog in the movie. He's a total gentle giant, but I wouldn't test him by getting too close to my *tía*.

"She may have taken the time to unlock the gate, but we had no reason to. Our men are already up and over. I can see them in the living room. We took out the guards following them already. Now there's no one to protect those two bitches. It's just a matter of time before we get into the basement. I'm sure that's where Elodie has the cunt."

He could be making up this play-by-play because he's given me nothing specific. Or these are things that could be happening in real time. I have no way of knowing, especially not when he described Maddy's outfit. He's still rambling as I notice lights flashing in the side-view mirror. I shift my gaze from straight ahead to looking at the cops approaching us. I hit the mute button, letting Drew continue to ramble.

"Fucking hell, this is the last thing we need."

"I'm doing the best I can, but I'm doing thirty over the speed limit and weaving through traffic."

"I know I'm not blaming you, but of all our fucking luck."

"Jav, they won't follow us into Jersey. Once we cross over, you know I can lose them on the side streets before they can radio in for a squad car to follow us."

I keep switching my gaze between looking out the windshield and peering in the side-view mirror, then glancing at my phone. I'm texting Pablo to get men over to Elle's house.

ME

Elle's house is under attack. Get men from tío's over there.

292

PABLO

We know. We got the alert. Men are already
headed over there.

ME

How far out are they?

PABLO

Less than a minute.

ME

Tell me exactly when they arrive.

PABLO

I'm watching the trackers right now. They
pulled onto tía's old street. They're about to
go through the gate now. How far out
are you?

ME

Five minutes

PABLO

By the time you get there, they should be
neutralized.

ME

They better be.

PABLO

Just get there in one piece.

I unmute the call. "O'Sheehan, if you had Madeline by
now, you'd be crowing like a fucking rooster. But we're cock
blocking you. You know you're not alone anymore."

"You don't know whether she's already dead."

"She's not because there's no way you would have her without
making sure I know. You'd boast about it and make her beg while

Sabine Barclay

I'm listening. Supposedly, you have men in that house. If you do, I'm sure they're nothing but corpses now. And why aren't you leading this mission? You sitting like a little bitch in some van two miles away, making sure nobody can get you rather than leading?"

There's noise in the background, and I hear a couple of voices. They're definitely not any of our men. I know this for two reasons. One, I can hear them. Our men would never draw attention to themselves like that. And two, the accents. None of what I hear is coming from native Spanish speakers.

We have guys from other Latin American countries besides Colombia. We have several Puerto Ricans and Dominicans as well. They have that unique accent that's a blend of Spanish and New York. That's not what I hear right now. These are the folks who barely speak English since they're fucking knuckle draggers. They definitely have Upstate accents.

All the noise goes silent, and my chest tightens. This could be very, very good or very, very horrible. I don't know which one yet. I point to a spot on the side of the road a block away from our *tía's* old house. Jorge pulls over as I take the call off the car speaker, then we move silently as we head to the back of the vehicle. He pops the trunk, and we pull out the tactical gear I have in our go bags. We slip off our suit coats to put on our bulletproof vests and shoulder holsters. We each slide a gun under our left and our right arms. We have one holstered at our lower backs, and we have knives in each pocket.

We slip the suit coats back on as we run back to the front of the car. Jorge has it in drive before either of us gets our door closed. It's convenient that our uncle developed the community our new aunt used to live in. Even though not every guy who works for the security company that patrols the neighborhood is one of ours, most have been there long enough to know everyone. My aunt and uncle met when *Tío* Enrique was on a run in *Tía* Elle's neighborhood.

Fortunately, it's one of our guys at the gate. He recognizes Jorge and me immediately. His eyes widen with a sense of urgency as he hits the button to open the gate. I know he has cameras for various parts of the neighborhood. Jorge winds down his window as we pass the guy.

"I haven't seen your ladies, but something's happening right now."

That means he hasn't seen them on camera or coming out of the neighborhood. That does nothing to reassure me they're safe. But at least it means they're not dead on the ground or been kidnapped. There aren't that many cars near the house, but there are three large SUVs along the street.

They must be ours, but we're not close enough yet for me to see the hubcaps that have our distinct markings. Because all of the Four Families use the same body shop to customize our vehicles, it's considered Switzerland. The only way for us to tell our vehicles apart in a hurry are the unique hubcaps the shop owner makes for each family.

I scan the street and look for cars that might have brought the O'Sheehans. I need to get a sense of how many men there are. Normally, we'd park somewhere away from our destination, but there's no time. Jorge pulls straight into the driveway. He barely has it in park before we're both opening our doors. He hits the ignition button and is outside before the engine is off.

I pull the gun from my lower back, ready to shoot first, ask questions later. Years of practice have Jorge and me moving together, taking turns looking forwards and behind us, twisting to ensure no one can sneak up on us.

"*Capitán.*"

I nod to one of our guys who hurries to open the back gate for us. Just as I pass through, I see a head of long blonde hair step out onto the back patio. I expect to see someone following Maddy, but she's alone.

What the fuck?

Nobody follows her out.

She steps onto the grass, looking around. I don't know if she saw me or not, but I spot Drew stepping out of a shadow.

"Bitch, if you don't want me to shoot you or your fucking bulldog, then get your scrawny ass over here."

"I'll come, just leave Elle alone. Leave all of these men alone. You win, Drew."

"Bull-fucking-shit. I don't win until they're all dead. But you might survive this after all. Get over here."

He points to the ground in front of him. He raises his gun and aims it toward the house. There's no noise coming from it, but I wouldn't expect there to be since their men will have silencers just like ours. I wonder for a moment where the fuck the new homeowners are. How have they not walked in on this shitshow? I may never get an answer to those questions, but I sure as fuck am glad they're not here.

At least I'm assuming not. If they were, I would know about it from Pedro, the guy who opened the gate.

"All right, all right, I'm coming."

Maddy runs toward him, her hands hidden at her side. The loose-fitting pants conceal what she has in them. If my heart was racing earlier, it's surely stopped now when I realize what she's about to do. I sprint toward her just as she draws back her right hand, then thrusts it forward, a knife going through Drew's belly.

He roars with pain, and his hands go around her throat. I see her twist and try to pull the knife free. It keeps him distracted. I know she only has moments to go before he stran-gles her. Her left arm rises, and she puts the gun to his right temple and pulls the trigger. Blood sprays across her, and he drops, pulling her on top of him.

His sightless eyes stare at the sky as he loses his grip on her neck. She scrambles to get off him and turns around. There's no surprise when she sees me, so I know she was aware I was there. She's lost her ever-loving mind if she thinks I'm okay with this.

Chapter Twenty-Seven

Maddy

I didn't spot Javi until I was almost at Drew. I had no room for error, so I only looked around enough to make sure I had a clear path to him. I was fully focused on my target. There was only one chance for me, and I had to time it exactly right. Otherwise, he would've gotten the gun and the knife from me. I'm an excellent shot, but I already knew his hands were far stronger than mine. When he would wrap them around my wrist and squeeze, then twist, there was no way for me to keep a hold on anything I had in my hand. I've learned that through plenty of experience.

I knew stabbing him wouldn't kill him instantly, but it would be much easier to penetrate the muscles in his abdomen than trying to drive a knife through his ribs over his chest. I wanted to stun him and distract him long enough to get the gun to his temple. I knew if I tried to shoot him as I ran toward him, he'd get off a shot that would kill me either before or at the same time as I fired my gun. I also wanted point-blank range with no room for error when the bullet entered him. Shooting him in the temple ensured I'd kill him.

I stare at his body as his vacant eyes look toward the heavens. I feel like I should roll him over so he can stare down toward hell. It only takes me a moment to come back to the present and drop both weapons. Hands grasp my shoulders and spin me. I'm prepared to defend myself, but I know within an instant that it's Javi. His grip is firm but not hard.

I gaze up into his whiskey-hued eyes, and the world feels better, but only for a moment. He's livid. I can't blame him, but he's pissed beyond words. He scoops me over his shoulder and hauls me toward the house. He says nothing to me as we pass through the back door. He says nothing to Jorge, who I spotted right behind him.

His men hurry out of the way, and Elle steps aside when Javi stops at the sink and grabs a towel, soaking half of it. He hands it back to me, and I scrub my face. I don't know how Elle found clothes, but she hands fresh ones to Javi. We pass through the rest of the kitchen into the living room. He keeps going until we get to the basement door. He carries me downstairs to the room I was in with Elle. The room I should've remained in but eventually abandoned. I'm trying to work through the story I'll tell Javi. It'll be the truth—but likely selective.

He doesn't quite drop me on the ground, but he's none too gentle as he lowers me. I glance at the clothes he holds, and I know I need to change. He has to dispose of the ones with Drew's blood. I hurry, then he presses my shoulder, silently instructing me to sit. I don't expect him to draw my hands behind my back, but he does. He holds my wrists together, and I'm certain this isn't kinky foreplay. I watch him reach into his pocket as he continues to lean over me. Before I realize what's happening, there's a zip tie around my wrists. Then he's doing the same to my ankles using some kind of combination of four of them. He picks up the towel I dropped, along with the soiled clothes, and is surprisingly gentle as he finishes wiping my face and neck.

"Madeline, you will stay put. If you move even an inch from this spot, I swear to all that is holy, you will not sit down ever again. I will spank your ass raw."

He says nothing else to me before leaving the room. The look he gave me while he issued that warning made my blood run cold. I don't fear him hurting me. That's not what causes my trepidation. I know he would never hurt me. I'm certain in his mind, keeping me here is the only way to ensure I won't endanger myself again. I can't blame him for feeling that way.

No, the look in his eyes makes me fear we're through, that what I did is too unforgivable in his eyes. I knew he'd be furious if and when he found out or if he saw me, but I didn't imagine he would end things with me. More fool am I for being that naive. It wasn't naivety that made me go out there. It wasn't a lack of considering all the things that could go wrong.

I thought through my actions, and it wasn't a heat of the moment decision. I doubt Javi will believe me when I try to explain, but it'll be the truth. Perhaps he'll believe my explanation, but I doubt there's any way he would agree with my rationale.

The minutes tick by, and I have no idea how long I've been down here alone. It's felt both interminable and far too quick when I hear the door open, then see him step through. If he's going to end this, then I'm in no rush. But if he'll listen to my explanation, then I want to be able to tell him my reasoning.

He's still not speaking to me as he cuts the bindings from my wrists and ankles. He helps me to my feet. I don't open my mouth, but he still shoots me a warning glare that keeps me silent. As we head outside, I realize there aren't any bodies in the house or in the yard like there were earlier. I look around, but I don't spot Elle anywhere. I don't know if she's upstairs or if she already left. I do wonder what they did with Drew. I watched her take out Timmy just as I came upstairs. So much for him being a rising star. He didn't make it through the first ten minutes of this mission.

We continue in silence as Javi takes me to his car. I wonder where we're headed. I figure it must be back to Enrique and Elle's house, which is only five minutes away without any detours or high-speed chases. I get in the car after he opens the door for me. His silence is nerve-wracking, and I want to demand he stop sulking and speak to me. But if he's not talking, then he's not breaking up with me.

I dart glances at him from the corner of my eye, and I can tell he's far calmer than he was earlier. I don't know if he's remaining quiet because he doesn't trust himself to speak, or if the silent treatment is part of my punishment. It's not so much him refusing to give me attention but knowing my imagination must be running wild.

It surprises me when we go past the turn for Enrique and Elle's neighborhood and get on the road to head back into Manhattan. We must be headed to his place. It's a solid forty-five minutes of silence. Once I know for certain he isn't going to talk to me, I rest back in my seat with my eyes closed as I let him drive us into the city.

We pull into his underground parking garage, and I look over at him. I assume even though he's pissed at me, the same rules apply. I don't get out of the car until he comes around to let me out. We enter the elevator with another couple. He maneuvers us so our backs are against the rear wall. He's positioned to step in front of me and shield me if needed. I don't think he's doing that purely out of a romantic sentiment for me. He would do that regardless for any woman.

His fingers brush against mine. I don't pull away, but I expect him to. Instead, his hand slips into mine, and he entwines our fingers. We ride up to the other couple's floor in silence. They must not know who he is because we stop at a floor we're not getting off at. He had to hit something on the panel, but now he enters his biometric pass code.

We continue up to the penthouse. The moment we're in his place, he doesn't quite slam his door, but it certainly doesn't close quietly. He grabs my upper right arm and yanks me back against him. He spins me until he can box me in against the door. Then his mouth is on mine.

His kiss is demanding.

It's overwhelming.

It fills every bit of my senses.

The way our noses press against each other, there's no finesse to this. I can barely breathe, but it continues on without any mercy. His hands roam over me touching as much of me as he can. His right hand yanks at the waistband of my pants. His hand drops beneath the material, and he thrusts his fingers into my pussy. His other hand goes up my shirt and yanks down my bra. He pinches my nipples hard enough to make me whimper.

He doesn't ease up even though he knows how much it hurts. He won't harm me. He would never harm me, but he definitely commands me. He doesn't stop me from running my hands over him as well. I want to touch every bit of him that I can. I have no idea what he was doing while I was locked in the basement. I assume organizing his men to clean up the mess left behind.

I know his fingers are toying with me. He has no intention of letting me come, but it still makes me whimper again. When he pulls them free, I clutch his shirt, hoping I can keep him near me, but he steps back. He still isn't talking when he leads me to the sofa. I squeak as he pulls me onto his lap.

I'm unprepared for the tender kisses he places across my cheeks and the tip of my nose. I remain quiet, letting him take the lead because I can tell he's still sorting through his thoughts. I won't rush him.

"*Chiquita*, I've been in a lot of situations over the course of my life that have terrified me. Times when I thought my mom would die. Times when I thought my brothers would die. My cousins, my uncles, and definitely times when I thought I was going to die. There has only been one other moment in my life that was worse than seeing you run toward Drew, knowing he was more likely to kill you than you were to succeed. It was the moment I watched a man murder my father."

That's more than just a gut punch. It steals my breath. I knew someone killed his father while they still lived in Bogotá. I had no idea he witnessed it. He must have been pretty young when it happened. Tears fill my eyes as I watch him. I can only imagine the pain he must have felt that day, so to think I caused him even a fraction of that is horrifying. But to know he ranks what I did up there with that experience crushes me. My lip trembles as the tears stream down my cheeks. That's not something I would ever want. I never meant to put him in a position where he would feel that way again.

"Maddy, I'm certain you have your reasons for what you did, and I've had to remind myself repeatedly that you've been in other dangerous situations. Hell, you were nearly killed today, more than once. But this felt completely different because you ran toward the danger rather than away. I'll listen to your explanation. I doubt you'll lie, so I'll believe it. But I can guarantee I won't agree with it, and I promise you I won't ignore the only consequences that can come from this."

I suck in a whistling breath as I freeze. My ears ring, and I don't feel like I can exhale or draw another breath. My chest feels like an elephant sat on it. I grasp his shirt and hold on as though I'm a helium balloon about to drift away.

"Maddy. Maddy."

I hear Javi call my name, but it feels like we're not even in the same room. His hands are on my shoulders as he gives me a little shake.

"Maddy, I'm not breaking up with you."

The words permeate the fog. He knew exactly what I most feared.

"*Chiquita*, I will punish you, but I'm not leaving you. I told you before I'm in this for good and that there are plenty of storms we'll have to weather together. I'm still upset with you, and I'm angry, but I'm no longer furious. But even if I were, that's still not enough to make me leave you. Neither of us is always going to agree with each other's decisions, but you told me you wanted domestic discipline, and I agreed to it. I warned you that endangering yourself was the surest way to wind up with a punishment. I can't think of a more dangerous set of choices than what you made today, so it's inevitable I will punish you."

"I—I—" I struggle to catch my breath and form the words to match my thoughts. "I figured you'd punish me, but I wasn't certain you'd stay with me."

"Maddy, I've been in love with you in one way or another since we were teens. If it didn't go away in all the time we've been apart, then it won't go away in the course of two hours."

"Yeah, but that was before I did what I did today."

"True, but I know you've been in other dangerous situations. I told you that. That wasn't enough to push me away. Neither is this, but it's something I can't and won't overlook."

The best I can do is nod.

"We're going to go in the guest bedroom. You will strip, and we'll start with a spanking and go from there."

"Javi, I'm sorry. I'm so, so sorry. I thought I was making the right choice. I didn't know you were there. I didn't know when you would get there. I knew you would. I just wasn't sure when. It was just Elle and me when it started. Then I could hear your men, or at least I assumed they were yours at first. It wasn't until I came upstairs that I was certain it was Diaz men and not some other syndicate along with Drew."

I watch him for a moment before he nods, encouraging me to continue.

"Elle and I already discussed what we could do to Drew. None of it involved me going to him and stabbing him or shooting him, but when the chance presented itself—"

I pause and watch him trying to tell what he's thinking as he allows me to explain. He told me he would listen, and that's what he's doing.

"It wasn't like the idea popped into my head, and I just took off. It wasn't like I gave it no thought. I did plenty of it. I knew Elle was capable of protecting herself. I know your men are definitely capable of protecting themselves and protecting Elle and me. I didn't take it upon myself because I thought there was nobody there to do it. It wasn't just about revenge, though some of it was about that. I needed him to know it was me. The dog he'd kicked too many times. I wanted to be the last person he saw before he died, but more than anything I wanted to know I could have some control of my life again. That he would no longer be part of it. That he no longer dictated where I could go, what I could do. That those choices were mine again."

I gaze at my hands in my lap as I gather my thoughts.

"I wanted to get past the fear I've lived in and know that I'm not as weak as he made me believe. That after all the times over the years he told me I was useless and worthless and that I was nothing but a pawn for him to move around, I could prove him wrong. But more importantly, to prove to myself that he was wrong. I suppose you could say I wanted to regain my agency, or whatever term you want to use. I wanted to feel free. I knew I would be free once he died, but I needed to feel free of the anchor he tied around my neck."

As I sit on Javi's lap, explaining why I did what I did, his hand strokes my hip and along my back and ribs. It's soothing and fortifying me. I'm not scared to share these things with him now that I know he won't reject me. However, it doesn't make it easy for me to sit here and wait to discover the full extent of my impending punishment.

"Maddy, I understand that better than most."

He looks toward the window, and I wait for him to continue, but the silence draws on. Instead, his hand continues to stroke my hip while the other wraps around my shoulder and presses me to lean against him. He strokes the hair back from my forehead and kisses the top of my head. He relaxes more the longer he simply holds me.

"Maddy, I told you I watched my dad die. Jorge was eight. I was nine, almost ten, and Joaquin was nearly eleven. Just a few weeks away from his birthday. *Mamá* was at work, and *Papá* was taking us to the movies. We'd begged him for a week straight to take us. My brothers and I knew the safety protocols, and we'd sensed there was something going on that was more than the usual danger our parents warned us to look out for. It wasn't like it was against my dad's better judgment to take us, but now I regret my brothers and I pushed so hard to do something that seems so insignificant now. We made it to the theater and had a great time while we were there. We got to eat all the snacks our mom would never let us have. It was the stereotype of a dad's day out. He completely indulged us and was the nice parent when my mom had to be the strict one, at least when it came to what we ate. By the end, all three of us had stomach aches, but we loved it."

He pauses to kiss the top of my head again, and I think that soothes him. He rests his cheek on my head.

"We were headed to the car with our guards. My brothers and I didn't notice the first guard to drop, but *Papá* did. He knew there was a sniper somewhere. He wrapped himself around the three of us and pushed us toward an alley. He didn't want us to go all the way down there because we would've been trapped, but he wanted a place where there were no doors or windows, where someone could creep up behind us. His men ran to block the entrance to the alley, but there wound up being two snipers who picked off half of them before they figured out where the hidden threats were. I watched a man fall out of a tenth-story window when one of our guys hit him, but the other sniper kept going. Then there were men on the street running toward us."

I rest my hand over his heart, and he sighs.

"Our SUV pulled up, and the remaining two guards and *Papá* hurried to get the three of us into the car. He'd just closed the door behind me when blood splattered the window. My brothers and I all saw it happen, but I was the one closest to him. I reached out, but the glass was in the way. There was nothing anyone could do. He died in order to protect us. He left himself exposed to make sure the three of us could get in the vehicle. He'd been our shield. He died being a dad before being anything else, but he died because he was in a cartel."

Chapter Twenty-Eight

Maddy

I sit in stunned silence as I listen to Javi's story. I can't imagine being nine and watching something so horrifying play out before my eyes. The Kutsenko brothers lost their dad to a grisly death when they were close to Javi and his brothers' ages. However, it happened while their dad was fighting in the Second Chechen War. His brother and brother-in-law were there when it happened, and they saw Kirill die. I can't imagine how horrible that was to see their brother step on a landmine, but the young boys weren't there to witness it.

Javi, Joaquin, and Jorge did. Talk about traumatic.

If I made him feel even an iota the same way he must have felt that day, I can't think of anything much worse than that. I cup his cheeks and offer him a soft kiss. It hardly makes up for anything, and I know it's not nearly enough to comfort him, but it's the best I can do since I have no words. They'd be useless platitudes anyway.

"*Chiquita,* I told you that story because I want you to know more about me. I told you that story so you'd understand just how dangerous it is to be near my family, but I also told you that story because I want you to understand you're just as important to me as anyone else in my family. I can't imagine surviving my *papá's* death all those years ago just to watch the most important person in my life now die too. That's more than I could bear. I don't fault you for your reasoning, but I still don't agree with it."

He eases me away from his chest, so he can gaze into my eyes.

"You got monumentally lucky because you were outgunned before my men arrived. If you'd tried that any sooner, you would've died before you even stepped outside. You did make it outside, and you even made it to him. However, it wasn't skill, but rather luck that prevailed today. I know you believed stabbing him was enough to distract him, so you could get the gun to his head. However, it was everything going on around you that was in your favor. It also was having all of us nearby in case you failed. Maybe Drew trained you a little to defend yourself. I know your parents taught you to shoot, but I guarantee nothing you know how to do matches what Drew knew."

He cups my cheek.

"Maybe you have no limits to what you would do just like the rest of us have none, but you simply were not matched in skill and strength to him. You were more likely to die for your efforts than not."

"Javi, I know."

"That means you were willing to take that risk—the risk of me losing the person I love. Risk Laura and your parents losing the person they love. You were willing to put us through that kind of agony."

I try not to let my temper rise, but what he says now is salt in a wound.

"Javi, you might very well be better trained than Drew was or were at least a match to him, but every time you leave to go do whatever it is you do, you put me in that same position. I've accepted that because that's who you are, and that comes with being with you, but don't for a moment act like I don't understand that danger or that I don't understand how you feel. I've watched Laura go through it when Maks has to leave. Now I'm going to live it too. I know you believe it was selfish of me to put you in that position, and it was, but—" I shake my head. "It's not like I want to say you got a dose of your own medicine or that misery loves company, but you do get some insight into what it's like."

He nods as he watches me. "That's fair, but as you said, I'm evenly matched with my adversaries, and you knew this from the get-go. You risking your life wasn't part of what either of us signed up for."

I swallow and nod. "I don't think I'll ever be in a situation like I was today. I certainly will never be in a relationship again like the one I had with Drew because you couldn't be more different from him. I accept all the things you're saying, and I feel guilty for how I made you feel. Hindsight being twenty-twenty, maybe I wouldn't do that again, but I don't feel guilty for reclaiming that freedom and feeling of closure."

"I don't expect you to. I don't want to take that from you. That's not what your punishment will be about. The punishment is about the danger, and I know in this case you couldn't get one without the other, but you could've waited until I got there. You could've waited for me to help you. I was standing right there. You looked at me and then went to Drew—"

"Wait, Javi, no, I did not see you. I looked around specifically for him and glanced for his men, but I didn't see you. Maybe you were there, but it didn't register with me."

"Then that's a problem in and of itself. To be that singularly focused without full situational awareness endangered you even more."

I nod because there's nothing to argue against that. I want to believe I would've noticed any additional threats, but I might not have.

"Little one, let's get your punishment out of the way, then we can take a bath together."

"Will it really be that simple to move on?"

"Maddy, I knew I would accept whatever explanation you gave. I'd even accept you not agreeing to a punishment, but you have, and you apologized. My forgiveness and acceptance are unconditional, but I think we'll both feel better after a spanking. It restores our balance. It gives us what we agreed to, and it'll allow us to move on from this."

I bite my bottom lip and nod. He's right about all of that. That's exactly what I want. I know plenty of people wouldn't understand this dynamic, but I couldn't give a flying fuck because it works for us.

I stand, and he offers me his hand as he rises. We walk side by side through the living room to the hallway. With his broad shoulders, it's a bit tight to continue down the hallway together, but it feels symbolic walking as his equal. It's not like he's leading me to my doom, or that I'm merely following him meekly. We're in this together, which is part of what accepting the punishment reestablishes or reminds us of because I did do things on my own rather than with a partner.

We step into the guest bedroom, and Javi lets go of my hand.

"It's not as though I think I'll be doling out punishments

left and right. This isn't the equivalent of a woodshed, but I don't want us to associate punishments with our bedroom."

He hesitates for a moment.

"Well, unless you want to move back to Albany...or move in with your parents, or Laura...you'd have to go to a hotel. While you make up your mind about that...I figured you could... maybe...stay with me."

His explanation is halting, and he sounds unsure of himself for the first time since he started talking to me when we got here.

"Javi, I definitely want to stay here with you, but being a guest here doesn't make it our room even if we share it."

His gaze locks with mine.

"It does when I hope you agree to make it permanent."

It's a moment before I nod. He knows that's not an agreement to the suggestion, but my willingness to consider it. It's a huge step to live with someone. And even though we've talked about our future being together since the very beginning, moving from the theoretical to the real is a huge step. I don't fear living with him despite my last experience cohabitating with a guy.

It's more that I want a minute or two to enjoy that control I got back today. It's not like I'd feel out of control living with Javi. Maybe independence is the better word, or freedom, or I don't know. There're no words I can think of right now that would make sense to someone else because it would sound like I don't want to live with him. That's not the case. I just need a minute or two on my own to breathe. Maybe next week I'll agree to live with him. Hell, maybe tomorrow morning. I'm just not quite ready today.

"Maddy, take your time. Neither I nor this condo are going anywhere. If you want to get your own place, then do that. If you want to live with your family again, do that too. Or we could find somewhere together when you're ready. Just know that being here with me—being anywhere with me—is an option."

"Thank you."

"Strip, and I'll be right back."

"Yes, Daddy."

It's easy for me to fall into that dynamic, not because I'm a Little and he's a Daddy Dom. It's not just because I'm about to receive a punishment, which would make plenty of people think we are in a DDLG relationship. It's not that at all. It's purely that I feel safe and protected by him. I feel loved and secure around him.

I heard the things Drew told Javi about me when they spoke on the phone. I turned on the intercom that was in the basement to get an idea of what was going on upstairs. Drew must not have known, or maybe he didn't care, or maybe it was even on purpose, but he stood close enough for me to hear that entire call. I couldn't hear Javi, but I know the things Drew said about me. It's not that I believed him, even though I'd heard him say it before. He'd still made me feel shitty at times about my body. Javi has never done that.

Javi steps back into the hallway, and I turn toward the bed as I take off my clothes and fold them. I don't know where he's going or what he's going to get, but I'm certain my spanking won't just be with his hand. My brow furrows when he returns.

I'm prepared to sink to my knees, but he shakes his head as he puts down an unfitted bedsheet and pillowcase. I watch as he twirls the pillowcase in order to coil it. He steps toward me and directs me to open my mouth. After I do, he secures it as a gag but then pulls it free and low enough so I can speak.

"Maddy, no matter what we do together, ultimately you decide if and when it stops. If you safe word or snap simply because you aren't enjoying a punishment or because it hurts, I won't be pleased, but it will stop. If you reach a limit where you truly can't take any more, then safe word or snap immediately. Don't try to take more than you can."

I nod.

"No, Maddy, I need to hear you for this. That's why I took the gag out."

"Yes, Daddy."

"We haven't had a chance to explore that much together. Do you have any hard limits?"

"Nothing specific that I can think of for a punishment. It's not like you've made me go out and cut a switch somewhere so you can cane me. I don't think you keep that sort of stuff here."

I raise my eyebrows, and he shakes his head.

"I zip-tied you earlier because it was all I had with me at the time, and I was too furious to speak, but I wanted to be sure you couldn't go anywhere. I didn't want you in danger again, and I didn't want you to see what was left behind while our cleaners got to work. I never set out with a plan to use zip ties on you, ever."

"I know, Daddy."

"I don't bring women here, so it's not like I have a stash of toys and implements sitting around. And even if I did, being intimate with you is not one of those moments where I want to reduce, reuse, recycle."

His lips twitch into a smile as I grimace. I definitely don't want to use anything that's been in another woman's vag.

"Thank you, Daddy."

"We can get whatever we want, whether it's something you know you already enjoy or something you want to explore, *chica*."

"Not just things I enjoy. I want to do things you enjoy too."

"I can't think of anything I wouldn't enjoy." He waggles his brow, and I can't help but grin.

"I feel the same way."

"In the meantime, these will just have to do. Snap for me."

I do, and the sound fills the room. Even if I were moaning, he would still hear me. After putting the gag back in place, he unfolds the sheet. He twists part of it like he did the pillowcase. I expect it to go around my wrists, but it doesn't. Instead, he creates a harness similar to what I might wear if we had Shibari rope.

It separates and lifts my tits, making them stand at attention. He draws the sheet down the center of my abdomen, then between my legs so that it splits my pussy. Only then does he draw my hands behind my back, using the last of the sheet to bind my wrists. Clearly, this was meant for a king-size bed, and I'm pretty short.

He turns me to face him before he leans forward and bites my right nipple. Once he catches it between his teeth, he tugs. I fight not to sway toward him but to remain in my spot. He pinches the other one, and the sensations shoot straight to my pussy. It hurts like a motherfucker, but not the kind of pain I want to avoid. Not even the type of pain I'd think someone would say qualifies me as a masochist. It's enough to keep my attention and remind me he's in control.

He reaches behind him and withdraws something I hadn't seen from his back pocket. It's a plastic spatula with slats. I'm certain he has wooden spoons, but I'm not sure if that would be too much of a stereotype or too painful or maybe not even painful enough. I'm certain he chose this implement for a reason.

He guides me to the bed and presses between my shoulder blades. I lean forward, my tender tits pressing into the mattress. He raises my arms, nudging me to bend them. It pulls the sheet taut, making it rub against my clit. It makes me want to writhe since I'm still wet and a little turned on from him fingering me against the front door earlier.

"This will hurt, little one, and it will leave marks, but I won't bruise you."

I nod my head because that's the most I can do. I inhale and brace for impact, but it doesn't come. I've squeezed my eyes shut, but now I open them and strain to see over my shoulder. Javi's watching me with appreciation.

"Turn your toes in."

I do as I'm told, and it naturally pushes my ass back. The first swat lands across my left ass cheek, and it makes me go onto my toes.

Holy motherfucker.

Immediately, another one lands across my right cheek. He alternates sides in rapid succession that burn so intensely I fear I'll hit my limit faster than expected. I didn't think I would reach a limit at all, but I might. As though he senses it, his hand reaches out and strokes my tender ass. He rubs away some of the pain.

Just as I breathe a little easier, his hand lands across both cheeks, catching me completely unprepared. I scream against the gag and try to shy away from him, but he lands another smack. I'd already stomped my feet several times, but now I want to climb across the bed to get away from him. I force myself to stay put.

I agreed to this punishment. It's not something he's doing to me. It's something we're doing together. He might be giving, and I might be taking, but it isn't one-sided.

I twist to see him better, and I can tell he's hard from the outline of his cock pressing against his pants. However, his expression doesn't match his dick's eagerness. There's an eroticism to this we both enjoy, but knowing it's the consequence of my bad choices tempers it a bit.

He eases me upright and turns me toward him. He shifts and brings the spatula head perpendicular to my chest. Rather than spanking down on each breast, he smacks each nipple head-on. His free hand is between my shoulder blades again, steadying me. I watch him as he studies me, ensuring he lands each one exactly on target. He tosses his tool on the bed, and I gaze down at my reddened and puffy tits.

They hurt nearly as much as my ass. He'd let me lower my arms for that, but now he guides me to bend them again, the sheet rubbing against my clit and between my pussy lips, reminding me of how empty I feel and how much I want him inside me. He undoes the gag, and I work my jaw and lick my lips.

"Maddy, how are you doing?"

"I'm all right. I can keep going."

"Do you need a break?"

"No. I'm ready for whatever is next."

He assesses me, looking at my chest and then my ass. He wraps his hand around the sheet where it lays against my belly. He pulls me forward as though it were a leash. There's a full-length mirror near his window. The natural light during the day must be useful, but it's dark now, and his blinds are closed. He's in one of the best neighborhoods in Manhattan. It didn't used to be, but gentrification has made Hudson Yards a highly desirable place to live. I'm certain with the blinds open, he has an excellent view out over the river and the bustling city below. For right now, we move to stand, staring at our reflection.

My blonde hair is a stark contrast to his deep chestnut. I used to be perpetually suntanned most of the time, but these days I'm far paler than I was. Even at my darkest, I'd still be lighter than him. I think we make a good-looking couple. Our differences are a complement to each other.

"Maddy, you're so incredibly beautiful. It's not just your

face and your body, though I love looking and touching both of those. Your strength and resourcefulness and intelligence are more attractive than anyone else I know because it's you. I wish we could stay like this so I can watch you and just enjoy."

"Daddy, that's so sweet."

He kisses my temple before he unfastens the sheet. He lets it fall to the floor before standing behind me and wrapping one arm around my ribs, bringing his hand between my tits and up to my shoulder. It draws me back against him, my tender ass pressing against his cock. His other hand toys with my clit, his index and middle fingers rubbing it while his ring finger and pinky dip inside me.

Just when I'm ready to shift restlessly, wanting far more, he freezes, his hand still on and in me, driving me to the point of my cunt burning with need. He slides three fingers into me, his pinky resting between my pussy and ass, his thumb just above my clit. He strokes the inside of me, close to my G-spot but not on it.

I tilt my head back, and he tsks.

"Don't look away. Watch in the mirror."

He insists I pay attention to how he edges me. There's no reprieve from it. I know he won't let me come. If he did, then it wouldn't be a punishment. I doubt he'll let me come at all tonight. He will, but I won't.

Around and around we go, him stroking me, then stopping, rubbing my clit, then stopping. I'm in a cold sweat by the time he pulls his hand away from me. I'm unprepared for him to scoop me into his arms. I wrap mine around his neck. He looks down at me, and his kiss is so tender that now both my heart and my cunt ache.

He walks down the hall to the main bedroom and takes me into the bathroom. I'm certain the punishment is done. He perches on the edge of the tub and pushes down the stopper before turning on the water. He squirts some bubble bath into the water. We sit quietly as the tub fills. The water's warm enough that steam curls above it. He turns it off when it's less than halfway full. I rise and help him undress. We hug, enjoying the nearness. The time it takes for us to strip him and enjoy the embrace allows the water to cool enough to be bearable. He helps me in and settles behind me.

"This is only phase two, little one."

Chapter Twenty-Nine

Javier

Maddy had relaxed against me when we settled into the water, but my comment jerks her away, then she freezes.

"Lean back, *chica*. It's not phase two of a punishment. It's phase two of this evening. The punishment is done. You took it so beautifully and with such strength and resolve. I know it hurt."

"Like a motherfucker, Daddy."

Her tone makes me smile before I kiss her cheek. I lap water over her chest and shoulders before rubbing them.

"I told you we'd take a bath together. I think we could both use a chance to relax."

"I love it. Javi, anytime I'm in your arms is the best time, but this is incredibly soothing. And being alone with you like this— I don't know—with a bathroom door, a bedroom door, and a condo door all blocking out the rest of the world. It just gives me peace we don't usually have."

"That's what I want too, little one. We need it, not just

today, but all the time. Your job is demanding, and mine pulls me in all different directions. I want to know that at the end of the day, not only will I come home to you, but that we'll have this solitude—just the two of us. It's our reprieve."

"It is, Javi. If a bath together is something we can do often, I'd love it. But even if it's not this, knowing you're who I'm coming home to gives me a sense of peace I've never had before."

I want to ask her if that means she'll agree to move in with me rather than just stay here as an extended house guest, but I won't push her. She needs to come to me when she's made that decision on her own. Too much has happened today for her to decide without me fearing she'll regret it.

"What's phase three?"

"I wondered when you would ask. I knew you wouldn't be patient enough to just wait and see."

"Definitely not patient enough to just wait and see."

"Phase three is me making you come for the rest of the night."

"You're going to let me come?"

I can't help but chuckle at her surprise. "Yes, *chica*. I didn't let you do it during your punishment, but that's over now. I intend for us to enjoy every bit of tonight, not just me."

She sits up and wriggles her hips between my legs. I groan as my cock presses against the top of her hips. My hands grasp her waist to make her sit still.

"Are you looking for a spanking of a different sort, *chiquita?*"

She freezes. "No, my ass definitely can't handle that."

That makes me pause. "Are you okay? Was I too rough? Was that—"

"Javi, if I wasn't okay with what you were doing, I would've stopped you. It's sore, and I definitely won't ask for anything

321

more tonight, but you didn't hurt me. I don't want you to fear that you did. Besides, the warm bath is definitely soothing."

"All right."

That reassures me, but I'm still going to be vigilant that I do nothing to add to the pain. From here on out, I want it to be purely pleasurable for her. I return to rubbing her shoulders again until the water cools. We step out of the tub and into my shower. I rub the shampoo through her hair as she runs the shower poof over my body, taking extra care with my cock and balls, which ache to be next to her cunt.

As she rinses the shampoo from her hair, I lather mine, making quick work of my short hair, so I can focus on lavishing her body with my attention. I run the poof I'd gotten out for her earlier over her body. I lower myself to my knees to wash her legs and then her pretty pink pussy. When she turns to rinse the suds from her, I cup her ass, gently spreading her cheeks. She pushes her hips back, and my tongue works from front to back as I finally taste her.

It's unbelievable how much has happened today. Being with her this morning seems like a lifetime ago. I've had other days where everything has gone wrong, and things have blown up—and not just metaphorically. I've had days where I thought they would never end, and I'm so exhausted I'm practically falling asleep on my feet.

But I swear I've lived at least five lifetimes today with all that's happened. But now I'm home with my *chiquita* where we belong, doing what we're meant to. Every moment I'm with her feels like it adds time back onto my life—something I need after what I saw her do today. She shaved years off of it.

I kiss each of her ass cheeks, which are still red. But just like I promised her, I left no bruises. However, she won't forget that punishment anytime soon.

"Face me, little one."

She obeys immediately, her palms pressing the wall next to her thighs. I nudge her legs apart before burying my face between her thighs. I do with my tongue what I did with my fingers earlier, toying with her clit, slipping it into her cunt. All the while, I stroke her ass with both hands, then over the sides and the front of her thighs, up her belly to her tits, which I'm also careful with. I massage them almost mindlessly.

"Daddy, please."

It's a whispered plea, and I know what she wants. I'm not edging her or giving her any more orgasm denial. Instead, I stand and lift her to wrap her legs around my waist. I saw earlier how she felt uneasy in Elle's clothes because they hung so loose on her. Whether she stays at this weight, goes back to what I remember, or gains more than that, I couldn't care less.

My brothers and uncles and Pablo all weigh around two-twenty, two-twenty-five. Alejandro's the biggest of all of us. He's easily two-forty but lean muscle like the rest of us. If I can fireman carry his ass along with everyone else's, then my *chiquita* is nothing more than a feather to me. But I wouldn't care what she weighs as long as she's willing to be in my arms.

I slide her onto my cock, and we both groan with relief. Then we're kissing again as the water runs over us. I have two rainforest showerheads angled, so we both fit beneath them. Usually, it's so I can soak under hot water, having it pound against my back and chest, or cold water to refresh me when I come in after a workout or a long day fucking up other people's lives.

Sometimes I'm in court, and sometimes I'm busting kneecaps. It just depends on the day of the week. My brothers and I are still enforcers whenever a more senior member fucks up. We have other men to handle the low-level soldiers. People know that if *Tres J's* shows up, they done fucked up.

But that's not what I want to think about now. All I want to think about is being with my *chiquita*. We revel in this moment of just being joined. But it's only a couple of minutes later that neither of us is satisfied without moving. Her fingers grip my shoulders as my hands grasp her hips to guide her up and down my cock. We'd both come sooner if I let her move faster, but neither of us is in a rush right now. We may both be eager to come, but neither of us wants this to end prematurely. I take a step forward, easing her back against the tiles.

"You're ready for more?"

It's somewhere between a question and a statement. She nods. I thrust harder, even if it's not faster. Each time I'm balls deep, I rock her hips, so her clit grinds against my pubic bone. I know this is what she needs. Her fingers flex and squeeze over and over.

"Javi, yes...Yes, just like that...More...Harder...Harder, Javi. Harder. Harder."

Who am I to deny her any longer? I broaden my stance and pound into her. If we were in bed, and I didn't worry about the hard surface behind her or me slipping, I'd be a fucking jackhammer in her pussy.

"May I come?"

"Yes, little one. I can't hold on much longer."

I can't hold on at all. Her legs squeeze my waist as her cunt contracts around my cock. Everything tenses in her body as her back arches away from the wall. I press her hips down, rocking her to keep grinding against me. As we come together, she goes lax in my arms and flops forward, her head against my shoulder. I know, from the way my kneecaps shake, I need to sit down in the shower or hurry up and get us out because I'm as spent as she is.

I push the glass door open only to realize I didn't turn on the extractor. The bathroom is full of steam. I feel like the condensation on the mirror stole my chance to see our bodies together. She kisses along my neck up to behind my ear before tugging on the lobe.

"Daddy, we can always go stand in front of the mirror in our bedroom."

I love that phrase—"our bedroom"—not just hearing it and saying it, not just thinking it and saying it, but hearing her acknowledge this is now our space. Something we share, just the two of us. I grab towels and drape one over her shoulders while wrapping the other one around my hips and over hers, fisting it closed. I head into the bedroom and lower her to her feet.

I hurry to wrap the towel around my waist, so I can rub her dry, but she pulls it open. She stares at my cock and licks her lips. We towel each other dry. I squeeze the water from her hair before glancing back at the bathroom. Since we have none of her stuff, and I don't know whether we'll be able to retrieve it from the estate, she doesn't have her regular toiletries.

"Wait here a moment."

I take the towels from her and head back into the bathroom, hanging them up before pulling open a drawer and grabbing what I want. She eyes the hairbrush as I come to stand before her. I see a moment's trepidation as she meets my gaze and cocks an eyebrow.

"Turn around, little one. Let me finish taking care of you."

She really thought I might spank her with it. I ease the brush through her hair, separating the tangles as gently as I can.

"Maddy, no more spankings tonight. Partly because your ass can't take much more, but also because I don't want you to think of anything else we do as being a punishment."

She nods and reaches back to pat my outer thigh.

"Thank you."

When I'm finished with her hair, I put the brush on the bedside table and draw back the covers.

"Do you want vanilla or kinky?"

She glances at my cock as I climb in next to her. It's coming back to life. The longer she stares at it, the faster it revives itself.

"Either. Both. I don't know." She grins at me, and I can't help but chuckle.

"All right, *chica*. Hands over your head. Cross your wrists."

"Yes, Daddy."

I slip out of bed and go to my closet. I grab four ties of various shades of gray. It takes me no time to bind her wrists together. Then I press her left leg up, bending it at the knee and hip. I use the second tie to wrap around her shin and thigh. I repeat that on the other side. She's spread and open to me. I take the last tie and make it a blindfold. I feather my fingers over her nipples and down her belly, skimming them along her pussy lips, then her clit.

I have a view of every part of her I want to be inside. I see how she's still full of my cum, and that's perhaps the most erotic and arousing thing I've ever witnessed. Every moment with her, every time we're together, surpasses the last. Each time, I think it must be the best it could ever be. Yet, it's not. There's always something more to come. In this case, it'll be her in the next couple of minutes.

I kiss the inside of her right thigh, moving up to the juncture with her hip. I kiss across the small landing strip she has above her pussy. Then over her belly to her tits. I kiss underneath and around and over and on her nipples. I kiss the dip in each collarbone, flicking my tongue when I move back down to her belly button. Then I ease onto the bed and settle between her legs.

"If having you blindfolded wasn't part of the allure, I'd want you to see just how spectacular you look to me. Your cunt is still full of my cum. It belongs to me. I can fuck it whenever I want."

"Yes, Daddy."

"You can fuck my cock whenever you want."

"I plan to." She says it with such seriousness I can't help but chuckle.

"You don't even have to ask, little one. Just take me out."

"If you say so."

She waggles her eyebrows above the top of the tie, and her lips twitch with a smile. I stroke myself until I'm completely hard again. Then I nudge the tip into her pussy, coating it before rubbing it over her clit, swirling my cum on it. I sink into her, and her neck arches as her shoulders press into the mattress, lifting her tits to me. I accept the invitation and lean forward, sucking on each. I don't thrust so much as coat my cock in my cum and her cream.

When I know it's fully covered, I withdraw. I use the combination as lube, lifting her hips, so I can press my cock into her ass. She relaxes, allowing me into her. She's so fucking tight I have to move slowly, so I don't hurt either of us. I know she's doing her best to continue to relax. I ease my way past the tight ring of muscle, stretching her.

"Do you know how hot you'd look with a jeweled plug?"

"I'd probably look hotter to you than to me, but if you say so, Daddy."

"Oh, I'm positive it's one of the things that will be on my Christmas list."

"Are you really going to make us wait that long?"

"Well, no. I'll probably come up with something else I want by the time Christmas rolls around. How are you doing, little one?"

"I'm fine for now."

"Does this hurt?" I remove the blindfold, so I can see her honest response.

"Javi, I want more. 'For now' means I'm being patient, but I ache to feel you move inside of me. Making me wait is its own type of torture."

"I won't deny you anything else tonight, little one."

I rock my hips before I withdraw, then thrust. We move together as we both bask in this intimacy.

"You're so incredibly tight, *chiquita*."

"You're so big, Daddy. I feel so full."

"You belong entirely to me now. I've had every part of you."

"You will always. Forever."

Our gazes lock, and while part of this might be dirty talk, I know we mean this all the way to our marrow. She nods, and I think she's telling me the answer to my offer earlier. This really is our bed now. That excites me as much as the physical feeling of being inside her. I continue to thrust until she writhes beneath me.

"Daddy, please more. Something...anything...just more."

I push up onto my right hand while my left thumb works her clit. I rub over and over until she can barely stand it.

"May I come, Daddy, please?"

"Yes, little one."

Watching her is exquisite. The flush that rises from her tits, up her neck, and into her cheeks. How tight her nipples are. The way she squeezes her eyes shut and opens her mouth in a silent scream that ends in a moan. She gasps before her eyes open, and she does her best to lift her hips, offering me all of her. It only takes four more thrusts before I fill her ass with my cum.

I'm careful as I lower myself, so we lie chest to chest. Our kiss is just as earth-shattering as our orgasms were. We both pour all our feelings into it. Ones that have developed over the years but lay dormant for so long. All the repressed and unfulfilled dreams we each had that now have the potential to come true.

I'm careful as I ease out of her. I free her from the ties and help her move her legs to get the circulation back in them and to loosen her joints. This shower is quick, just to freshen up. Then we're climbing into bed together. She nestles against my side, her cheek on my chest as her fingers run through the smattering of hair on my chest.

"I know you can't tell me much, but can you tell me anything that's going to happen next?"

It's a fair question, and one I need to answer even if it's only a fraction of the truth.

"Even though Drew is gone now, that won't end things. It'll embolden them even further when they believe honor requires them to retaliate, even though all we did was defend ourselves against their attacks."

"What do you think they'll do?"

I remain silent. She tilts her head back to look up at me before she nods. She knows I can't answer that question as much as I'd like to. Anything I tell her they might do will hint at how we strike back. That would make her complicit to the crimes. She's already entrenched in this life now, even before we reconnected. But I won't make it worse.

Just the opposite. I want her as far removed as I can possibly get her after today. I refuse to see her in danger like this ever again. I don't think my heart can take it.

"Will you have to go away for a few days?"

"Most likely. If it's more than three, I want you to stay with *Mamá*."

She pushes up her elbow, digging into the mattress as she supports herself. We stare at each other before she closes her eyes.

"*Chica*, I know you'd rather go to Laura or even to your parents."

"I made my choice, Javi." She opens her eyes. "And I don't regret it. I never will. But that doesn't mean it's easy."

"If anything happens, I need you to promise you'll come to me and my family first. Only go to Laura if you have no other choice."

"I know, Javi. You are my first choice. Laura understands. But I don't know your mom as well as I know my sister, so I think it's understandable why she would be my second choice. But I trust everyone in your family as much as I do you."

"I'm sorry you're in this position. If it's too much—"

"No!"

The word flies from her mouth. I doubt she intended it to be so loud, but her adamance is clear.

"Do not give me a way to back out of this, Javi. If I wanted out, I would've left already. I would've bolted today. It wouldn't have been easy, but there were chances for me to go. You would've taken me if I asked, but I didn't. I agreed to go to Laura and Maks's because you believed it was the right thing to do. If and when you tell me to go to my sister's, then I will. But I'm not asking during a crisis."

I brush hair back from her forehead as I roll onto my side and prop myself up on my elbow. My hand rests on her waist.

"There will be times where the hostilities between the Kutsenkos and my family reach a boiling point. But what goes on between the men is never meant to affect the women. It would be stupid to believe it doesn't. I hate knowing it may strain or test your relationship with Laura. And I hate knowing it means your parents are caught having to divide their loyalty. Do you believe they would stand by us?"

"Absolutely. I don't doubt that at all. Can we tell them anything that happened with Drew?"

"You can tell them as much or as little of your relationship with him as you want. They're not blind to who Laura's in-laws are. And you know your family has its own history. But you should decide how soon you want to tell them. Your dad is not a man without skills. If you tell him before my family resolves things with the O'Sheehans, he will rightfully demand to be part of it."

She stares at me for a long moment before she nods.

"I understand. I don't want any more people I love to be in danger. But I won't turn down the offer of one more person to look out for you. Just how involved was Maks's family?"

Again, I fall silent. I believe Misha's ignorance about Maddy's involvement in the O'Sheehans operations. But he still accepted the risk that went with associating with the O'Sheehans when she could be so nearby. Yet again, I also have to question Maks's judgment in allowing Maddy to be with Drew since I'm certain he knew Drew's reputation with women. I'm struggling, but I'll give him the benefit of the doubt. Maybe he figured the douche had turned over a new leaf, especially since Maddy was with him for four years.

However, as her big brother, he should've kept a better eye on her relationship. He might have trusted her, but he never should've trusted Drew. I'm hard-pressed to forgive him for that. I don't know that I ever will.

"*Chiquita*, there's a tenuous balance among the families. We know we can fuck with one another, and we can fuck each other over. But we never directly target each other now that so many of us have wives and children. There's no guarantee what may or may not happen if things erupt, but the goal is no longer to kill each other. Maim, maybe. Kill, no. There are a lot of unwritten, unspoken rules. But no one wants to leave the women of the Four Families as widows. I sure as fuck don't want to be responsible for that."

Her eyes water as she nods, and I know she's thinking about the story I shared earlier. She wouldn't want her sister to be in the same position as my mom. And I sure as fuck don't want Maddy to ever be alone like that. There's so much more to my mom's story I haven't shared.

Being without a husband with young children put her at risk. When my grandmother became a widow, *Mamá* and my *tía* and *tíos* were already adults. The risk wasn't the same for her as it was for *Mamá*. After my father died, my mother became one of the most desirable women in the Latin American underworld—probably in the entire underworld—not just because she's a stunning woman, but because of her family connections and the wealth my father left us that was independent of his cartel dealings. As a Diaz and a Cardenas, she was connected to two of the most powerful families.

My father's family runs Medellín, one of the major Colombian cities, and controls all the poppy fields in the country. My mother's family, *los Diaz*, have been what they are today for generations. The ruling family of Latin America.

More than once, there were kidnapping attempts. Men tried to pressure her into marriage, even threatening my brothers and me. Street gangs targeted my brothers and me. But if leaders of major cartels couldn't bend my mother's will, then piddly street gangs stood no chance. Between that and how gangs targeted Joaquin, Jorge, and me, we had no choice but to leave our home in Colombia. Once our *abuela* was no longer with us, there was little reason for us to stay. There are things about our life in Colombia that I miss, but not much. I don't need to miss anything with all my family being here.

I know Galina Kutsenko faced much the same danger as *Mamá* did, and that's part of the reason she and her sons fled to America with her sister and her family, along with her brother-in-law and his family. The difference was they thought they could escape the bratva by coming here. Escaping the Cartel was never an option.

"Javi?"

My focus settles on Maddy again. "I'm sorry, little one. My mind wandered, thinking about making sure I can keep you safe."

She inches closer to me and offers me a soft peck on my lips. "Nothing will be solved tonight, Daddy, so we can deal with everything in the morning."

Chapter Thirty

Maddy

Something rouses me from the deepest sleep I've had in ages. It takes me a moment to recognize the sensation. It's Javi's lips sucking on my nipple, then traveling up my chest to the crook of my neck. His fingers are in my pussy, working me.

I can't help but moan as I come round a little bit more. However, I'm so tired I can't get my eyes open.

Then I feel his cock against my pussy.

"Yes, Daddy...Yes."

Part of my mind is fully awake, even if my eyes still won't open. I force them to, and they flutter a couple of times, taking in how gorgeous he looks as he hovers above me, his abs contracted and his pecs flexing as he eases into me. There's just enough light filtering in through the blinds for me to see his muscular outline. I let my eyes drift closed again, reveling in the sensations.

"*Chica*, I couldn't wait till morning."

"You don't have to. I want it."

"You were so beautiful, lying here next to me. Too much of a temptation."

I slide my hands up his abs over his chest and wrap them around his neck. His lips brush mine, and his kiss is intoxicating. In my half-awake state, he moves inside me, thrusting as I lift my hips to match him. I dig my heels into the mattress for any leverage. He grinds against me, already knowing exactly what I love.

My hands slide down his back to cup his ass. The feel of chiseled muscle under my hands makes me moan. Everything about him is perfection. The way he takes care of me, the way he—dare I say—loves me, his intelligence, his humor, his body. All of it combined is better than I ever hoped for.

Certainly far better than I believed I deserved all that time I was with Drew. He's the last person I want to think about right now. My groggy mind returns to what's happening as Javi and I make love.

I'm still fighting to keep my eyes open. I'm not entirely sure this isn't a dream.

"Javi, am I awake?"

He chuckles. "Yes, not very, but enough."

"Can you wake me like this every night?"

"Gladly."

We continue to kiss as his hand massages my tits. Then I'm pulling him down to be chest to chest with me. He already knows how much I love to feel him pressing against me.

"Daddy, I'm so close."

"So am I, *chica*." He works my body into a frenzy.

"May I come?"

"You don't have to ask when we're like this."

My abs tighten as my body goes rigid, straining to get there. The first hints of my orgasm tighten my lower belly. Then the wave of pleasure radiates from my pussy upward.

"Fucking hell, Daddy!"

I don't intend to scream, but I can't help it. I think my mind is finally fully awake as my eyes snap open.

"Fuck, little girl."

He buries his face in the crook of my neck, and I know he's coming. We lay panting together for a moment before he withdraws from me.

"I'm going to keep all your cum in me. I'll wake up sticky with it on the inside of my thighs as a reminder."

"That's right, *chiquita*. A reminder that I can't get enough of you. I can't even make it through a night without being inside you."

"Were you really watching me sleep?"

"Yes. You're so damn beautiful."

I roll onto my side, and he spoons me, drawing me back against his chest. He creates a cocoon around me. He reminds me he'll always be a shield, protecting me from a world I'm still learning about. As I drift off to sleep, he kisses my shoulder.

"You're everything to me, *chiquita*."

"There will never be anyone else, Daddy, because you're everything I could ever want."

This time, when I wake, sunlight streams in through the slats, illuminating the room. I'm in the same position as I was when I fell back to sleep after Javi made love to me. I'm more fully aware than I was last time.

Yesterday's events are a jumble in my mind. They jump from one thing to another, almost impossible to keep straight. Drew's men found me at my hotel. They followed me when I bolted. Javi came to my rescue, taking me to one of his family's businesses in Jackson Heights. We didn't stay long before we thought we could hide on his family's private estate in Greenwich.

He told me several times it wasn't my fault—that the attack wasn't my fault—but waves of guilt crash over me as I think about the significance of that property to his family and how I'm the reason men violated that sanctity. Reasonably, I know it also had to do with the pressure the bratva and the Albany mob put on one of Javi's men. But I definitely still played a part in that. Returning to the city did nothing to shield us. Going to Jersey wasn't any better. Another chase and another attack. It shocks me that being in Manhattan has been the quietest place so far.

Shame and fear claw at me since I know this isn't done yet. Drew may be gone, but the O'Sheehans aren't. Javi and the Kutsenkos may have called a truce, but Javi won't forgive them. I pray it doesn't cause problems between Laura and Maks. Choosing Javi will inevitably strain my relationship with my sister. I can't imagine it won't. The weight of all of this is crushing me.

"*Chiquita.*"

I look over my shoulder at Javi. His hand runs over my ass, and it's so fucking soothing.

"You're thinking about everything, aren't you?"

I nod, a lump forming in my throat.

"Do you want me to listen, or hold you, or do you need space?"

He practically chokes on that last option. I know he fears my rejection now that we're in the cold light of day.

"Daddy, space is the last thing I need right now. The only thing that's keeping me from falling apart is you being here with me."

"I'll stay with you as long as I can."

I nod, but that's what finally makes the tears fall. Not as

long as he wants to be, not as long as I need him to be, but for as long as he can. Something might call him away from me. I don't doubt he wants to be here with me. However, the choice may not be his. It was much easier to say I could accept that yesterday when I was running on adrenaline. Now the aftermath leaves me depleted, even hollow.

He eases me to roll over and face him. He sits up, adjusting the pillows, so he can lean against the headboard.

"Come here, little one."

He encourages me to sit up too. Then he lifts me to straddle him. I could feel how hard he was when I woke, his cock tucked between my ass cheeks. I'm still wet with his cum from the middle of the night. He lowers me onto his dick, his hand pressing my head to his shoulder. We simply sit like this together.

This isn't about getting off. I rock my hips periodically and do Kegels to keep him hard even though I don't think I even have to.

This is what I need. The intimacy without having to explain myself. I need him to be the strong, silent type for me. He gets that, and I couldn't ask for more.

"I know Maks and Laura's is the last place you want to go, but there's no way my sister will calm down until she sees me in person. A video call isn't enough."

"*Chiquita*, I don't blame her. That's completely a reasonable request for her. And no, I never want to see Maks, and I especially don't want to see him now, but I certainly won't stand in the way of you being with your family. There's just no chance in hell you're going anywhere out of my sight today."

"Will it cause an argument between you guys when we arrive?"

"It might, but Maks knows enough of what happened yesterday to understand how serious we are and why I won't just drop you off. In the future, I would. You'll go by yourself, but for now, not a chance."

I lean my head against his shoulder as we ride in the second row of the monstrous SUV. I had a big one up in Albany, but this one makes it look like a little toy Tonka compared to what we're in now. These SUVs are veritable tanks. They're indestructible battering rams. I feel completely safe, which is the trade-off for not having privacy like we would in a town car. There's no glass separating us from the driver and bodyguard up front.

It doesn't help that Joaquin is in the front passenger seat, and Jorge and Pablo are in the third row. To top it all off, Alejandro's driving. It's not like all five of them showing up won't antagonize my in-laws, but the other guys have promised to wait outside.

There might be some staring contests and posturing, but Javi reassures me Maks's men who patrol his property won't instigate anything. The neighborhood my sister and her family live in is the Switzerland of the underworld in New York. It's one that nearly every syndicate family lives in.

Most of them grew up in this neighborhood, but Maks and his family didn't. They moved in after they bought Galena a house in the neighborhood, which was after all four brothers were out of the home. Maks had a house in Queens he and Laura sold not long after the twins were born.

They now live in the same neighborhood as everyone else. Enrique and Elle, along with Luis and Margherita, are the only ones in Jersey. Everyone else is in this neighborhood or the adjacent one. The mob boss lives on the corner that connects the two neighborhoods.

We pass through the community gate and make our way past several Mafia and mob houses and two other bratva homes before we get to Laura and Maks's. Alejandro's barely put the vehicle in park before the front door opens, and Laura dashes out with Maks on her heels.

I'm certain he's not thrilled with her leaving the house without a protective circle around her. Just getting me into the house without leaving me exposed to anyone driving by or another drone attack is why all five guys are here. Javi steps out of the SUV, and I slide over, but he makes me wait until his brother and cousin climb out of the third row on the other side and come around the vehicle. Joaquin does the same.

I disappear in the midst of these enormous men in their perfectly tailored suits. My sister disappears too as Maks's brothers and cousins filter out of the house. The men glower at each other, but they remain quiet. It's not until we're through the front door that Maks's family steps back and allows Laura to leave the center of their circle. Only Javi crosses the threshold with me.

Laura clings to me, and I gladly return the hug. I don't notice who's still around us, but I sense most of the guys are gone. When we pull apart, it's just Maks and Misha along with Javi in the foyer with Laura and me. I turn to look over my shoulder at Javi and follow his gaze to Misha. I shift my focus to the blonde Russian who's staring back at Javi with just as much disdain. I'm not sure what to make of the standoff.

Javi's hand rests at my lower back as he steps beside me. He smiles down at me, and I feel my shoulders lower. They were practically brushing my earlobes.

"Enjoy your visit with your sister. I'll hang out here. Just let me know whenever you're ready to go."

"You can't just loiter in my entryway." Maks practically huffs, but Laura shoots him a look that makes him shake his head.

Javi smiles at my sister. "Laura, it's fine. I don't want to impose, but we all know I won't go anywhere, so I'll remain unobtrusive over here until Maddy's ready to leave."

"Don't be ridiculous. You might be sitting alone, but you can at least go into the living room."

Javi offers her a gracious thank you before Maks and Misha glare at him one last time, then disappear into the office Maks and Laura share. She and I head into the sunroom where the twins are playing.

"Auntie Madeline!"

Mila greets me and slams into my right leg while Konstantin wraps himself around my left. I squat down to hug them both. They were certainly a surprise to everyone so soon after my sister and brother-in-law married, but I can't imagine Laura and Maks without their twins. The four of them are a package deal.

Laura speaks to them in Russian, and I'm certain she tells them to go to the playroom upstairs. I get a hug and a kiss from each of them before they run off together. Laura and I sit on the sofa, turned so we can look at each other. I'm waiting for her to unleash the tirade of questions I'm certain she came up with yesterday. It'll feel like a cross examination since she's still the best lawyer I know.

I'm utterly unprepared for her to burst into tears.

"Laura!"

I reach out and wrap my arms around her again while she shakes her head and swats at her tears.

"I don't know where the hell that just came from. I should be comforting you, not the other way around. Maks wouldn't tell me much yesterday. 'It's a developing situation.'" She uses air quotes around that last comment. "There have been threats to the family before, and you know we're all very close. The women who've married into this family consider each other sisters, even when many of us are cousins-in-law. I've feared for them over the years, but there's something vastly different—exponentially worse—when it's your actual sister in danger, and there's nothing you can do."

I cock an eyebrow.

"Yes, I know." She closes her eyes and shakes her head. "But you didn't know what was happening in real time."

"True, but finding out everything after the fact was its own kind of horrible."

"I wish you'd told me about Drew, but I understand why you didn't."

"I look back at it now, and I know there were times when I could've spoken up in person, and reasonably, I understand how much stronger Maks's family is than the O'Sheehans. But when you're in the thick of it, it doesn't feel that way."

"Mads, you don't have to justify anything to me. I understand. I won't question your decision about being with him. I'll do whatever you need from me, but I won't shame you for it or doubt your decisions."

"Thank you."

She stares at me for a long moment. "You expected me to do that, didn't you?"

I shrug. "You're my big sister."

"I am, but you're also an adult. I know you weren't thrilled about my getting together with Maks, but you supported me."

"Because I'd never seen you happier than you were with Maks, and now with the twins as well. Though it's not the same since I was miserable with Drew for so much of it."

"But you hid it."

"I did, and I will regret that for the rest of time."

"It is what it is. It was what it was, Mads. It's all right. The main thing is, you're moving past it. With Javier." Her smile is lukewarm at best, but she doesn't disagree with me.

"Laura, you knew how I felt about him. You never spoke up. You allowed me to have that secret. My feelings for him never went away completely. It wasn't exactly that they dwindled, either. They were just put on pause. Being with him feels as natural as breathing. That's how you described Maks."

"It's obvious just watching both of you. When's the wedding?" She grins at me the same way she did before she got me in trouble alongside her.

"We haven't set a date. He hasn't proposed or anything, but we've agreed our future is together."

"So, I can look for a gown and make sure it's ready for next week. What color should I pick?"

"You're so bossy."

"I'm practical."

I huff a pretend sigh. "Lavendar."

"Figured."

We laugh together, and it feels good to have a reprieve from everything that happened yesterday. I'm just hanging out with my sister. But I know we can't avoid discussing things. If Maks hasn't filled her in, there must be a reason. I know he consults her on a lot of shit he would deny ever discussing with his wife. If he hasn't told Laura much, there's bound to be a reason. That won't stop us from talking about what we can.

"I know you won't judge me, so I need to tell you more about the past four years. You know it took me two solid years before I was ready to move in with Drew. After what happened with my last relationship and how things fizzled when I thought we were moving toward marriage, I was hesitant to commit. He was persuasive, but I took my time. It was within a couple months of me moving in that he inherited his title."

I keep to myself that I suspect Elle had something to do with Drew's father's death.

"Everything changed. I didn't know what was going on at first. I thought it was grief that made him lash out. When I found out who he'd become, it infuriated me that he hadn't been upfront since Maks never hid from you who he is. But I rationalized that Drew and I aren't you and Maks. I tried to leave after the first time he hit me. His reaction made it seem like leaving would only make everything worse. Things settled down, and I figured we were back to normal. I didn't forgive him, but I decided to move on."

No greater fool was I than not to go to Maks when it happened.

"Even though I'm a midwife and hadn't patched anyone up since nursing school, he insisted I stitch up his guys when they got injured. After two guys died of wounds medical care could have treated, it progressed into me going on missions but staying out of sight. He claimed he didn't want to lose any more men to stupid shit that could've been cured in the field."

I throw my voice into a mockingly deep one when I repeat the bullshit he spewed.

"You can't 'cure'—" My turn for air quotes. "—GSWs and stabbings, but he made me go. He picked me up and shoved me into the SUV the first two times. Again, it was just easier to go along with it. There was an incident where a rival fired over my shoulder and hit a guy I was patching up in an SUV's trunk. I didn't think twice about grabbing the gun in front of me and shooting back. I hit the guy three times and killed him. Traumatized the fuck out of me, but I lived and so did Drew's mobster."

Laura's holding my hands as I confess my sins. I know her temper's on a steady simmer because Drew is already dead. If he were alive, it would be boiling over.

"I feared how Drew would react to me getting involved. It

344

was the nicest he'd been since I moved in. He was back to the guy I originally dated. But it was his usual subterfuge. Less than a month later, he coerced me into taking three duffel bags of money to Rochester. I didn't know the money was counterfeit or that I'd be picking up product to bring back to him. It shocked the shit out of the guy when I showed up. He didn't expect a woman. It made him suspicious until he realized I was far less likely to get pulled over after leaving a known mob neighborhood than if I were a man. It just went downhill from there. I became his best mule. I even negotiated some of the deals."

"You worked for the mob."

"Pretty much. After the shit I saw and heard, I didn't doubt Drew would target you, Mila, and Konstantin."

He sent me the photo of them at the grocery store. That wasn't the first time he used them to blackmail me. It just didn't work this last time because I had Javi with me.

"I didn't want to cause a war between Maks and Drew. I knew it would wind up being a proxy war that was really about Maks and Dillan. I feared it would explode into something way bigger, so I sucked it up."

"How did you wind up with Javi?"

"We had a chance encounter at the hotel where I hid in Brooklyn. I recognized him immediately, but I'm a lot thinner than I used to be. He spotted some bruises on my wrists that weren't completely healed. He came back to see me once he realized who I was."

I won't give away more than that because that's Diaz business.

"How long had you been there?"

"Nearly a month."

"And you still had bruises? What the fuck? I'll resurrect that motherfucker and kill him myself."

"They were faint, but you know these guys. You know they're more observant and recognize shit like that far more than the average person. If anyone else would've asked, I would've said my boyfriend and I were into kinky shit that got too rough. That tends to shut people up fast."

Laura nods and darts a glance in the living room's direction before cocking an eyebrow. I grin and nod. We giggle. That's as open as we'll be about our sex lives. She's never shared intimate details about Maks and her, and I would never reveal intimate things about Javi. But I've known she's been into BDSM for years, so it never surprised me when I figured out she and Maks are into it together. She knows I've preferred it in the past. Luckily, Drew wasn't into it. I never would've willingly given him that much control. Even during the good years—the first two—something kept me from suggesting it, so we stuck with vanilla. I'm far better sexually matched and fulfilled with Javi than any previous partner.

"When do you think the O'Sheehans will strike next?"

Laura knows like I do—it's inevitable.

"I don't know. Javi was taking care of something yesterday, but I don't know what. I fell asleep at Elodie and Enrique's and then shit went crazy. I didn't ask, and I know he won't tell me."

Laura isn't on friendly terms with anyone in the Diaz family, so it feels a little off to use Elle since it's a nickname. It's a little too familiar.

"Javi has his family guarding you around the clock, right?"

"Yeah. I figure it'll be like your family. One of the men in his will be with me if he can't."

She sighs. I know she wants to ask if I'm all right with that. If I think it's adequate protection. But she's trusting my judgment. That's saying something after the shit ton of errors I made.

"Javi's as devoted to me as I am to him. His family knows

346

we're serious. It's the same as when you started dating Maks, and his family realized you were Maks's future. They get what Javi and I mean to each other. They're as dedicated to my safety as the Kutsenko and Andreyev men are to yours."

Maks's cousins on both sides of the family were Laura's guards from the get-go.

"If anything like this ever happens again, you go to Javi's family immediately. If you need me to get you there, then I will. Only come to a bratva house if you can't get to a Cartel one. You have to be on the edge of death before you go to a mob or Mafia one, but you will get sanctuary until Javi or his family can get to you."

"I know, but thank you for confirming that. Laura, is this going to get between us?"

"It might make it tough, but I refuse to allow it to. I'm still as close to Michelle as I ever was, and she married Lorenzo. Neither he nor Maks ever stand in the way of Michelle and me hanging out. I don't believe Javi would ever keep you from me unless there was a viable and imminent threat. Just the opposite, I think he'll be like Maks and encourage us to spend more time together now that you're back down here. Are you moving in with Javi?"

"Pretty much. He asked, and I told him I needed time to decide. I wanted to breathe on my own for a bit. But I made up my mind last night. I don't want to be apart from him after all. Would you be comfortable coming to our condo?"

"Of course. And before you ask, yes, I will bring Mila and Konstantin when it's appropriate. We've known the Diazes our entire life. Fucked-up shit has happened between their family and mine. Things will change now that you're a Diaz for all intents and purposes. It can't not. You're truly part of Enrique's family now, so we'll have a truce. Juan was responsible for the shit that happened to me, not Enrique or any of the others.

347

Yeah, Javi and the others played a part in shit that happened to other bratva women, and I haven't forgiven them that. But this is just different."

I test the waters with my next question.

"Do you think bratva women were targets or collateral?"

"Mostly collateral, but that's because they didn't care enough to think about how it inevitably made them targets."

"Enrique's never changed his tattoo."

"He never will. No matter how I've felt about him, he's always been devoted to us as much as he was to Pablo and Juan. I think he keeps the J as a memory of the kid he once knew and the man he thought Juan became. He keeps our initials on the cross's points because he's never given up hope that he and I could reconcile. He's never thought of you as anything less than an adopted niece."

"What if I was collateral damage?"

Laura stiffens and once again looks toward the living room, but this time, I think she's picturing her shared office with Maks.

"Maks knew who and what Drew was and never spoke up, never confronted me about it. Did you tell him not to?"

"No."

"He never expressed any concerns about me being with Drew?"

"No. I would have gone straight to you if he had. He doesn't know Drew that well."

I stare at Laura. She's too intelligent to believe her husband, who leads the NYC bratva and pretty much controls all the Russian syndicates along the Easten Seaboard, doesn't know a mob boss in Upstate New York. I figured Maks knew who Drew was but chose silence because he believed Drew was an okay guy for me to be with, that he didn't know what Drew was like behind closed doors. Elle's comments yesterday make me question why Maks was never suspicious.

Before either of us can say more, voices float past the window. The men are speaking Russian, but I recognize Maks, Misha, and Sergei's voices. My sister's been a fluent Russian speaker since college. Her professor was a former Soviet instructor and dogmatic in making sure his students sounded like native speakers. She listens to what the men say as they pass by. Something catches her attention because she rises and heads to the door leading outside. She eases open the window to eavesdrop. I watch her before creeping next to her. Whatever Sergei is saying makes Laura clench her jaw.

"Should we be listening?" I more mouth the words than whisper.

"No. But I don't care. It's about you, so there isn't a fucking chance in hell I'm not listening."

She puts her lips to my ear to whisper all of that. She doesn't move away, instead interpreting for me. It's Sergei still speaking.

"We are going to lose a shit ton from this, Maks. I warned you something was up between Madeline and Drew. I didn't know what happened behind closed doors, but I told you it was something shady."

It's Misha who responds instead.

"It's my fault. Don't get pissed at Maks. I pushed for the deals with Drew to fuck over the Tremblays and the O'Rourkes. When we heard they were using a woman mule, I should've backed off. That it was Madeline only makes it worse."

Sergei's not done and isn't letting Maks off the hook.

"It was ultimately Maks's decision. You and I are not Elite Group members, but his brothers are. They should have spoken up too. I should have dug deeper for more intel. We're all guilty."

Laura's cheeks are a deepening shade of red as she listens. I believe she's telling me everything. I'm too stunned to react yet. She narrows her eyes as Maks finally speaks up.

"We got the information about the men working for the Diazes. That's what mattered at the time. How were we supposed to know Drew would turn around and use that to go after Javier while Madeline was with him. We didn't even know she was down here."

"Because she ran away from her abusive boyfriend. I should have kept a closer eye on her the moment we found out four years ago that she was dating him. We've always known what a piece of shit he was."

I can't understand Sergei without Laura, but his tone sounds distressed.

There's a pause before I hear Misha.

"Look, what's done is done. We can't undo it. We do our best to make amends without Laura or Madeline finding out our involvement. Obviously, Javier knows. We take it on the chin when he retaliates. Whatever it is, we accept it. I'll own that this is my fault."

I watch Maks sigh even if I can't hear it. "It's just as much mine. I'm the *pakhan*, and she's my sister. There were gaps in our intel, but even if she wasn't working for Drew, I still knew he had a history of abusing women. I should've known he hadn't changed. I should've known he'd take shit out on Madeline. How the fuck am I going to look Laura in the eye?"

My sister opens the door and stands where I'm certain Maks, Misha, and Sergei can see her.

"That's a good fucking question, Maks." She speaks in English for my benefit.

Maks's face becomes a thundercloud as he marches over to

his wife. If I didn't know to the depths of my soul Maks would never hurt Laura, I would fear for her.

"You know not to listen."

"You've never nearly killed my sister."

Maks looks at me before returning his focus to Laura.

"You're right. I took a chance and failed. I didn't know Madeline's involvement in the business, but I should've told you what Drew was like. I should've spoken up. I should've forced him to end things with Madeline. I should've done almost everything differently. But you have no right to listen to these conversations. You know you endanger yourself and the kids by hearing things like this."

"Maybe so, but would you have told me the truth?"

"Selectively."

Laura's jaw ticks. She looks at me as I stand here on the verge of tears. I don't want to cause a rift between her and her husband. I know it's Maks's actions that are to blame, but it's still over me. I want to shrink into the floor.

Laura takes a deep inhale, and I know she's forcing herself to calm down before she speaks.

"I know you don't make these decisions lightly. I know that whatever you did, you did for the bratva, not for yourself. I'll have to remind myself of that whenever I think about this. I hold you responsible, Maks, but I don't blame you. There's bound to have been far more going on, but that's no consolation when I find out that douche abused my sister for *years*. That whatever this information was that you sold him made him target Javier and use it as a way to get to Madeline. You didn't know she was with him, so I get that. But it still put her in danger."

"*Malyshka*, I'm sorry." He looks at me. "I will never stop regretting this. I'm so sorry, Madeline. I've called you my sister since I married Laura, but I didn't take care of you like a brother should have."

"I forgive you, Maks. This doesn't rest solely on your shoulders. There was plenty I could've done, but like you, I did what I thought was best for the people who matter in my life."

Laura watches me as I speak, and I know her heart's breaking. She shifts her focus to Maks, and I know she's conflicted. She wants his comfort, but she's still angry at him. He draws her out of the doorway and into his arms. She sags against him.

"I'm still angry, *solnste*, but I forgive you."

He rubs her back as she wraps her arms around his waist. I want to be with Javi right now. Laura looks over her shoulder at me and smiles weakly. She nods. She gets it. I retreat to allow them to have time alone. Misha and Sergei, who could practically be twins, even though Misha's a few years younger than his older brother, also nod. They turn around, and I head to the living room to find Javi.

Chapter Thirty-One

Javier

It's been three days since Maddy visited Laura. She wouldn't tell me what happened in the sunroom, but she came out and walked straight to me, wrapping her arms around me. She didn't appear upset, but Laura didn't look pleased at Maks. I figured Laura figured shit out or Maks told her shit that pissed her off. If it were just Maks, I'd gloat. But I don't wish any of Maddy's family to be unhappy. Maddy was quiet the entire way home, so I didn't press the issue.

We went to bed early, then I waited until she fell asleep before slipping down the hallway to my office to call Maks. It got contentious, but we came to a truce. He accepted that I will strike back, but I agreed not to do anything that could affect Laura. I've waited a few days, so Maks can wonder when and how.

He's about to find out.

"Is everything set?"

"Yeah."

Pablo's a trained biologist and chemist. We are Colombian, after all. It comes in handy for our family business. He's not the only one with a fascination with science. I may be a lawyer, but I also double majored in electrical and mechanical engineering. I've always had a fascination with physics. I can remember a hell of a lot more than the rate of gravity is nine-point-eight meters per second and Newton's three laws of motion.

In this case, if Maks hadn't bothered me, I wouldn't have been bothered back. An object at rest remains at rest. If he hadn't pushed me, I wouldn't be pushing back. When an object exerts force on another, the second object will react with an equal and opposite force. If he hadn't fucked up so badly, I wouldn't have gotten so pissed so fast. The acceleration of an object depends on the mass and force applied. I'm a big fucking guy who's big fucking pissed.

Right now, the laws of motion and gravity will apply to the fireworks my brothers, cousins, and I are about to watch. I built the explosives, and Alejandro set them with no problems. The Kutsenkos' security is slipping. My cousin shouldn't have approached the warehouse with such ease, but he did. Then again, Alejandro is a fucking ghost.

He's the biggest of us but the most light-footed. He can disappear right before your eyes. He's been like that since he was a toddler. He'd just slip away, and no one would know where he went. It would terrify *Tía* Catalina and *Tío* Matáis until they realized he usually went one of three places: the kitchen, the swings in their backyard, or his room to read. It's why he spends so much time going back and forth to Colombia. He's our best spy.

"In three, two, one."

The sky illuminates with a burst of red and orange. The noise is a cacophony of shattered glass, rattling metal, and bricks crashing to the ground. I grin like a fucking fool.

"That'll be inconvenient."

Even though talking is often my job as the family lawyer, I can be the master of understatement. This warehouse is their equivalent to our bodega. It's where they handled—blessedly past tense—the shit no one can see. It's where they disposed of their refuse. Now they'll have to find somewhere else to hide.

That won't be easy since we just bought several abandoned warehouses in Queens that we'll flip. We also knocked down ones that weren't on city records because they were already so fucking dilapidated most people wouldn't even look in their direction.

We watch the blaze for a few minutes, no feelings of remorse for the men inside who never saw this coming. When I'm certain nothing will rain down on me at those nine-point-eight meters per second, I stroll over to the blast. I leave a bouquet of seven *Flor de Mayo*—May Flower. They're really Cattleya trianae orchids—the Colombian national flower. There's one for each of us: Joaquin, Jorge, Pablo, Alejandro, *Tío* Enrique, *Tío* Luis, and me. A little calling card, so they know who's pissed at them today. Besides, I don't want the fucking Mancinellis or O'Rourkes claiming this win. Those fuckers would. Fucking cheaters.

It's broad fucking daylight as we drive away in our SUV. It takes some *huevos* to pull that off when anyone could have seen us—when men should have seen us.

"How soon do you think you'll get a call?" Jorge looks at me in the rearview mirror while he drives.

"Five minutes?"

"No. He won't call. He'll know about the building and figure out it was you. If he calls, he has to admit that not only did we find their lair, we also got one over on them." Pablo frowns and shakes his head.

We make it back into Manhattan without any of our phones

ringing, and we didn't get a call from *Tío* Enrique who sanctioned this retaliation. Jorge drops me off at my place, and I head up to the penthouse. Maddy was looking at hospital and clinic openings for midwives when I left. I'm not sure what she'll be up to now.

"Honey, I'm home."

I call out to her, loving the cliché since she agreed to move in on our way home from her sister's. She steps out of my office, and I know something is wrong. Did Maks fucking call her? Or did he make Laura call her?

"*Chiquita*, what's the matter?"

"My license is suspended."

"What? Driver's or nursing?"

"Nursing. I can't find any history of complaints or reprimands, but the state system shows it as suspended for misconduct."

I walk over to her, and she steps out of the way, pointing to my computer monitor. I move around the desk and take a seat. Sure as shit. She's not allowed to practice in the state of New York. I look over at her, unsure how she's feeling since I could only sense something was off.

Is she scared? Angry? Confused?

"Javi, I'm pretty sure I know who did this."

"Really?"

"Yeah. Drew's mother."

"How could she do this?"

"She might not have hacked the system herself, but she knows several people at the Board of Regents and State Education Department. They're who oversee midwives. We usually don't have direct oversight but rather are independent practitioners who work for a hospital or private practice. But we still have to have our license, and now I don't."

"Does it say what kind of misconduct?"

"It claims 'failure to report and treat' as the grounds. It doesn't give specifics about an event, but it states I didn't give adequate care to a high-risk pregnancy which resulted in miscarriage at twenty weeks. That's when a pregnancy is generally deemed viable."

"Did you search for any alleged malpractice suits?"

"Yes. Nothing came up, but I hoped you could check. I figured you can probably get into shit I can't since you're admitted to the bar here."

I pull up a couple of sites and do some searches. Fortunately, nothing comes up.

"It looks like she settled for this."

"Fucking cunt. I always disliked her, but I made nice for Drew's sake. Now that I look back on it, she probably resented me for my bratva connections. She asked about Laura a few times when Drew and I first got together, but he changed the subject each time. She tried when we were alone, but I mentioned it in passing. He got quiet, then she never asked again. Reflecting upon that, I think she hoped to find something to leverage."

"I'll have Joaquin sort this out. He'll get it reinstated by morning."

She shakes her head as she stares at the computer then looks up at me.

"That's not enough. She won't stop. They might have named Drew's successor already, but she'll still be eyeballs deep in their shit. She'll prod whoever's the new boss until they give in. She controls the books, according to Elle. If that's the case, she'll make life financially difficult for anyone who gets in her way. She's a fucking battleax. I saw how she treated Drew's dad. Talk about pussy whipped. Drew usually ignored and avoided her, so I didn't have to spend time with her often.

When I did, she fucking nagged Drew's dad like it was her fucking full-time job."

"We have things in the works, *chiquita*. They'll all know you're untouchable now."

"It's not like I don't take everything else personally. But this strikes deeper. I gave up my career because it was my choice. I knew I wouldn't practice under an assumed name. I accepted that. This is about her revenge for her son, for me dating her son, and for me escaping her son. You won't strike her, but I will."

"Stay out of it, Maddy."

She practically bares her teeth at me when she crosses her arms and lifts her chin. She hasn't been defiant since we reconnected. She's digging her heels in now.

"I won't tell you not to be pissed or want revenge, but if you get involved, I will punish you."

"Fine."

She's not backing down. She's telling me she'll take whatever I dole out.

I rise and push in the desk chair. I prowl around the desk until I'm standing in front of her. She's unprepared for how fast I move. I spin her and press her to lean over the desk. She's wearing a dress she ordered a couple days ago since she packed light when she ran away. My brothers went back up to inspect the estate. The surveillance was down, but there was next to no damage besides losing the garage. They brought back her bag that she left up there. Even with that, she didn't have a full wardrobe.

I flip the dress up and find her without panties. I crack my hand down, landing it across most of both cheeks. I spank her four more times in rapid succession.

"This is a warning. It's a hint of what I'll do if you involve yourself, Maddy. Stay out of it."

"It's better to ask forgiveness than permission."

The next swat is far harder than I intended, and I fear I went too far. But her comment infuriates me.

"You sorely underestimate my creativity, little one. I told you my forgiveness is unconditional, and it always will be. But that doesn't mean I'll forego punishing you. I'm warning you, Maddy, stay out of this. If you endanger yourself recklessly or purposely, you will find yourself under house arrest. I will lock you in this penthouse until I can trust you again. There is nothing I won't do to protect you, so don't push me into something neither of us will enjoy. That might break us, but I'll do it to keep you safe."

She freezes at my last comment before looking back at me. "You'd break up with me?"

"That's not what I said. It's more likely you'd leave me if I tried to imprison you. But I will if I can't trust you not to do something that'll put you at risk."

"Then help me."

I run my hand over her pinkened ass before taking her hand to guide her away from the desk. I know I'll regret asking.

"What do you want to do?"

"The money and product I buried. I want to go back to Albany and get it. I want your family to have it to do what you want with it. I know where other shit is stashed in the place I shared with Drew. Shit no one knows about. I wasn't supposed to, but he wasn't the only one who watched our place. It wasn't hard for me to figure out the login to the app he used. I'd wipe my activity on it, so he never knew I spied on him just like he spied on me."

"Tell me where to look and what I'll find."

"He never knew I added my biometrics to lockboxes and safes. Unless you want to blow shit up in a residential area, you need me to slip in and out of the house."

359

"No. I'll find a way to get the shit out of there and bring it to you."

"He had it sunken into the foundation. You can't take it out. That was the point. Apparently, he had a small team of guys work on the foundation. A fire burned some of the building materials at a warehouse, so it delayed the build. Really, it kept people away from the site while the foundation set and the slab was laid around these safes. He killed the guys on that first team, including the foreman. People knew they went afoul of him, but they never knew why. It kept his new team from asking questions. I found out all of this a few months ago when he was talking to Jacob. His cousin warned him about a potential raid, and Drew reassured him shit was so well hidden, the feds would never find it."

"If it's in the foundation, it means removing the flooring."

"Yeah, which is tile in the areas above the safes. There are lockboxes hidden in the attic insulation too. There's cash and drugs. My guess is also forged documents and identification. There could be more, but I don't know what. I know which tiles are loose and how to get them out without disturbing the ones around them. There was a power outage during a storm while he was in LA a year ago. I went into the attic and found the lockboxes and added my biometric credentials to them. We had a cable and internet outage six months ago, which meant the app couldn't record or transmit anything. I used that opportunity and him being down here in the city to deal with the safes. You need me, Javi."

It would be faster to take her up there, but I don't like it. We don't *need* anything the O'Sheehans have, even if I might *want* the shit. It'd be impossible to excavate the place without knocking it down first. Someone might notice.

I can have a wry sense of humor even at times like this.

"Let me talk to the others before I rule this out. I won't advocate for it, but I will share your ideas."

"That's fair. If you agree to it, I will follow whatever rules or instructions you give me, Javi. I want a long life with you. I'm not looking to end it because I fuck up the mission."

"You also don't want the sore ass and needy pussy I leave you with after I punish you."

"I definitely don't need those, Daddy. Thank you for listening."

"Always."

Chapter Thirty-Two

Maddy

It shocked the shit out of me when Javi told me Enrique agreed to me going up to Albany with the guys. You could've knocked me over with a feather when I discovered Maks and his family are coming too. I guess they have their own grudge to settle with the O'Sheehans after learning what Drew put me through. The bratva are going to shake up some shit and draw the O'Sheehans' attention to them while the Diazes—I consider myself one now that Javi and I have been together for nearly a month—ransack the house I used to live in.

It's taken three weeks of coordinated planning to make sure the plan is solid. I think it also took that long because Javi and Maks kept getting into arguments about how to handle this. They needed to walk away and cool off. I'm certain neither family encouraged them to simmer down. Just the opposite.

But here we are. Javi, his cousins, brothers, Enrique, and I just pulled up outside the house. Luis is back in Bogotá dealing with his and Enrique's uncle. Apparently, after all these years of house arrest, Humberto has reached the end of his usefulness. I think Luis is giving him one last chance. It had something to do with Elle, but I only pieced that together. I didn't dare ask. I took my garage door opener with me when I left. It was in the car I left in the underground parking lot in Jackson Heights. Someone got it for me, so I use it now.

Arrogant bastard. He didn't replace it or change the frequency. Not because he was too lazy or didn't worry about someone getting ahold of it and breaking in. No. He assumed I'd come back to him.

The door rises without a sound. He made sure the chain was always well oiled, and the door never rattled. How the motor makes no noise is beyond me. He must have left his car somewhere before he flew to New Jersey because both spaces are empty. That's how he got down there so fast. It's only an hour flight. We discovered Elle's contact was double dipping and delayed sending the photo, and he tipped off Drew that people were asking about him. That's why we thought Drew was at the pub when he was really on his way to Jersey. Elle went out of town for a day. That's all I know for sure. I can guess what no one told me.

Once both Diaz SUVs are inside, I hand the clicker to Javi. He closes the door, and we all pile out. Javi, his brothers, and I were in one vehicle while Pablo, Alejandro, and Enrique were in another. Technically, all seven of us could've fit in one SUV, but these men are huge. It would have been uncomfortable, even with me in the middle of the third row. It also means they have construction tools in the back of both. We weren't sure what they might need once we arrived. My key still works, and the fucker didn't change the alarm code either.

"Javi, there are cameras and mics all over the place. Do you want to destroy them before we get to work? Even if you cut the power, there's now an emergency generator backup

Drew installed after the storm that gave me the chance to go in the attic. There are four lockboxes in the attic you can bring down to me, and the safes can be accessed from the basement."

Javi looks at his brothers who nod and head to the stairs to lead them to the second floor. They'll take care of the surveillance devices up there. They'll easily be able to reach the hatch to the attic and pull down the ladder. Javi leads the way to the basement, his gun drawn. Even though I'm certain we're alone, he won't risk taking me anywhere without his weapon handy. Pablo remains on the first floor to keep watch and to find the cameras and mics there while Alejandro and Enrique follow Javi and me to the basement.

It's finished, so I point to the workout equipment that covers one of the safes. Javi looks at me in surprise.

"You moved that by yourself?"

It was a fucking struggle to move that. "I had to take all the weights off the rack, then move the rack. I was exhausted and sore the next day and needed a shower afterward, but I was highly motivated. The other one is over here."

I point to where we kept our Christmas ornaments and other holiday decorations. Moving those tubs was annoying but not challenging on my own. Javi tackles the tubs while his cousin and uncle handle the weight rack. They lift even the heaviest dumbbells as though they're as light as a scrap of paper. I nearly broke my toes a few times trying to lug the heavy ones off the bottom rack. I let them fall more than lifted them.

I remain quiet while the men work. There's no need for me to prattle, and they haven't asked any questions. They work in silence as well. Javi moves the tubs faster than the others move the weights, so I show him which tiles he can pry loose to access the safe.

"This one should have a cache of weapons as well as product."

I use my fingertips to press against the screen, allowing it to read my prints. We hear the lock mechanism slide free, and Javi opens the door. I don't know what he expected to jump out at us, but he's pointing his gun at the safe as he eases it open. There's a stack of handguns and knives like the last time I explored, but there're even more drugs than I realized. There're blocks of cocaine and bags of pot and pills. I push Javi back and slam the door shut.

"I don't know what those are."

My fear is they're carfentanil. The kind that's even more powerful than regular fentanyl, which can be used as a prescribed narcotic. Carfentanil is the type where you even breathe in a speck of it, and it could kill you. It's a hundred time stronger than fentanyl and ten thousand times stronger than morphine.

"*Chiquita*, it's all right. I recognize the markings on the pills and the bags. You're right to be cautious. Those are ecstasy."

"Are you sure? I didn't think they came in pills that look like those."

"Yeah, I know exactly which family they bought these from, and it wasn't anyone north of the border, and it sure as fuck wasn't the O'Rourkes."

Javi reaches in and pulls out a baggie, holding it up so Alejandro and Enrique can see. None of them name a syndicate. Since they don't volunteer, I don't ask. Javi empties the safe into several duffel bags. I move on to the one the other guys uncovered. I open that, and Alejandro does the same thing Javi did, a gun ready to fire if needed. I peer around Enrique's shoulder.

I stand gawking at the safe, trying to value the stash I see in front of me. This one is full of bricks of cocaine and marijuana.

I've never seen so much in my life. This was far more than he ever made me run. I can't help but be practically irate knowing all this stuff was in the house while I lived here. Yeah, sure, he had a cousin in the DEA to distract them and keep the target off the O'Sheehans, but that wasn't a guarantee. A different law enforcement agency could've raided the house while I was here.

Even though we weren't married, my name is on the deed. It was one of my stipulations to moving in with him. I refused to have no stake in the house in case we broke up. I wanted to be protected. New York is an equitable division of property state, so if and when we married and then divorced, it wouldn't have automatically been fifty-fifty. More would've gone to Drew than me since he paid cash for the house, but I still would've gotten something.

Not being married meant I would've been shit out of luck without my name on it. I wasn't prepared to do that. I wanted to know I could get some equity out of it if we went our separate ways. Now, I get all of it.

I know his mom and dad gave him shit about putting me on the deed since they claimed I would live rent-free and get something for nothing, but putting up with Drew should've been payment enough. He handled the household bills, but I still did my part when it came to things like groceries and incidentals. I cleaned the whole place every single week.

It wasn't like I was the queen of the castle with minions to take care of me. That was fucking Drew, and I was one of those minions. There's so fucking much I regret now, even though I try to tell myself regrets are pointless.

I look up at Javi, my eyebrows raised. He's staring at the contents. When his gaze shifts to me, he answers my unspoken question.

"There's close to a million dollars' worth of product in there."

"Holy sh—smokes."

I catch myself before I swear in front of Enrique. It still feels wrong.

"It surprises me no one has emptied out these safes. I assumed someone over the years figured out they existed, or he let it slip or confided in someone, but I guess not."

They're secrets he took to the grave, and now they're ones that benefit the Diazes. I can't think of a better ending to all of this. I notice the bricks have the same marking on them that the bags of pills had. Curiosity gets the better of me.

"Whose branding is that?"

"It's not branding so much as a tracking system. I know you figured out we recognized it. It's better if I don't say who it belongs to."

"Is it Maks?"

"I can tell you this much. No, it's not."

That makes me wonder if it's the O'Rourkes or Mancinellis. Nothing on the packaging gives me any hints, but then I don't truly know what to look for. It takes them no time to empty this safe as well. Once again, I follow Javier upstairs. Except this time Alejandro and Enrique go ahead of me.

I'm certain it's to protect me in case anyone should attack and go after the duffel bags. This way no one can trap me in between. Jorge and Joaquin are in the dining room with the lockboxes on the table. I'm quick to have those open, and Javi and Joaquin rummage through the contents. There are stacks of fake passports for Drew and even a few for me. There're more for his mother than me.

Of course, it shouldn't shock me. Weak ass, little bitch, mama's boy.

There's also a stack of envelopes. I'm not sure what they

Sabine Barclay

contain. Javi thumbs through them, and it turns out a few are fake birth certificates. Others are what I'm sure are forged or fraudulent customs declarations. They're in a variety of languages. I look among the men, and I sense they want to discuss something I can't be around for.

"Is it okay if I go up to my room and gather things I left behind that I still want?"

I watch Javi hesitate, but he winds up agreeing, knowing the others have already swept the house. No one is reaching me without going through them first.

"I won't take long."

"Take as long as you need, *chiquita*."

"Thank you."

I dash upstairs, not wanting to spend any more time in the bedroom than I have to. I look at the bed and would love nothing more than to burn the motherfucker. I move to the closet instead and pull out the clothes I like most. I lay them on the bed. I line up shoes on the floor, then move to the dresser to get stuff out of there.

Wouldn't it be funny if I took everything but my panties? Let whoever comes in here to clear the place out wonder why that is.

I gather everything from the drawers and put the stack on the bed. I sweep my gaze around the room to see if there's anything I want to take. I sure as shit don't want to take the framed photos of Drew and me. I walk around the other side of the bed before climbing on. I take down the crucifix my maternal grandparents gave me for my confirmation. Drew spotted it in my old apartment and insisted we hang it above the bed for good luck—that no one would kill us in our sleep. It felt like sacrilege to have Jesus looking down on us while we fucked.

I head into the bathroom, but there's nothing I want. I took

368

all the necessary toiletries with me. I just wanted to double-check. I make my way downstairs, calling out before I can hear the men.

"Javi?"

"Yeah."

"I need to get a couple suitcases from the basement. I didn't think of that earlier."

"I'll get 'em."

I recognize Pablo's voice. It makes me wonder what they're doing down there if I can't walk around the corner from them to go to the basement myself. They could just pause their conversation. If they don't want me to see, then it's definitely something I shouldn't want to know about.

Pablo's quick, and it only takes me five minutes to put my belongings in the two cases he brings me. Joaquin spies me struggling to get down the stairs with them, so he rushes up to help. I was so focused on handling the luggage that I forgot my pledge not to witness what they had out. There are scales and testing kits on the table, and there are three ficus trees nearby. I didn't see those get loaded into either SUV, but I'm certain it's how they'll transport the drugs.

I pretend like none of this fazes me, but it's a stark reminder I'm jumping out of the frying pan and into the fire by binding myself to the Diaz family, the most notorious and wealthiest narco-traffickers in the world. I remind myself no one in their family's gone down for shit, and Enrique even goes to the grocery store like he doesn't have a care in the world. He comes across as a typical—albeit hot—middle-aged man.

"I'm going to take you back to the hotel, Maddy. The others have an errand to run."

I can't help it when my gaze darts to everything laid out across the table. It's organized and neat. Clearly, they've done this before.

"I'll—"

Javi's interrupted by his phone ringing in his pocket. He pulls it out and checks the screen.

"Misha."

The bratva must be done with whatever their contribution was to the revenge. That or something went wrong.

"*Madeline está con nosotros.*" Madeline is with us.

Javi and I discussed my Spanish skills, and he knows I can understand some stuff. But most goes over my head. I can sort of follow a conversation, but I miss more than I get. Since I know Misha and his family speak Spanish along with Russian, it doesn't surprise me when Javi continues in Spanish after putting the call on speaker.

"*Esos pedazos de mierda bebedores de Chianti hicieron esto.*" Those Chianti-drinking pieces of shit did this.

Fuck.

I understood pieces of shit, and I know what Chianti is. He didn't want to name the Mancinellis, but I'm certain he's talking about them since he named an Italian wine.

"*Descubrimos lo mismo.*" We figured out the same thing.

Something about the same thing. It was a short sentence, but I don't know the first word.

"*Quiero saber cuál.*" I want to know which one.

Yo quiero Taco Bell. Quiero una cerveza. I want Taco Bell, and I want a beer are the only things I know how to say using *quiero*. One of those came from a nineties commercial with a talking chihuahua.

"*¿Alguna idea de quién?*" Any idea who?

I understood what Misha just said. They must want to know which Mancinelli got involved. I want to know that, and I want to know what they did and why. If I can't follow all of this conversation, I don't know whether Javi will tell me.

"*Supongo que es el segundo hijo.*" My guess is the second son.

Second son?

Marco.

What the fuck did I ever do to him? Does he even know I'm involved?

"*¿Qué quieres hacer al respecto?*" What do you want to do about it?

I didn't understand any of what Misha said.

"*Revienta toda su porquería. Supongo que le compraron esto para venderlo en Buffalo o Rochester y expandirse. Se arriesgaron a enfadar a los pelirrojos. No me sorprendería que no le hayan comprado desde hace tiempo. Probablemente así es como te pagaron por la información.*" Blow all their shit up. My guess is they bought this shit from him to sell in Buffalo or Rochester to expand. They risked pissing off the redheads to do it. It wouldn't surprise me if they haven't been buying from him for a while. It's probably how they paid you for the information.

Javi spoke way too fast. I didn't catch anything besides the two cities.

"*Tienes que descubrir lo que sabe.*" You need to find out what he knows.

"*No jodas. Lo haré.*" No shit. I will.

"*Manténganos informados.*" Keep us informed.

I understand the last thing Javi said and what Misha responded with. Javi basically grunts. He's not promising the bratva anything more.

"*Como sea. Guarda tus secretos. Vaciamos sus cuentas. Los bancos están vacíos. También las cajas fuertes de sus restaurantes y clubes de striptease. Conseguimos lo que buscábamos. Están desesperados por averiguar qué pasó.*" Whatever. Keep your secrets. We cleared out their accounts. The banks are empty. So are the safes in their restaurants and strip clubs. We

371

got what we came for. They're scrambling to figure out what just happened.

"*Gracias.*"

Javi sounds seriously pained to say thank you to Misha.

"*De nada, cabrón.*" You're welcome, asshole.

"*Vete a la mierda.*" Fuck off.

They end the call with Misha laughing. They just hang up on each other. I'm certain countless calls have ended that way.

"Let's head to the hotel then the airport."

We flew up here. A few of their men drove up in the SUVs. They set off before dawn to meet us here. They're waiting down the block just in case. Javi and his family wanted their custom vehicles as a precaution. Better safe than sorry.

Chapter Thirty-Three

Javier

We made it back from Albany last night without incident. I didn't love having Maddy with us, but it wound up profitable. The stuff in the safe was a windfall we already have out for distribution. The money's in our offshore accounts. We know the bratva did more than just steal a shit ton of money—though not as much as the street value of the stuff we took—they also ransacked several O'Sheehan establishments. They took them down to the studs. It'll be an expensive endeavor with a lot of scrambled answers and lies to explain what happened.

It pissed Maks off to discover their warehouse was gone, but he accepted our reprisal. We worked together in Albany, but that's only because we had separate tasks. The truce was temporary. No one in my family is looking to be buddy-buddy with them, and the feeling is still mutual. But those portions of the problem—the O'Sheehans and the bratva—are resolved. It's the Mancinellis who still need their asses handed to them.

I'm at Joaquin's while he's been digging to find out what the deal is. As best we can tell, Marco wanted to expand the Mancinellis' influence upstate because he's in a snit over something Shane and Sean did. The twins bought stock in a biotech company he wanted, then flipped their shares for a hefty profit, which is what Marco planned. To get back at them, he wanted to give Drew a bigger share of the market. He also wanted the Albany Italians to remember the Mancinellis are either with them or against them. I don't know what they did to piss off Salvatore—I couldn't give a shit—but they're against the Scarpacis right now.

"Do you know whether Marco was aware of Maddy?"

"As best I can tell, he knew there was a woman running drugs, but I don't think he knew it was Madeline."

"He knew there was a woman who could've been caught in the crossfire."

"Yeah, but you know how that goes. They're one step below female mercenaries who are completely fair game. We try to avoid the female mules, but they know the risks they take."

He's right, but I hate hearing it since it reminds me of how much danger Maddy faced. I think she was only aware of the threat law enforcement posed. I don't think she fully realized she could've died at the hands of a rival, and it would've been deemed justifiable if it wasn't just killing for the sake of killing. That's fine for a male mark, but women aren't supposed to be targeted to send a point or for shits and giggles.

"So, you got nothing that links Marco to Maddy?"

"I might. Nothing I've found indicates Marco knew Madeline was involved with Drew. However, there is a text where Drew says 'My girl'll take it out there. She's good. She knows what'll happen if she fucks it up. She learned fast not to piss me off now that we live together.'"

"Marco still did fucking business with the *malparido ñero*, even though he just confessed to abusing his girlfriend."

There's not an equivalent English word for *malparido* which means badly born. The closest is despicable. Ñero suits Drew since he was a lowlife criminal.

"We've been accused of a lot of shit over the years, *hermanito*, but we've never supported anyone we know abuses women. Marco turned a blind eye to it. What're you going to do about it?"

Little brother. Joaquin's called Jorge and me that since we were kids. He started after *Mamá* forbade him from calling us babies when we were each at an age where that word is super triggering. What toddler wants to be called a baby? Now, it's said with affection.

"I have to tread carefully. He's married to Laura's best friend's sister. That ties Elizabeth to Maddy. They've known each other since they were kids. I can't do anything that might affect his wife."

I think about it for a moment before I laugh.

"That fucker won't have his new polo pony for the match next week. He'll lose his ever-loving shit when I ride onto the field with it."

As much as things change, they stay the same. The O'Rourkes, Mancinellis, and *los Diaz* competed against each other in peewee and little league sports. My brothers and I didn't arrive in the States until we were too old for that, but we played club sports. Since, in a fucked-up turn of events, we all went to high school together, many of us played on the same teams. Marco and I wrestled the same weight class, so we scrimmaged all the time. Dumbass coach never took a hint what a bad idea that was.

We both started riding polo ponies when we were four. We had polo mallets in our hands before we were seven. I wound up joining the same polo club as him when we moved here. We lasted a month on the same team. We bet each other who could score more in a game. His ass wound up finding a new team after playing for the same club since he was in elementary school.

"That's going to piss him off more than anything. He had that horse bred specifically for him, and he's been waiting for it to be trained and ready for five years. Promise me, you save me the best seat!"

"Second best. I want Maddy to see me in all my glory. I gotta go. I have calls to make."

"I'll fucking kill you, motherfucker."

"Good morning, Marco."

My grin stretches ear to ear. Shit eating is what I heard it called when I moved here.

"That's my fucking horse."

"Mmm. No. I have papers that say otherwise."

"Fucking forged ones."

"Possession is nine-tenths of the law. My ass in this saddle on Mercury's back says he's mine."

Mercury—the Roman god of several things, including thieves. Fucking poetic justice.

"I'm serious, Javier. Give me back my pony."

I snort.

"Do you hear yourself. Do you know how ridiculous you sound at your age?"

I nudge the horse past him, tempted to take my foot out of the stirrup to kick him. Too many people around for that. I make the horse practically prance before swinging out his hindquarters as I turn him around. So far, he's the best trained horse I've ever ridden. We'll see how he performs on the field, but just grooming, saddling, mounting, and now walking him tells me he'll be excellent.

I smirk as I ride past Marco, who has no horse today. He didn't know he lost the trusty steed until he arrived. He'd put a down payment on the horse, if you will, contingent on it being trained well enough to compete. Before he made the final payment, I swooped in. The bank draw was supposed to go through once Marco checked over the animal. I went to the stables three days ago. Bribed the fuck out of the stablemaster to not say a damn thing about me looking at the horse. Then I paid twice the agreed-upon price to the breeder. It cost me half a million dollars, but I recently came into some money. Thank you, Drew. May you rest in hell.

We sent men to the cemetery to retrieve what Maddy buried. I wouldn't agree to her being somewhere so exposed. We came home with that bounty too. It's what paid for my new mount. We definitely came out the winner that day. Since getting back to New York, I've had a lengthy conversation with the Albany mob's new leader. Granted I had to wait until Dillan was done housebreaking him, but he understands Maddy is completely off limits. He's likely to always walk with a limp after I had his shin broken in three places with a hammer. *Misery* was such an inspiring movie.

I wave to Maddy as I ride onto the field. Then I'm focused for the next two hours. It's a long game with seven chukkers— periods. Mercury and I are exhausted, but we won. It's the cherry on top since I scored the most points. Marco looks ready to murder me as Maddy showers me with kisses after cheering for me during the entire match. Elizabeth looks nearly as pissed as Marco until she has to be gracious when they walk past Maddy and me. She congratulates me with a grimace, but she's genuinely warm to Maddy.

"Watching you ride that horse was exhilarating, Daddy."

Maddy's whispering in my ear as we walk to the clubhouse for the post-match celebration.

"Do you want to go for a ride?"

When our gazes meet, she knows I'm not talking about my horse.

"There's definitely a stallion I plan to mount." She waggles her eyebrows at me.

"*Chiquita*, these bloody pants are too tight to make jokes like that around me."

"Who's kidding?"

"One glass of champagne, *chiquita*, then we're leaving."

"Party pooper."

"You can award the winner at home."

My hand slides low on her hip as I give it a squeeze. Her arm's wrapped around my waist as she leans into me.

"To the victor goes the spoils, Daddy."

Epilogue

Maddy

"Javi, would you stop?!"

I swat my husband's hand away from the *tres leches* cake *Tía* Margherita brought over for our son's fourth birthday. Apparently, she was the favorite snack mom because she'd bring cakes to peewee soccer games whenever it was a kid's birthday. It meant a field full of kids went home on a sugar high at least once a month.

"If you won't let me have this cream, then there's a different kind I want."

"You already had two servings of that today."

Javi still wakes me often in the middle of the night despite having been together for eight years.

"*Mamá?*"

"*Sí*, Josue."

"Don't let *Papá* eat all my cake like last year."

We named our son after the grandfather Javi never got to meet. He was Luciana, Catalina, Luis, and Enrique's father.

379

Apparently, Javi bears the closest resemblance to him, and our little one is the spitting image of his father.

"*Papá* didn't eat all your cake, *mijo*."

"But I heard you tell *Papá* that last year that he left you wanting more."

Javi chokes on his laughter, and I'm glad Josue is too young to understand what he overheard. Otherwise, my face would be on fire.

We're saved when Elle joins us at the table in the backyard. She's trying to smother her giggle, but she can't.

"Josue, *Tío* Enrique promised to take you to see your pony before everyone arrives. Are you ready?"

"*Sí, Tía!*"

He runs as fast as his little legs can carry him toward Enrique, who swings him up onto his shoulders. He's been like a surrogate grandfather to all the kids in Josue's generation. He loves every moment of it. Elle isn't far behind him as she joins them.

"Did you send that photo to Marco?"

"Yes. Salt in the wound, and I loved it."

"It wasn't enough that you got his pony eight years ago. Now you send him a photo of your son riding the pony that one sired. You just can't let things go, can you?"

"Once I got my hands on you, *chiquita*, I didn't let go."

I turn in his embrace as he wraps his arms around my waist. I tilt my head back and accept his kiss that would be inappropriate if anyone was around to see us.

"I wouldn't have let you, Daddy."

I'm where I've always meant to be.

Pablo never expected he'd come face to face with the daughter of the man who stole his aunt's happily ever after and left his cousins without a father in the heart of the Colombian underworld. But the woman he nicknames *reina*—queen—needs him when she finds herself in the midst of a plot to destroy her and the Diazes in *Cartel Prince*.

Bonus Epilogue

Javier

Pablo will kill me if he finds out what I'm doing with Maddy when we're supposed to meet the woman I know he's fallen for. But Maddy's too tempting to ignore.

"Daddy, someone is going to see us."

"I know."

I steer her into the dimly lit corner of the restaurant where we're all gathered for Sunday dinner. Neither Maks nor I accompanied our wives to Mass today when Maddy and Laura went with their parents. Maybe I should have, so I could've confessed my sins, though I hadn't thought of the one I'm about to commit.

Instead, I'm trailing my fingertips along the back of Maddy's right thigh until I can slide my hand beneath her dress and palm her ass cheek. She's regained the weight she lost while she was with the douchebag whose name we never speak anymore. I slip my fingers between her cheeks.

"I could take you in the restroom and fuck this glorious little ass right now."

I feel her shiver and see the goosebumps on her arms. She likes the idea. I press my fingers into her pussy, but I don't go deeper than the first knuckle.

"Javi."

It's a breathless plea with a tinge of fear.

I ease into her a little deeper, my fingers now halfway. I stroke the silky skin inside her cunt, and my cock's begging me to free it from my trousers and boxers. I look around and spy a chair a couple feet away. Everyone's mingling as they sip wine and cocktails before going to our table. My free arm slides around Maddy's waist, my hand resting on her belly. I press low on it as I twist my other hand. She spreads her feet enough for me to stroke the front of her pussy. Her moan as I find the sensitive spot that's made her squirt—the things it does to me. She shifts restlessly until she catches herself.

"What do you need, *chiquita*?"

"Relief from your tormenting. You edged me the entire way here."

"You did the same thing to me. Your hand felt divine, but you didn't let me come. You purposely took your time."

"So did you."

"Mmm. I was enjoying the taste of you and lost track of time."

She snorts quietly.

"You did no such thing. You knew you got me close over and over, then supposedly ran out of time just as we pulled up. Javi, *please*."

"I thought you were worried someone would see us."

"I'm almost to the point where I don't care. Fuck, Daddy. My pussy burns to have you inside me."

We're whispering everything as we smile at our family.

Pablo isn't here yet, and I don't know when he'll arrive. It could be five minutes, or it could be five seconds. I'll take my chances. I back us toward the chair and let go over Maddy's waist. I slide my zipper down just before I sit and bring Maddy down onto my lap. The moment she feels the tip of my cock brush against her pussy lips, she adjusts to take me inside her.

"Javi, I can't believe we're doing this. Someone is going to figure out what the fuck we're doing."

"Do you want to stop?"

"No."

I've fingered her when others were around, but we've never had sex in public before. At least, not anywhere but the club we now belong to. She was curious, so I agreed to take her to one. It wasn't where I used to belong. The last thing I needed was a ghost from my past. Instead, we nearly ran into Gabriele and Sinead Mancinelli. I pushed Maddy into a room before Sinead saw us. I'm certain Gabriele did. We ignored each other.

Maddy shifts to take me all the way inside her. She Kegels over and over since she can't rock or slide up and down my dick. I can see her reflection in the window, and I know she has a smile plastered on her face despite how nervous she is.

"Daddy, do something."

She shifts, and I want to groan. This wasn't such a good idea after all. I want to thrust into her until we both come. I can't reach around her to finger her since everyone would see that. My mother would crucify me.

Instead, I widen my legs slightly since Maddy's are between mine. I rest my left hand on her hip and pull back. She tilts them then pushes them forward as though she's wriggling to get more comfortable.

"Fuck."

She hisses the word as my cock hits her G-spot. Now she

wriggles for real until she catches herself. I shift enough to see her cheeks grow pink.

"If you keep blushing, people will wonder why."

"I'm sitting on your lap when neither *Tía* Elle nor *Tía* Catalina nor *Tía* Margherita are sitting on their husband's lap."

"We're newly engaged."

"*Tía* Elle and *Tío* Enrique are newlyweds, but they're not like this."

I love that she calls my aunts *Tía* and my uncles *Tío* just like my brothers and cousins do.

"They wish they could be. Shh, *chiquita*. Enjoy our secret."

"It is pretty scandalous, isn't it?"

She Kegels extra tight and long. I think I'm about to blow my load right now. She's going to squeeze the cum right out of me. It's my turn to tilt my hips. When her hand grips my thigh before she catches herself, I know I'm hitting the right spot. I watch us in the window's reflection to make sure none of our movements will draw attention. We're slow as we get each other off.

"Daddy, I'm close. May I come?"

"Yes, because I'm about to fill your tight little cunt with all my cum. You're going to wear it throughout dinner. No one but us will know you're dripping with every step. When you stand, and your thighs stick together, you'll remember that you're mine. In the town car on the way home, I'm going to fuck you in this position, but I'll be in your ass. By the time we get home, you'll be overflowing with my cum."

"Yes, Daddy. Can we skip dessert? Can that be my dessert?"

I chuckle, and she moans as I twitch inside her.

"Anything you want, *chica*."

"If that were true, I'd be bouncing on your dick right now, then we'd be leaving the minute after we come."

She sounds so aggrieved that we have to make it through a meal with our family. I wrap my arm around her waist again and draw her back to my chest as I whisper in her ear.

"Your impatience got you edged on the way over here."

"And your toying with me is what got you edged on the way over here."

"Tilt your hips back again, Maddy."

She does as I say, and I rock mine once more. She tenses, and I know she's coming from the way her breath hiccups, then she holds it. My cock pulses inside her as I erupt. I don't know how I'm coming so hard when she's basically just warming my dick. It's being inside my fiancée. She gets me too excited too fast. I blame her for not being able to last like I once did.

"Javi, everyone's moving to the table. We have to go."

"I see them. Stand up, little one."

I rise at the same time she does and slide out of her. She doesn't move, knowing I need to adjust myself. She brushes down her dress in the back, and the back of her fingers graze my sensitive tip. I know it was an accident, but it makes me want to maul her and go for round two.

"Remember, Daddy. No dessert."

I get my pants zipped without catching myself in it. Small miracle since I'm still semi-hard. When we're sure we're both presentable, we head to the table. I spot Pablo with Florencia Aguilar. I thought I could handle seeing the woman whose father murdered mine, but rage consumes me. It fizzles the post coital high I was on. Maddy looks up at me, worried since she knows why my mood shifted.

"I can say I suddenly don't feel well."

"No. I have to give her a chance. She's not her father."

I keep repeating that to myself as I glance at my brothers. I know Jorge and Joaquin are thinking the same thing. *Mamá's* doing her best to be gracious to the woman who looks like she wants to sink through the floor. Pablo's arm around her waist is probably all that's keeping her from bolting.

"I'm so, so sorry. So sorry."

Florencia blurts her apology before Pablo pulls her in for a hug. She leans against him as he kisses her forehead. I look down at Maddy again, and our gazes lock. She slips her arms around my waist, and I immediately feel calmer. She's my soul-mate. She knows what I need, and she knows she's the only one who'll ever bring me true peace in this fucked-up world.

"Javi?"

"I'll come to terms with it just like everyone else."

"Lean on me while you do. I love you."

"I love you too, *chiquita*."

As I kiss her, I know no one caught us having sex, but everyone can see how much I adore my fiancée.

Don't miss the next installment

Meet Pablo and Reina in *Cartel Prince*.

Pablo—I'm dark. When people call me that, they don't just mean my hair and eyes. I'm the enforcer. The man in your nightmares. But her...*I want her, but I can't trust her.* Her family is my enemy. She works for the one man we despise more than anyone else. But she doesn't fear me when everyone else does. She doesn't back down. She's the one woman who could help me rule my family's empire one day. My r*eina*—my queen. I'll give her body pleasure and leave her breathless. Touch her, and I'll leave you breathless...But there'll be no pleasure.

Florencia—In the Colombian underworld, my father robbed Pablo's aunt of her happily ever after and left his cousins father-less. Now I'm the woman who's supposed to destroy his family. I didn't ask to work for his uncle. I didn't ask to be a repayment for my father's debts—a man I never met. I'm so far in over my head I'm drowning, and the last man I should rely on is the only one willing to save me. *I want him, but I can't trust* *him.* His touch makes me crave more, makes me dream of something that should never be. He's the prince of darkness who steals my heart. There's nothing I won't do to protect what's mine.

Preorder Cartel Prince now!

Thank you for reading

 Sabine Barclay, a nom de plume also writing Historical Romance as Celeste Barclay, lives near the Southern California coast with her husband and sons. She loves her days at the beach soaking up way too much sun, a good Netflix binge, and a strong hot chai. Her heroines are independent women who can defend themselves but love their Alpha heroes who want nothing more than to protect their soulmates in her Mafia Romances. She's Gen Y/Oregon Trail and loves creating engrossing contemporary romances that will make your toes curl and your granny blush.

Subscribe to Sabine's bimonthly newsletter to receive exclusive insider perks.
www.sabinebarclay.com

Join the fun and get exclusive insider giveaways, sneak peeks, and new release announcements in
Sabine Barclay's Facebook Dubious Dames Group

Do you also enjoy steamy Historical Romance? Discover Sabine's books written as Celeste Barclay.

The Cartel Brotherhood

Cartel King
BOOK ONE SNEAK PEEK

ENRIQUE

She's going to fall off that fucking ladder.

I slow my pace to a jog as I approach a house with a woman far too high on her ladder, leaning far too much to the right as she tries to fish something out of her gutters. She's got to be about five-five to my six-three.

I could reach whatever she's fishing around for. She's more likely to fall off and break something. I should mind my own business and keep going with my run, but there's no way I'm doing that. I wouldn't if it were a woman of any age, and I wouldn't if it were an elderly person, either.

If it were a guy my age, maybe I'd let him deal with it, but for her—there's something in how she's reaching. Some frustration I can feel even from here. I approach slowly as I walk up the driveway. I'm only halfway to her when a humongous dog comes bounding toward me.

393

No wonder there's a baby gate across the entrance to her open garage. The massive beast doesn't bark, but he growls. It's a Mastiff, much like the one Laura Kutsenko has, except this one is a different color and easily weighs about fifty pounds more than her giant companion. I wonder if this one is as much of a love bug as Laura's. At least, that's what she's always claimed.

The woman on the ladder speaks to her dog, giving him a command.

"Hush, Constantine. Lie down."

The dog immediately obeys, but he inches closer to the baby gate, still growling at me. It's only then that the woman notices me. She grips the ladder as she jerks away. I hurry over and grab the ladder, tempted to demand she come down from there.

"Who are you?"

If anybody's going to do the demanding, apparently it's her. Not that I can blame the woman, since I'm a complete stranger.

"I'm Enrique. I saw you as I was running. You looked a little wobbly up there."

"Well, I was okay until I was startled—but thank you."

Dismissive is the only way to describe her now. I don't blame her for that either. She's a woman in a precarious position with a strange man looking up at her. Now that I'm certain the ladder won't fall over, I step away. I don't need to look like a perv staring up her shorts.

"Would you like some help? I can easily reach whatever you're going for."

Cartel Viper
Cartel Prince

The Ivankov Brotherhood

Bratva Darling
BOOK ONE SNEAK PEEK

LAURA

As I sit across from the four Kutsenko brothers, I press my lips together to keep from drooling. No four men should be so strikingly handsome. Not all from the same family, anyway. I fight a valiant battle against letting my gaze drift toward the eldest, Maksim, whose ice-blue eyes bore into me. After years of negotiating billion-dollar investment contracts while facing countless ruthless businessmen, I've learned to keep my expression studiously blank. But it's a true struggle today. Instead, I focus my attention on the squirrelly lawyer sitting across the conference table. While he's disingenuous with each comment, he's a good negotiator. But I'm better. How cliché am I?

While I feel Maksim watching me, I focus on Dmitry Yakovitch as he continues to argue the merits of the venture capitalist company I represent, RK Capital Group, merging with

Kutsenko Partners. What he means is the merits of Kutsenko Partners acquiring RK Capital Group, then stripping it and making it another money-laundering shell corporation. While most people in New York have little awareness of the Russian mafia, I do. The Kutsenko brothers' names appear on no titles or deeds anywhere in New York City, but it wasn't difficult to determine which shell companies likely belong to them. Their assumption that I'm unfamiliar with them is proving beneficial to me as they continue to whisper amongst themselves in Russian. I think they may even believe they're convincing me that they don't speak much English.

The senior partners of RK Capital Group know who I'm negotiating with, though they may not know I'm aware of these Russians' more nefarious operations. They've given me the go-ahead to agree to a merger with an eventual acquisition, but only for the right price. A price to the tune of twenty billion dollars. Considering an investment firm like Goldman Sachs is worth nearly one-hundred-and-twenty billion dollars, my clients' asking price appears reasonable.

"Mr. Yakovitch, I shall stop you now." I raise my left hand, pen caught between my index and middle fingers. When I have his attention, I lean back in my chair and casually twirl the pen over my index finger and thumb. "Fifty billion is my clients' asking price. You know that. Your clients know that. RK doesn't oppose the merger. What they oppose is the insulting offer you've made. It's nearly noon, and I'm hungry, Mr. Yakovitch. I have a delicious ham sandwich waiting for me. I even have three chocolate chip cookies waiting for me. If we aren't going to make any progress, I shall let you go, so I can move onto my eagerly anticipated lunch."

I cant my head just enough for me to appear as though my gaze rests solely on the opposing attorney's face, but I can see each

Kutsenko brothers' reaction. My face battles yet again against showing my emotions as I fight not to smirk. Their muted but surprised expressions confirm what I already know.

"Please tell your clients to make a reasonable counteroffer, or I will conclude this meeting and enjoy my ham sandwich and cookies."

Dmitry glares at me before turning to Maksim and his three brothers. In rapid Russian, he doesn't interpret my suggestion. Oh no. There's no need for that. I can't catch every word because his voice is too low. But I catch something along the lines of "The bitch refuses to budge. What now? A fucking ham sandwich. More like a stick up her ass."

Maksim swivels his chair to look at his brothers. In Russian, he says, "Fifty billion is ridiculous. She's not so stupid or naïve not to know that. My guess is they'll settle for twenty billion. We offer fifteen."

"That's barely better than what we already offered," Aleksei, the second-oldest brother, argues. "She'll be eating the fucking sandwich and dipping her cookies in milk before we walk out the door. We need the buildings."

"We offer twenty, Maks," Bogdan, the youngest, insists.

As I watch the brothers discuss, their voices barely lowered, I pull my lunch sack from the black leather satchel by my feet and set it beside my laptop. It's a ridiculously pink floral bag with an embroidered monogram, the L and D overlapping. It's an empty prop, but they don't know that. I watch as five sets of eyes narrow. I offer a smile that would appear innocent in any setting other than this meeting. It's patronizing, and I know it.

Bratva Sweetheart
Bratva Treasure
Bratva Beauty

397

Sabine Barclay

Bratva Angel
Bratva Jewel

Do you also enjoy steamy Historical Romance? Discover Sabine's books written as Celeste Barclay.

The Mancinelli Brotherhood

Mafia Heir
BOOK ONE SNEAK PEEK

LUCA

This asshole is pissing me off. We've been going around in circles for five minutes, and the longer we stand out here, the greater the likelihood someone will spot us. I have a sixth sense about these things. It's why I'm still alive at the ripe old age of thirty-one.

"Espinoza, enough already. Either sell to us or don't, but we set the price. Your tequila is good, but it isn't nectar from the gods."

I'm watching Carlos Espinoza, some lackey for the Mexican Culiacán Cartel, try to maneuver me into paying more than the agreed upon price. I know it's so he can skim off the top.

"It's as close as you're going to get. You've upped the order, so the price per case goes up."

My uncle, Salvatore Mancinelli, is the New York don. He negotiated this deal, and I warned him it was a bad idea. But what do I know as his underboss and heir? I'm not backing down.

"Haven't you ever heard of a bulk discount? The more I order the better the price should be. No one else around here is buying from you. You know we're your only choice in three out of five boroughs. You aren't going to the Bronx because you won't get more than pennies there. You aren't going to Queens because you don't want to run into the Colombians. You aren't going to Manhattan because then you face the bratva along with us. And what are you going to do in Staten Island? Sell to us anyway? We control Staten Island and Brooklyn when it comes to liquor stores, so take the money and go."

"Luca, there are plenty of liquor stores in Brooklyn that aren't owned by Italians. I'll go there."

We aren't friends. He's patronizing me by using my first name. Fuck him and the horse he rode in on. I have other solutions for this shit.

"And I'll just take what I want from them for free. That's not a half bad idea. The deal's over. Take your shit with the worm in it and go."

"Motherfucking racist. Not all tequila has a worm in it."

"You're selling Mezcal. It's known for the fucking worm. I wouldn't start calling me names, you *penche hijo de puta*."

Fucking son of a bitch.

He has twenty-five crates of stolen tequila that he's trying to offload because he knows he can't sell it at his own liquor store.

"What did you call me?"

Carlos takes what he thinks is a menacing step forward, and his two bodyguards do the same. Not smart. Neither of my two bodyguards nor I react, but the three men in each of my cars open their doors. They won't do more than that. It's just a reminder that the Culiacán can try, but the *Cosa Nostra* still run New York City.

"This is the third and final time I say this. Sell or leave."
Every head turns toward the liquor store's back door as it opens.
A gorgeous blonde steps out, and I wish I had the time to
appreciate her beauty, but she's about to die. Carlos and his
men draw their guns and pivot toward her. My men pull their
weapons too, but we keep them pointed at the Mexicans. The
woman stands like a deer in the headlights for a second before
ducking behind the industrial garbage dumpster like a frightened rabbit. Three shots hit the metal almost at the same
moment. That's all it takes for my men and me. The two bodyguards standing with me aim for a guard each, and I set my
sights on Carlos. We squeeze our triggers, and the men fall.
Screeching tires tell me Carlos's driver takes off. I hear more
gunshots as at least one soldier in my cars tries to shoot the
escaping vehicle. Glass shatters, but the sedan keeps going. I
hear more tires squeal as one of my SUVs takes off and chases
the guy. I holster my gun and wave my men to do the same.
I inch forward toward the trash can, but I see the shadow shift.
The woman bolts from the other side. She's still the frightened
rabbit, but I'm the fox pursuing her. She's fast, I'll give her that.
But she has to be at least a foot shorter than me. My legs are a
lot longer and cover a lot more ground with each stride.
She weaves among the cars, most likely believing it's harder to
hit a moving object. She isn't wrong, but I have no intention of
shooting her. I push myself harder and pounce as she darts out
and tries to cross the last stretch of parking lot to reach a better
lit area near a bus stop. I lunge.
"Stop running, *piccolina*. I won't hurt you."
I wrap my arms around her and pull her back against my chest,
but I'm quick to spin her around and put space between us as I
grasp her arms. Of course, she fights me.
"If I wanted you dead, I would have shot at you, too."
"It doesn't mean you won't kill me after."

401

She's breathless as she continues to struggle. I almost let go to take a step back, insulted at what she implied. But I can't blame her. If I were a woman, I'd be terrified of the same thing.

"I'm not going to rape you. I'm going to talk to you."

"Talk? You are not a man who talks if you just killed a guy."

"To keep him and his men from killing you. I told you, if I wanted you dead, I would have shot at you too. And I wouldn't have missed."

She stops struggling against me, but her eyes continue to dart from one place to another, trying to find somewhere to flee. I know I can keep her in place with only one hand, so I release her left arm. I still have a firm hold on her right one, but I haven't held it nearly as tightly as I could.

"I'm Luca. I know you figured out you interrupted something you shouldn't have. Did that man know who you are?"

"Yes."

"What about his driver? Would he know you?"

"Yes."

"Do you have a name?"

"Yes."

"*Piccolina*, we won't get very far if yes is all you can say. Are you willing to answer me with more than one word?"

"No."

I knew that was coming, and I grin. I can't help it. I wasn't wrong about her being gorgeous, but I doubt she wants to know that's what I think. At least, not if I want her to know I won't assault her.

"Fine. I have more than twenty questions I can ask that you can answer with one word. Do you work at the store?"

"Sometimes."

Ah, an improvement.

"Did Carlos know you were still working?"

"No."

"Do you have a car, or do you take the subway or bus?"

She raises her chin and remains silent. Smart but counterproductive.

"The subway or the bus will get you killed. You're too easy to find and follow. Do you have a car?"

"Yes."

"Can you stay with someone instead of going home?"

She refuses to answer.

"If that man knew you and you sometimes work in the store, then he knew where you live. If he found that out, so will someone in his cartel."

"I know. Let me go. The longer I stand here, the more likely someone is to come back for me."

"No one will touch you while I'm here."

"Arrogant. If he shot at me, he would have shot at you."

"And he would have died, anyway. What's your name?"

"Jane."

"Look, I know you won't get in one of my cars and let me drive you somewhere. In most cases, I would say that's a smart move. But you did nothing wrong tonight except for leave work at the wrong time. I know that, and you know that. But the Culiacán won't see it that way, *piccolina*."

She freezes for no more than five seconds before she trembles so much that I can see it. I don't know what drives me next, but it's the same instinct that's made me call her little girl three times. I pull her to my chest and tuck her head against it. I stroke her hair down to her shoulders, rubbing my hand up and down her back. This is the most inopportune moment to notice she isn't wearing a bra. I will my body not to react.

"What does that mean?"

Her voice is barely more than a whisper, but I know what she's asking.

"It means little girl."

"I should be insulted, but the way you say it..."

"It has nothing to do with your height. I know you're not a child."

God, do I know she's not. She feels amazing. Her tits are soft as they press against me, and I can see she has the most delectable ass. I'd love nothing more than to cup it and squeeze until she goes up on her toes and begs for me to wrap her legs around my waist and fuck her. For fuck's sake. Stop, you disgusting asshole. That is not what you need to be thinking about.

"Why didn't you shoot me? Whatever you were talking about, if it was with a Cartel member, then it wasn't completely legal. Carlos didn't want me alive to talk about seeing you together. Why are you letting me live?"

"I told you. You did nothing wrong but try to leave work. He should have checked the building before starting the meeting. That was on him. The only thing I take issue with is you leaving by yourself and walking into a dimly lit parking lot. I suspect you do that often, and that's too dangerous. Jane Doe, I don't hurt women."

Mafia Sinner
Mafia Beauty
Mafia Angel
Mafia Redeemer
Mafia Star

Do you also enjoy steamy Historical Romance? Discover Sabine's books written as Celeste Barclay.

The O'Rourke Brotherhood

Mob Boss
BOOK ONE SNEAK PEEK

DILLAN

I hate meetings like this. I don't need to wear pants from some shitty off-the-rack suit that are too tight to *try* to make my dick look bigger. I'm secure in my cock size, and I don't need to show how big my balls are for people to know I run this part of the city. I loathe strip clubs too. I'm past the point where naked women make my jimmy do jumping jacks. I can appreciate a hot bod and gymnast level strength, but it does nothing for me. These douchebags? They're practically ready to come in those cheap arse pants. Why am I here? I keep asking myself that. Seamus and Shane are doing just fine with these negotiations. I'm just here to look good. I'm the muscle today. Or rather my name and my position. Who the fuck thought— way, way back in the day —that giving the mob hierarchy nautical names was a good idea? Fucking Skipper. This isn't motherfucking Gilli-

405

gan's Island. None of these numb nuts are the Professor, even if
they think they're fucking Mr. Howell.

But who is that? If this is *Gilligan's Island*, then she's
Mary Ann.

I glance at Seamus, but he's focused on the Albanian he's trying
not to lose his shite at. Shane smirks at me when I dart my gaze
to him. I cock an eyebrow as the waitress walks over. She's definitely not a dancer. She has too many clothes on. But you can
barely call the pieces of thread she's wearing clothes. She's got
on a bikini top that's barely more than pasties, and the skirt
she's wearing would make my Catholic grandmother do somer-
saults in her grave.

It's the standard uniform for this place, but somehow it doesn't
look right on her. Not because she doesn't have a banging body
because she does. Not because she's a butter face— but-her-
face —as in great bod, not so great face. She's beautiful in a
super understated way. That's part of what makes her look out
of place. She has next to no makeup on. I think those are even
her real eyelashes. The natural beauty is drawing way too much
attention.

"'Scuse me."

She tries to step around Zef Hoxha, the *kyre* of the Albanian
mafia here in New York. When he reaches out to grab her
wrist, I'm out of my seat with my hand around his. He never
gets a chance to touch her because my hold is so tight he can't
bend his fingers. I keep squeezing until it must feel like I'll snap
the bones.

"No touching."

Zef drops his arm as much as my hold allows. I let go and stare
at him before I tilt my head toward the waitress. I narrow my
eyes, and he knows what I expect.

"I apologize, miss."

"That's all right, sir. Here's your drink."

She's polite as she hands him his glass. Unfortunately, to put down the rest, she has to bend forward, giving everyone a view of her glorious cleavage. Tits and arse are what sell here, and she has them in spades. I'm certain it's why my cousin hired her. If I sit down, everyone will know I'm just as guilty as these fuck nuts because she's made my dick do something that hasn't happened in a strip club since I was like twenty-three. I'm now thirty-three.

Mob Boss
Mob Star
Mob Princess
Mob Saint
Mob Bride
Mob Knight

Do you also enjoy steamy Historical Romance? Discover Sabine's books written as Celeste Barclay.

www.ingramcontent.com/pod-product-compliance
Lightning Source LLC
Chambersburg PA
CBHW020523110726
47899CB00004B/1220